RAVE REVIEWS FOR HEIDI BETTS!

"Nobody spins an entertaining, sexy yarn better than Heidi Betts, and *Walker's Widow* is her best to date."

—*Reader to Reader*

"*Almost a Lady* is a top-notch winner."

—*Romance Reviews Today*

"*Cinnamon and Roses* is an engaging and fast-paced tale . . . a well-crafted debut novel that will leave readers eager for Ms. Betts's next one. Excellent!

—*Rendezvous*

"Books like *Cinnamon and Roses* are few and far between. The story will tug at your heartstrings and tickle your funny bone. . . . *Cinnamon and Roses* is a keeper."

—*Reader to Reader*

"A delightful romance that enthralled and enchanted me from the beginning. An outstanding read."

—*Rendezvous* on *A Promise of Roses*

"Snappy dialogue makes this a quick read."

—*Romantic Times* on *A Promise of Roses*

"The dialogue is dynamic, the writing superb! Ms. Betts is an absolutely wonderful writer. . . . Don't miss any of [the *Rose* trilogy]! FANTASTIC! 5 BELLS!"

—*Bell, Book & Candle* on *A Promise of Roses*

"Ms. Betts's *Rose* trilogy is well worth reading."

—*Old Book Barn Gazette*

NEEDLESS WORDS

"You could tell them all to go to hell," Clay suggested.

Regan gasped, her mouth falling open in astonishment. "I could never to that."

He took a step toward her, dipping his head a fraction and fixing her with a determined glare. "Sure you could. You just say, 'Go to hell.' Try it."

An appalled puff of air escaped her lungs. "I couldn't."

With her back to the barn wall, Clay took the opportunity to move closer, laying his hands flat against the rough planks on either side of her head.

"What are you doing?" she rasped.

"Maybe you just need the proper motivation," he told her, slanting his head to one side and studying her mouth. "I'm thinking about kissing you, Regan Doyle. And if you don't want that, then you're going to have to tell me, plain and simple, to go to hell."

Her eyes widened and she kept her gaze locked on his lips as they descended toward her own. He stopped a hairbreadth from her mouth, giving her one last chance to deter him.

Her fingers curled into his shirt. Her breathing was shallow.

"Too late," he murmured as he captured her lips with his own.

WALKER'S WIDOW

HEIDI BETTS

LEISURE BOOKS NEW YORK CITY

A LEISURE BOOK®

January 2002

Published by

Dorchester Publishing Co., Inc.
276 Fifth Avenue
New York, NY 10001

ISBN 0-8439-4954-6

The name "Leisure Books" and the stylized "L" with design are trademarks of Dorchester Publishing Co., Inc.

Printed in the United States of America.

Visit us on the web at www.dorchesterpub.com.

*This book is dedicated to two of the educators
who had the greatest impact on my writing career:*

*To my sixth-grade teacher, Miss Shoemaker (now Mrs. Judy
Larson)—thank you for making every Friday "Creative
Writing Day" and helping me to discover my love of story-
telling. I promise never again to write about poison pepper-
oni at the school carnival.*

*And to my typing teacher, Mrs. (Sheila) Kovalcin—thank
you for giving me a valuable tool I use every single day.
(Who knew I would spend this much time at a keyboard,
huh? <g>) If not for you, I would be destined to a life of
two-finger typing and could never meet my deadlines.*

ACKNOWLEDGMENTS

I would like to extend a very special thanks to my editor, Kate Seaver, who increased the potential of this story tenfold by uttering two simple words: "cat burglar." As soon as you said that, Kate, a lightbulb went on in my head, and *Walker's Widow* took on new and even more exciting dimensions. Thank you.

WALKER'S WIDOW

Prologue

Martha Doyle gazed out the window of her bed-room on the first floor of the sprawling, two-story house that her son had built more than seven years before. James had been a good boy. A loving son, a decent husband.

Just not the ideal husband for dear Regan.

Martha studied the figure of her daughter-in-law for several minutes more, watching as she weeded Martha's favorite flowerbed—the only one she could see from the confines of her room. She took in the fading fibers of Regan's black daydress, worn for grieving a full two years since her husband's passing. The tight, fiery red curls pulled tightly into a chignon at the top of her head and already escaping to run riot around her pretty Irish face.

Regan had been as good to her as James, Martha

thought. Better, if the truth be known. Even after James's death, when Regan could have gone off on her own and abandoned her aging, decrepit mother-in-law, she had stuck around and cared for Martha. Been a friend to her.

But it had been two years since James's death. Time enough for Regan to put away her widow's weeds and move on with her life. To find another husband. A young, sprightly one who could give her love and laughter and the children she deserved. The children Martha suspected Regan wanted . . . badly.

Martha smoothed a hand over her sister's most recent letter, hoping her plan wouldn't fail. Hoping Regan . . . or worse yet, Clayton . . . wouldn't balk too badly when they found out what she'd done.

She cast one final glance out the window to where her daughter-in-law knelt, covered in damp soil. And then she began to write out a very special request of her sister. And her sister's son.

Chapter One

No one locked his doors in Purgatory. Not even after eleven incidents of burglary had been reported.

This made The Ghost of Ol' Morty Pike's job much easier.

Regan stifled a giggle at the ominous nickname as she crouched in the bushes outside the kitchen of Dorisa Finch's luxurious home, dressed in black trousers, black shirtwaist, and dusty black boots. A black kerchief was tied about her head to hide her hair. The tightly knotted mass was so bright, so red, that she suspected it could be seen for miles, no matter the time of day or night. That alone would identify her to anyone who happened to catch her sneaking about, which was why she took such pains to cover every stray strand.

She also had been cursed with pale, porcelain

Irish skin that she knew would glow like a full moon in the darkness. It had taken her two or three of these excursions before she'd come up with the idea of fashioning a bit of a mask out of yet another black handkerchief. She'd cut out two small holes for her eyes, and tied the material at the back of her head. It was folded so that it ran all the way to her hairline and then hung down in a point to cover the rest of her face. All in all, she thought it did the job quite well.

And she had to admit that it made her feel just a bit . . . wicked. Like an outlaw or highwayman. Or the Ghost of Ol' Morty Pike.

To think that someone thought her dangerous enough to link her with the long-dead and much-feared specter of Mortimer Pike. Pike had been Purgatory's first undertaker, setting up shop soon after the town was founded, and who—it was rumored—enjoyed his occupation a little *too* much. The parents of Purgatory used stories of Ol' Morty Pike and his ghost to scare their children into behaving properly. And the children of Purgatory used stories of Ol' Morty Pike's ghost to scare each other.

Now, due to her recent vocation, tales of Morty were making the rounds again. The *Purgatory Prophet* had even begun to print weekly reports of his supposed activities.

While her only true crime was walking off with one or two valuables from the households of the town's wealthier residents, the *Prophet* seemed to enjoy blaming the ghost for any number of misdeeds. At last count, he was accused of stealing Ida

Jefferson's wedding dress and replacing it on the scarecrow in her husband's sorghum field, spiking Mrs. Shoemaker's batch of lemonade so that she got all of the Sunday school children snookered, and spooking Joe Don Hawbaker's cattle through Eldon Carter's sheep field and nearly sparking a range war.

In reality, Regan Doyle had done none of those things. But it was kind of fun to think that everyone in town believed she had.

Not that they had any idea the thief they called Ol' Morty's Ghost was really the woman they knew as sweet, innocent, still-grieving Widow Doyle, wife of the late James Doyle, whom everyone in Purgatory had liked and respected.

Regan popped her head out of the shrubbery where she hid and peeked in the nearest window to make sure the house was vacant. No light shone from within. The Finches were in town this evening, celebrating little Cissy Finch's eleventh birthday with a family dinner at the Eat 'Em Up Café. A big party with all of Cissy's school friends would follow this Saturday afternoon—Regan should know, she was baking six dozen tiny, individual frosted cakes for the children—but tonight's outing gave Regan the perfect opportunity to sneak into the house and steal a bit of the fine jewelry Dorisa Finch had been so enamored of after church last Sunday. Poor Dorisa would be terribly upset to discover that Morty Pike's ghost had walked away with her favorite, rather expensive necklace and earbobs.

Let that be a lesson to Thomas and Dorisa Finch

17

that they should be more generous with their money when Regan asked—quite politely—for a donation to the Purgatory Home for Unwanted Children. And less inclined to brag about their newest high-priced baubles only moments after declining to contribute to a very worthwhile fund.

Sneaking around the side of the dark house, Regan opened the back door to the kitchen and slipped inside.

This was the hard part, she thought. Making her way through a strange house, around unfamiliar obstacles without the aid of a lantern. Even though she'd been a guest in many of these homes, she had gotten a number of nasty bruises on her shins and upper thighs from crashing into tables and other unseen furnishings while she skulked around her neighbors' dwellings.

The discolorations always caused her a pang of guilt when she saw them, reminding her that she *was* committing crimes.

But the orphanage was in need. And her neighbors didn't seem inclined to help, even though she knew perfectly well many of them had the financial advantages to do so.

Which was why she found herself once again breaking into a home to take personal items worth just about as much as a donation that should have been given willingly.

Feeling her way in the dark, Regan moved through the kitchen and into the foyer. From there, it was easy enough to climb the stairs to the bedrooms, though it took her a little longer to find the room Thomas and Dorisa shared. Once she did, she moved directly to the bureau where she suspected Dorisa kept most of her jewelry.

Sure enough, an ornately carved teakwood box sat in the middle of the dressertop, and when Regan lifted the lid, an assortment of jewels—likely quite real—glittered in the pale moonlight spilling through the open window over her shoulder.

She picked through the collection and found the lovely emerald choker and matching diamond-cut earrings Dorisa had been wearing the Sunday before when Regan had asked the Finches for a donation to the orphanage. It was just the set she'd been looking to steal.

Slipping the cool jewels into the front pocket of her trousers, Regan left the teakwood box open— the Finches needed some small hint that their home had been broken into, after all—and turned to leave the room. She made her way downstairs as silently as she'd gone up and exited the house through the same back kitchen door she'd used to enter.

These nighttime burglaries were going so well, she thought. It was almost routine now, from leaving her house with the excuse that she was looking for little Lucy-fur, to changing back into the nightclothes she had hidden beneath a burgeoning pecan tree.

If she didn't feel so guilty for what she was doing, she almost would have been proud of her exceptional expertise at being the female version of a modern-day Robin Hood.

*　　*　　*

Purgatory might be smack-dab between Heaven and Hell on the map of Texas, but as far as Clayton Walker was concerned, it was much closer to Hell. The real one.

Of course, that assessment could have something to do with the fact that Purgatory, Texas, was the last place he wanted to be right now. He wanted to be back in Sweetwater working at capturing the band of renegade Army deserters who had been terrorizing the local townspeople.

And he would be if his mother hadn't demanded, harassed, and browbeat him into making this trip. If his mother hadn't gone to his superior, asking that Clay be given a few weeks away from his job to visit his elderly, ailing, hard-of-hearing, wheelchair-bound aunt who was concerned enough about the string of robberies in her town to ask her nephew to come and investigate.

But instead of simply giving him some time off from his job to deal with this family situation, Jake had been so moved by Clay's mother and her lengthy diatribe that he'd *assigned* Clay to the robberies in Purgatory and ordered him to stay with his aunt until the culprit was caught.

Caesar nickered softly and Clay grunted, agreeing with the gelding's sentiments at having to travel so far out of the way to catch a thief that any two-bit, small-town sheriff should have been able to apprehend.

Spending the next few weeks with his taxing, needy, invalid Aunt Martha didn't exactly toast his oats, either.

Clay was just about to start on another path of self-misery when he noticed a movement out of the corner of his eye. Maybe he was seeing things. Maybe he was desperate enough to capture this burglar that he was creating apparitions out of thin air. Because he could have sworn he saw a lone figure, crouched low, dashing across the dry, bare space between a shadowed, two-story house and a copse of trees several yards away.

Pulling his mount to a halt, he blinked once and studied the area more closely. A moment later, he caught the movement again. There was definitely someone there, sneaking about in dark clothes near a seemingly empty house.

Clay blinked again just to be sure.

Could he be so lucky as to happen upon the thief his first hour in Purgatory? Before he even reached Aunt Martha's house?

No one could be that lucky, could he?

Of course, the way his luck had been running lately, maybe he was due this one, blessedly fortunate event.

And if this wraithlike creature was the burglar vandalizing the town, and he caught the bastard tonight . . . why, he could be on his way back home tomorrow morning after only a cursory visit with his aunt.

That thought had Clay spurring his horse forward, in the direction of his coveted prey. The blood rushed in his veins as fast as Caesar cut across the field and around the tree where he'd last spotted the crook.

Clay couldn't see him now, hidden in the dark and shadows of the trees. But he was here, Clay could feel it.

He slowed Caesar, slowed his breathing, and listened. His eyes were already well-adjusted to the darkness, so he had no trouble watching for movement. The rustle of a branch, the flutter of leaves stirred by the slight breeze.

And then there it was. An unnatural sound. One that had him urging Caesar forward another few steps.

His quarry—seemingly unaware that he was being tracked—broke away from the cover where he'd been hidden and continued his crouched run. He moved at a quick, steady pace, but Clay didn't think he was running out of a sense of panic. Merely to get away from the site of his latest crime.

Clay drew one of his Colts out of its holster, holding it flat against his thigh as he leaned forward over his mount's neck and spurred the horse even faster after their prey. Caesar's hooves pounded on the hard-packed earth, catching the stranger's attention. The man froze, arms out and legs bent. And then he turned—just his head—and Clay knew he was right. The mask alone identified the fleeing figure as the burglar who'd been robbing Purgatory blind. This was the criminal who would make Clay's life a hell of a lot easier just by being caught and thrown in a jail cell.

Yes! he wanted to cry. He had him.

Clay spent a moment too long rejoicing, giving the culprit a chance to dart forward and away from him. The man took off at a dead run and Clay kicked his mount to race after him.

But Clay didn't know the area, the terrain, and wasn't willing to risk a broken leg by pushing Caesar to unsafe speeds. Still, he kept his target in sight, watching as he darted left, darted right, ducked and weaved.

And then they entered another stand of trees and Clay lost him. One minute the thief was there, the next he'd disappeared. Vanished like so much smoke.

Clay cursed, long and steady, and pulled Caesar to a halt. Where the hell could the bastard have gone?

He began walking his mount in short paces from side to side, covering the periphery of the wooded area. Then he moved in, studying every shadow, every outcropping. He searched the area twice, to no avail, and drove a fist down hard on the pommel of his saddle in frustration.

One impeccable chance to capture the thief plaguing Purgatory; the perfect opportunity to cut his forced stay short, and he'd blown it. Now in all probability he would have to endure an extended visit with dear Aunt Martha.

Damn.

Regan held her breath until her lungs burned. Until her arms shook and her eyes crossed. Even after her pursuer seemed to have called a halt to his chase and vanished back into the dark of night, she released the air from her diaphragm only in low, short bursts.

She listened carefully, pretended to be Lucy-fur, with pure, nocturnal cat-vision. She didn't hear or see anything, but that didn't mean he wasn't out there, watching and waiting.

Who was that man? Dear God, she'd been so careful, so positive that she was alone. And then there he'd been, coming out of nowhere and chasing her until she'd thought her legs would buckle. Out of fear or physical exhaustion, she wasn't sure. But she had known that she couldn't run much farther when she'd landed on the idea of climbing this pine tree with the nice, low branches.

This man, this pursuer who had frightened her more than the real Morty Pike's Ghost could have, was a complete stranger. In the fraction of a second she'd whipped around to look at him, she'd caught a glimpse of his narrow face with its high cheek-bones and intense eyes, glowing almost silver in the moonlight. She wasn't sure, but she thought his hair might be dark in color. From what she'd seen, any-way, beneath the brim of his well-worn Stetson.

As dark as it had been, and as little time as she'd had to study him, she was fairly certain all of those features put together did not produce a face with which she was familiar. Definitely not the face of anyone she'd ever met, and she knew most of the residents of Purgatory.

New neighbor or passerby, the fact remained that he'd scared the starch right out of her bloomers. Her heart was only now beginning to regain its regular rhythm, and her breath was still coming in quick, sharp pants.

Several minutes had passed since her pursuer had presumably disappeared. She'd heard nothing, seen nothing. And though a jolt of panic raced down her spine at the idea of showing herself when the man *could* still be out there, she knew she couldn't stay in this tree all night.

Forcing her fear-stiffened limbs to move, Regan unbent her legs and let them dangle from the branch where she perched. Cautiously, she reached out with one foot until she found a solid hold and then, wrapping her arms around the trunk of the tree, she scuttled her way down to the ground.

The soles of her boots hit with a thump and she tensed a moment, wondering if the noise would attract the attention of her foe—if he was still out there.

When no steely arms locked around her waist or grabbed her by the hair, she began to believe she might—just might—be safe.

But she wasn't taking any chances. Without a backward glance, Regan turned and raced toward home as fast as her feet could carry her.

She stopped several yards from the house, hunkering at the base of the pecan tree where she kept her stash of clothes. Pulling the dusty burlap sack from its hiding place, she removed a nightdress and robe.

Both were black, as were all of her garments now that James had passed. But that simply made things easier for her. Whether wearing her nightclothes or her burglary outfit, all were dark enough to blend with the black of night and give her that much more protection.

She tugged the coverings from her face and hair and stuffed them to the bottom of the sack. Her boots came next, followed by the black trousers and shirt until she crouched in nothing more than her sinfully scarlet camisole and drawers.

Her flesh tingled wickedly at the decadence of the fancy, colorful satin underthings. They were her one indulgence. Given that every other stitch of clothing she owned was black, black, black, she'd discovered six months into her grieving that she had to wear *something* of color or go stark raving mad.

And so she'd begun to order rather expensive, wanton unmentionables through the mail. From catalogs her mother-in-law didn't realize she had and likely didn't even know existed.

James would roll in his grave if he knew what lay beneath her proper and respectful widow's weeds, but he'd left her enough money for this one small extravagance. And she had to admit that the caress of soft, slinky material against her skin made her feel more feminine than her late husband, with his effusive compliments and tender touches, ever had.

And all the rest of her inheritance she put towards caring for Mother Doyle or the orphans at the Purgatory Home for Unwanted Children. That had to count for something.

Embarrassed to be crouching in the dark in ruby red drawers, Regan quickly shrugged into her gown and wrap. With comfortable ebony slippers on her feet, she palmed the stolen necklace and earbobs, shoving her burglary clothing back into the hutch at the base of the tree and straightening.

And then, running a hand over her mass of unruly corkscrew curls, she made her way to the back entrance of the house.

Lucy-fur sat waiting on the porch step, right where she always was when Regan returned from her late-night excursions. Regan smiled broadly and scooped the drowsy feline into her arms.

"My sweet girl," she cooed as she ruffled Lucy's soft, midnight fur. Even her beloved pet was black, she noted—not for the first time—with irony.

But though she needed an occasional reminder, she really did like her life this way. The simplicity, the privacy, the freedom. She had no room to complain, which was why she rarely did so.

Even with tonight's frightening events, Regan had escaped unscathed and doubted anything like that would ever happen again. That man had stumbled upon her quite by accident, after all, and had likely given up and moved on. Her identity was safe, as was her secret sideline.

Dorisa's emeralds rested securely in the pocket of her soft cotton nightrail, the Purgatory Home for Unwanted Children could continue to provide for the orphans a while longer, and Lucy-fur once again seemed content to act as her alibi for being outside so late at night.

Regan couldn't wait to visit the orphanage tomorrow and deliver her latest donation to Father Ignacio. He and the children would be thrilled, even if the contribution was made anonymously.

"Come on, Lucy-fur, let's go check on Mother Doyle."

She pushed open the back kitchen door with a smile on her face. Only to drop both the grin and Lucy as soon as she got a clear glimpse of the two people sitting across the room, porcelain cups and saucers on the table before them.

"Reee-ow!" The cat hit the floor with a screech of annoyance and raced to safety. Likely upstairs beneath Regan's bed.

Regan couldn't work up even a token of concern for her beloved pet. Because there, making himself at home in her very own kitchen, was none other than the man who had chased her from the Finch house.

He gave a polite nod and rose to his feet to greet her. And that's when she noticed his chest. Or more to the point, the silver star pinned there, glinting in the bright lamplight.

It was the badge of a lawman. But not just any lawman—a Texas Ranger.

Regan swayed for a moment and then toppled over, hitting the floor with a loud thump.

Chapter Two

Clay lurched forward and almost caught the woman before she went down. He was a fraction of a second too late, though, and the passably attractive redhead fell like an oak. Flat on her face.

Ouch. That had to hurt, Clay thought. And then he remembered his gentlemanly duty—partly because of his Aunt Martha screeching at him over his shoulder to help her dear, sweet daughter-in-law—and went to her aid.

He rolled the woman to her back, cushioning her head with the palm of his hand. Her tight, flyaway curls caressed his skin and caused him to rub a strand, for just a moment, between his fingers.

She was really quite beautiful. Clay had thought her only passably attractive a moment ago, what with all that rusty-gold hair sprouting out around her head like a forest fire, but now that he had her literally in the palm of his hand and took a moment to study her delicate features, he found himself willingly elevating his opinion of her looks.

During the fifteen to twenty minutes before Regan's arrival, Martha had talked his ear off about her daughter-in-law. And whatever other personality traits Martha might have embellished, she was right about one thing: The woman had fine Irish skin and bone structure. Not to mention pouty pink lips.

Of course, that could be partially due to the swelling. Her nose was a big round cherry at the tip, with blood trickling from one nostril, and it looked like her mouth might have taken a bit of the blow, as well. She'd be black and blue in the morning, but she'd survive.

He untied the blue bandanna from around his neck and used it to dab at the blood. Martha was still screaming frantically behind him, working to move the squeaky wheels of her invalid chair in their direction.

"She's fine," he assured his aunt. "Just a bit of a fainting spell."

"A fainting spell?" Martha cried, shrilly enough to send coyotes running. "Regan has never fainted in her life, not even at my dear James's funeral." And then she spotted the blood, giving Clay a swift cuff to the shoulder. "What did you do to her, you ruffian? She's *bleeding!*"

His head whipped around and he fixed his aunt with wide, disbelieving eyes. "Me?" he said, offended. "I didn't do anything. She dropped like a stone. I'm trying to help!"

"Well, you're only making matters worse," she blasted him. "Move. Move away, let me see her."

Martha was tugging on his arm and before he could warn her to be careful, she'd pulled him away from Regan, causing his hold on her head to slip and her skull to hit the hardwood floor with another sickening thud.

He winced . . . and then gave an approving grunt when the second blow actually seemed to rouse the unconscious woman.

"Uhhhhhh," she moaned.

"Regan. Regan, dear, are you all right?" Martha wheeled her chair as close as possible to her prostrate daughter-in-law, and then, because she still couldn't reach her with her hands, took to nudging her gently with the toe of her shoe.

Clay rolled his eyes. What in God's name had he gotten himself into? A woman who passed out cold at the sight of a man in her kitchen and an aunt who thought kicking an accident victim was the best way to revive her. He'd have to remember to thank his mother for sending him into this mess— if he ever spoke to her again.

With a hand pressed to her obviously throbbing temple, Regan sat up. Clay didn't miss the slight shift of her body that took her out of range of Martha's pointy-toed shoe.

Ignoring his aunt's proprietary manner, he went down on one knee beside his cousin's widow. "Are you all right?" he asked gently.

31

Regan lifted the hand that partially covered her eyes and fixed him with a wary, confused gaze. Her eyes were a beautiful, sparkling green that put him in mind of soft, cushiony moss, tall, majestic fir trees, and hot, passionate evenings spent tangled in the sheets.

Clay sat back, his chin jerking up with a snap. Where the hell had that thought come from? And why did he have the rather jarring impression that the young lady he'd been about to picture in those twisted bedlinens with him would look suspiciously like the woman sprawled on the floor in front of him?

"Are you all right?" he asked again, clenching his fists to keep from reaching out to touch her.

Her glance held his for a moment before traveling down to his shirtfront and then a little to the side. If possible, her already pale face blanched even more and her eyes rolled in their sockets like marbles.

Fearing she was about to swoon again, he reached out to grasp her upper arms and steady her. But the minute his fingers came in contact with the soft, thin material of her black wrap, she bolted backwards and scurried across the floor.

Clay's brow furrowed. Just what the hell was going on here?

First his aunt seemed ecstatic to see him, insisting he push her wheeled chair into the kitchen and sit with her over a cup of tea until Regan returned from her search for a missing cat. Meanwhile, Martha couldn't say enough about her daughter-in-law, even hinting that he might find the woman attractive.

Well, he did that, but it would take more than a comely face to cause him to make advances toward his cousin's widow. *His cousin's widow*, for god's sake! Though he hadn't been close to Aunt Martha's son, he didn't even want to consider how many commandments he might be breaking by thinking so much as one improper thought about a relative by marriage.

Then the mysterious Regan returned from her task with the elusive black cat in hand, took one look at him, and immediately set about introducing her nose to the floorboards. And his aunt, who only moments before had been gushing over what a wonderful nephew he was to come for a visit, acted as though he'd hit her beloved daughter-in-law in the face with a skillet and knocked her bodily to the floor.

Now Regan was leaning against the cookstove, looking at him like horns had sprouted from the sides of his head. All because she'd gotten a glimpse of his badge.

Hmm.

"Clayton. Clayton, dear, help Regan to her feet and then to a chair," his aunt instructed.

Clay wasn't so sure Regan would appreciate his help, so he stood where he was and held a hand out to her, offering peace as well as assistance, if she wanted it.

Regan studied him cautiously, but started to rise, using the stove at her back for leverage. She didn't take his hand, moving under her own steam toward the kitchen table.

Afraid of once again incurring his aunt's wrath, Clay followed close behind, his arms out in case Regan lost her balance and started to sway.

She made it all the way to one of the spindleback chairs and plopped down on the seat. Clay released a breath he hadn't been aware he was holding and began to lower himself into the empty chair opposite her.

Only to notice his aunt, still facing the other direction in her invalid chair. He jumped up and made quick work of turning Martha around and wheeling her to the edge of the table near Regan.

Martha reached out a hand to cover Regan's where it rested on the tabletop. "How are you feeling, dear?"

Regan lifted wary eyes to Clay where he sat across the long oaken table from her. "I'm fine." She offered a small, fragile smile to Martha, turning away from Clay.

"That's quite a bump on the nose you've taken," her mother-in-law pointed out.

Regan lifted a hand to her face to find that her nose was about twice its normal size. It felt bulbous and throbbed painfully. It would likely be worse in the morning, however. Her top lip was sore, too, and she tested her front teeth to be sure she hadn't knocked anything loose.

She still couldn't believe she'd fainted. She'd never fainted before in her life. Never even suffered a dizzy spell and thought she *might* faint.

Not when her older brother had held her upside down by her ankles over the bridge near their childhood home. Not when James Doyle—thirty years her senior—had taken her from the brothel where she'd been serving drinks and brought her home to meet the rather intimidating Mother Doyle. And not when she'd walked into James's office one afternoon, only to find him slumped over on his desk, dead.

Why, then, had her pulse fluttered and her brain become fuzzy the minute she'd spotted the man who'd chased her sitting at the table with her mother-in-law?

Well, because he'd chased her, for one thing. The pursuit had scared her witless, and just when she'd thought she was safe, she'd opened the door of her very own house to find him staring right back at her.

But it wasn't that. Or not that entirely, at any rate. The dizziness had only truly begun when she'd recognized that tin star pinned to the left breast pocket of his shirt. That had frightened her even more than being chased in the dark because, for one split second, prison bars had danced in front of her eyes and she knew she'd been found out. She knew he was here to arrest her and drag her off to jail.

Even now, fear pumped through her. She looked at Mother Doyle, then the dark-haired stranger, then back to Mother Doyle. Why weren't they saying anything? If he was here for her, why didn't he say so and get it over with instead of sitting there, drilling that heavy gray gaze into her trembling body?

He hadn't arrested her yet. Why not? Maybe he didn't recognize her. He hadn't gotten a clear look at her tonight, of that she was sure. Her mask covered all of her face and hair, and the men's clothing she wore should have been enough to throw anyone off her trail unless he already suspected a woman of committing the crimes. Regan was equally confident that he hadn't followed her. Unless he was very, very good and very, very quiet.

So maybe he wasn't here for her at all. The wave of relief that washed through her body at that thought took Regan by surprise. It was almost too much to hope for. But if he *wasn't* here for her . . . if he had no idea that the woman sitting across from him was the same person he'd chased earlier tonight . . . then what did he want? What was he doing in her house?

She cast a questioning glance at her mother-in-law.

"Regan, dear," Mother Doyle said, taking the cue, "if you're sure you're feeling better, I want to introduce you to my nephew, Clayton Walker. Clayton, this is James's wife, Regan." She cast Clay a sidelong glance. "He had excellent taste, didn't he, my James?"

She didn't give Clay a chance to answer Mother Doyle's question. "Your *nephew?*" Regan asked loudly.

If it was possible, the Ranger's eyes grew even

more intense, turning a stormy shade of slate and making her want to squirm.

Wait a minute. Regan's spine snapped straight and her vision cleared. This was Mother Doyle's nephew? She didn't remember her mother-in-law ever mentioning a nephew, especially one who happened to be a Texas Ranger! If he was a relative merely here to visit his aunt, then maybe that badge wasn't a threat to her. Maybe it was just a coincidence and he wasn't here for her, after all. Oh, mercy, please let it be true.

Clearing her throat, she said, "It's a pleasure to meet you, Mr. Walker. I'm sorry about causing such a commotion. I promise you, I'm not usually inclined to swooning."

"No need to apologize," he offered in a low, bone-melting drawl. "I'm just sorry I wasn't a mite faster on my feet. I might have saved you a bloody nose if I had been."

At the mention of her nose, Regan raised her fingers and felt a small trail of what was likely dried blood. Her cheeks heated in embarrassment, turning even hotter when Clay passed a sapphire-blue kerchief to her across the table.

She wet a spot of the cloth with her tongue and dabbed it beneath her nose, hoping to erase all signs of her foolish accident.

When her mortification had passed enough to meet the man's eyes again, she raised her head and made herself ask the question foremost on her mind. One of the questions, anyway. "Are you just passing through, then, Mr. Walker?"

Please say yes, please say yes. . . .

"Call me Clayton, or just plain Clay," he told her, flashing a grin that revealed a set of straight white teeth against the sun-dappled bronze of his skin. "And, actually, it seems I may be staying for a while. That is, if you don't mind my imposing on your hospitality."

Regan opened her mouth to reflexively assure him that his visit would be no imposition whatsoever. Even though it would be, and every fiber of her being was screaming for her to tell him so.

"Now, Clayton," Mother Doyle interjected, patting an age-spotted hand over his. "You know good and well you're welcome to stay as long as you like. I invited you, after all."

That news had Regan swinging her head in her mother-in-law's direction, wondering what in all the heavens would possess Mother Doyle to invite a man—a man who also happened to be a Texas Ranger—into their household.

And then Mother Doyle answered Regan's unasked question, and Regan wished the thought had never even crossed her mind.

"Clayton here is a Texas Ranger," Mother Doyle confided, as though the silver badge declaring just that hadn't put Regan in a spin all night. "And I asked him to come because of all the trouble that's been going on around here lately. Why, this boy is going to catch that terrible thief who's been plaguing our town. Isn't that wonderful, dear?"

Chapter Three

Regan didn't look like she thought it was wonderful. She looked like she'd just swallowed a bug.

This was not going well, not well at all. Martha wrung her hands and tried not to let her concern show on her face.

When Clayton had arrived less than an hour ago, all of her dreams had materialized in her mind's eye and taken root in her heart. She'd been eager for Regan to get back so she could introduce the two. The idea of them discovering a mutual attraction that would lead to courtship, marriage, and babies had her so excited, she'd sat Clayton right down and started listing all of Regan's countless admirable qualities one by one. And she thought Clayton had been suitably impressed. If he had any sense whatsoever, he certainly would be.

But then Regan had come in through the back kitchen door, taken one look at Clayton, and swooned like an overprotected maid at her first glimpse of a naked man on her wedding night. Martha still didn't know what that had been about. No matter her inexperience before marrying James, Regan was not one to turn into a wilting water lily at the mere sight of a man sitting at her kitchen table.

Regardless of the reason for Regan's fainting spell, however, the fact remained that Martha had not handled the situation well at all.

She wanted Clayton to fall in love with Regan, to see her as the answer to his every hope and desire. He may well have been on his way to thinking just that, too—until Martha had taken to swatting at him and ordering him away from her injured daughter-in-law.

Good lord, what had she been thinking? Regan's fainting spell—whatever the cause—had been an ideal chance for Clayton to play hero. To run to Regan's rescue, nurse her back to consciousness. For Regan and Clayton to look deep into each other's eyes and see the generations of children they would create by their coming together.

It had been so perfect! And Martha had let her natural protectiveness toward Regan ruin the whole thing. If she hadn't been confined to her invalid chair at the moment, she would have kicked herself. The only solution was to repair the damage, though she hadn't one iota of an idea how to go about it.

From the looks of things, Clayton and Regan weren't exactly taking to each other. She'd seen warmer looks in icehouses in the dead of winter. And Regan kept shifting wary glances from Clayton's face to his silver star and back again.

Martha found the gesture more than a little odd. If she didn't know better, she would almost suspect that Clayton's position with the Texas Rangers made Regan nervous. But that was a ridiculous notion. Regan had never been frightened or intimidated by lawmen before. Whyever would she start now?

Maybe it was simply Clayton's standing as a *man* that had Regan acting so skittish. It had only been two years since her dear James's death. Martha knew her son and his wife had shared a true marriage in every sense of the word. She also knew in her heart that James had treated Regan kindly in their marriage bed. Martha would have given her son a stern dressing down if she had suspected he'd been anything but gentle with the girl.

Even so, Regan had been significantly younger than James. James had loved Regan, and if she hadn't exactly returned that love, Regan had certainly respected her husband and been grateful to him for all he'd done for her.

The possibility existed, however, that even though Regan had shared an intimate relationship with her husband, she was not comfortable with a gentleman her own age.

Why, that must be it! Regan was apprehensive. She was so used to being a dutiful wife to James, and now to being totally independent these past two years, that she didn't know how to act around an attractive, unattached male. Especially one who sent shivers down her spine. And Martha so hoped Clayton sent shivers down Regan's spine!

Martha cheered inwardly. It was all she could do to keep from rubbing her hands together in glee. Now that she understood the dilemma, she knew precisely how to solve the problem. Regan and Clayton needed to spend time together, to get to know each other and become comfortable with one another. And Martha knew exactly how to give them the necessary privacy.

She opened her mouth and feigned a loud yawn, using the back of her hand to add to the performance. "Oh, I'm so terribly tired all of a sudden."

Her declaration brought both youngsters' gazes around to her. It took a moment for Regan to remember herself, but as soon as she did, she jumped up and moved to Martha's aid.

"I'm so sorry, Mother Doyle. I should have realized how late it was. And tonight's events must have taken a toll."

On the contrary. Martha hadn't felt this invigorated in years. But if her plan was to work, she had to feign exhaustion as an excuse to leave Regan and Clayton alone together.

Regan turned Martha's wheeled chair with a low squeak and pushed her toward her first-floor bedroom. Clayton, Martha was delighted to notice, trailed close behind.

Regan positioned the chair close to the bed, turned down the quilted coverlet, and circled around to help Martha onto the feather mattress.

Martha had donned her nightdress hours earlier, before Regan had gone out looking for Lucy, so there was no reason to ask Clayton to leave. In a gentlemanly manner, as she'd known he would, Clayton slipped his hands beneath Martha's arms and lifted, and they had her situated in record time.

"Now, Regan, dear. You'll be sure to get Clayton settled, won't you? I thought he might be most comfortable in the Cherub Room next to your own. Fresh sheets and extra blankets are in the hall linen closet."

She didn't miss the withering look Regan shot in Clayton's direction.

"Regan is a wonderful hostess," Martha added as she laid back against the pillow and pulled the covers up to her neck. "If you need anything . . . anything at all, Clayton . . . you just tell Regan and she'll see that you get it."

There. That should do it. She'd opened the door to all kinds of interesting opportunities for Clayton and Regan to get to know each other. They would have to manage the rest on their own—at least for tonight.

Mother Doyle's comment made Regan's mouth turn down in annoyance. She would rather suck lemons than cater to her mother-in-law's nephew. But she made a conscious effort to mask her expression as she turned toward Martha.

"Do you need anything before I go, Mother Doyle?"

43

"No, no, dear. You go on and get Clayton settled, I'll be just fine."

"All right." Regan moved toward the door with steely determination, giving Clay no choice but to back into the hall. As she passed the bedside table, she turned down the oil lamp, casting the room into a shimmering darkness, lighted only by a pale shaft of moonlight spilling through the window opposite the bed. "Goodnight," she whispered and pulled the door closed quietly behind her.

Clay stood in the shadowed hall, his thumbs hooked over the well-worn leather of his gunbelt, and watched her. The steady, penetrating heat of his gaze caused gooseflesh to break out over her arms and made her want to squirm.

And then Mother Doyle's voice broke through the heavy silence, raised so they would both hear her words through the closed bedroom door. "That Regan is an absolute gem, she is. *A gem.*"

Regan closed her eyes and sighed at her mother-in-law's antics. Martha had turned quite vocal this evening and seemed to be striving to make a point. Regan couldn't for the life of her figure out what that point was, but knowing Mother Doyle, she would keep at it until everyone saw it clearly.

When she lifted her head, she found Clay grinning at her, obviously as amused by Martha as she was. She almost smiled back . . . but caught herself just in time.

What was she doing nearly smiling at this man? A Texas Ranger who could hog-tie her to his horse and drag her to jail for theft, no less. Lord have mercy.

"I suppose I should show you to your room," she said, guarding herself against those silver-gray eyes and the even more powerful force of his smile.

"Actually," he drawled, pushing himself away from the wall with his elbows, "I was hoping you'd point me toward the barn."

"The barn?" she asked, confused. Why would he want to stay in the barn when Mother Doyle had already told him there was plenty of room for him in the house? Granted, Regan might prefer he spend the night with the livestock—and after he got a good look at the Cherub Room, he might decide a pallet of straw was less frightening than Martha's decorating skills—but she wouldn't feel right leaving him out there after Mother Doyle had been so specific in her orders for Regan to see to Clayton's comfort.

"I need to unsaddle my horse," he told her, "and grab my saddlebags before I settle in for the night."

Ah, yes, the horse he'd used to chase her. Regan concentrated on keeping her expression neutral as she moved away from the stairwell leading upstairs and instead headed in the opposite direction and out the front door. Down the steps and only a short walk away stood the large, weather-worn barn. It had been built at the same time as the house and so was fairly new, but already the wind and rain had turned the unpainted boards a dull grayish-brown, and in tonight's moonlight, the wood seemed almost silver.

Clayton retrieved his mount from where the animal was tied tight to a front porch post, grazing contentedly, and followed a few paces behind her to the barn door. Grasping the heavy iron handle, she threw her weight backwards and pulled open one side of the large double doors.

The inside was black, with only a few thin slivers of light spilling in through gaps in the walls. One horse nickered softly at their entry, another shuffled her hooves in the straw bedding of her stall.

More than a little familiar with her surroundings, Regan moved directly to the lantern hanging on the center post, raised the perforated tin, and struck a match. She turned the wick up just enough so that they could see, then replaced the lantern on its hook and stuffed the burnt wooden match into the pocket of her dressing gown. Her fingertips brushed Dorisa Finch's jewels as she did so.

Glancing over the edge of several empty stalls, she found one with a soft layer of straw on the floor and swung the door open for Clay. "This one looks clean. You can keep him in here," she said.

Clay led his horse into the enclosure and began to loosen the saddle's cinch strap.

Regan moved to the feed bin and filled a metal bucket with several scoops of oats sweetened with molasses. "What's his name?" she asked as she dumped the contents of the pail into the trough built along one wall of the stall.

"Caesar. But he also answers to Jackass."

Her brows knit while she stroked the horse's warm muzzle. He looked like a perfectly delightful animal to her. "Whyever would you call him that?" she asked, a tad annoyed by his owner's seeming insensitivity.

Clay hefted the scuffed brown leather saddle from Caesar's back and carried it outside the stall. Then he returned and began to rub down his mount with the remaining saddle blanket. "Caesar has a tendency to wander off if he's not tied tight enough. It's not the best habit for a Ranger's mount to have." Though he cast a scowl at his four-legged companion, his strokes across the horse's back remained gentle and caring. "I've been in a fair share of scrapes where it would have been nice to jump on Caesar and race to safety. But Caesar, here, seems to think that once he gets me to my destination, his job is over. Don't you, boy?" He gave one of the gelding's ears a quick squeeze and Caesar snuffled in reply, blowing bits of oat and corn out of the trough where he was busy eating.

"I guess I lost my temper a few times and called him some choice names once I tracked him down. Now if he hears the word 'jackass' he comes trotting."

Regan chuckled. "Why don't you just get a new horse?"

Clay's head whipped up at that, and his dark eyes bored into her. She didn't miss the sidestep that brought Clay close enough to loop his arm over Caesar's neck. "A man doesn't just dump his mount at the nearest livery. Caesar and I have been together since I joined the Rangers."

"Sorry, I didn't realize," she said solemnly, but

47

inside she was biting down on a laugh.

She stopped petting Caesar and wiped her hands on the sides of her robe as she moved out of the stall. "I'll get some hay and a pail of water to hold him through the night." Grabbing the same bucket she'd used to hold Caesar's feed, she headed for the pump, which was outside at the corner of the barn.

She heard the crackle and snap of straw beneath heavy bootsteps only a second before Clay came up behind her. His quick movements and close proximity made her jump and she pressed a hand to her heart to slow its hastened beats.

"Let me get that," he said softly, taking the bucket and heading outside.

Regan stood for several moments, watching him move with fluid grace through the wide open doorway, watching the moonlight gild with silver his inky black hair.

And then with a huff, she shook off whatever had possessed her to stand there ogling a near stranger and turned toward the pile of hay at the back of the barn.

Retrieving a pitchfork from its hook on the wall, she moved to scoop up her first load of hay when she heard a movement behind the great mound of dried grasses. She paused, waiting to see if the noise would come again.

It had sounded like a horse shuffling in its straw bedding, but the stalls were behind her. Perhaps it was one of the barn cats or a rodent it might be chasing. But the noise hadn't sounded like a cat or a rat. It had sounded much larger.

After several long moments of silence, she decided she must have been hearing things and resumed the task of gathering hay for Caesar. But just as she heard Clay returning through the barn door at her back, she both heard and saw something moving around the hay stack. And it wasn't a horse or a cat or a rodent. It was a person.

Before she could stop herself, she let out a short shriek of panic. The shape shifted from a crouched position to standing at his full height, moving toward her.

Behind her, she heard the pail of water drop from Clay's hand and the distinct sound of a gun being whipped from its holster, the hammer being cocked.

"No!" she cried out. Letting the pitchfork fall from her grasp, she turned toward Clay, throwing up her hands and blocking his shot at the trespasser with her body.

"Get the hell out of the way, Regan," he snapped, taking a step forward and adjusting his aim.

The form behind her moved, made a dash for the back entrance to the barn. "Don't shoot," she ordered Clay before twisting around once again. "Don't run," she told the shadowed form. "Please, David, don't run."

Chapter Four

The boy stopped with his hand on the latch of the back barn door. Then he turned slowly to face her.

With a sigh, Regan moved forward and brushed specks of hay away from his long, straight hair. "What are you doing here, David?"

His eyes darted over her shoulder toward Clay and she could feel that he wanted to run. She half-turned to look at Clay who, sure enough, still had his revolver aimed directly at David. She tried not to be offended or frightened by the fact that in order to hit him, Clay would have to shoot *through* her.

"You can put the gun away, Mr. Walker," she told him softly but firmly. "David is one of the children from the local orphanage. He isn't here to hurt anyone."

"I'm not a child," the boy said. "And my name isn't David. It's Little Badger."

His angry words drew her attention back around, but not before she saw Clay returning his pistol to the holster on his hip. "You're right, I'm sorry," she offered amicably. "You're nearly an adult now, aren't you? But I first met you when you were still a little boy and didn't mind going by your Christian name, so you'll have to forgive me if I forget sometimes that you're growing like a weed. Do you think you can do that?"

David's mouth was a thin line of rebellion, but he nodded. At sixteen, he was already taller than she was. Taller than all of the other orphans at the Purgatory Home for Unwanted Children. Taller, probably, than a lot of full-grown men. Nearly as tall as Clay.

And he was so very angry. When she'd first started visiting the home, David had been a fairly happy child. He hadn't yet realized his skin was a darker shade of brown than the other children's. That the straight black hair the Sisters insisted upon cutting short was a clear sign of his Indian bloodlines. That the name his mother had given him shortly after his birth—Little Badger—had been replaced by a white man's name—David.

Now, though, he knew everything. And he hated it. He hated that he was a half-breed and that many of the townspeople, even some of the other children at the orphanage, never missed an opportunity to remind him of his heritage. He hated that he didn't know who his real parents were. He hated that the white man had taken his Comanche name and given him a new, Christian one they thought more appropriate.

Frankly, Regan didn't blame him a bit. Which was why, more often than not, when David ran away from the orphanage, he ran *to* her. Especially if twelve-year-old Hannah just happened to be staying in one of the guest bedrooms upstairs.

"Have you eaten yet?" she asked, hoping to draw the look of abject hurt and betrayal from his dark eyes.

Shoving his hands into the front pockets of his threadbare trousers, he hunched his shoulders and shook his head.

"Come inside, then, and we'll fix you a plate."

Ignoring his defiant pose, she looped an arm through his bent elbow and started forward. "Dav— I mean, Little Badger, this is Clayton Walker. He's Mother Doyle's nephew visiting from . . ." Her nose crinkled and she gave Clay a curious look. "I'm afraid I don't know where you're visiting from."

"Sweetwater."

"Sweetwater," she repeated. "Did you ever learn about Sweetwater in your geography classes, D— Little Badger?"

He kept his head solemnly slanted toward the barn floor, but shook his head in response.

"Well, then, maybe Mr. Walker can tell you a bit about the town where he lives over a slice of apple pie. You could impress all the other children with your new knowledge."

David shrugged his shoulders again in an uncaring gesture and Regan had to bite her tongue to keep from groaning in frustration.

"Did you know that Hannah is staying with us this week?" she tried instead, thinking that if anything could get through his thick outer shell, it was the mention of blond-haired, blue-eyed Hannah.

David's head snapped up and his eyes turned from cold and angry to warm and concerned. Regan knew that David had a small crush on the girl.

Pretending she didn't notice his reaction, she continued as though he wouldn't care any more about this than about Clay being from Sweetwater. "You know how I like to bring at least one of the children home with me after every visit, and it seemed like Hannah's turn again. I hope you don't mind," she said with a motherly pat to his arm. "It's been a while since you've stayed over, too, I know, and I'd have likely invited you, but you were nowhere to be found when I was getting ready to leave."

"Hannah likes it here," he mumbled, almost too low for her to hear.

"Yes, she does," Regan agreed with a smile. All of the children loved coming to her house, if only because it made them feel special for a short while. Having an adult's undivided attention was a great rarity in an orphanage filled with so many other children.

Before leading David the rest of the way to the house, she cast a glance over her shoulder to study Clay, who stood there watching their interaction.

"Are you hungry at all?" she inquired.

He shrugged a shoulder, much the way David had only moments before, and Regan found herself thinking that it must be a ubiquitous gesture men used to keep from having to answer direct questions.

And then he did answer her. "I could eat," he said simply.

"Wonderful," she said, ignoring his gruff tone. "Come into the kitchen when you're finished bedding down Caesar and I'll have a nice, warm slice of my special apple pie on the table for you."

His eyes narrowed for a minute and then one brow shot up quizzically. "What's so special about it?" he asked.

Regan just managed to bite back a laugh at his suspicious words. "You'll have to wait and see," she told him primly.

Tightening her hands on David's arm, she turned and pulled the boy toward the house, and tried her best to pretend Clay's low chuckle didn't cause her stomach to flip-flop in delight.

He wasn't jealous. All right, for a minute there he *had* wanted to take the kid by the scruff of the neck and toss him through the barn door head-first. But that was only because he'd seen the way Regan's face lit up as she brushed loose strands of hay out of the boy's hair. And straightened his suspenders. And linked her arm through his.

She had looked at Clay and fainted dead away. An orphan half-breed nearly attacked her in a dark barn and she took him to her breast like a long-lost child.

"Shit," he muttered, as the image took form in his head. Only there was no child in his mind's eye, just a bare breast. Regan's bare breast.

"Beans and bacon," he began, muttering to himself as he went about forking hay into Caesar's stall and refilling the water bucket he'd dropped when he thought Regan was in danger. "Blisters from new boots. Saddle sores. Hardtack." He gave a little shudder at that. "Jake's missing pinky finger. Aunt Martha's screeching."

There. His mind started thinking of other things and the heat in his loins began to dissipate. "Mom's apple pie." Another shudder shook him. His mother was a good woman, but she'd never made a pie in her life that didn't taste like it came straight from a cattle pasture.

Now, Regan's pie. . . . Compared to his mother's baking, it could taste like sawdust and still be an improvement, but he had to admit he was eager to see just what made her believe it was so all-fired special.

"Dammit," he cursed again, and fixed a scowl on Caesar, who was chewing contentedly on a mouthful of hay. "Why didn't you stop me before I circled back around to thinking of her?"

Caesar gave a disgusted snort and a look that pretty much reminded his master he'd been gelded years ago and Clay's problems in that area were his own.

"Thanks a lot," Clay returned glumly. He arranged the pail of water where he didn't think Caesar would overturn it during the night, then closed and locked the stall door before resting his arms on the edge to look back in at his mount. Thanks to the often solitary existence of being a Texas Ranger, Caesar also happened to be one of Clay's best friends. At least he was a good listener, and Clay did have a tendency to talk to himself when he had a problem.

"I'm going to go back in there and have a slice of apple pie. That's it."

Caesar ignored him.

"She's not even pretty," he added. "All that fiery red hair busting out all over. Aunt Martha told me she's Irish, so with all that red hair, you can bet she has a powder-keg temper. I could be just walking through the house, minding my own business one day, and she'd come up behind me and flatten me with a rolling pin. Who needs that?"

Caesar continued chewing with that casual, side-to-side motion of his, blinking sleepily.

"She's my cousin's wife, you know. It's not smart to lust after another man's wife."

Caesar gave a great shake of his head, blowing bits of hay and spittle in Clay's direction.

Clay swore—out of habit more than anything else—and brushed the bits of wetness from his shirt. "I know Cousin James is dead, you don't have to tell me that. Ma reminded me before we headed out, Aunt Martha mentioned it at least a dozen times after I arrived, and Regan is dressed in black from head to foot."

Unfortunately, the black Regan was wearing happened to be a nightdress and wrap, and didn't do all that good a job of hiding her womanly curves. And before she'd thought to tie the little ribbon at the front of the frilly robe, he'd quite enjoyed the sight of that shadowy area between her breasts. Not to mention how nicely her breasts had filled out the gown.

"I know what the problem is, Caes," he said with utter confidence. "It's not her, it's just that she's a woman and I haven't had a woman in quite some time. I'm bound to get a little . . . worked up at the sight of any female after this long."

Caesar huffed and began pawing the ground with his hoof. One, two, three strikes.

Damn horse, always acting as his conscience when there were things he'd rather forget. "I don't know what you're talking about," Clay insisted.

One, two, three more strikes on the ground. "All right. Christ, you're stubborn for having four legs and not being able to talk." Clay let his gaze drift to the back of the stall, away from Caesar's too-knowing eyes. "So it hasn't been all that long. Three weeks, as you're so eager to remind me. But that doesn't mean I couldn't still be in need of another quick tumble. Maybe it's a full moon, or something in the water here in Purgatory."

Another equine snort made him admit that the moon was a quarter-size crescent in the sky and he hadn't tried any of Aunt Martha's god-awful-smelling tea, so the only drink he'd had since entering town had been from his own canteen.

"I hear tell Thurston Mueller is looking for new stock," he bit out, fixing the horse with a warning glare. "You wouldn't want me to send you to Mueller's glue factory, would you?"

Caesar turned away from Clay. Then he lifted his tail and a loud, prolonged squeak filled the barn.

The smell sent Clay stumbling back several steps, waving a hand in front of his nose. "Jesus God, horse. What have you been eating?" One last, tiny squeak was Caesar's only response.

To keep from gagging at the stench, Clay grabbed his saddlebags and hurried out of the barn, slamming the big, sliding door closed behind him.

He kept waving a hand in front of his face, trying to dispel the odor lodged in his nostrils and take in large lungfuls of fresh night air before he reached the house.

He hadn't come to any great conclusions about his attraction to his cousin's widow, and thanks to Caesar's sudden case of flatulence, he didn't think he'd be sharing his troubles with his trusty mount again anytime soon. He did, however, think he might take a trip into town tomorrow and see if there was any kind of entertainment at the local saloon. A tasty morsel with red hair and dainty white ankles who might help banish Regan's countenance from his brain. And his trousers, he hoped, as he climbed the front porch steps, readjusting the course material around the area of his crotch before opening the front door and stepping into the house.

Aware of his aunt sleeping in the downstairs bedroom only a few feet away, he stepped lightly as he made his way to the kitchen. Pushing open the swinging door, he found Regan sitting at one end of the table with her back to him, that bright red nest of hair tied with a thin black ribbon that did nothing to tame the wild curls. Across from her, David froze with a forkful of dinner raised halfway to his mouth. The boy's eyes, which had been friendly and open only a second earlier, turned wary and watchful.

Noting the change in David's demeanor, Regan turned to look at Clay.

"There you are," she said pleasantly enough, and rose to cross the kitchen. "Have a seat. Your pie should be plenty warm by now." She motioned to the chair she'd just vacated, then grabbed a nearby dishtowel and used it to protect her hands while she opened the door to the oven warmer and removed a plate with a large chunk of pie resting on it.

Around a bite of food, David butted into the conversation and mumbled to Regan, "What happened to your nose?"

Her motions slowed as she gingerly lifted two fingers to test the still-red and slightly swollen appendage. "I bumped it, is all. I'm sure it will be fine by morning." Her brusque tone put an end to that line of questioning.

She grabbed a fork from the silverware drawer as she passed and placed the dessert in front of Clay, then took a step back. Hands on hips, she watched him, awaiting his response to her baking skills.

"Well? Aren't you going to try it?" With a slight shift of her head, she looked at the boy. "Finish your pork roast, David, and you can have a slice, too."

As wary as the boy seemed of Clay, the promise of Regan's apple pie spurred him into action. Even her use of his Christian name, which he'd been so offended by out in the barn, didn't seem to bother him as he shoveled bite after bite of meat and potatoes into his mouth, barely bothering to chew.

Clay picked up his own fork and moved to eat, but was stopped by the roll of Regan's eyes.

"I told you to *finish* your dinner." She laughed at David. "I don't recall saying you should *inhale* it. What will Father Ignacio think if I send you back with a stomachache?"

David turned soft, hopeful eyes to Regan.

Her own lashes narrowed. "I suppose you think that because it's so late, and because you'll likely be sick from eating so fast, I'll invite you to stay the night."

The boy shrugged his shoulders, but Clay had a feeling that's exactly what he was hoping for. Worse yet, he suspected Regan had planned that very thing all along—she was just toying with David to keep from seeming like too much of a push-over.

Not likely. Clay had noticed her entire change in demeanor the minute she'd recognized the intruder in the barn as a runaway from the orphanage. With Clay, her eyes were chips of emerald ice and she acted as though simply being in the same room with him was enough to bring on a case of consumption. With David, her eyes turned warm and maternal, and she either didn't realize or didn't care that the boy had nearly gotten them both shot by sneaking around in the dead of night.

Even as he dug into his pie and tipped a large chunk onto his fork, Clay was beginning to tack days onto his original estimate of how long it would be before he spoke to his mother again. An invalid aunt, a fainting cousin-in-law, a farting horse, and two bloody orphans under the same roof. And he had to put up with all of them until he caught that damned thief.

He stuffed the bite of pie into his mouth and began to chew. He didn't even much care that his mother had nothing to do with Caesar's offensive ailment. He was still going to hold it against her, since it was her fault that he was stuck in this no-account town to begin with.

The longer he chewed, the more he began to realize his mouth didn't taste like sawdust. Neither did it taste like day-old cow shit. In fact, it tasted good. Damn good.

"Mmmm." The uncontrolled utterance passed his lips before he had time to think. "Mmmm-mmm. This is . . ." The best thing he'd ever tasted.

"Special?" Regan offered, a wicked, almost challenging gleam in her eyes.

" 'Special' doesn't even come close," he admitted, but couldn't think of a single other word to describe her pie that didn't have something to do with sex. And somehow he didn't think she would appreciate having her wholesome dessert compared with a mind-shattering climax.

Accepting his comment as enough of a compliment, she bustled about the kitchen fixing an equally large slice for David. "The secret is in the pecans. And the brown sugar. I use a lot of brown sugar." She divulged her secret with the impish lift of one side of her mouth.

Clay could taste the brown sugar. The apple slices were buried in the stuff. And with every bite, there was also the crunch and nutty flavor of pecans.

He finished the dessert in short order and slouched down in his chair. "God, that was good."

"I'm glad you enjoyed it," Regan said on a chuckle.

She brought David's slice straight from the warmer and Clay eyed it greedily. "Would you like another piece?" she asked solicitously, catching his covetous staring.

"More than I want to wake up in the morning," he replied with conviction.

This time, her amused laughter rang through the room, sending a shock of desire straight to his groin. Delicious food delivered by a beautiful woman. God was in His heaven and all was right with the world. Now if he could only get that woman into his bed . . .

She placed his refilled plate in front of him and he murmured a word of thanks. "You know, they say the way to a man's heart is through his stomach," he told her, digging in.

"That's not the way I heard it," she returned, brushing crumbs from the oaken tabletop with the yellow-striped towel in her hands.

Clay sat back and chewed. "Oh yeah?" he asked once he had swallowed. There was something about the slight flush to her cheeks and the way she'd sucked her lower lip between her teeth. As though sorry she'd said anything at all. "Just what did you hear?"

Her hand froze, pausing her nervous movements. For a moment she simply looked at him, as though weighing her next words carefully.

"I think I'll go upstairs and find some extra blankets for you, David. There's more milk in the icebox out back. Help yourself to more pie, if you'd like."

She ignored Clay completely, moving back to the sink to fold and replace the dishtowel she'd used to protect her fingers from the heat of the oven. And then she headed for the kitchen door, refusing to make eye contact with either of them.

Two steps before she reached the swinging door, she stopped. Clay chewed thoughtfully, watching her chest rise and fall as she took several deep breaths. Then she turned.

"The way to a man's heart . . ." She paused for a moment, as though steeling herself to continue. Still refusing to meet his gaze, she leaned over his shoulder. Her words were barely a whisper as her warm breath stirred his hair and tickled the lobe of his ear. "Is through his belt buckle."

Chapter Five

Oh, how she enjoyed watching him choke and sputter and turn red around the ears.

She shouldn't have said it. She should have tamped down on the impulse and reminded herself that she was no longer a green girl working at Madam Pomfrey's Hospitality House—which is where she'd originally heard the crude remark, of course—but an experienced, ladylike widow who would never utter such suggestive words.

But the rebel in her, the same one who changed into trousers and broke into her neighbors' homes, had to admit that she liked watching this big, bad Texas Ranger squirm. From the moment he'd arrived, he'd thrown her off balance, sent her into a panic, and caused her to swoon—an act that still mortified her right down to her toenails. It was past time for him to be caught off guard.

Regan stood in the upstairs hallway, a heavy woolen blanket pressed to her face to keep her laughter from being heard. After making that totally out-of-character remark, she'd rushed from the room, her own face flaming, but not before she'd caught a glimpse of Clay's stunned, startled, *flabbergasted* reaction.

Oh, she was terrible. A horrible, nasty person, no doubt bound for the fiery depths of hell.

Another bubble of merriment worked its way up her throat and she quickly stepped into the linen closet and buried her face in a whole *pile* of blankets to muffle the sounds of her amusement.

The scrape of wood against wood warned her that either Clay or David had pushed his chair back and would likely be making his way upstairs at any moment. The fear of being caught in the midst of her mirth sobered her immediately and she began pulling sheets and blankets from the closet. Just as she heard footsteps on the stairs, she raced into the spare bedroom and began shaking out new sheets to make the bed.

This room was rarely used. It was Martha's favorite, as she'd decorated it from ceiling to floor, but even though the children loved to sneak in and stare at all the bare-bottomed babies gracing the walls, they never wanted to sleep in here. Regan couldn't fault them for that; she didn't spend any more time in the Cherub Room than she had to, either.

Clay crossed the threshold as Regan tucked the final corner of the bottom sheet beneath the mattress. David stood a foot or so behind him, his hands tucked into his pockets. The normally belligerent tilt of his chin seemed softened for a change. A warm dinner and sweet dessert must have done him some good, but from the quick shifting of his eyes, Regan didn't think he planned to trust Clay anytime soon.

Regan agreed with David's caution on that point, at least. Being a Ranger, and Martha's nephew to boot, Clay was probably a trustworthy enough sort—for anyone who hadn't broken the law. But she *had* broken the law. Several times over the past months, in fact. And there was no way she'd trust him not to put her in jail if he ever found out. Which was why she had to be so very careful around him. Careful about what she said, what she did, how she acted . . .

Lord, but these next few days were going to be the longest of her life. She hoped Clay's visit was a short one.

"You've got quite a . . . flair for decorating," Clay said from behind her, and she could have sworn from the mumbled sound of his voice that he was biting his tongue.

"Isn't it lovely?" She pretended to be unaware of the hideous furnishings. "But I'm afraid I can't take credit for any of this. Your aunt decorated every inch of it herself."

She thought she heard him mutter something like, "I should have figured," as he began taking in more of the details of the room. The lamps were turned up enough for him to see just about everything.

The lamps themselves were very, very feminine, with pink teardrop crystals hanging from the painted caps. And painted on those caps, of course, were little blond and brunette cherubs with feathery white wings and tight red lips.

Just about every inch of the room was covered with bare-bottomed babies floating on gossamer wings. The wallpaper had vertical rows of the heaven-sent children separated by dark pink slashes of ribbon and bows. The carpeting matched those lines of ribbon, as did the lace draperies and the lone armchair stationed in one corner of the room. The throw pillow arranged artfully on the seat of that chair had been embroidered with a cherub. Not a full cherub, merely the head and wings of one poor, auburn-haired baby.

The cherub-covered walls even boasted framed lithographs of cherub-related paintings. Cherubs bringing the message of love to two fifteenth-century star-crossed lovers. Cherubs fluttering above the heads of two longtime and devoted lovers. Cherubs dancing on the clouds of heaven. So many cherubs . . .

And if that wasn't bad enough, every available surface of furniture was covered with tiny cherub figurines that Martha insisted be dusted frequently and with the utmost care. Little did Martha know that Regan put off that particular chore as long as humanly possible. Only when Mother Doyle rolled her wheeled chair to the base of the stairs and threatened to pull herself up to the second story on her hands and knees to do it herself did Regan rush around her with a cleaning rag and blow the little darlings free of dirt. She would never surreptitiously break one of Martha's beloved knick-knacks or deny her her fondest desire, but Regan absolutely *hated* being alone in this room.

A niggling voice in the back of her mind suggested that her feelings stemmed from the fact that the bare-bottomed toddlers on the pillows and walls served as a poignant reminder that she didn't have children of her own—and likely never would—though she'd wanted babies so badly. But that was ridiculous, considering that these were cherubs and therefore not really babies at all. Besides, she had all the progeny she could ever desire in the children from the orphanage. Any time she got heartsick over not having a baby of her own, she only need ride into town and cuddle little girls like Hannah or little boys like David when he'd been younger.

Shaking off the depressing thoughts, she smoothed out the ruffles of the pillowslip and turned down the top coverlet.

"There, that should keep you plenty warm for tonight."

Clay stared at Regan's long fingers on the pink bedclothes and tried to block out every other detail of the room. This place was enough to give a grown man nightmares. He wasn't the least surprised to learn it was his aunt's handiwork.

He'd rather bed down in the barn with Caesar than spend the night in this room, surrounded by all these big-headed, bare-assed, smiling angel babies, and he suspected Regan knew it. Which was why he wouldn't give her the satisfaction of complaining.

"This'll be just fine, thanks." He glanced over his shoulder at David as he set his saddlebags at the foot of the bed. "You gonna catch some shut-eye with me, kid?" He didn't want the snot-nosed orphan spending the night with him any more than he wanted to toss and turn till dawn in this room, but if he had to suffer, the sour-mouthed brat could damn well suffer right along with him.

David shook his head, backing up a step. To get away from the Cherub Room or the idea of sleeping with Clay, he didn't know. But with a comforting smile on her face, Regan moved to David's side and slipped an arm around his back.

"You two will be very comfortable in here," she told him.

The boy didn't budge. "I'm not sleeping in here. With him," he spat out.

Blinking innocently—when Clay was sure Regan Doyle was anything but innocent—she said, "But I thought you wanted to spend the night. It's much too late for you to walk back to the Home by yourself, but if you're set on returning tonight, I'm sure Mr. Walker would be happy to see you there safely."

Clay would do no such thing, but he didn't say so, having seen before how Regan wrapped this kid around her little finger. Give her another two seconds and she'd have him scrubbing her floors.

"Why can't I stay with Hannah?" David asked, not giving up just yet.

Regan moved around the room, fluffing a pillow here, rearranging a glass trinket there. "Because Hannah is already sound asleep and I won't have you waking her. And even at the Home, the boys and girls sleep in separate rooms. You know that." She turned to face him, her arms crossed loosely beneath the swells of those breasts Clay was doing his damnedest not to think about. "I'm afraid sharing this room with Mr. Walker is your only choice. Unless you prefer to return to the orphanage."

David's mouth turned down in an angry frown as he stared at the scuffed toe of his boots. Then he raised his head and shot daggers at Clay. "I'll stay, then, on account of Hannah, but I ain't sleepin' with *him*. I'll sleep on the floor."

"Oh, what a fine idea," Regan put in cheerily, as though he'd just suggested they hold a royal ball. "I'll get you an extra blanket." And she disappeared into the hall.

It was just as well David was being mule-stubborn, Clay thought. He didn't particularly want to curl up next to a prickly kid any more than the boy wanted to curl up to him. At least this way he'd have the nice, wide mattress all to himself. It had been a while since he'd spent the night on anything more than an uncomfortable one-man cot. And spending the night on a hardwood floor might be just what the kid needed to drive that surliness out of him.

Regan swept back into the room, blanket in hand, just as Clay was kicking off his boots. She helped David fold it into a little pallet on the floor, then bustled about turning down all the lamps that earlier had blazed bright. She left only the one beside the bed burning, apparently trusting Clay to turn that one down himself.

Considering the remark she'd made in the kitchen, he didn't stop undressing just because she was still in the room. He did move more slowly than usual, removing his socks, then unbuttoning but not taking off his shirt. He waited until she'd turned back to him before moving a hand to his belt buckle and letting it rest there.

"If you need anything . . ." Her words stopped as rose-pink heat filled her cheeks. She averted her gaze, but her blush continued to grow. "I'll, um . . . be right . . ." Words failing, she lifted a hand and pointed at the wall. "Right over . . ." She pointed even more fiercely. "There."

"I'm sure we'll be fine," Clay drawled. "Goodnight."

Regan looked his way once more and he saw courage building in her eyes. With a slow grin, he flipped the silver buckle beneath his fingers.

And she ran.

"Goodnight," she called out quickly before she disappeared, all but slamming the door behind her.

Clay chuckled, then finished shucking out of his clothes. David, he saw, was sitting cross-legged on

71

the floor, glaring at him. A little terror down to the bone, he thought. Well, as long as he didn't try to attack Clay in the middle of the night, Clay certainly wasn't going to worry about him.

Stripped down to his drawers, he wrapped the straps of his gunbelt around the holster and set the weapon on the bedside table. Then he blew out the lamp and climbed under the covers, propping his folded arms and head on the soft pillow Regan had just fluffed to perfection.

He closed his eyes and envisioned his cousin's widow bustling about her room, primping for bed. Untying the bow of her wrap, letting the silky material slip down her arms. Drawing a soft-bristled brush through her long hair. Or maybe not . . . he didn't imagine even a hard-bristled comb could be dragged through those tight, untamed tresses. So she would likely crawl straight into bed. Under warm, soft covers. Hugging a plump pillow to her breast like a lover . . .

Ah, yes, like a lover.

Clay drifted off to sleep with a smile on his face.

Chapter Six

It was the scream that woke him. He was right in the middle of parting Regan's milky-white thighs and exploring a whole new patch of tight red curls, but instead of savoring the low moans he knew he could induce, a high-pitched shriek nearly shattered his eardrums.

He bolted upright in bed, cursing, blinking his eyes to adjust to the dark, and taking a moment to remember where he was. Not bothering to pull on his trousers, he grabbed his gun and headed for the hall, in the direction of the screams.

David, already wide awake, bumped him aside as he opened the door. He was about to cuss the kid out when Regan's bedroom door opened and she disappeared behind David into the room across the hall.

Why did it seem that everyone knew what was going on around here but him?

Heaving a sigh, he went back for a shirt and pants, buttoned both, then followed the others, not even wondering what he would find. Given his experiences in Purgatory so far, he doubted even an ongoing burlesque show behind the opposite door could surprise him.

He started across the hall, only to step on something soft and furry. Regan's black-as-midnight cat let out a wake-the-dead screech and tore down the stairs, further tripping Clay in the process. He lurched forward, catching himself against the wall with the palms of his hands. For a moment, he remained in that position, breathing in and out and trying to quell the urge to commit bloody murder.

He yearned for the open trail. For nights spent in complete isolation out in the middle of nowhere. For long days of travel when the only sign of life he came across was the occasional hawk or rattlesnake.

Feather mattress or no feather mattress, he'd have gotten a better night's sleep bunking down in the barn with Caesar. It was still an option, he reminded himself, and pushed away from the papered wall.

Although his temper had dissipated, he still had to concentrate on breathing in and out to keep from cursing. He'd known this trip was a bad idea. He'd told his mother it was a bad idea. And now he was stuck here with an aunt he barely knew and wasn't even sure he liked, a woman who'd apparently never met a homeless child she didn't want to adopt, and a lightning-quick cat who was going to break his neck if he wasn't careful.

Why the hell didn't anyone ever listen to him?

With a sigh of resignation, he pushed open the door to the room David and Regan had both entered and took in the scene that had awakened him in the middle of a very nice dream, dammit.

Even in the dark, he could see Regan's shapely form sitting on the edge of a low bed, her arms wrapped around a small child. David was crouched on the floor beside them, his face strained with worry as he patted the girl's back. This must be Hannah, Clay thought.

The creak of the door had all three figures turning toward him. The little girl looked terrified, David looked like he wanted to scratch Clay's eyes out, and Regan looked . . . maternal.

It was not a thought that placated his already off-kilter frame of mind.

Regan murmured calming words to the child on her lap, then gazed up at Clay. "It was just a nightmare," she told him, still holding the little girl. "She has them sometimes."

Brushing a loose strand of hair away from Hannah's damp forehead, she kissed the child's temple. "But we're all better now, aren't we, darling?"

The little girl nodded.

"What do you say we go downstairs and make some nice, hot cocoa while we decide what to fix for breakfast? Would you like that?"

Hannah nodded again, but kept her head burrowed against Regan's neck.

"David," Regan began, but the boy obviously knew what Regan was going to say before she got the words out because he grabbed a blanket off the bed and draped it over the little girl's fragile frame.

Clay glanced out the window. Not so much as a spot of light broke out over the horizon. "Breakfast?" he asked. "Already?" He was used to early mornings, but this was bordering on the absurd.

"It was almost time to get up, anyway," Regan said as she stood up and gently guided Hannah out the door and toward the stairs.

"Just what time do people get up around these parts?"

She chuckled. "Whenever little girls have nightmares and need a cup of cocoa to calm them down."

Trailing behind her as she negotiated the dark stairwell, he said, "I think I'm going to need more of a reason than that."

"Well, there are always the chickens."

"The chickens?"

"Yes, the chickens. And the horses. And Pansy."

"Pansy," he repeated, wondering what the hell they were talking about now. Swear to God, the longer he spent in this house, the less hold he seemed to have on reality. At least Regan's and Aunt Martha's reality.

"Pansy is our cow. She'll need milking before long. The horses and chickens will need to be fed, and eggs collected. I usually do all of that not long after sunup."

They'd reached the kitchen now. David had lit a lamp on the wall over the table and was piling wood into the cookstove.

"But the sun isn't up yet," Clay argued.

Regan set Hannah on a chair near the table and wrapped the blanket more securely about her shoulders, then turned a serene smile on Clay. "Well, sometimes I get an early start."

An early start. Hmph. He wondered if it would be downright uncivil of him to go on back to bed. Probably.

"You're welcome to go back to bed, if you like," Regan suggested sweetly, practically reading his mind.

David's nod of agreement was accompanied by a smug look that set Clay's teeth on edge.

So they'd both prefer he carry himself back upstairs, huh? Well, there wasn't much chance of that now. No matter how loud his tired, gritty eyes screamed for him to do just that, his stubborn pride would no longer let him. If a woman and kid could wake up—and stay up—at such an ungodly hour, then so could he. Damn it all to hell.

Dropping into one of the three remaining chairs, he let his body slide down until he had a nice slouch going. He'd stay awake, then. He'd even help feed the chickens and milk that ridiculously named cow—*later*. But he'd be damned if he was going to help make cocoa and an early breakfast for a couple of orphans who should have had the decency to let a man sleep through the night.

Besides, the boy seemed to have everything under control. He was crinkling old pieces of newspaper and stuffing them in between the cuts of wood he'd piled up a moment ago.

Clay maintained his sulk while he watched Regan bustle around the kitchen. First she set out a tin of cocoa powder and a canister of sugar, then she collected milk from the outside icebox. By the time she'd gathered all her ingredients, David had the stove warming up and she moved to mix hot chocolate for Hannah.

While the milk was heating, she gathered eggs and smoked bacon from the porch. She cracked and sliced and had both frying on the stove before Clay could blink. In one smooth move, she turned from stove to counter and emptied the pan of cocoa into four tin cups. It was when she tried to carry them all to the table in one trip that Clay decided he'd better get up and help her.

Pushing to his feet, he crossed to the counter and took the hot cups from her hands. They nearly scalded his fingers as he delivered them, setting one in front of each child and the remaining two at his and Regan's places.

He turned back, only to have a stack of plates all but shoved into his belly. "Be sure to let them cool," she said to Hannah and David as they reached for the mugs of cocoa. To Clay she said, "After you get these put out, you can add forks and knives. They're in that drawer." She tapped the drawer in question

as she passed on her way back to the stove to flip
the bacon and eggs.

This was why he hadn't wanted to get up, Clay
groused beneath his breath. Show a woman a little
consideration and the next thing you knew, she had
you setting the damn table. What was he, a scullery
maid?

And just how the hell did Regan manage to be so
chipper at . . . he wasn't sure what time it was, but
he'd guess even roosters were still sleeping soundly
at this hour.

As he stomped across the kitchen for forks and
knives, he caught Regan eyeing him, a greasy spatula in her hand.

"What?" he barked, and added a scowl for good
measure.

"Are you always this pleasant in the morning?"

"Only when I'm forced to be up before God."

She chuckled and rested the spatula on the coun-
tertop. "Oh, I think God is awake by now."

"Don't be so sure," he grumbled, clattering uten-
sils as he counted out four knives and four forks,
then stalked his way back to the table.

"Well, let me fix you breakfast and then you're
welcome to go back to bed for a while longer."

Was it his tired imagination, or did she sound
cheery about the idea of him going back to sleep?
He finished off the place settings, then cocked his
head and studied her prim figure in that black nightdress. The toes of her black slippers peeked from
beneath the hem.

"You going back to bed, too?" he asked. Last

night, he'd have made sure there was suggestive inflection and second meaning to his words. Now, he just wanted to know what she would be doing while he was snoring his way back into his dream. If he was lucky.

"Oh, no. I have plenty of chores to do around here, and then I thought the children and I would go into town."

He watched her a moment more. She held his gaze for several seconds before taking up the spatula and turning back to the stove.

"Come to think of it, a trip to town doesn't sound like such a bad idea. I'm sure I'll be more awake after a bite to eat, and I need to talk to the sheriff about all the robberies you've been having around here, anyway."

Regan's body tensed. Why had she told him she was planning a trip to town? Why couldn't she have kept her fool mouth shut and let him go back to bed so she could carry on with the errands she needed to run? Now he would be underfoot and she'd have the devil's own time getting away from him long enough to exchange Dorisa Finch's jewels for cash.

The strip of bacon she'd been in the process of turning slipped from the end of the fork and back into the iron skillet, sending hot grease sizzling. A drop jumped from the pan to land on the side of her hand.

"Ouch!" She gasped with surprise and a touch of pain and brought the spot to her lips.

Clay rounded the counter and came to stand behind her. "Let me see."

"It's nothing, I'm fine," she said, moving her hand away from her mouth and inspecting it for grease burns. There was barely any red visible, and most of that was from her sucking on the spot.

He took her arm anyway, wrapping his big, dark hand around her slender wrist. His touch didn't alarm her nearly as much as the sight of those strong fingers, with just a sprinkling of hair covering them, against the nearly porcelain whiteness of her skin. He was tanned to bronze perfection, she was cursed with pale Irish skin that burned at so much as a hint of sunlight. He was large and commanding, she felt tiny and delicate next to him.

He was a man. She was a woman. And that single thought seemed to steal the breath from her lungs. She jerked her hand out of his grasp and took an unsteady step away from his towering expanse. "It's fine, really."

His dusky lashes narrowed a fraction as he watched her. He was probably thinking she'd lost a marble or two to jump back that way.

"You should put some butter on it."

"Father Ignacio washes burns with cold water," David put in from his seat by the table. He didn't seem overly concerned, but then, he'd seen her receive worse burns than this and knew if she was really hurt, she would have yelped much louder.

"Butter works better," Clay maintained, shooting David what could only be described as a challenging glare.

She'd never seen a grown man so intent upon disliking a child. Or a young man so intent upon despising an elder. She didn't even know why they had daggers for each other, only that the tension between them was palpable. That was another reason she'd made them stay in the Cherub Room last night—in hopes that being confined together would dispel some of their animosity toward each other.

"Cold water takes away the sting."

Regan knew that if she didn't interrupt, this ridiculous argument would turn into a full-scale shouting match. "I'm not sure it matters what would work best, as it doesn't hurt at all any longer."

"My mama used honey," Hannah murmured quietly, her face tipped over her cup of cocoa, concentrating on stirring the liquid inside with the tip of one finger.

"That's a wonderful idea, Hannah. I'll use honey." She shot Clay and David both quelling glances as she skipped to the cupboard and dabbed a bit of honey on the now nonexistent burn. Then she moved back to the stove and took the sizzling skillet from the heat.

Clay took his seat at the table while she scooped fried eggs and crispy bacon onto everyone's plates. She poured tall glasses of milk for the children and freshly brewed coffee for Clay and herself.

"Ah," she sighed once she was seated. "This is nice." She smiled at her three breakfast companions, imagining for a moment that they were a family. It was a ridiculous notion, she knew. She would never marry a man like Clay, who harbored such obvious animosity toward David . . . not to mention his occupation as a lawman. She would also never have kids of her own. But it was nice to pretend she had two beautiful children, just like Hannah and David.

For a few minutes, she let herself daydream. Let herself pretend Clay was a nice man—as opposed to a surly one—and *not* a Texas Ranger. And that David and Hannah were her flesh and blood. The illusion would break apart the moment Clay claimed the bacon was too crisp and David said it wasn't crisp enough, but for now, it was a perfectly lovely fantasy in her mind's eye.

"David," she said, while her imagination was still firm, "would you like to say grace?"

They all lowered their heads and waited for David to begin.

"Oh, Great Spirit . . ." he began.

Clay's head snapped up. She didn't see the motion, but she sensed it and quickly raised her own to meet his eyes. With a shake of her head, she warned him not to say anything. David had only recently discovered his true heritage and was obsessed with learning everything he could about his people and exercising his new knowledge at every opportunity. Especially when he thought it might upset those around him. He was exerting his independence, behaving under the notion that whites had treated him like an outcast all his life, he was now going to give them more than enough reason to hate and fear him.

83

Clay glowered, but bowed his head once again and let David pray over their meals in his own way. When he finished, everyone reached for their forks and dug in, the soft clinks of silver tines against metal plates filling the room.

"Regan?" a shrill voice cut into the near-silence, making Regan jump. "Regan, are you up?"

"Oh, my lord," she whispered, getting up so quickly, she nearly overturned her chair.

She'd forgotten Mother Doyle!

Chapter Seven

The line of people rushing to Martha's room looked like a funeral procession, with Regan in the lead, followed by Clay, who was followed by David, who was followed by a blanket-clutching Hannah. They all stood in the hallway as Regan opened the door and hurried to light a lamp.

Martha sat on the edge of the bed, the covers thrown back, her weak and crippled legs dangling over the side.

"Mother Doyle, you're awake," Regan exclaimed in a falsely bright voice.

"I don't know how a body could sleep through all the racket," her mother-in-law grumbled. "I expected you to come for me after you started breakfast, but you never did."

Martha's guilt-tipped arrow went straight to Regan's heart. She'd been so preoccupied with Clay and the children that she'd forgotten her mother-in-law even existed. With a silent groan, she thought, *I am going straight to hell*. And a hundred little old ladies with pitchforks would be there to greet her.

But even though Martha was making a fuss about being forgotten, she would be heartbroken to know it was actually true. So Regan put on her most innocent face and let not a hint of guilt color her words.

"I didn't want to disturb you, Mother Doyle. You need your sleep, and you know I'm happy to fix your breakfast whenever you get up."

"Nonsense," Martha snapped with a wave of her hand. "I'm perfectly able to join everyone else for a family meal. Now close the door and help me dress. Then, Clayton, you can get me situated in my chair and wheel me into the kitchen."

Clay straightened from where he'd been lounging against the doorframe and sent Regan an amused wink over Martha's head. "Yes, ma'am," he drawled. "It'll be my pleasure."

He all but saluted, and Regan quickly stuck her face back into the open closet before he spotted the smile tugging at the corners of her mouth.

Because she had no control over her failing health, Martha liked to control everything else. She made a habit of handing out clipped orders and expecting them to be carried out to the letter. And she loved anyone who immediately complied. If Clay continued to be so acquiescent to Martha's demands, he would soon have the elderly woman's sole devotion. Regan wouldn't be surprised if he was fully aware of this fact. She suspected the man could charm the garters off just about any woman, be she seventeen or seventy—and every age in between.

It was fortunate, then, that Regan had no interest in men whatsoever. She was quite happy being a widow, and her fancy San Francisco garters were tightly tied in place, thank you very much.

The door clicked shut as Clay closed the two women in together, and Regan turned to Martha with a lovely blue calico dress in hand.

"Not that one, dear. Stuck in that bloody invalid chair, that dress makes me look like a moving meadow of wildflowers."

"It does no such thing," Regan protested, but she was already on her way back to the closet to try again.

"Grab that nice lavender one I wore just last week."

"Your church dress?" Regan asked in surprise. "But I thought you saved that for special occasions."

Martha raised her nose and gave a little sniff. "It's not every day my nephew is here for a visit. I want to look my best. Now bring it here, and while I change, you can look for my new button-up boots."

Oh, no, not the button-ups. Lord, but getting those things on Martha's feet would take all day, and half the evening besides. What a woman confined to an invalid chair needed with so many pairs of shoes, Regan would never know. No one ever even *saw* her feet!

"I'm not sure they're here, Mother Doyle," she tried, pretending to look for the things.

"Of course they are. Check the back of the closet," Martha insisted.

With a sigh, Regan dropped to her hands and knees and began sorting through the many pieces of footwear at the bottom of Martha's closet. And there, at the back, right where Regan had stuffed them the last time she'd had the displeasure of tying and untying them twice in one day for her mother-in-law, were the dreaded twenty-button-high walking boots. Walking boots for a cripple.

"Did you find them?" Martha demanded.

"Yes," Regan replied without joy or enthusiasm and returned to Martha's side.

Martha had her nightgown off and her new dress pulled on over her head to her waist. They went through the same routine every morning, and Regan automatically knelt to slip stockings on Martha's legs. One sensible thing, anyway, was that Martha never expected Regan to pull her stockings on all the way. If she rolled them only to the knee, Martha was happy.

When it came time to fasten Martha's shoes, Regan plopped all the way down on the floor and began threading the laces back and forth about the tiny metal studs. By the time she finished, her back ached and her fingers were cramped. She could barely feel the reddened tips.

But Martha was dressed, and now it was Clay's

turn to transfer her to her wheeled chair. She opened the door and waved him in gladly.

"What would you like for breakfast, Mother Doyle?" she asked while Clay lifted Martha into her chair and helped her arrange her skirts about her legs.

"I smell bacon. Is there bacon?"

"Of course. And eggs, if you'd like them." The wheels of Martha's invalid chair squeaked as Regan maneuvered her through the doorway and down the hall toward the kitchen. "Or I can fry up some ham, if you'd prefer. Or oatmeal porridge."

Martha reached back to pat her hand where it rested on one of the chair's handles. "Bacon and eggs will be fine, dear. I don't want to put you to any trouble."

Regan just managed to bite back on a chuckle. A day didn't go by without Martha putting someone out. Sometimes Regan wondered if she didn't do it on purpose, to see how far she could push people. Of course, Regan loved her and didn't mind catering to her mother-in-law's needs. Most of the time, anyway.

"Why is everyone up so early?" Mother Doyle wanted to know as Regan situated her behind the table and went to the stove to put on another serving of breakfast. Everyone else had already gone back to eating, afraid their food would get cold.

"Hannah had a nightmare."

Martha's expression turned sad and she stroked Hannah's fine cornsilk hair. "Don't worry, dear heart, you won't always have bad dreams about your mama and papa."

Hannah's eyes filled with tears, but she nodded and turned her face back to her plate.

In a soft aside to Clay, Martha said, "Hannah's parents were killed in an Indian raid on their wagon train."

Regan had to swallow past a lump of emotion before she could continue. "Since most of us were awake, anyway, at that point, it seemed more sensible to get up and start the day."

"Hmph," Clay huffed and shoved another strip of bacon into his mouth.

Martha's gaze met hers over Clay's head. "He isn't used to rising so early," she told her mother-in-law. "But the children and I were happy to get up. We thought we'd take a trip into town today."

"A trip to town," Martha repeated. "Just what I need to work the kinks out of these old bones."

How she managed to do that, when she never left her invalid chair, Regan wasn't sure. And taking Martha along was bound to add both time and duty to the trip. But it would do her good to get out. Maybe she would even run into some of her friends and they could spend the afternoon chatting over a cup of tea. Or better yet, she might be able to foist Martha off on Clay and get away for a few minutes to conduct her business.

The more she thought about it, the more she liked the idea. She began to hum and flipped the bright-yolked eggs with a smile.

*   *   *

It took Clay a minute to place the tune Regan was humming. When he did, he nearly choked on his coffee. God in heaven, it was a bawdy song. A ditty most often whistled by men on their way out of a whore's room at the local brothel.

So what in the Sam Hill was his cousin's widow doing singing it to herself while she cooked? At five o'clock in the morning. In front of his aunt and two young children.

How did she even know such a song?

And he couldn't help wondering if she knew the lyrics as well as the tune. Something about a fair-haired farm girl losing her cherry to a less-than-reputable cowpoke in her father's barn, as he recalled.

If she did. . . . If she did, Regan Doyle had some explaining to do. He'd suspected from the first time they'd met that there was more going on behind those emerald eyes than she let on, but for her to be familiar with the type of music she was humming, she had to be harboring even bigger secrets than he'd first suspected.

And wouldn't it be interesting to do a little investigating and find out just what those secrets were.

That thought had him whistling right along with her in his head, words and all.

Chapter Eight

"All right, everybody up." Clay lifted tiny Hannah under her arms and into the back of the buckboard. Aunt Martha and her chair were already strapped in, and David climbed up on his own.

That left Regan. She was busy making sure Martha was comfortable, seeing that the children had all their things with them for the return to the orphanage, and checking to be sure she had enough money in her reticule for any provisions they might need in town.

Clay watched her bustle around distractedly, wondering what she would look like in anything other than black. She was once again dressed head to toe in widow's weeds, and he had the irrational urge to wrap her in a blanket or tablecloth just to see her in a bit of color.

Not that Regan's plain black frock didn't make a pleasant display of her feminine curves. There were some things a woman couldn't hide, even in sackcloth. And Clay figured that if he had to stare at the dull, fading fabric all day, he might as well take every opportunity to look his fill of her shape without her knowing it.

His perusal had just passed the indent of her waist and settled on her rump when she turned and cleared her throat. He lifted his head and smiled guilelessly.

"Are you quite ready to go?" she asked primly, and he knew she was aware of exactly where he'd been looking.

"Ready when you are," he replied, and offered his hand. "Let me help you up."

She allowed the bare minimum of physical contact as he held her elbow and she climbed up to the seat on her own. She fussed with her skirts and matching black parasol until he walked around and hauled himself up beside her. Then her movements seemed to freeze and she sat ramrod straight beside him, the tiny umbrella acting as more of a shield against him than the early morning sun.

If he didn't know better, Clay thought with a grin, he might get the idea she didn't particularly like him.

Of course, that was plain nonsense. He flicked the reins and clicked the horses into motion. Anyone with eyes could see Regan Doyle was half in love with him already. Why, if she mooned over him anymore, it would get downright embarrassing.

And if he watched the sky long enough, he might just see a jackrabbit take flight.

"Do you have a lot to do in town today?" he asked, deciding that holding a conversation—however grudgingly on her part—would probably make the time pass more quickly than if they sat in stony silence all the way into Purgatory.

She gave an impersonal nod and for a minute he thought she'd refuse to speak. Then she said, "I thought we could take the children with us to Heaven before taking them back to the Home."

"Heaven?" he asked.

"Yes, it's on the other side of Purgatory."

He knew what she was talking about, but decided to tease her a bit. "So the Good Book says."

She actually smiled at that. Or at least one side of her mouth lifted and caused a small hollow in her cheek. He liked to think that qualified.

"I thought we were going into Purgatory," he continued when she remained silent.

"We are. After we stop in Heaven for a few things. I also want to give the children one more full day away from the orphanage before they have to go back."

He had to admire her dedication. She didn't take these kids in out of civic duty. Instead she truly cared for and about them. She wanted to make them happy and give them enjoyable experiences away from the orphanage. He didn't care for children himself; not the young ones and not the older ones. Tilting his head at the spot where David sat cross-legged in the wagonbed, he frowned and decided he *really* didn't like the older ones. Too surly, too undisciplined, too set in their ways.

But he supposed when parents couldn't or didn't want to provide for their own, someone had to see to the responsibility of food, clothing, and shelter. And it seemed Regan was only too eager to pitch in.

"What do you need in Heaven?" he asked, just to keep her talking.

From the corner of his eye, he saw her shoot him a sidelong glance. He couldn't decide if her expression conveyed annoyance or concern.

"Errands," she finally answered.

"Mm-hm." She was being less then forthcoming, but then, Clay never had been one to give up easily. "Anything in particular?"

This time the look she gave him was anything but sidelong. She turned to face him full-on, her brows drawn together in a vee of irritation. "I don't see what concern that is of yours. We make a trip into town at least once a week and never have we been questioned about our reasons. Do you mind?"

His mouth tightened as he fought not to laugh. "Not at all," he managed. "Just so long as you don't mind if I run a few errands of my own."

Regan twisted back to stare straight ahead. "Not at all." Not at all. In fact, that was exactly what she wanted. If Clay went off on his own, or stayed with Mother Doyle and the children so *she* could go off on her own, then she would be able to accomplish her most important task of the day.

His statement had the immediate affect of lightening her mood, and she found herself grinning as the buckboard bumped its way past the outskirts of Purgatory toward Heaven. When necessary, Regan pointed Clay toward the proper trails to get them to town, but otherwise avoided speaking to him for the rest of the journey. Thankfully, David and Hannah kept up an ongoing dialogue with Mother Doyle and only rarely directed a query toward the front of the wagon.

Once they arrived in Heaven, the children jumped from the wagon and dashed into the general store, leaving Clay and Regan to untie Martha's chair and lift her down to the boardwalk. From there, Regan shook off Clay's offer to help and wheeled Mother Doyle into the mercantile. Martha insisted she be taken directly to her favorite spot, the bolts of material.

Regan was more than happy to arrange her mother-in-law's chair in the aisle and leave her there, since the wide array of fabrics would keep Martha occupied for quite some time. Long enough for her to accomplish her most pressing errand, anyway.

To keep the children busy, Regan bought a peppermint stick for Hannah and a bag of lemon drops for David.

Clay was drifting slowly through the aisles toward the back of the store, looking at saddle soap, chaps, and assorted stacks of cambric shirts and denim trousers.

This was going to be the tricky part, she thought. Clay had been nothing but helpful and accommodating so far, but she was afraid that when she tried to sneak away, he would become suspicious and insist upon accompanying her. And that would never do. Oh, no. She had to get away—alone—to deal with this bit of business.

Taking a deep breath, she swept down the row of ready-made clothes and stopped beside him. She reached out to finger the folded edges of a cream-colored shirt, anything to keep from looking directly at him.

"I need to run across the street for a moment," she said quickly, before she lost her nerve. "I was wondering if you wouldn't mind staying with Mother Doyle and the children until I get back."

Clay turned his head to look out the front windows of the general store, at the painted signs hanging over the shops across the way. A dentist's office and jeweler's were in full view.

"Got a toothache, have you?" he asked, returning his perusal to her face.

She fought off a wave of conscience and prayed her alabaster skin wouldn't betray her deception with a tell-tale rise of color to her cheeks. Mustering her courage, she regally answered, "Of course not. But I do have things to do, so if you would just stay with them until I return."

Not giving him a chance to respond, she stepped around him with a sweep of her skirts and made her way to the front of the store. A tiny bell over the door tinkled as she opened it, then closed it just as firmly behind her.

Her pace was quick as she bustled across the

street and onto the opposite sidewalk. Though she suspected Clay might be watching her from inside the mercantile, she didn't look back. He wouldn't be able to see her once she got a little farther down the street, anyway. She passed the dentist's office and a German baker's that smelled wonderfully of fresh-from-the-oven bread, and headed straight for the saloon several yards away.

It was early yet, and few patrons were inside. A young black boy was busy sweeping the rough-planked floor and a middle-aged woman with platinum blond hair washed down the bar and tables. The bartender—or at least a man she assumed to be the bartender—stacked clean glasses and re-stocked bottles of whiskey and barrels of ale.

As the batwing doors swung closed behind her, her gaze found Mr. Sawyer.

He sat at a table in the back, dealing out a game of solitaire. They met here every few weeks, and every time she found him at the same table, shuffling the same worn deck of cards.

He was a dandy, and Regan knew it. His black suit and embroidered silver vest were tailored, not a spot or wrinkle in sight. His black hat carried not a speck of dust, and if his boots had ever taken more than the shortest of strolls on the softest terrain, they sure didn't look it.

But despite his outward citified appearance, Regan liked the man and trusted him to help her when she needed it.

She made her way to the table and took a seat opposite the gambler—at least she assumed that's how he amassed the bulk of his income. "Good morning," she greeted.

"Morning," he returned. "How are you this bright and sunny day?"

"Quite well, thank you." She didn't have time for polite banter, but neither could she bear to be rude. "How was your trip?" she asked, just as she did each time they met.

Their business arrangement was simple: Regan brought the property she'd stolen to Mr. Sawyer here in Heaven, and Mr. Sawyer took it to St. Louis to sell. At each meeting he would have money for her from the last sale.

She knew, of course, that she wasn't receiving the full value of the items she gave him. An old acquaintance from Madam Pomfrey's Hospitality House had put her in contact with Mr. Sawyer, and when they'd first met, he had told her he expected to be paid, and paid well, for his part in her scheme. Knowing that a fair amount of money for the Purgatory Home for Unwanted Children was better than none, and that without Mr. Sawyer she would have no way of turning the stolen trinkets into useful cash, she was more than willing to allow him his cut.

"My recent stay in the city was very lucrative, I'm happy to say." He gifted her with a cocky grin, straightening the cards in his hand before setting them in front of him on the felt-topped table.

Regan leaned forward eagerly, watching as he reached inside his jacket and removed a hefty stack of greenbacks. A shiver of excitement fluttered low in her belly and radiated outward into her limbs. That same bolt of exhilaration ran through her every time she saw the monetary results of her late-night exploits and thought of all the necessities that money could provide for the children at the Home.

"That opal ring you gave me last time was quite a prize, it turns out. A jeweler in St. Louis paid a pretty penny for it." He handed her the doubled-over bills. "I've already taken my share off the top. That's all yours."

Regan took the money, resisting the urge to count it before putting it away. She let her fingers fan the edges just a bit, then opened her reticule and stuffed the bills inside. While the bag was open, she shifted items around until she found Dorisa Finch's emerald necklace and earbobs. She set the pieces on the table and slid them slowly toward Mr. Sawyer.

Sawyer lifted the necklace and held it up to the muted rays of light shining through one of the dirt-specked windows of the saloon. He gave a low, appreciative whistle and returned the choker to the table before doing the same with the two earrings.

"Very nice," he offered. "Very nice, indeed. These should bring a hefty sum on my next trip." And then he fixed her with an inquisitive gaze. "You're sure you want to part with them?"

She swallowed a lump of guilt that threatened to close her throat and nodded. "I'm sure."

She didn't know what Mr. Sawyer thought brought her here once a month or so, but he always acted as though the baubles she chose to exchange for cash were her own. He never asked how she came by such a large collection of valuables or how she used the money, for which she was infinitely grateful.

"Well, then," Sawyer murmured. "I guess that squares things this time around." He picked up his deck of cards and resumed shuffling.

All of their meetings ended with these words, and Regan felt her body relax. Glad to be finished with this task for another few weeks, she inclined her head and rose from her seat. "Thank you, Mr. Sawyer. Until next time."

He touched the brim of his hat with one finger and gave her a small salute. "Always a pleasure, ma'am."

Regan held her spine ramrod straight as she made her way outside, refusing to make eye contact with the others in the saloon. Not that they paid her the least bit of attention. She doubted they cared what business she had with the gambler, each seemed intent on indulging his own misery or pleasure.

She strolled quickly down the boardwalk and crossed back to the mercantile, where she found everyone pretty much as she'd left them. Mother Doyle was now lecturing David on the wisdom of accepting new clothes when they were offered to him instead of walking around in too-short pants and torn shirts, while Hannah stood farther down the aisle, silently stroking the delicate fingers of a porcelain doll.

Clay, however, stood somewhat apart from the others, staring directly at her. Arms crossed, slate gray eyes boring into her. "Get that errand taken care of?" he asked, accusation dripping from every syllable.

Swallowing a slither of nervousness, she forced a smile to her lips and replied, "Yes, it went quite well, thank you."

Not the least put off by her answer, he continued to press. "Care to tell me just what you were off doing?"

Her answer came quickly and easily. "No, I wouldn't."

"None of my business, huh?" His tone had softened, but the force of his gaze warned her not to be fooled.

Her lips curled even wider. "None whatsoever. It was just a small personal matter I needed to attend to. But I appreciate your concern."

He studied her a moment longer, then gave a resigned nod. "Since I kept an eye on everyone while you were off on your errand . . ." He dragged the word out, further implying that she'd been up to no good. "I don't suppose you'd mind returning the favor while I conduct a little business of my own."

Her smile faltered a bit. He'd only arrived the evening before, what business could he possibly have in Heaven? But she couldn't pry into his affairs after making such a fuss about keeping her own secret.

"Not at all." She toyed with the string of her reticule. "How long do you think you'll be?"

One side of Clay's mouth lifted in a cocky grin—a thousand times more daring than Mr. Sawyer's, and Regan felt sure Mr. Sawyer used his on a regular basis to bluff his way through many a game of poker.

Clay hooked his thumbs over the top of his low-riding gunbelt and leaned forward conspiratorially. His breath fanned the hair at her temple and tickled her ear. "Don't worry, I won't be able to stay away from you for very long."

Her heart all but stopped and she had to swallow hard to get it beating again.

Then he straightened and said casually, "I reckon it's about time we found somewhere for lunch. I'll take care of my errand when we get back to Purgatory. There's a sheriff I need to speak with."

And before she could offer a word of protest on either count, he'd turned and was striding toward the others.

Chapter Nine

Clay pulled the buckboard to a stop in front of the Purgatory Home for Unwanted Children, set the brake, and jumped to the ground. Regan folded her parasol and started climbing down on her own, so he moved around to loosen the ropes holding his aunt's chair in place.

Regan was the damnedest woman. Independent to a fault, and so proud Clay usually ended up grinding his teeth in frustration.

She was also hiding something. Clay had been a lawman most of his life, and he knew when people were harboring secrets. Her reluctance to tell him where she'd hied off to this morning in Heaven, her skittishness when he touched her or made a move to touch her, her surprise and agitation when he'd announced his intention to talk to the Purgatory sheriff. All of these things roused his suspicions and made him want to find out just what she was concealing.

For the time being, though, he had a few more important issues to deal with. He'd been sent here to catch a thief, and that's just what he was going to do.

With Regan's help, they guided Martha out of the wagon and let her lean against the tailgate until Clay lifted down her chair.

For once, David and Hannah weren't in a hurry to run off. They followed along sedately as Clay wheeled Aunt Martha up a rickety wooden ramp set over a portion of the front steps and into the adobe mission that fronted the orphanage. As soon as they stepped inside the house of worship, Clay removed his Stetson. Aunt Martha would likely slap him if he didn't.

"Regan! Señora Doyle!" A short, bald man in the long brown robes of a Mexican clergyman hurried over as soon as he saw them. He lifted Martha's hand to his lips and kissed the knuckles.

"To what do we owe this great pleasure, señora?" he asked, his *r*'s and *s*'s rolling thickly. "We are used to our dear Regan gracing us with her presence," he said, shooting a twinkling grin in her direction, "but rarely do we get to see you."

Martha blushed like a schoolgirl and smoothed her skirts in a nervous gesture. "It's not as easy for me to get around anymore, padre. These old bones don't move the way they used to, and it's not fair to ask my dear daughter-in-law to drag me along every time she comes into town. But my nephew is here now," she added, and her shoulders straightened with pride. She wiggled her fingers at Clay, waving him forward. "Clayton. Clayton, come here, dear."

Clay stepped forward dutifully and put his hand in hers. "Father Ignacio, this is my sister's son, Clayton. Clayton, this is our local man of God, Father Ignacio. But you can call him Padre, everybody does."

Clay smiled as he and the older man shook and mumbled polite greetings.

"Clayton is a strong boy, thank heavens," his aunt went on. She reached up to squeeze his upper arm, smoothing his shirt over the hard muscle of his bicep as proof of her statement. "He doesn't mind wheeling me wherever I need to go, and when I decided to come along this morning, why, he just picked my chair right up and tossed it into the back of the wagon."

Father Ignacio's mouth lifted in a kind smile. "Well, we are very pleased you were able to visit us this day."

Moving to the side, the priest focused his attention on Regan and the two youngsters standing silently at her side. "I see you found our David. I'm glad to see you came to no harm," he told the boy without a hint of censorship in his voice. "But from now on, we would greatly appreciate it if you would tell someone where you are going before you run off."

David glared at the padre mulishly, then without

a word took Hannah's hand and led her away through a side doorway that Clay assumed led to where the rest of the children were housed.

"That boy . . ." Father Ignacio shook his head. "I do not know what to do with him. He fights us at every turn, creates anger and hostility where there is no need."

"He knows the townspeople consider him a half-breed," Regan put in softly. "He's feeling out of place, unsure of where he belongs. It's hard enough to grow up without parents and family. David is also dealing with the fact that his skin is red, when everyone around him is white."

"We do not hold that against him here," Father Ignacio responded firmly. "You know that."

"I know." Regan took a step forward and laid a hand on the priest's cloaked arm. "But not everyone shares your attitude. He'll be all right," she added. "He just needs time."

"I pray you are right," the father said, still shaking his head in doubt. "Enough of this," he brightened. "Come, come. Let me get you some refreshments and we will talk."

Father Ignacio began pushing Mother Doyle away, but Clay grabbed Regan's elbow before she could follow. She turned her head, then gave his hand on her arm a pointed look.

Normally, he would have released her. He would have released any young woman who so obviously didn't want him touching her. But Regan was different. Her cool stares and upturned nose pushed points of annoyance in him he hadn't even known existed. And her soft lips and warm gazes heated places in him he wasn't sure he should be thinking about.

Because he wanted to hit a few of her hot spots, he kept his hand where it was, going so far as to tighten his grip half a fraction when she tried to pull away.

"Yes?" she asked, her chin lifting in that regal way she had about her, her tone cool.

"You think you'll be all right while I run my errand?"

"Your visit with the sheriff?" she asked, and he thought he felt a tremor run through her body.

"Yes. The sooner I talk to him, the sooner I can be on my way."

Her shoulders went back and Clay thought her haughtiness alone added an inch to her usual height. "Then by all means, go. Please. And take your time. Mother Doyle and I will probably visit with the children for several hours."

With that, she pulled her arm free and walked away.

If she only knew how much Clay relished the sway of her hips, she wouldn't have been in such a hurry to follow Martha and the padre.

That didn't keep Clay from looking his fill, though. He stayed where he was, enjoying the view until she disappeared around the corner. Then, with a sigh, he plopped his hat back on his head and left the church.

His boots kicked up dust as he headed for the main street of town. The sheriff's office was located in the center of town, right across the street from the Painted Lady saloon. Clay figured this wasn't such a bad idea, as most of the ruckus in small towns like these was usually caused by drunken cowboys, anyway.

Clay reached the jail the same time as another man. He was a big fellow, in both height and width, with an enormous roll of fat hanging over his belt and floppy jowls hanging from the ends of his mutton chop sideburns. When he removed his hat, the sun glinted off his shiny head, visible through the few strands of dark hair combed in a sideways sweep.

Before he'd known this man was headed for the sheriff's office, too, Clay had noticed him exiting one of the doorways no more than a hundred yards down the street. The air wheezed in the other man's chest like a pneumonic horse ridden well past its endurance, apparently from the exertion of walking the length of the boardwalk.

Clay lowered his eyes and noticed the badge pinned to the man's chest. Good God, this man was Purgatory's sheriff. This corpulent, puffing, red-nosed, glossy-eyed man was entrusted with maintaining law and order and keeping the townspeople safe.

No wonder the bandit who broke into houses and stole people's valuables hadn't been caught; it probably took a week for the sheriff to drag himself to the victims' residences.

Well, Clay didn't have to work with him, he just had to get some information about the robberies so he could conduct his own investigation.

"Howdy," the sheriff greeted after a moment of sizing up Clay the same as Clay'd been doing to him. "Name's Jensen Graves. I'm the sheriff here in Purgatory." He held out a hand with fingers that reminded Clay of pudgy white sausages.

"Pleased to meet you, Sheriff. Clay Walker." When Graves opened the door, Clay followed him inside.

"I see you got a tin star pinned to your chest," the sheriff stated amicably as he took a seat behind a scarred, cluttered desk. The joints of the chair screeched in protest as he shifted his massive bulk. "You're a Ranger, huh?"

"That's right," Clay answered, but didn't elaborate. He wasn't sure he liked Sheriff Graves much yet and didn't want to kick up a friendship with him just because they both wore badges.

Graves studied him for a long minute, his sallow eyes narrowing suspiciously. Reaching into the low pocket of his vest, he pulled out a polished yellow coin and began to rub it absently between his broomstick-size fingers. "So what brings you to Purgatory? You got business here?"

Clay pulled an extra, less auspicious chair away from the opposite wall and brought it closer to the sheriff's desk. "In a manner of speaking," he replied as he straddled the seat and rested his forearms along the back. "I've got an aunt who lives just outside of town. Martha Doyle."

Sheriff Graves gave a knowing nod. "Good woman, Mrs. Doyle. And that daughter-in-law she's got living with her." He winked at Clay as though they'd shared a ribald joke. "Quite a looker, that one."

Clay's jaw clenched. Now he was sure. He didn't like the town's sheriff one little bit. "Her name is Regan," he ground out. "She's my cousin's widow." He didn't quite know why he'd felt the need to add that last part. He spent most of his time trying to forget that, strictly speaking, Regan was related to him. However, for some reason he'd felt compelled to remind Jensen Graves that Regan wasn't simply some young lightskirt staying with his aunt, but a respectable widow, Clay's cousin by marriage, and therefore under his protection.

"Of course, of course," Graves replied with a chuckle. "A lot of the menfolk around here were real proud of James when he brought the girl home with him. Weren't sure why he bothered marrying up with her, though, if you know what I mean. Heh heh heh."

The sound of the sheriff's vulgar laughter made Clay's hands curl into fists. He thought they ought to get onto another topic of conversation right quick before he plowed a nice big hole through the middle of this smirking bastard's face.

"The reason I'm in town, Sheriff," he started brusquely, "is because my aunt wrote me about some burglaries going on here in Purgatory. She's real worked up about it and was hoping I could help catch the culprit before many more people are robbed."

The sheriff's jowls quit bouncing as his amusement was cut short. His eyes constricted to snake-like slits as he glared at Clay with obvious hostility. "You think you can catch this guy quicker than I can?" he spat, practically daring Clay to oppose him.

Clay hadn't planned to upset the local law. In fact, before he'd met Jensen Graves, he'd intended to downplay his presence in Purgatory, to emphasize that he was just doing his silly old aunt a favor, and to act as though he had little interest in whether he caught the bandit or not. But now he didn't much care if the town sheriff liked or disliked him. He didn't even care if the man helped him, he just wanted to piss him off.

"I'm sure gonna try," he answered indolently.

Graves flushed angrily, the tiny lines of broken blood vessels in his cheeks growing even redder. "Well, good luck, boy," he stormed. " 'Cause that sneak thief don't never leave no trail to follow. There's been talk that the Ghost of Ol' Morty Pike is up to his old tricks again."

"A ghost," Clay put in, letting those two short words convey his skepticism.

"Yep. Ol' Morty Pike is a real legend 'round these parts. People don't cotton to his specter floatin' in and out of their houses." The sheriff scratched his massive stomach and leaned farther back in his chair. "You want my guess, though, I'd say these rich folk who keep getting robbed ain't really gettin' robbed at all. I'd bet one of them made it up, just for attention, then the rest thought that was a right-fine idea and followed suit." He shrugged, as though he couldn't care one way or the other. "Either that, or it's one of those damn orphans from over yonder. Get more trouble from them than from ten drunks on a Saturday night."

"Is that right?" Clay asked.

The sheriff stopped the rocking of his chair and glared at Clay. Hatred radiated from his beefy body. "That's right."

Clay stood and swung his chair back against the opposite wall in one smooth motion. "Well, then, I guess I'll be on my way."

Graves pushed and shoved his way to his feet as though from a standing position he could better threaten Clay. "You find out anything, you come tell me, you hear?"

"Sure will, Sheriff," Clay replied amicably, as he moved for the door. "After all, I'll need one of your cells to hold the culprit till the circuit judge comes around for his trial."

Chapter Ten

Martha Doyle was humming "Rock of Ages," arranging hymnals on the polished wooden pews, when the doors to the mission opened, letting in a dusty shaft of light. Without waiting to see who it was, she bustled as quickly as her stiff and creaky legs would carry her back to her invalid chair. She had just gotten her shoes lifted onto the footrests, her skirts straightened, when the sound of boot heels clacking in her direction stopped.

She turned her head and beamed at her nephew. "Clayton!"

He'd removed his hat and was absently twisting the brim in his hands. "What are you doing all alone, Aunt Martha? Did Regan go off and leave you?" His brows knit and a displeased look came over his face as he glanced toward the doorway to the side of the vestibule.

"No, no," Martha corrected quickly. "Regan and Father Ignacio are off with the children. I asked them to leave me here so I could straighten some of the hymnals before Sunday services. I don't do enough to help the church now that I'm stuck in this chair." She tapped the wooden arm with the palm of her hand, then began rolling the wheels to turn herself around.

Clayton hurried forward, turning her the rest of the way, then pushing her in the direction she pointed.

"I must admit, I miss coming here every week," Martha continued. "Regan offers to bring me, the sweet girl, but I hate to put her out. Being here alone gives me a chance to think and talk to God the way I would at Mass."

That was true enough. She'd thought and thought of how she could convince Clayton and Regan that they belonged together. And she'd prayed for the good Lord's guidance.

The matchmaking business was not as easy as she'd expected it to be.

For one thing, Regan didn't seem as open to the idea of courting as Martha had hoped. In fact, she seemed downright wary of Clayton, and darned if Martha could figure out why. For another, Clayton wasn't nearly as charming as Martha remembered. She thought he'd come in, take one look at Regan, and sweep her into his arms. Instead, he'd done

115

something to spook the poor girl and she'd ended up with a bloody nose that still looked a little red around the edges. Since then, Clayton hadn't made any advances toward Regan that Martha saw as bridging the gap between them.

"Over there, dear," she instructed as Clayton pushed her around the corner of the church and into the orphanage play yard.

If Clayton and Regan didn't start moving in the right direction soon, she would be forced to take drastic action. Locking them in the root cellar until they fell madly in love. Or concocting a love potion to make them realize they were meant for each other.

Martha mentally reviewed her knowledge of such potions and spells as Clayton wheeled her over the dry, bumpy ground. Was it a bay leaf under a maid's pillow or in the toe of her slipper? Or perhaps it was rose petals in her tea or in her bath. But what about apple peels? Martha distinctly remembered something about apple peels and finding your one true love.

Oh, drat. How was she ever supposed to get these two young people together if she couldn't even remember a simple love concoction?

Regan lifted her head from the crown of wildflowers she was weaving together in time to see Martha and Clay coming her way. Her heart flipped over beneath her ribcage in the most annoying way at the sight of him, his hat tipped low over his forehead, shading his dark eyes, his blue cotton shirt stretched taught over his broad shoulders and solid chest, his faded denim trousers hugging his thighs and calves and backside like a caress.

Well, now, that was quite an unladylike thought. And it must have come from some part of her memory because very little of Clay's lower body was visible behind Martha and her invalid chair.

Regan swallowed a wave of embarrassment at her wayward musings and turned her attention back to the little girl on her lap. Four-year-old Bonnie lifted her wide, innocent eyes to Regan and smiled around the thumb tucked securely between her teeth. Regan smiled back and set the wreath of daisies and bluebonnets over her dark hair, then helped her to her feet so she could run off to play with Hannah and the other children.

Leaning forward on both hands, she started to rise from her seat on the bare ground only to feel a pair of distinctly masculine hands curl around her waist and lift her to her feet.

The air stole from her lungs at both the sudden movement from sitting to standing, and the shock of Clay's gallant behavior. She wasn't sure whether to be flattered or incensed. She settled for a polite, if clipped, thank you as she brushed the dirt from her black skirts.

"Regan, dear, I'm getting a bit drowsy. Are you about ready to go?"

"Of course, Mother Doyle. I don't want you overtaxing yourself." She continued batting light brown soil from her black skirts, and then . . .

Regan tensed abruptly, her spine snapping

straight like a ruler. Her breath caught and her mind raced to find another explanation for what she was feeling. Nothing came to her.

In a careful, intentional motion, she tilted her head just so to look behind her. And saw one of Clay's tanned hands stroking her rump.

"What do you think you're doing?" Her voice was brittle, each word terse and succinct.

His eyes sparkled devilishly and one side of his mouth lifted in a grin that warned her he was about to lie through his teeth.

"Dirt," he said simply, giving her skirt one last pat for good measure.

Her eyes narrowed. She drew in a great breath of air, ready to tell him just what she would do with his hand the next time he put it anywhere near her person without permission, when Mother Doyle—unaware, as usual, of the tension between her nephew and her daughter-in-law—cut off her tirade before it could even begin.

"Are you ready, then?" she asked again, clearly in a rush to get going.

"Yes. Yes, of course." Regan shot Clay one last look of irritation, then walked around Martha's chair to take the handles. "Let's go get one of the children. I'm afraid Paul and Lillian are arguing over who gets to go home with us this time. They both seem to think it's their turn, and I haven't been much help because I honestly can't remember whose turn it is. Do you know?"

"I know you like taking one or two of the chil-dren home with you each week, Regan," Mother

Doyle began, "but would you be terribly disappointed if we spent this week alone?"

Regan paused on her path to where several young boys and girls were running in circles, playing with a battered ball and fighting over who was on whose team. "You mean not take anyone home with us this time?" she questioned incredulously. They had never not taken a child home with them, except for the rare times when Mother Doyle was feeling too under the weather to deal with youngsters racing around her house.

"Are you feeling all right, Mother Doyle?" Concerned, she came around to face her mother-in-law, laying a hand on the older woman's forehead and studying her eyes for any sign of illness. She felt Clay at her shoulder, equally concerned about his aunt's health.

Martha waved her away. "I'm fine. A bit tired, but nothing to work yourself up about. I just thought that since Clayton is staying with us, it might be nice to spend a few days alone, enjoying his company. It's not often I get to see my nephew, after all."

Regan took a step back, studying Martha and Clay both. Clay shrugged a shoulder as though he didn't care one way or the other. He hadn't seemed overly fond of David or Hannah, but he also hadn't seemed eager to carry on a conversation with his aunt.

And certainly Regan had no desire whatsoever to be alone with Clay. If anything, she wanted as many children between them as possible. David to scowl at him, Hannah to ward him off with her sad eyes and nightmares, Jeremy to howl like the dickens when he got too close to the cookstove, and Bonnie to wet on his lap because she hadn't quite mastered the use of the outhouse yet.

But what could she do? She'd never denied Mother Doyle anything, and she wasn't about to start now. Not if her mother-in-law truly didn't feel well, and if she wanted to spend time alone with her nephew.

"I . . . suppose that would be all right." Regan said hesitantly. "Paul and Lilly will be terribly disappointed, but I'll promise they can both come to stay next week. And maybe I'll slip them an extra sweet to make up for it."

"That's a dear." Martha smiled up at her and patted her hand. "You deal with the children and tell Father Ignacio we'll see him soon while Clayton takes me to the wagon. Clayton, dear . . ." She gestured to the back of her chair and Clay quickly stepped around to follow her command.

He shot Regan a lopsided grin, amused by his aunt's demands. "Guess this means we'll have plenty of time to get to know each other," he said, then turned and started pushing Martha toward the front of the church.

Regan stood for several long beats, watching their progress—and struggling very hard *not* to watch the way Clay's legs moved in those dungarees. Despite the preoccupation she seemed to have with his tall, muscular form, she didn't want to get to know him. She didn't want to spend so much as a minute with him.

He made her skin tingle, her heart do funny things inside her chest that she didn't think were at all healthy. Those things could be caused by the fact that he was a lawman. In the beginning, no doubt they had been. Now, though, she wasn't so sure.

She didn't find herself glancing at his tin star as much as his silken hair and soft-looking lips. His storm-gray eyes and high cheekbones. His standing as a Texas Ranger had nothing to do with her impulse to run her hands over his stubbled jaw.

She needed him to go away before she did something foolish. Before she touched him. Or he touched her and she didn't move away. She needed him to leave Purgatory so that her life—and her pulse rate—could return to normal.

Unfortunately, Mother Doyle wanted him here. And what Mother Doyle wanted, Mother Doyle most often received. Regan would just have to deal with Clay's presence and hope he didn't discover her secret.

Which reminded her . . . After explaining to Paul and Lilly why they couldn't come home with her this time and tucking an extra piece of candy into each of their pockets, Regan made her way into the church. Glancing around to be sure she was alone, she slipped the thick roll of bills from the pocket of her skirt and tucked them into the poor box.

On Sunday, Father Ignacio would discover the money. It would be put to good use, and the donation would never be linked to her. The longer she stole for the orphanage, the more she worried that the money would somehow be connected to her. She had to be careful that no one noticed her visits often coincided with the rather large contributions that sometimes appeared in the poor box.

Her favorite and best course of action was to place a little of the pilfered cash in the collection plate each week in order to make the additional income as inconspicuous as possible. Today, however, she wanted to be rid of the bills in case Clay somehow discovered them and became suspicious.

Having taken care of that task, she met Clay and Mother Doyle at the wagon, and even let Clay help her up to the seat. Without the children on the ride home, the drive passed in near silence. Regan couldn't think of anything to say, not that she felt much like talking, and for once, Mother Doyle didn't seem interested in conversation.

When they reached home, Clay helped Martha down from the wagon and carried her into the house. Regan followed, dragging Martha's chair behind her across the yard and up the front steps.

Clay met her at the top of the stairs and in one quick motion took the chair away from her and set it on the porch. "She's in the kitchen," he offered before she had a chance to thank him. "Says you'll make her a nice cup of tea before she takes a nap."

"Oh." Regan's eyes widened in consternation at her own forgetfulness. She'd been watching the muscles of Clay's arms bulge as he lifted Martha's heavy wheeled chair up the last few steps onto the porch. And how the sun highlighted his raven hair and glinted off the round silver badge pinned to his left shirt pocket.

She'd completely forgotten that Mother Doyle wasn't feeling well. That she always fixed her mother-in-law a cup of hot tea in the afternoon before she laid down for a few hours. Forgot that she should not—could not—find this man attractive. He was a threat not only to her freedom, but to her peace of mind.

"Oh," she repeated, struggling to string more than two words together. "Yes, I'd better set some water on to boil."

Clay inclined his head in a soundless, masculine nod of approval. "I'll unhitch the horses and put them out to pasture," he said, moving down a step beside her. Then another. And another.

Regan let her gaze trace his almost lazy departure.

Once his booted feet hit the hard-packed earth, he stopped and glanced over his shoulder at her. "As soon as Martha's down for her nap . . . we need to talk."

She swallowed and carefully wet her lips before answering, hoping her voice wouldn't betray the alarm skating around the outer edges of her belly. "About what?"

"My trip to the sheriff's office."

Chapter Eleven

Regan watched him walk away, her heart beating like an Apache war cry in her chest.

He wanted to talk about his visit to the sheriff? Why? What had Sheriff Graves said to him? Did Clay suspect her of the robberies? Was he going to question her, then take her away in manacles and leg irons?

A wave of dizzy panic washed over her and she clutched the porch balustrade for support. Her life passed before her eyes as she pictured herself being thrown into a tiny cell in the Purgatory jail; sitting in the makeshift courtroom that would be constructed for her trial; being found guilty and sent to a larger prison like Huntsville where she would be housed with lunatics and hardened criminals, fed moldy, worm-infested bread and fetid water.

Oh, lord, she would never survive such a thing.

When she'd first begun stealing for the Home, she hadn't thought of the repercussions. Of the penalty should she be caught.

And now a Texas Ranger was living under her roof, searching for the thief, and threatening to lock her in a dark, dank prison cell.

Her breath came in short, shallow pants as terror overcame her. Her nails dug half moons into the painted wooden railing and she sank to the top step of the porch as her knees buckled beneath her.

She thought of running. Of simply taking off across the field and not stopping until she reached the Mexican border. Once there, she could dress in the bright colors and flowing skirts of the Mexican people, cover her tell-tale curls with a long mantilla, and take a position as a maidservant at some wealthy don's hacienda.

Yes, that would work . . . if she actually made it to the border. Regan suspected Clay would track her down before she reached the outskirts of Purgatory.

If she could make it out of town, she could hide out in Hell, the well-known outlaw camp on the other side of Purgatory. She deserved to be trapped there, with all the rest of the robbers, rapists, and murderers. She may not fair well, being a woman, but at least she would be with her own kind. It was no less than she deserved.

The idea of turning herself in *did* cross her mind, but only for a fraction of a second. Confessing would probably be the noble thing to do, but it would only result in the same nightmare actions she'd envisioned a moment ago. Incarceration, misery . . . and death, because she could never withstand so much as a week behind bars.

Regan suddenly became aware of her name being called. She lifted her head and heard Martha yelling for her from the kitchen.

Martha's tea. Good heavens, she'd forgotten *again*.

Yet another reason—besides her cowardice—that she could never run away. If she left, there would be no one to care for Mother Doyle. Her mother-in-law needed her. And even without her regular financial contributions, Regan knew that the orphans needed her. The children loved her as much as she loved them. Whether she brought them gifts or not, she brightened their lives with her visits—just as they brightened her life with their innocence and youthful antics.

"Regan! Where are you?"

Regan inhaled deeply and pushed herself to her feet. "Coming, Mother Doyle."

She would deal with Clay when the time came and hope for the best. Perhaps he didn't suspect her at all. Perhaps he had noticed the sheriff's overt lack of interest in halting or preventing crime in Purgatory. Everyone in town knew Sheriff Graves for the shiftless incompetent that he was. Unfortunately, no one else had ever volunteered for his position, so they were stuck with him.

And if Clay did question her in relation to the robberies, she would simply answer his questions as best she could. Without implicating herself, of course.

"Regan Doyle, are you going to fix me a cup of tea or not?" Martha's frustration echoed through the house and out to the porch.

"Coming!" Regan cast one last look toward the barn where Clay had disappeared, then turned for the kitchen and whatever fate awaited her.

By the time Clay returned from unhitching the team from the buckboard, Regan was helping Aunt Martha into bed for her nap. Two nearly empty, flower-patterned china cups and saucers sat on the kitchen table, along with one less dainty mug.

A pot of coffee bubbled on the stove and, not for the first time, Clay noted Regan's homemaking skills. She made a fine cup of coffee, a mean bacon and egg breakfast, and an apple pie that could cause a saint to sin.

It wasn't much of a jump for Clay's mind to go from thinking about Regan's proficiency in the kitchen to imagining her talents in the bedroom. He could see her fixing an early dinner, sending the children off to bed, then meeting her husband in the bedroom for a little tussle between the sheets. He could see slim fingers slowly working loose the buttons of her dress. Something peach or yellow or violet—anything but black. Slowly revealing hidden inches of her porcelain skin with a light spattering of freckles on her shoulders and the tops of her breasts. Her dark nipples puckering as her husband ran his thumbs over the tightened peaks, her copper curls brushing the top of her buttocks as her head fell back, her moan of delight as her husband swept her into his arms and deposited her on the bed so that he could further explore her luscious body.

So many things could be done with a woman as beautiful as Regan, Clay thought. So many touches and tastes. So many sounds of pleasure. The possibilities rushed through his brain and heated his already simmering blood.

And it didn't set well at all that when he pictured Regan's second husband, the man had his face.

Admit it, Walker, a voice in his head prodded. *You want her.*

And just how bad would it be if he had her? The thought was a sudden one. Jarring, and yet somehow comforting.

He'd spent so much time trying to convince himself that lusting after his cousin's wife was a bad idea, he'd never stopped to consider the positive side of the situation.

Regan was a widow. That gave her more freedom than if she were unmarried or her husband were still alive. She could easily take a lover if she chose and was discreet about it. Perhaps she already had.

Clay's jaw clenched. He didn't want to think about that possibility. About another man relieving her of her form-fitting widow's weeds, revealing her pale skin and high, pert breasts. Kissing her full, moist lips and making her moan the way she had in last night's dream.

But once the idea forged in his head, it took root and grew to mammoth proportions. Maybe that was why she was so nervous around him. Maybe she had a lover she didn't want him or Martha to know about. It would explain a few things . . . like her being out so late the night before with the excuse of looking for her cat. And her reaction to his unannounced appearance in her kitchen.

What if she'd sneaked off to meet a lover? What if she did this several times a week—or every night, for all he knew? How dare she behave like such a brazen hussy under his aunt's roof.

Clay let the anger and resentment curdle in his gut for a moment, then took a deep breath and let it out. All right. He was overreacting and he knew it.

His mind had conjured up the idea of Regan running off to meet a lover and he was suddenly on the verge of accusing her of betraying his entire family. He'd known the woman all of twenty-four hours and she had him wavering between thinking her an angel or the devil's spawn.

He hooked his thumbs into the gunbelt at his waist and cocked his hip to the side while he considered. He'd give Regan the benefit of the doubt. She could very well be everything she seemed to be, everything Aunt Martha crowed about. Sweet, innocent, caring, kind . . . sexy as hell out of those mourning clothes.

When she came back into the kitchen, he'd talk to her about his chat with Sheriff Graves and see if she knew anything more about this burglar he was supposed to capture. If he managed to drop a few questions or hints about her virtue and activities, and he didn't like her answers . . . then he'd worry about her after-dark excursions and unexplained errands in town.

Her soft voice wishing his aunt a good nap carried down the hallway, followed by the uneven rhythm of her footfalls on the hardwood floor as she neared the kitchen.

Clay turned at her entrance, and she hesitated when she saw him. Then she seemed to recover herself.

"Did you get yourself some coffee?" she asked politely as she crossed the room.

He tracked her with his eyes. "No."

She wrapped a towel around the handle of the blue-speckled pot and brought it to the table. "I thought you might like this better than tea," she offered as she poured a generous portion into his cup.

He grunted his thanks, not taking his gaze off her.

She returned the kettle to the stove, neatly folded the towel and set it aside, then turned toward him like a felon facing a firing squad.

"You wanted to discuss your visit to Sheriff Graves," she said curtly.

This was the first time she'd ever looked him directly in the eye without squirming. He wondered what she was up to. "That's right."

"I'm sorry, but I can't take the time to sit down and chat right now. The trip to town has already eaten up more of the day than I can spare. I hope you don't mind."

He took a threatening step forward. Not to frighten her, but to show her he meant business. "I do mind."

Clay should have known she would not let herself be intimidated by him. At his tone, her brows lifted and she fixed him with a stare of her own that told him if he messed with her, he might just end up walking with a limp.

"I'm sorry to hear that," she replied in the prim, clipped tone of an experienced schoolmarm, "but I have work to do." Spine like a branding iron, she marched to the back door, took a wide-brimmed straw hat off a pegboard on the wall, and stuffed it on her head. "You're welcome to the rest of the coffee," she said as she tucked away loose curls and tied the bits of ribbon beneath her chin. "And there's pie in the warmer. Good day."

Good day? *Good day?* Clay's gaze narrowed as he watched her bustle out of the house. Did she really think she could offer such a flimsy excuse and flounce off without talking to him? Apparently so. Well, he wouldn't be brushed aside that readily.

Downing the steaming coffee in one long swallow, he set the mug back on the table with a clunk and headed out the back door after his headstrong widow.

Chapter Twelve

Regan heard the kitchen door slam and cursed her dratted luck. Why couldn't this man leave her alone?

Everywhere she looked, every time she turned around, there he was. Bad enough he was a lawman, her mother-in-law's nephew . . . now he was her shadow, as well. And it was obvious the man couldn't take a hint.

She didn't want to talk, which she thought she'd made clear as leaded crystal. And yet here Clay was, trailing her out to the garden to harangue her with questions about Purgatory's unidentified burglar. How she was supposed to answer his inquiries without turning suspicion on herself, she hadn't the first notion.

At the very least, she would have to put him off a while longer.

She went to the small tool shed behind the house to collect a wicker basket and several gardening tools. Digging in the dirt was not her favorite pastime, but she often weeded Mother Doyle's flowerbeds, and the vegetables *had* been left to linger a bit too long, so this was as good a way as any to look busy and to put off conversing with Clay.

Even from a yard away, where he stood just off the back steps of the house, his gaze burned across her flesh like a flame. The feel of his eyes following her every movement caused her palms to sweat, but she dried them distractedly in the folds of her skirt as she knelt in the soil beside a row of tomatoes and began turning the dirt near their bases. She pulled stray weeds from around the plants and tossed them aside, breaking off ripe tomatoes when she found them, and setting them gently in the basket at her hip.

She sensed rather than saw Clay's approach. He wasn't going to leave her alone—she should have known that from the outset. If she had faced facts twenty minutes ago, she would be inside where it was at least a few degrees cooler, being interrogated over a nice cup of mint tea instead of kneeling out here on the ground, bent over wilting tomato plants.

"Need some help?" he asked charitably.

Not for a minute did she assume he'd lost or forgotten his main focus. Oh, no, he was simply trying to lull her into a relaxed state so that she would be more likely to answer his questions quickly and honestly, without thinking, when he finally got around to asking them.

Of course, if he was offering to help . . .

Tipping her head to the side, she studied him from beneath the brim of her wide sunbonnet. "That's very kind of you, thank you." She leaned on the short handle of her trowel for leverage as she held her skirts aside and rose to her feet. Then she handed him the gardening implement and gestured to the rest of the bushy green plants in the row.

"Pull any ripe tomatoes you find and put them in the basket. Mother Doyle will be delighted to see that her vegetable patch is doing so well. Do the same with the peppers and corn, if you would, please. And pull as many weeds as you can from around the plant stems. It will help them hold more moisture when I water them."

Regan brushed dirt from the palms of her hands and light brown spots from the knee area of her skirt to keep from laughing at Clay's stunned expression. Based on his reaction to her instructions, she thought he'd likely expected his polite query to be met with an equally polite "no, thank you," or the simple request of taking the basket of fresh vegetables into the house.

"As soon as you finish that, perhaps you'd help me gather some carrots and potatoes. Those are always the most difficult for me because they require digging with the big shovel." She didn't bother telling him that Emmett, who came by to clean stalls and care for the livestock each morning, often helped her with larger chores. Occasionally, she would also hire a man from town to work around the house, giving him the jobs that were too big or physically challenging for her to accomplish on her own.

She hadn't planned to do so much today, hadn't even planned to garden at all. But as long as Clay was handy and willing to help, she might as well put those wide shoulders and strong back to good use.

Clay regarded her carefully, kneading the handle of the trowel she'd passed him. "And just what will you be doing while I'm busy harvesting your supper?"

Her lips turned up in momentary amusement. "Unless you've taken a room in town, it will be your supper, too," she reminded him, then averted her eyes before responding to the other part of his question. "I thought I would go inside to clean a bit. The parlor needs dusting and Mother Doyle's silver is in dire need of a good polishing. I really will have to start dinner soon, too."

Reaching up to loosen the tie under her chin, she began to turn. Only to feel Clay's large hand close on her upper arm. Regan lifted a brow, looking pointedly at where his fingers folded over the dark sleeve of her daydress. He didn't release her.

"I don't think so."

His low voice ran like syrup down her spine, warming her at the same time the dangerous tone brought out chicken flesh on her skin.

She forced herself to swallow past the lump in her throat. "I really do have things to do."

"That's right. Which is why I followed you out here." His hold loosened a fraction, but then he further impaired her concentration by rubbing his thumb back and forth along her arm. Back and forth, as though they were flesh to flesh, with no fabric whatsoever between them.

The very thought caused her mouth to run dry. She hadn't been touched since James died. Not intimately, the way Clay was touching her now. Oh, he was only stroking her arm, and they were both fully clothed, but the heat in his eyes and the reciprocal pounding of her heart told her this was much more than a casual caress.

She could deny it. She could fight it. She could dredge down deep for some modicum of guilt over betraying her late husband by lusting after Clayton Walker.

Or she could admit—if only to herself—that she wanted him. Craved his touch. Had been attracted to him from nearly the moment they'd first met.

It was wrong, it was dangerous, it could potentially shorten her life on this side of prison bars. But that didn't keep the tips of her fingers from tingling, or heat from pooling low in her belly.

"Let's get started."

Clay's words broke into the myriad images cluttering her mind and brought a light stain of embarrassment to her cheeks. "Started?" she almost croaked.

He chuckled, as though he'd seen inside her head

and knew exactly what she'd been thinking.

"You fetch some water for these poor thirsty plants, and I'll gather what I can. Then I'll dig the potatoes while you tell me what you know about this thief who's been stealing from your neighbors."

The increased temperature of arousal that had engulfed her body only moments ago now plummeted to near-freezing. "I thought you spoke to Sheriff Graves about that," she said carefully.

One corner of his mouth lifted. "Your sheriff wasn't as forthcoming as I'd hoped," he told her wryly.

That sounded like Jensen. He never worked any harder than he had to, and if things got too wild in Purgatory, or someone caused more trouble than he cared to handle, he did his best to convince the miscreant to move on. He'd even point him toward Hell, where he could find harder liquor, more willing women, and higher stakes poker than in Purgatory's Painted Lady saloon.

"What do you want to know?" she asked, because she knew trying to avoid the topic any longer was futile.

When Clay wrapped an arm around her waist and pulled her close to his side, she struggled to break away. But he held her tight and steered her toward the tool shed. Once there, he gathered a rope-handled bucket and large dipper, and pushed them into her hands. Then he grabbed a shovel and turned her back around to head for the garden.

"Get some water," he instructed. "I'll begin over here."

Regan stood for a confused second, wondering how Clay had gone from stoic lawman to light-hearted farmer so suddenly. How she had gone from avoiding him to working side-by-side with him in the sweltering Texas sun.

Ah, well, she sighed. It was bound to happen. From the moment she'd met him, she'd known he was no easier to deter than his aunt. Both Clay and Martha would forever get their way in all things. They had the determination and obstinacy of a hundred mules.

Heading for the barn on the other side of the house, she worked the pump, then hauled the full bucket back to the garden. Clay was several plants ahead of her down the row, breaking off ripe tomatoes and pulling up clumps of fat orange carrots as she began tipping the ladle to circle each set of roots with fresh water. The ground soaked up the moisture gratefully.

From the corner of his eye, Clay studied Regan as he shook loose dirt off a clump of freshly yanked carrots. She must be sweating like a chicken on the chopping block under that heavy black dress.

He had to admire her doggedness, though. He'd given her the harder job—lugging a full bucket all the way from the barn—while he'd stayed put to do nothing more than clip vegetables from the vine. But she hadn't uttered a word of complaint.

It was obvious she didn't want to talk to him, that she would much prefer to remain half a mile from him at any given time. And yet she was sticking around. Biting the bullet, so to speak, in order to answer his questions about Jensen Graves and the robberies he and the sheriff were supposed to solve.

"Tell me what you know about these burglaries," he ventured out of the blue, hoping to catch her off guard, keep her from thinking before she spoke.

It didn't work. At least not completely. He saw her body tense at the sound of his voice, her muscles tighten as she let the rest of the water in her dipper trickle into the earth. Then she returned the scoop to the bucket and turned slowly to face him.

"I don't think I know anything more than anyone else. We believe they began a year or so ago. That's about the time people started talking and admitted some of their things had gone missing. After that, more and more people came forward to report thefts." Her mouth lifted in a gentle smile. "I'm sure some of those claims are exaggerated, but everyone wants to be a part of the excitement. Everyone wants to be able to say they were victims of the Ghost of Ol' Morty Pike's antics."

She laughed at that, bending slightly to set the bucket of water on the ground. "You've heard that rumor, haven't you? That a ghost is the culprit?"

Clay returned her grin. "The sheriff mentioned something of the sort."

"Sheriff Graves would love a ghost to be responsible for the burglaries. Then he wouldn't have to do anything to stop him." She slanted him a sly glance. "In case you haven't noticed, Sheriff Graves doesn't move around much more than he has to."

"I noticed. 'Course, I can't blame him. Just getting that wide girth out of bed in the morning has to be a full day's work."

Regan chuckled. The first humorous, all-belly laugh he'd heard from her since his arrival.

"Ol' Morty Pike was Purgatory's first undertaker. He died long ago, but the townspeople still love to blame him for assorted peculiar and unexplained occurrences. Or rather, they blame his ghost. You wouldn't believe the things Pike's ghost has been accused of."

Having abandoned his vegetable picking when she first started to speak, Clay nudged the basket a little to the side with the toe of his boot and hitched his thumbs over the edge of his pockets. "Do you believe in ghosts, Regan?" He wasn't sure if he was serious or teasing, but awaited her response with curiosity.

"I believe in rambunctious spirits," she answered lightly. "I'm not so sure about actual ghosts."

Clay was mesmerized by her beauty. She stood there in the sun, her wide-brimmed straw bonnet shading her eyes, her pale Irish skin dappled with perspiration. Her cheeks were flushed with healthy color, her full pink lips tipped up in merriment. Joking about ghosts and the town's rotund sheriff.

He didn't want to mar the moment with more interrogative questions, but he couldn't think of a single other thing to say. He wanted to march over, tip that hat off her head, and kiss her breathless. He wanted to rip the pins from her swept-up hair and tangle his fingers in the mass of tight red ringlets.

His aunt would kill him, and he'd probably burn in hell for all eternity, but at the moment, Clay didn't much give a shit. White-hot desire did that to a man.

"Do you believe in ghosts?" she asked, drawing his attention straight to her mouth. He watched her tongue dart out to wet her lips and nearly groaned. That one small movement had sucked all of the blood out of his brain and sent it straight to his groin. If Regan lowered her eyes even a fraction, she'd notice his aroused state and run screaming. Then his aunt would wheel herself out to the porch with a shotgun and fill his ass with buckshot.

Funny how that thought didn't help to thin the blood flow in that region any.

Regan cocked her head and studied him. "Clay?" she prompted.

"Hm?" The sound passed his lips without a conscious thought on his part. His attention was still stuck on her mouth and the slow rise and fall of her breasts.

"I asked if *you* believe in ghosts."

He imagined she used that same tone with the younger or less attentive children at the Purgatory Home for Unwanted Children, but damned if he could work up an intelligent response. So he settled for a firm shake of his head. He believed in a lot of things, but ghosts weren't one of them.

"What would you do if this thief broke into your house in the middle of the night?" he asked, his voice sounding harsh and gravelly even to his own ears. He imagined Regan sound asleep in bed, stripped down to her camisole and drawers, covered with little more than a sheet while a stranger tiptoed around her room. The idea caused a jolt of anger to pummel his solar plexus.

Her gaze darted away while she seemed to consider his question. When her eyes met his once more, he could see they held a wariness that hadn't been there seconds before. "I can't say the prospect frightens me much," she said in a forced bright manner. "Mother Doyle and I have very little of value these days. Neither of us buys expensive jewelry or other trinkets; we both like to put most of our extra funds into the orphanage. So, you see, even if a burglar did make his way inside, he would be disappointed by what he found."

Clay disagreed with that statement. Even if they had no gold or jewels in the house, their most prized possession was standing right in front of him. A man could easily hurt her, use her for his own filthy pleasure. And what was to say this robber—who had held himself to merely stealing useless baubles thus far—wouldn't increase his crimes to rape or murder?

His brows knit in consternation. What the hell was he doing, expanding this string of fairly minor robberies into something much darker and more dangerous?

Had Regan crawled so far under his skin that he was beginning to worry about her, concern himself with her welfare? His legs moved him forward of their own accord and he realized the answer to that question was a resounding *yes*.

Yes, he wanted her to be protected. Yes, he wanted to catch Purgatory's housebreaker if it would keep her safe. And if that deed forged him as a hero in her eyes, all the better. But mostly, he just plain *wanted* her, dammit.

He stopped not an inch from her black-clad form. Her eyes widened at his sudden advance and she leaned back a fraction, watching him carefully.

His hand came up to caress her face, his fingers stroking the long line of her jaw, the determined tilt of her chin. Her skin felt like satin against the rough, callused pads of his fingertips.

Her eyes dilated, the emerald green irises growing wide. Her lips parted in a tiny O of anticipation, and his gaze zeroed in on the innocent lure. "What would you do if I kissed you, Regan Doyle? Right here between the sweet corn and tomatoes."

He saw the muscles in her neck contract as she swallowed and he wanted to press his lips to the pulse point there, feel the beat of her heart pounding through every vein of her body.

"I . . . I don't know," she admitted softly, cautiously.

His thumb brushed over the warm flesh of her lips as he tilted his head closer. He could feel the warmth of his own breath fanning her face.

"Let's find out," he whispered.

Chapter Thirteen

Regan's eyes remained open as Clay closed in on her, as his fingers cradled her cheek, as his face drew near and he leaned forward to kiss her. She watched his slate-gray eyes soften and felt the pad of his thumb drift across her suddenly dry lips.

And then he kissed her and her heart stopped beating. The air froze in her lungs, her head began to spin, and she could do nothing more than lean against him and savor the flavor of his hot, sensual mouth.

Her lids grew heavy. She heard a low moan of pleasure and realized it came from deep in her own belly. Her arms lifted to twine about Clay's neck as she parted her lips beneath the onslaught.

His tongue delved inside, tangling with her own as his hands slipped from her waist to the curve of her hips. With his fingers digging into her buttocks, he pulled her forward to press against the hard swell of his desire.

James had never made her feel like this. He'd never kissed her like this—so heated and desperate and passionate. He had never wanted her so badly that he'd grabbed her in the middle of the vegetable patch, out in the open where people might see them. His tongue had never mated with her own the way Clay's was right now.

And all she could think was, *Oh, what I've been missing!*

She'd been raised in poverty, her parents barely able to put enough food on the table for their seven children. Her youngest sister had died of a fever when Regan was only five because Da and Mum hadn't had the money for proper medical care. Soon after, her parents had passed away, and she and her brothers and sisters had had to fend for themselves.

At the age of only thirteen, Regan had ended up working for Madam Pomfrey at her Hospitality House—a polite expression for nothing more than an upscale whorehouse. Regan's position at the brothel had been innocent enough in the beginning; serving drinks, laundering the girls' clothing and bedlinens, keeping the house clean. But she'd never deluded herself about her future prospects. She was being cultivated to one day be a prostitute, as well.

So when James started visiting Madam Pomfrey's, then courting her in a manner that didn't lead to one of the upstairs rooms, she'd been filled with gratitude. His marriage proposal was one of the nicest things that had ever happened to her, and she'd accepted his offer with appreciation. She'd loved James, just not in the passionate way she'd always believed husbands and wives could love one another. But he'd rescued her from life as a prostitute, and provided her with a sense of security she'd never before known.

And he'd been good to her. James had never raised a hand to her or spoken a cruel word. He'd given her everything a woman could ask for while he was alive. And after his death, he'd left her a fortune large enough to sustain her independence.

But he'd never turned her knees weak, or made her heart pound like a drum. He'd never caused sweat to break out over every inch of her skin, or made her want to sink to the ground right here, right now and make love in the bright sun.

And that was exactly what she wanted. With Clay. Only with Clay.

Her eyes popped open and she gasped in stunned disbelief.

What was she doing? Thinking? Picturing Clay and herself naked, writhing on the grass like crazed animals. Lord, but she should be ashamed of herself.

Laying her palms flat on the solid expanse of Clay's chest, she took a decisive step backwards and broke the kiss. His breathing was as ragged as her own as they stood staring at each other, wondering what to do or say next.

He was her mother-in-law's nephew, for heaven's sake. She was an independent, respectable widow . . .

who happened to break into houses around town and steal people's belongings. And Clay was a Texas Ranger who'd come to Purgatory with the sole intention of capturing her and bringing her to justice.

And she'd kissed him. Worse yet, she'd liked it. She wanted to do it again. That and more.

Mercy, the man addled her brain better than a four-day fever.

Step by step, she began to retreat, keeping him in her sights the entire time. "I have to . . . I'd better . . ." She waved a hand over her shoulder, pointing in the general direction of the house.

She saw the Adam's apple bob in Clay's neck, which had already begun to darken with a day's growth of beard. He looked none too steady himself and merely nodded at her stuttered pronouncement.

With that, she turned on her heel and ran the rest of the way to the house, locking herself away where it was safe.

But there was no latch and key inside her head, and she couldn't stop the images that raced through her mind, making her wish she'd stayed outside to see where that kiss would lead.

The next few days were so dull, Clay actually considered shooting himself in the foot just for a bit of excitement.

He'd gone around town, questioning the handful of robbery victims for any information they might be able to give him about the Purgatory bandit. No one seemed to know anything and by the time he'd

147

interrogated everybody, he was no further along on the case than before he'd begun. It was even possible he'd regressed.

Despite all those visits to fill his days, time still seemed to pass so slowly that, at one point, he'd thought he actually witnessed the blades of grass growing. And Regan avoided him so completely, he might as well have been walking around in the shroud of a leper.

She wouldn't discuss the kiss they'd shared, wouldn't meet his eyes, and wouldn't remain in a room alone with him if there was any way she could possibly avoid it.

Even Aunt Martha seemed to sense the tension between them. She'd taken to her bed several times, forcing Regan to busy herself at some task that took her far away from his presence.

He'd had no luck prying more information out of Regan about the local thief, either. He'd made a few trips into town, hoping to stumble across some new information, or a witness—even an unwitting one—to no avail. Sheriff Graves was worthless, Regan's lips were sealed, and no one else in the whole of Purgatory seemed to know a damn thing about what was really going on. They enjoyed blaming the Ghost of Ol' Morty Pike more than they cared to catch the real culprit.

Clay rolled over in bed, punching his pillow into an angry point. What the hell was he doing here? He didn't give a frog's webbed foot whether Purgatory's burglar was ever caught. His aunt and her assorted maladies were getting on his nerves. And

Regan was a damn fine cook, but he sure as hell wanted more from her than a plate of fried chicken and stewed tomatoes.

He wondered if Regan was sleeping peacefully in the room right beside his. He hoped not. If he had to spend his nights tossing and turning because he couldn't get the taste of her mouth and texture of her lips out of his head, then she should toss and turn with him.

Bad choice of words, Walker, he thought grimly. Because now all he could see was a splendidly naked Regan tossing and turning *with* him. On the bed, on the floor, across the grass of the yard . . . His forehead crinkled with a scowl that would have sent grizzlies scurrying.

The sky overhead rumbled, as though mimicking his dark mood. The skies had been gray all day, warning of an impending storm. And now it seemed the clouds were about to part and send the rain the parched fields could certainly use.

He was just flopping back to his other side when he heard the creak of a floorboard. He cocked his head to listen and this time heard the squeak of hinges on what sounded like the door of Regan's room.

Was she up and moving about? Or was someone breaking in?

The tail end of that thought had Clay swinging his legs over the edge of the bed and quickly shrugging into his trousers. He grabbed his gunbelt, which was always close at hand on the bedside table, and tiptoed across the room.

149

He put his ear to the door, but didn't hear anything. No footsteps or signs of an intruder. Maybe he'd imagined the noise altogether.

Another bout of thunder shook the house and a flash of lightning lit the night sky. He'd better check, just to be sure everything was all right.

He pulled the door back, thankful for its silent hinges, and stepped into the hall. Two steps showed him that the door of Regan's room stood open and her bed was empty. He cursed beneath his breath, not knowing if this meant she'd simply gone downstairs for a cup of warm milk, or if something was wrong.

Careful not to make a sound, he headed for the stairwell and made his way down to the first floor. He used the walls to guide him through the pitch dark house, checking every room, listening at his aunt's closed door for any sign that she was awake. He met with only empty rooms and more silence.

What the hell was going on? Where had Regan disappeared to?

Clenching his jaw in frustration, he yanked open the front door and stepped onto the porch.

Wind buffeted his half-dressed frame and rattled nearby tree branches, and the sky flashed in fury. Summer rain was falling in torrents, hitting the ground with hard, staccato splats and soaking into the thirsty earth.

A light flickered inside the barn, visible through the partially opened door, and Clay moved forward, certain he had found Regan.

Damn woman. What the hell was she up to now?

Then the far side of the barn came into view and Clay's heart stopped.

Regan was halfway up a rickety wooden ladder, the rain tangling her skirts about her legs and the laces of her too-big boots threatening to trip her up. And if that wasn't bad enough, she was trying to hold on to the sides of the ladder with a hammer in one hand and a small sack of what he assumed was nails in the other.

Clay's heart started again, tripping over itself to see her in such a precarious position, and he found himself bellowing to be heard over the noise of the storm. "What the hell do you think you're doing out here?"

Regan gasped and swung toward him, grasping the sides of the ladder as she began to lose her balance.

Clay lurched forward, ready to catch her. She caught herself just in time and readjusted her footing, all without dropping a thing. Jesus, she was a one-woman walking disaster, he thought with disgust.

"Good lord, Clay, you scared ten years off my life," she scolded, the hand with the hammer in it pressed to the area of her heart.

"Just returning the favor," he said through clenched teeth. And then louder, he asked again, "What are you doing out here?"

"There's a hole in the roof that we haven't gotten fixed yet, and I forgot to cover it before the storm hit."

"And that's a reason to come out here in the dead

of night, in your nightclothes, in the pouring rain?" he demanded.

Even in the dark and rain, he saw her shoot him a quelling glance.

"If too much water gets in, it will turn all the hay and straw and feed moldy," she replied primly. "Then we'll have sick horses—if they haven't already caught pneumonia from spending the night in a damp barn."

Regan stood in the middle of the ladder, rain pouring down on her, and Clay thought he'd never seen anyone more beautiful or more all-fired independent and donkey-stubborn in all his life.

"Get down from there," he ordered. Surprisingly, she didn't argue, but began backing her way carefully down the rungs, and he moved to the base of the ladder to hold it while she descended. As soon as she reached the ground, he took her elbow and propelled her around the corner and into the barn.

"What are you doing?" she asked, balking now that she was out of the elements. "I have to get that hole covered."

She stood only a few feet from him, arms crossed over her chest as she waited for him to respond. He tried not to notice how the stance lifted the swell of her breasts. Or how the thin, soaked-through fabric of her black nightrail showed the shape of those tautened swells and perfectly outlined her pebbled nipples.

He grew hard within the confines of his own rain-tightened trousers and prayed to God she didn't notice. He'd better help her get the roof covered and get them both back to the safety of their separate beds before something happened. Something he knew she'd regret in the morning.

"Fine. Where's your tarpaulin?"

Shaking a clump of hair away from her face, she blinked at him. "On the roof, of course. Emmett spread it out a few weeks ago, but it's since come loose and I forgot to fasten it down again. Why? What are we going to do?"

"We." He gave a contrived chuckle. "I like that, we." Turning serious, he took the hammer and nails from her and said, "*I'm* going to climb up that stupid ladder and tie down the tarpaulin so your hay doesn't get moldy."

A surprised expression widened her eyes. "You'd do that? You don't have to. I don't mind taking care of it; that's what I'd do if you weren't around. It would be fine until Emmett could get here to repair the damage."

She sounded like a child desperate to convince an adult that she didn't really need something she wanted so badly her mouth watered. Which swung his mood right back from furious to half-smitten.

This woman had his insides twisted up in knots. He wanted to leave so he wouldn't be tempted by her bow-tie mouth and fiery red curls, but the idea of actually mounting Caesar and riding off for good caused a physical clutch of pain in his gut. He wanted to make love to her more than he recalled ever wanting anything in his life. And yet he knew it would be a mistake because she was his cousin's widow and his aunt's companion, and his job took him far away for long periods of time—if he came back at all. It was just as likely he'd be killed on one of his missions for the Rangers.

"I don't mind," he told her quickly, before his hands shot out and pulled her against him. Before his mouth started betraying the secrets of his mind and promising her things he could never deliver.

Despite his protests, she accompanied him back outside into the drenching rain. He readjusted the ladder against the side of the barn and began his ascent, with Regan cautioning him about his bare feet with every step on the slippery wooden rungs.

Lightning crackled overhead, lighting his way. The hole was close enough to the edge of the roof that he could stay on the ladder and reach out to grab the flapping corner of the tarpaulin. Pulling the hammer from the waistband of his pants and a nail from his pocket, he began to hammer down the protective covering. It wasn't an ideal remedy, but it would do until he or the man Regan called Emmett could permanently repair the damage. And it would keep any more rain out of the barn for tonight.

That taken care of, he carefully began backing down the ladder. Regan stood at its base, her hands curled around the sides as though she had a prayer of keeping the thing upright if it started to topple.

It was sweet, though, that she would stand out in the drenching rain while he covered the hole in her barn roof. That she would worry about his safety and want to keep an eye on him to make sure he didn't get hurt.

He hit the ground with a splat. He had mud up to his ankles, and even though Regan wore an old pair of what looked to be men's work boots, she hadn't fared much better. She let go of the ladder and rubbed her arms for warmth. Her hair was plastered to her head, straighter than he'd ever seen it—or ever would again, he'd wager—and her teeth were chattering.

But she smiled at him and blinked the rain out of her eyes. "Thank you."

The muscles in his throat suddenly spasmed and he wasn't sure he could speak. Before he even realized he was doing it, he'd reached up to push a swath of hair out of her face and tuck it behind her ear. He didn't move away, and she turned her face a fraction into the warmth of his palm.

She blinked again and he saw a chill shake her body.

"Let's get inside." His voice sounded husky even to his own ears. "We should make sure no water is leaking in at the edges of the tarpaulin."

They turned and raced back to the barn. Regan was laughing and squeezing water out of her long hair when he slid the door closed behind them.

"It's not cold until you get soaked to the bone," she chuckled as she faced him.

He nodded brusquely, mesmerized by her beauty. She looked like a drowned rat, with one long, bedraggled plait of hair thrown over her shoulder, her black robe so wet it clung to every inch of her body, and scattered drops of rain rolling down her face, her arms, her chest.

"I'll go up in the loft and check the roof. You should try to get dry."

Her head bobbed in a positive gesture and she walked across the barn to a distant stall. Clay followed her with his eyes, drawn by the sway of her hips in the water-tight garments.

Then he shook his head and headed for the loft. The tarpaulin was working just fine, and as Clay turned to call down the good news to Regan, she appeared at the top of the ladder clutching a rough woolen Army blanket around her shoulders. Their eyes met and a bolt of awareness shot between them. It rocked him to his toes, and he knew she felt it, too.

He grasped her hand to help steady her as she stepped into the loft. Her eyes never wavered from his, and it seemed only natural to release her fingers and take her into his embrace.

Her arms wrapped around his waist, her chin tilting upwards as she strained to hold his gaze. The length of her feminine body pressed against the planes and angles of his own.

"I tried to resist this," he muttered.

"I know," she whispered softly.

"Are you sure?" he asked. He wouldn't go any further if it wasn't what she wanted, too. He would release her and watch her walk away . . . and then he would go outside, into the storm, and pray for lightning to strike him dead.

"I shouldn't," she said carefully. "But I want to. More than you can imagine."

One corner of his mouth quirked up in a grin.

"Oh, sweetheart, if you want me half as much as I want you, you've got to be in a terrible, terrible state."

Her face remained impassive, but her green eyes danced with merriment. "I am," she replied solemnly. "A terrible, *terrible* state. You do know how to remedy that, don't you?"

He threw his head back and laughed. "Darlin', I'm sure as blue blazes gonna try."

Chapter Fourteen

Regan twined the fingers of one hand with Clay's and led him to the middle of the loft. She didn't need seduction and romance, or rose petals and satin sheets. She just needed Clay.

Except for a thin layer of straw cluttering the floor, the loft was empty. When James was alive, it had been used to hold extra hay and straw. But knowing what a chore stacking the bales on this level was, Regan let Emmett keep them on the main floor of the barn.

She shook out the blanket and started spreading it on the ground when she felt Clay's hands slip around her waist. She straightened and leaned back against him, letting her head rest in the curve of his shoulder. His lips brushed the side of her neck and she moaned in pleasure.

He turned her in a pirouette. His chest was bare and covered in raindrops, but radiated heat right through the dampness of her cotton robe. She lifted her arms to toy with the wet strands of hair that curled around his ears and dripped onto his fore-head. Her fingers drifted down to his shoulders, his biceps, the tapering line of his waist. She could feel the even ridges of his ribs beneath the warm skin and heard him suck in a breath as she ran her nails lightly over the slight delineations.

His hands rose to the nape of her neck, sliding into the tangle of her heavy, rain-logged hair and holding her face so that he could stare into her eyes. "You're too beautiful," he whispered, kissing one corner of her mouth and then the other. "No one has a right to be this beautiful."

His words warmed her like a crackling hearth, dispelling any remaining chill from the summer storm.

"I'm glad you think so," she responded breath-lessly. "The first time I saw you, I thought you were handsome enough to make angels weep."

He chuckled, still framing her face with his wide, masculine hands. "That explains your little fainting spell."

Even his mention of that night—and the memory of her true reason for swooning—couldn't tarnish her spirits this evening.

His head swooped down and their lips locked. She let him take her, mold her, concentrating on nothing more than her heightened senses and the havoc Clay wreaked on every nerve ending.

Slowly, step by step, he backed her over to the blanket and carefully lowered her to the ground. Her legs parted, creating a cradle for his long frame as he settled atop her.

The deep, soul-altering kiss continued as they explored each other's bodies, as her fingertips trailed up and down his abdomen and he loosened her wrap. Parting the ties all down the front of her robe, he slid his hands beneath—and jerked his head up in surprise.

She hadn't had a chance to change into her nightdress before she remembered the uncovered hole in the barn roof, and had simply thrown a wrap on over her camisole and drawers. She hadn't even laced up her boots, only slipped them on to protect the bottoms of her feet. And though her soles had been covered, mud and water had leaked in through the open fastenings. She'd shucked the awkward, waterlogged boots before climbing up to the loft.

Clay stared at her face—his chest heaving from their vigorous kiss—then down at the soft satin of her special-order underthings. Today she'd worn the purple ones that reminded her of a queen's imperial robes.

"What have we here, Widow Doyle?" Clay fingered the delicate material. "A wild streak beneath that dour exterior?"

Was he serious or toying with her? "It wouldn't be right for me to wear anything but black this soon after my husband's passing," she told him, striving for a dignified air.

160

Clay quirked a brow and shot her a quizzical glance. "Your husband has been dead for two years now. The standard mourning period is only one year."

She didn't know what to say to that, so she didn't say anything.

"You know what I think?" Without waiting for her to answer, he continued. "I think you like wearing black because people leave you alone. If you came out of mourning and started wearing regular gowns with a bit of color again, men would look at you, maybe try to court you. People would expect you to move on with your life, probably marry again."

His index finger slid down her bare torso and over her hip, raising gooseflesh everywhere he touched. When that devilish digit reached the bottom of one leg of her fancy drawers, it dipped beneath to bare skin and Regan sucked in a breath.

"You don't want that, do you?" he went on, his voice deep and husky, seeping into every fiber of her being. "You enjoy living alone, with only Aunt Martha to care for. You enjoy your independence. That your time is your own. No one to ask permission of, and no one to answer to. Am I right?"

She thought for a moment, afraid to give him any sign of just how independent she'd become—and how close to the mark he was in his speculations. "You're not . . . wrong."

He chuckled at her noncommittal response. "I like that I'm the only one who knows your secret." Then he looked at her, an expression of mock concern on his face. "I *am* the only one who knows about your purple dainties, aren't I?"

She fluttered her lashes and averted her head, pretending to hide her true reaction from him. "The purple ones, yes," she said slowly.

His eyes widened. "You mean there are more?"

Still acting the prim miss, she listed her inventory of erotic-colored unmentionables. "I also have some in red, and yellow, and blue, and green, and a sort of pink that's not quite rose and not quite magenta."

"Lord, woman," Clay groaned, resting his forehead against her own. "Now I'm really glad I'm the only man privileged enough to see them. Any chance you'll let me see them *all?*"

Her lips lifted as she gave a low, throaty laugh. "If you're very, very good, I might."

A wicked glint came into his eyes and she knew she was in trouble. "Oh, darlin'. You can count on it."

His mouth returned to hers as he slid his hands into the waist of her satin drawers and pushed them down her legs. Then he lifted the hem of the royal violet camisole up over her breasts, pausing to stroke the soft globes before removing the item altogether.

Although Regan was now completely nude, Clay's body pressed so closely against her own kept her quite warm. But something about their dissimilar states of undress seemed unfair to her. Curling her hands over his shoulders, she said, "You can't be the only one with clothes on."

"No?"

She shook her head, watching him intently. "What are you going to do about that?"

Her heart fluttered at the obvious challenge. She'd never undressed James; he'd always met her in bed and they'd disrobed beneath the covers. Just coming up to the loft and agreeing to make love with Clay was aeons beyond the experience of her marriage.

But that was the beauty of this moment, of her time with Clay. It was forbidden, yes, but it was also exciting and rash and more sensual than anything she'd ever done before in her life.

Taking a deep breath, she let her hands trail from his shoulders to the band of his denim trousers and flipped open the top button before her daring deserted her. But, surprisingly, the action didn't send her courage scurrying. Instead, it increased by leaps and bounds, and she suddenly wanted to act the wanton. Wanted to do some of the things she'd seen and heard about while working at Madam Pomfrey's. And she knew that with Clay, she could. Without the fear of chastisement or embarrassment.

She undid the next button on the fly of his jeans, and the next, and the next, until her hand fit between the thick fabric and his searingly hot skin. He wasn't wearing drawers, she noted with surprise. Likely because he'd dressed in such a hurry to follow her out here.

The lack of a second layer of clothing allowed

her knuckles to come into direct contact with the rough hairs forming a narrow triangle down his lower abdomen, her fingers to bump the long, hard length of his erection, which strained upwards and gave an involuntary quiver when she wrapped her hand around it. She felt Clay's body tense, the muscles of his stomach spasm and his chest rise sharply with a deep inhalation of air.

Regan lifted her head to look at him, only to find his gaze burning back at her. For a moment, she considered stopping, considered returning to the passive role and letting Clay take over. But then the brave, willful woman inside her came to the fore once again and she not only left her hand where it was, she began kissing the smooth flesh of his chest. She started at his collarbone, parting her lips and licking all the way across the protruding ridge.

As she moved lower, Clay's fingers curled into the hair at her temples. With her free hand, she traced the curve of his pectoral muscle, reveling when it quivered beneath her fingertips. She kissed his tiny male nipples, circling them with her tongue.

Clay's grip tightened and he arched an inch off the ground. "You're killing me," he groaned.

She lifted her head—at the same time tightening her grasp on his throbbing manhood the tiniest bit. "I can stop," she offered.

"Don't you dare," he said with a strangled laugh. This woman would be the death of him. He wanted her so badly, his blood boiled in his veins. Her hand on his manhood was enough to end their encounter in a matter of seconds, and he didn't want that.

Considering this might be his only chance to make love to Regan, he wanted tonight to last and last.

He wrapped his fingers around her wrist at the opening of his pants, breaking her hold on him. Coming to his knees, he quickly shucked his jeans, then brought Regan up to kneel beside him.

"I love what you're doing," he told her, feathering the ends of her drying hair, which was already returning to its usual unruly curliness. "And I'll let you finish later, believe me. But for now, it's my turn to drive *you* to the brink of insanity."

Regan licked her lips in what Clay assumed was a nervous gesture. A nervousness that certainly hadn't been there moments before when she'd seduced him like a practiced courtesan. And he doubted her current anxiety was due to any real fear of what he was going to do to her. A healthy dose of anticipation, he thought smugly. And he'd make sure it was well worth the agitation.

He settled his hands at the indentation of her waist, massaging the pads of his thumbs up and down on her silken skin. Nuzzling the lobe of her ear, his caress traveled over her ribcage, to the undersides of her breasts.

Her breath was coming in short little pants that raised his temperature to an almost fever pitch. He wondered if his cousin had ever shortened her breathing this way. Ever caused her to shiver and lean toward him like a baby rabbit seeking sustenance.

And then he wiped the thought from his mind. His cousin was dead, and Regan's past was her

165

own. None of it had any bearing on their time together. Besides, even if James had been the greatest
lover north of the Mexican border, Clay had every
intention of erasing the man's image from Regan's
memory. She could hang on to any shred of her
everyday life as a married woman that she chose,
but after tonight, she would know she had never
truly been loved until Clayton Walker touched her.

"Lie back," he whispered, and was filled with
lofty delight when her lashes drifted closed and she
let herself fall backwards simply on his say-so. He
held fast to her waist and lowered her to the blanket
as though she were the most delicate of hothouse
flowers.

Following her halfway down, he crossed her arms
and positioned them below the cushion of her
breasts. She cast him a questioning glance, and he
grinned.

"Trust me."

She raised a doubtful brow, but held the pose
he'd orchestrated.

Knowing he had her full—if not most confident—
cooperation, he brushed his hands past her hips,
over her thighs, beneath her knees. When he bent
her legs and lifted them wide apart, she gasped, her
mouth forming a small O of astonishment.

His grin only widened. "You'll like this, I promise."

She didn't seem to believe him.

Silly girl. He'd just have to prove it to her.

Chapter Fifteen

Supporting her hips, he lowered his head and began to explore the soft inner folds of her body with his tongue. She was already wet and smelled of musk and woman.

When she whimpered and tried to clamp her legs tight together, he knew he was on the right track. He slowed his ministrations, taking more care with the budded pulse point at the very center of her femininity until she tensed from head to toe, arched her back, and gave a high, keening scream of pleasure.

Clay brought her down slowly, kissing her inner thighs and belly as he made his way to lie above her.

She raised glassy, satisfied eyes to his and smiled.

"You were right," she sighed contentedly. "I enjoyed that very much."

He'd never in his life seen a smile like that, so wide open and at ease. Just knowing he'd been the one to put that look on her face made him feel ten feet tall.

"There's more, you know."

She stretched languidly. "Mmm, I can't wait."

He chuckled. God, she was marvelous. So honest and enthusiastic about her passion. So eager and willing to trust him.

But truth be told, he couldn't wait much longer, either. He brushed his lips over her swollen, pouty mouth. Explored her deepest corners and recesses. Drank in her warmth and desire.

With her breasts pressed flat to his chest, he raised her legs to wrap high around his waist and thrust inside. They both gasped at the sudden contact, the heady feel of his engorged shaft fitting so snuggly within her damp heat.

Regan's white, even teeth appeared as she bit down on her bottom lip. Clay imagined she did it to keep from yelling out. He was gnawing hard on his own control to hold back the clamoring ecstasy pounding through his veins.

The storm raged on outside the barn. Thunder boomed and rain barreled down on the shingled roof. Inside a completely different tempest raged, one punctuated by rustles and moans.

Her legs tightened about his waist and her nails dug into the solid flesh of his back. She sighed as wave after wave of pure delectation washed through her body.

"Clay." His name tumbled from her lips as her head tipped back and her breath began to come in shallow pants.

He stroked deep, pushing into her welcoming warmth, then pulling out, only to plunge in once again. "Say it again," he commanded. "Say my name."

She obeyed at once, bringing her hips up to meet him thrust for thrust. "Clay," she repeated breathlessly. "Clay, Clay, Clay."

"Regan, Regan, Regan," he followed suit.

Accelerating his movements, he grasped her hips and pummeled into her. She welcomed the pressure, the pounding, the rapid motions that promised to bring much-sought-after release.

And then it did, as her entire body tensed, and her inner muscles convulsed around Clay's hardness. She cried out as the climax hit her, shaking with its intensity.

A moment later, he followed her over the edge. With a few last, quick thrusts, he stiffened and came inside her, gripping her close, his arms around her waist.

For long minutes afterwards, they lay perfectly still, their chests rising and falling as they gasped for air, the thunder rumbling about them and livestock shuffling below.

Clay's head rested between her breasts on her bare chest, and she raised a weak arm to run her fingers through his silky, short-cropped midnight hair. "Thank you."

At her soft statement, he lifted up and fixed her with a surprised, questioning stare.

She tried to shy away, embarrassed by her abrupt admission. But he wouldn't let her hide. He captured her chin and turned her to face him.

She expected him to demand an explanation, to, at the very least, ask why her voice had trembled when she'd spoken. Instead, he kissed her lightly on the lips, reminding her of why she decided to follow him up to the loft in the first place.

"I'm the one who should be thanking you," he told her, his mouth still resting against her own. His arms bracketed her body while his hands cradled the base of her skull.

Even though she never wanted to move . . . even though she'd have liked to stay in the barn with Clay forever, she knew that was impossible. It was the middle of the night, but morning would come soon enough. Mother Doyle would wake, and Regan would die if Martha or anyone else discovered she and Clay had been rolling around in the hay loft.

She wasn't ashamed—far from it. Her time with Clay was her concern and no one else's. But that didn't mean she wanted people privy to her business, or to know with whom she'd been spending private, intimate moments.

"The rain has let up," she said quietly.

Clay gave an answering grunt, pressing light kisses along the line of her jaw. He was still inside her, and she felt him once more growing firm. She was afraid to let things get carried away, to let their passions kindle and burn and blaze again like an out of control forest fire.

"Don't you think we should go in?"

He sighed—a deep, ragged, rueful breath—and let his brow rest against hers. "I'd rather stay here and make love to you again."

Even as he said it, though, he rolled aside and tugged the corners of the old Army blanket about her shoulders. "But if you're determined to protect your reputation"—he shot her a teasing wink— "then I suppose it's my duty as a gentleman to help you dress and see if we can get you back to the house with some degree of dryness."

He was trying so hard to be noble that she laughed. "And what do you plan to do with me once you get me into the house?"

He'd gathered her discarded clothing into a pile at her side and was tugging on his still-drenched trousers when her words stopped him cold.

The question had popped out before she'd thought it through, and a stain of color flew into her cheeks as she realized its double meaning.

With the button fly of his pants still half open and his eyes burning bright, he stepped forward. He reached down to where she sat, grasped her hands, and pulled her to her feet. The blanket began to slip, but he caught the edges and tucked them around her bare form.

"Is that an invitation?" he asked huskily.

She pictured him in her room, in her bed, yellow

flowers and eyelet lace tucked to his ears. The thought made her smile. Until Mother Doyle entered the vision and she realized how mortified she would be if Martha found out that her daughter-in-law and her nephew were cavorting about naked.

In answer to his query, she shook her head vehemently. "No. No, no. I don't think that would be wise at all."

His gaze fell to her mouth, as though he was considering kissing her. A very big part of her wanted him to—wanted that, and everything she knew would follow. A more intelligent part of her realized the foolishness of such an action, however, and she did her best to tamp down on her own desires.

Unfortunately, his attention remained focused on her lips, even as he spoke, which continued to distract her and sent little shivers of need dancing down her spine.

"You're right. Spending the night together under Aunt Martha's roof probably isn't the smartest idea. But if you ever change your mind . . ." His hands slipped beneath the ends of the scratchy woolen blanket to stroke back and forth along her upper arms. "Just give a whistle, and I'm there. A herd of stampeding longhorns couldn't keep me away." He gave her arms a little squeeze. "Got it?"

His meaning couldn't have been more clear, and her heart swelled at the knowledge that this man seemed to want her so very much.

"Got it?" he asked again.

She nodded. It took all her strength not to put

her lips together right now and trill, just to see how quickly he would move.

He bent to retrieve her clothing, handing her the camisole and drawers. "You'd better get dressed," he said, "before the storm kicks up again."

Keeping the spread around her as best she could, she struggled into her wet purple underthings. Then Clay held the blanket while she covered herself with the equally damp black robe.

Their eyes met and they seemed to inhale the same reluctant breath.

"Ready?"

She moved toward the ladder, turning to back her way down. She reclaimed her boots at the bottom and made her way to the front entrance. Clay followed and slid open the wide barn door, using the blanket as an umbrella to protect her from the rain as they ran across the muddy yard. Hurrying up the steps and onto the porch, they wiped their dirty feet as best as they could with the overused Army blanket and left it and Regan's oversized boots to be washed the next day.

They headed upstairs, being sure to tiptoe past Martha's room. And even though their rooms were side by side, Clay walked Regan to her door.

She considered inviting him in, once again replaying her earlier daydream. But the end result remained catastrophic, and she stepped past the open doorway before the impulse to pull him with her became overwhelming.

Turning to face him, she offered a quiet, "Goodnight."

Clay ran his wide, callused fingers through the hair at her temple and gave her a temperate smile. "Sleep tight, green eyes. I'll see you in the morning." And then he leaned in to press his warm mouth to her slightly parted lips.

As soon as the contact was broken, he turned and entered his own room, closing the door behind him.

Regan stood where she was, committing to memory every stroke, every breath, every nuance of that kiss. And wondering how she would ever fall asleep now, with the taste of Clay lingering on her lips, and the man only one thin wall away.

Regan awoke the next morning to the sound of her name being called. She rolled over and stuffed her head under the nearest pillow. She was too tired to deal with life right now. Another hour and she'd be good as new, but at the moment, she was simply too exhausted to move.

She had just drifted back to sleep, was enjoying the hazy edges of a lovely dream, when someone knocked at her door. With a groan, she let the pillow fall away and rolled toward the side of the mattress.

"*What?*" she bit out, knowing it was completely out of character for her to snap at anyone; to laze about past dawn and not jump up to immediately see to Mother Doyle's needs. But she was so *tired*.

"Regan?" came a muffled male voice. No doubt Clay's.

At the thought of Clay, she shot out of bed like a pebble from a sling and grabbed for her robe. In her struggle for a few more minutes of peace, she'd forgotten the probable reason for her exceptional lethargy.

"Regan?" he called again, before another knock sounded and the door slowly squeaked open.

Though it was a futile gesture—since he had already seen her in much less the night before—she put a hand to her collar to hold the sides of her hastily donned wrap closed. She was naked beneath it, because she'd only taken the time to remove her wet garments last night before falling into bed.

Clay wore his characteristic outfit of denim trousers, dusty cowboy boots, and a light cambric shirt—this one an off-white that brought out the bronze of his skin and black of his hair. He'd shaved and apparently gotten a good night's sleep, as he didn't look the least bit tired.

Regan wanted to hit him. Worse yet, she wanted to take two steps forward and run her fingers over the material of his shirt to see if it was as soft as it looked. That way lay madness, of course, but for just a moment, she let herself imagine doing that very thing.

It didn't help that he was watching her, studying her with those gray, penetrating eyes that had captured her attention almost from the first moment they'd met.

She saw his gaze travel to where she clutched the folds of her robe, then back to her face, one side of his mouth quirked in a lopsided grin. As though he knew what she was trying to do by covering herself, and that it would do no good if he decided to launch an attack.

"I thought maybe you'd climbed out the window to escape Martha's screeching."

Her lashes fluttered guiltily. "Is she all right? I didn't mean to ignore her, I was just so sleepy."

Clay's lips curved even wider. Cocky. That was the word; he looked cocky, correctly assuming that he was the reason she'd been unable to get out of bed at a decent hour.

"Aunt Martha's fine. She was a little surprised you weren't up at the usual time, but I told her how hard you worked in the garden yesterday"—he slanted her a wicked, knowing glance—"and fixed her some breakfast so she wouldn't have to wake you."

Ignoring his suggestive mien, she zeroed in on the second part of his statement. "*You* cooked breakfast?"

With a bark of laughter, he said, "Don't sound so shocked. I've spent a lot of time on the trail. Not to mention, my mother is a lousy cook. Growing up, I often had to choose between a couple hours over a hot cookstove or the risk of starvation."

She frowned, not completely convinced. "What did you make?"

"This morning, or when I was a kid?"

She shot him a quelling glare.

"Porridge and fried ham," he answered quickly, tempted to stand at attention and give her a mock salute.

When her nose crinkled in distaste, he rushed to justify his choices. "It's what Martha wanted. I'll admit the oatmeal mush was a little . . . well, mushy, but she seemed to enjoy it. And it bought you a couple more hours of sleep."

He couldn't believe he was defending his cooking skills. If he was smart, he'd tell her he'd over-cooked the ham and almost burned down the kitchen so he'd never be expected to prepare a meal again.

"I suppose I should thank you for that," Regan said, her tone uncertain. His actions seemed to have thrown her for a loop. "Thank you."

Her throaty, just-awakened voice was all it took to tear his attention from the matter of his aunt's breakfast to the fact that Regan looked beautiful, all mussed and sleep-tousled. Her hair was a wild crown of rampaging red all about her head, and her robe was a wrinkled mess. He wondered if she was still wearing her colorful dainties beneath.

Just the thought of those fancy purple drawers rubbing against her silky white skin, and then being pushed down her legs was enough to bring him to full, instant arousal. If he never saw another piece of women's unmentionables, the memory of those satiny violet underthings would have no trouble carrying him to his grave.

"Where's Mother Doyle now?" Regan asked, breaking into the sudden silence.

Which reminded him of his original reason for coming to her room. "She's downstairs. With Father Ignacio."

"Father Ignacio?" Her brows knit. "This early in the morning?"

"It's nearly ten," he informed her, and smiled at

177

the stunned expression that crossed her countenance. "And the padre needs to talk to you about
the orphanage. I guess the storm did some damage
over there last night."

Regan's reaction was immediate, as he'd expected. It didn't take a top-notch investigator to recognize that the Purgatory Home for Unwanted
Children held a prominent place in her heart.

"What kind of damage? How bad is it?" she
asked, racing around the room looking for a change
of clothes.

"I'm not sure, but I take it a tree came down and
caved in the roof."

His poor choice of words struck him the minute
he saw all the color drain from her face and she
started to sway. He leapt forward, hoping to catch
her this time before she hit the floor nose-first.

Chapter Sixteen

For a few short seconds, the room seemed to swim around her, the yellow bud roses of the wallpaper swirling into fuzzy, nauseating streaks.

Clay rushed forward to grasp her arms and keep her upright, but despite past incidents in his presence, she wasn't going to swoon. Far from it. The news frightened and sickened her, but with the orphans in danger, possibly hurt, she was infused with the need to move, to take action, to *do something*.

"The children," she forced past her tight throat. "Were any of the children hurt?"

"No," Clay responded quickly. "Everyone's fine. I don't know all the details—I came up to wake you as soon as I realized you'd want to talk to the padre yourself—but from my understanding, the portion

Heidi Betts

of the roof and wall that came down were well away from where the children sleep."

"Thank God," she breathed. She dumped a pile of fresh clothes in the middle of her bed and began shrugging out of her robe. She was about to let her robe fall to the floor when she noticed Clay was still in the room and it doubtless wasn't a good idea to strip in front of him.

Doing her best to cover her barely concealed chest with her hands and arms, she shot him an uneasy look. "If you'll give me a minute," she prompted, "I'll be right down."

A devilish glint came into his kohl-gray eyes. "You don't have to hide from me, Regan. I recall seeing just about all of you last night."

His voice was low, suggestive, and she flushed to the roots of her hair. She thought about castigating him. Or going ahead and dressing, ignoring him altogether. But despite the intimacies they'd shared, she couldn't bring herself to be that bold. And she was in such a hurry to get downstairs, to see what could be done to help the children.

"Please," she finally managed, the word quavering slightly on her tongue.

Clay seemed to sense her urgency and discomfort. He stepped close and lifted a hand to cup her cheek. "You're a beautiful woman, Regan. You shouldn't be so shy about letting people see that."

And then he stepped back. "I'll keep Aunt Martha and Father Ignacio occupied until you're ready." With a gentle smile, he pulled the door closed behind him, leaving her alone to dress.

180

Once again, he'd left her speechless. He had a way of doing that. No matter the situation . . . no matter how confident she might be feeling at the moment . . . the barest touch, the simplest word from Clayton Walker, and she was struck dumb.

He'd told her she was beautiful—both the night before and just now. She didn't know if he meant it, or if he was merely trying to soften her up for the next time he wanted to seduce her, but regardless, his compliment seeped into every pore of her being. Warmed her through and through, and made her *feel* beautiful.

Given her provincial lifestyle and two years of wearing nothing but black, she hadn't felt comely in a very long time.

Her stomach gave an excited little flip, and she quickly shook off such distracting thoughts. She didn't have time to stand here mooning over her mother-in-law's nephew. Father Ignacio and the orphans needed her.

Scrambling out of her wrap, she hurriedly washed with tepid water from the bowl and pitcher on her dresser before outfitting herself in a sunflower yellow camisole and drawers, and a lightweight black cotton gown that would hopefully be comfortable for a trip into town and any work she had to do to assist in the restoration of the orphanage.

Grabbing a bonnet from the top shelf of her closet and pulling on her walking boots as she hopped down the stairs, she burst into the kitchen already short of breath. Clay and Mother Doyle sat at the uncovered oak table nursing steaming cups of tea and coffee while Father Ignacio paced back and forth, wringing his wrinkled hands. He looked much more upset than she'd expected, given Clay's description of the storm's damage to the Home.

"Regan! Oh, Regan," he exclaimed the moment he saw her, rushing forward. "It's terrible, simply terrible. The storm, it was so violent, the wind so strong it woke many of the children. *Gracias Dios*, no one was sleeping on the side of the building that collapsed."

The priest clutched Regan's wrists as she tried to calm him. "Clay told me no one was hurt, Father Ignacio."

"*Si, si,* it is true." His voice was filled with relief. "Sweet *Madre de Dios,* no one was harmed. For that, we are all grateful. But the orphanage . . . Regan, it is destroyed. The tree fell into the west wall, and a great portion of the roof has crumbled around us. The wind and rain flooded everywhere. The children have no decent place to stay."

"Where are they now?" she asked, remaining composed even though she was gravely concerned.

"They are in the church. The Sisters and I collected all that we could—blankets, pillows, food— and settled the children on the pews. But this will not do for long, Regan, and we do not have enough money to rebuild."

Regan cast a glance over her shoulder at Clay and Martha. Licking her lips, she carefully inquired about the cash she knew she'd been leaving for the orphanage on a fairly regular basis. "What about the poor box, Father? Or the money from the collection plates?"

"We have been very lucky in that regard, I admit." He made a sign of the cross in thanks. "We have had enough to care for the children very well. Very well, indeed. But it is not enough to pay for repairs. Believe me," he said fervently, "I have counted and recounted, trying to find a way to stretch every peso. I simply do not see how we can have the orphanage rebuilt and still feed the children. Oh, Regan." He grasped her hands and squeezed. "What will we do?"

Regan took a deep breath. "We'll do what we have to. The children will be fine, Father Ignacio, I promise."

And it was true. She would see that the Home was repaired and the children cared for, no matter what she had to do.

She turned a wary, sidelong glance in Clay's direction. Since his arrival, she'd put a halt to her late-night excursions in hopes of convincing him the robberies had stopped, and making him lose interest in catching the burglar. Now, though, she suspected the Ghost of Ol' Morty Pike would have to reappear.

She wasn't sure she had any other choice.

After Martha assured them she would be fine at home alone, Regan and Clay returned to town with Father Ignacio and spent most of the day calming the children and trying to figure out what could be done in regard to the collapsed portion of the orphanage.

Clay thought it best to clear away the fallen tree and rubble first so they could see just how many repairs needed to be made and how to go about them. He, Father Ignacio, and a few of the men from town who'd offered to pitch in, spent several hours removing broken boards and crumbled stone.

For the most part, Regan stayed inside the church, helping to make up a number of pallets for the children, playing, reading stories, and assisting the Sisters at meal times.

When the sun was beginning to set in a breathtaking splash of orange and lavender, Regan took a platter of sandwiches out to the men, along with a stack of glasses and a pitcher of fresh lemonade.

Welcoming the much-needed break, the men took their food and drinks and found places to sit while they ate dinner. Clay, however, remained standing at Regan's elbow, chewing slowly on a bite of bread and cheese, washing it down with a long gulp of cool, sweet lemonade.

"You're really making progress," she said by way of conversation. The wall that had been nothing but a pile of rubble hours before was nearly down to bare ground, and most of the cracked rafters had already been carted away.

"Uh-huh."

"There's still a long way to go."

He grunted and took another bite.

Regan refilled his half empty glass. "I thought it might be a good idea for me to go home and check on Mother Doyle," she began. "Will it be all right if I leave you here?"

He gave her a crooked smile. "I think I'll survive your absence," he teased. "Besides, that's why I brought Caesar along into town. The question is, will you be all right taking the buckboard back by yourself?"

"I'll be fine. I've driven the wagon plenty of times."

Glancing past her to the horizon, he nodded. "You'd best get going, then, if you want to make it home before dark. We'll likely keep working here several more hours. We've already gathered some lanterns to light once the sun goes down."

Confident that Clay would be stuck at the orphanage for a few more hours, at least, and that she could get Mother Doyle settled soon after she arrived home, Regan started to turn away. Only to halt mid-step and turn back.

"Clay, I just want you to know . . . I really appreciate . . . I can't thank you enough. . . ."

He chuckled over her stuttered attempt at conveying her gratitude. Still holding his glass of lemonade, he ran his knuckles along her jaw. "Do you realize, green eyes, that this is the third time you've thanked me in the past twenty-four hours?"

Regan opened her mouth, but no sound came out. She didn't have the foggiest notion how to respond. Once again, he'd left her speechless.

This time, however, she wasn't as enamored as the last. In fact, she was beginning to feel like an imbecile, unable to form the simplest thought when Clay was near.

"If you're not careful, I'm going to get a swelled head. Then what will you do with me?"

Brow winging upward, she studied him, thinking this at least was an easy enough question to answer. "Drill a hole in your skull to relieve the pressure?" she ventured.

He threw his head back and laughed. A loud, booming chortle that brought the other men's gazes swiveling in their direction.

"You're quick, sweetheart, and so funny, I could kiss you."

Her eyes flew wide and she stepped away, afraid he might do exactly as he threatened, out here, where everyone would see.

He took a step toward her and she started to retreat again, but he grabbed her wrist. Lemonade sloshed at the bottom of the near-empty pitcher she was holding.

"I won't, of course," he added softly. "It wouldn't do for all these nice people to see me kissing the curl from your hair. But tonight . . ."

He paused and the effect was immediate; her breath caught and her heart's natural pace doubled, maybe even tripled.

"Tonight," he went on, "we may just have to take another trip out to the barn. I'm thinking that tarp might have come loose again."

His tone ran like honey through her weakened bone structure. The imagery he created, the memories of what they'd done together in the barn while rain beat down around them nearly caused her knees to give.

In the same tone he'd used to make those highly erotic propositions, he flawlessly returned to the earlier thread of their conversation. "I'm glad you appreciate what I'm doing here, but I'm happy to help out. Now you'd better head out before it gets too dark to see the road. And when you get home, leave the wagon and horses out front; I'll unhitch them when I get there."

His hold on her wrist loosened, changing to a slow stroking of her fingers between his own. "Sound good?"

She inclined her head, too thrown off balance to speak. Moments ago, she'd had a distinct plan and was prepared to carry out that plan. She'd only come outside to see that the men got something to eat and let Clay know she was heading home to check on Mother Doyle.

Now, her blood was pounding in her veins, her mouth was dry as a gulch, proving Clay was a dangerous distraction.

She needed to shake free of him and get back to the matter at hand—locating cash for the repair of the orphanage.

Inhaling deeply, she set her shoulders and lifted her chin. "I'll see you at home, then." She turned on her heel and practically ran from his too-charming countenance.

Chapter Seventeen

Regan crouched in the darkness, waiting for the carriage to pull away from Nolan Updike's house. The Updikes were fine, upstanding citizens of Purgatory and were usually quite generous when it came to local charities. They had actually been fairly low on Regan's list of possible marks for robbery.

Until tonight. Tonight, she was desperate. She needed something valuable to turn over to Mr. Sawyer for cash, and she needed it now.

She'd spent the entire ride home from town wondering whose house she could break into this evening, and the Updikes' had come to mind again and again simply because it was common knowledge they spent every Wednesday night in town. After dinner Veronica attended a quilting circle, where the ladies chatted and worked, and the children played hard enough to fall straight into bed when they got home. And since the rest of the family was busy in town one evening a week, Nolan took the opportunity to put in extra hours at the bank and then ride home with his family.

Regan had hidden in the bushes, watching as Mrs. Updike and the children bustled about the house getting ready. As soon as she heard their black landau rock into motion, she made a crouched run to the back of the house.

There were lamps burning inside, which meant a servant or two might be around, even though Regan thought she recalled the Updikes mentioning they let their help go home early on quilting nights. Still, she would have to be extra careful to remain undetected.

Sneaking toward a first floor window, she silently eased open the frame, then searched for some way to boost herself up to its level. This would take some doing, but it was better than going through the kitchen and risking being caught if some of the staff were still cleaning up from dinner.

She ended up sprinting for the dark barn several yards away and returning to the open window with a bucket. Turning it over, she used it to boost herself onto the sill. It took some doing—several bounces on her precarious perch and a lot of stifled grunts as she braced herself with her elbows. Relying on her questionable upper body strength, she pulled herself through the opening and fell to the carpeted floor with a thump she prayed no one would hear.

When no one burst through the door to catch her in the act, she straightened and brushed herself off. She was in a bedroom. One of the children's or servant's quarters, she suspected, but took the time to rifle through the things on the dresser, just in case.

When she found nothing valuable enough to exchange for cash, she tiptoed to the door and opened it as quietly as possible, slipping into the hall. She stood against the wall, the waist-high molding digging into the small of her back. Slowly, step by step, she made her way through the dim passage toward the stairwell leading to the house's second story.

Once upstairs, she began searching for the master bedroom. Nolan was a collector of expensive, intricately designed pocket watches, and she thought one of them might bring a hefty sum in St. Louis.

She made quick work of navigating Nolan and Veronica's chamber, finding the very masculine cherrywood and crewel box that held Nolan's prized timepieces. There were too many to choose from, and she truly didn't want to take anything too valuable or sentimental. She liked the Updikes and didn't want to cause them any more distress than absolutely necessary.

Without a lamp or candle, it was hard to distinguish one watch from the next. She could only carry the box to the window and use the moonlight as a guide. She handled each one, fingering the detailed etchings and trying to decide which to take. She checked for inscriptions or signs of age—anything that might hint of an emotional attachment. Finally, she settled on a fairly large one with the carving of a locomotive that looked to be made of real gold. At least she hoped it was real gold.

She returned the box to the dressertop, and was about to sneak back out of the room when she heard raised voices drawing near. Before she could stop herself, she let out a small squeak of alarm.

The house was supposed to be empty. No one should be tromping around below. And it wasn't simply a servant; this sounded like Nolan Updike himself. His hardy, rather nasally voice was quite distinctive. He was speaking to someone in a rapid, enraged timbre, and furious footsteps stomped up the stairs to the second floor, coming ever closer to the room Regan occupied.

Her heartbeat raced out of control. A cold sweat broke out over her brow.

What was she going to do? If Nolan and his companion came into the master bedroom, she would be found out. There were very few places to hide, and little time to do so even if she found a spot to conceal herself. Her only option might be to jump from the window, which would surely result in broken bones—possibly including the ones in her neck!

The voices grew even closer, and she began to draw great gasping gulps of air into her lungs.

"I don't care what you want!" she heard Nolan bellow. "You're not getting another damn dime from me, you stinking bastard."

"You owe me," the other voice barked.

The doorknob rattled as someone grabbed it and began to twist. Sheer terror shot through Regan and she threw herself against the opposite wall, behind the door, not knowing what else to do.

"I don't owe you anything. Now get out of my house before I throw you out."

"I won't let you do this, Updike," the stranger replied in such a cold, savage tone, Regan shivered.

The brass knob rattled again and the door opened a fraction, sending Regan's heart into her throat. Then she heard a thud and the sounds of a scuffle in the hallway.

"What are you doing? Dammit, get your filthy hands off of me!" And then Nolan gave a shout of horror. *"No!"*

Thump, thump, thump. . . .

My God! Was that what she thought it was? With a hand clamped tight over her mouth to keep from crying out, she envisioned Nolan falling down the steep stairs.

"Now who's the bastard?" she heard through the crack of the door, followed by a satisfied grunt. Then a muffled noise, like something falling to the carpeted hallway on the other side of the door, and heavy footfalls leading back downstairs as the killer left the scene of his crime.

Killer. Dear God, it was true. She wanted to deny it, but deep in her gut, she knew what she'd heard. Nolan had been pushed down the stairs—and it didn't sound like he was getting up anytime soon. Had she just witnessed a murder?

Squeezing her eyes tight for a moment, she took a deep breath and gathered her courage. She had to go and check on Nolan. What if he needed her help?

Worse, what if he was dead? He had always been a kind, decent man. Why would anyone want to hurt him?

Shaking off the disturbing thoughts, she pushed away from the wall and wrapped her hand over the edge of the door. She peeked around the corner to make sure the hall was empty. When she saw that it was, she made her way slowly, reluctantly to the top of the stairs.

She could see Nolan, sprawled on the floor below. His leg and neck were twisted at odd angles, confirming her worst fears. He was dead.

Even so, she bit back a sob and started carefully down the stairwell. Clinging to the wall at her back and listening for the sounds of another person in the house, Regan crouched beside the body and felt for a pulse in Nolan's neck. Her touch met with nothing but the cold stillness of death.

The house was eerily quiet and Regan sensed the man who'd pushed Nolan was already gone. She was safer that way, certainly, but she hadn't even caught a glimpse of the man who'd murdered Nolan.

She rose and hurried to the foyer. The front door stood wide open and she quickly scanned the outside area for some sign of movement. There was no one there and she instinctively knew the killer had escaped.

Her shoulders slumped as she sighed in defeat. Cautiously, she checked the rest of the house in case she'd been wrong about the killer fleeing, but, as expected, found nothing.

What should she do now? she wondered. If she alerted the sheriff he would wonder how she'd come to be in the house in the first place while most of the family was in town. But she couldn't very well leave Nolan to be discovered by his family. What a horrible scene to come home to.

No, she couldn't do that to Veronica and the children.

She wracked her brain for several long minutes until she devised a plan that she thought might work. She would hurry home and change garments, then she would come up with some reason that she needed to visit the Updikes immediately. Once she arrived at her neighbors' home, she would "discover" the body. Perhaps she would even take Clay along with her. Being a lawman, he would know how to handle the situation and no one would ever suspect she'd been in the house when the murder took place.

Yes, she thought, that seemed plausible.

With a strategy planted firmly in her mind, she quickly sneaked back out of the house and raced toward home. By the time she reached her secret stash of nightclothes beneath the pecan tree, she was panting with exertion. She hastily traded her robbery outfit for the black shift and robe she'd hidden earlier and headed for the back of the house.

Her breathing was still ragged and uneven when she opened the door to the kitchen—and came face to face with a visibly perturbed Clay Walker.

"Where the hell were you?" he snapped the minute she shut the door behind her. His arms were crossed over his broad chest, reminding her of an ancient Roman sentinel ordered to guard the royal palace.

Her mind raced for a plausible explanation. It took all of her willpower to keep from fidgeting with the sleeves of her wrap. "I was . . . out looking for Lucy-fur."

He narrowed his eyes and pinned her with a suspicious glare. "Don't give me that," he forced past tightly clenched teeth. "Your cat is asleep on your bed, right where she's been since before I got home."

Knowing she had no choice now but to stick with her original story, she pressed a hand to her heart and feigned relief. "Is she? My heavens, I looked everywhere for her. She certainly wasn't there earlier." Hoping this confrontation could be put to rest with a few more guileless words, she stepped around him as though nothing was out of the ordinary. "Mother Doyle has a tendency to put Lucy out for the night, but I prefer she remain inside. It's not easy to track her down once she's been let loose, though," she ended with a chuckle.

"Regan."

His tone sent coils of apprehension spiraling down her spine, but she pasted a smile on her face as she turned back to him. "Yes?"

"I don't believe you."

Chapter Eighteen

"You don't believe me?" she retorted with a nervous giggle while caterpillars did somersaults in her belly. "That's the silliest thing I've ever heard. What is there to believe?" She shrugged a shoulder nonchalantly and sauntered to the stove to put on water for tea. Anything to keep from having to meet Clay's accusatory gaze.

"No one has that much trouble with one pint-size feline, Regan."

She tossed him a placating smile. "I take it you haven't spent much time around cats," she said amicably. "I admit, Lucy-fur can be more vexing than most, but that's part of the reason I love her. I'm afraid she's never been much of a lay-about lap cat. Even when she was just a kitten, I spent a fair amount of time rescuing her from trees or the corners of horse stalls before she got trampled. And she almost always thanked me for my efforts with a nice dead bird or mouse at the foot of my bed." The kettle began to gurgle and she removed it from the hot burner. "Who wouldn't dote on such a generous pet?" she finished with a smile.

Unfortunately, Clay wasn't buying her story for a minute. He stood in the center of the kitchen, a muscle twitching in his jaw.

"You're not going to tell me what you were really doing out there this late at night, are you?"

"I told you," she insisted, pouring water over the loose tea at the bottom of her cup. She took a seat at the table to let the shredded leaves steep and met his belligerent gray stare. "It's not my fault you think I'm lying."

"Then you have no plans to go back out," he stated, leaving her little to no room for negotiation.

She had meant to go back out, of course, had even intended to ask him to go with her as a second witness when they discovered Nolan's body. But as suspicious as Clay seemed this evening, she thought it wiser to go along with his proposal.

"Not at all. As you can see, I'm already dressed for bed. Which is where I'm headed as soon as I finish my tea. Would you care for something?" she asked casually.

Taking a seat across from her, he stacked his arms on the rim of the table and studied her intently, giving a stiff shake of his head in response to her question.

She thought the silence might strangle her. They

sat in the stuffy kitchen, gazes locked on each other while Regan sipped her drink and Clay surveyed her as though she was about to sprout wings.

After fighting the urge to flee as long as humanly possible, she gulped down the last of her tea—which was supposed to calm her, not set her nerves even more on edge—and jumped to her feet. "Well. I think I'll peek in on Mother Doyle and then go up to bed. See you in the morning."

Clay watched her brisk movements as she took her empty cup and saucer to the cast iron sink, then darted out of the room.

She sounded sincere. Looked as innocent as a newborn babe. And even though his instincts and inherently doubtful nature told him there was something going on, he couldn't honestly picture any sinister reasons for her to be running around in her nightclothes after dark.

So maybe she had simply been looking for her cat.

God knew, he wanted to believe her, but damned if *something* in this household didn't feel out of place.

Extinguishing the kitchen lamps, he ambled toward the front of the house in time to see Regan slipping out of Martha's room. She pressed a finger to her lips, signaling for him to be quiet to keep from waking his aunt.

She started up the stairs and he followed suit, not missing the gentle back and forth rhythm of her hips only inches ahead of him. He wondered what she would do if he swept her off her feet and carried her into his bedroom. Would she throw her arms around his neck and nuzzle his ear?

He gave a mental scoff. Not likely, given the way he'd browbeat her downstairs. Chances were, she'd scream her lungs out and punch him in the head for daring to touch her two minutes after interrogating her like an accused horse thief.

You're an idiot, Walker, he chastised himself. If he had half the brain God gave a tumblebug, he'd have kept his mouth shut when Regan came in through the back door. He'd have kissed her and run his fingers through her hair and done his best to woo her into his bed for the night, to hell with figuring out what she'd been up to. After all, a good lawman knew that if you kept your mouth shut and your eyes open, you'd eventually find what you were looking for.

But he'd been so damn concerned about her when he'd arrived home to discover Aunt Martha asleep in her room and Regan nowhere to be found. At first, he hadn't thought much of her absence. Then, as the minutes ticked by and there were no signs of her, he'd gotten worried. Scratch that. He'd been downright frantic, imagining any number of horrific things that could happen to a woman left alone— things he'd been unfortunate enough to encounter on more than one occasion during his years with the Rangers.

Still, he'd ruined his chances of seducing her tonight. He'd envisioned so many nice fantasies of repeating last night's experiences, too.

He sighed.

Out loud, apparently, because Regan stopped on the second floor landing and turned to regard him with shadowed, doe-like green eyes. He loved those eyes.

"Are you all right?" she asked.

"Fine." Except for the fact that he would never be able to sleep tonight without a nice, cold dip in the horse trough.

She walked the last few steps to her bedroom door, tilting her head for a last glance in his direction. "Goodnight, then," she said softly.

He stood where he was, waiting as she stepped into her room and closed the door behind her with a gentle click.

This was not good, he thought to himself, panic skittering through his blood. He was watching her much too closely, found her much too attractive. Wanted her way too much. And he was starting to worry, which meant he cared for her.

No, this was definitely not a reassuring turn of events. If he knew what was good for him, he'd get on the ball about catching Purgatory's resident thief and hightail it out of town with all due haste.

Then maybe a green-eyed, flame-haired Irish beauty would stop haunting both his waking *and* sleeping moments.

A pounding on the front door woke everyone early the next morning. Clay was the first out of bed, and made his way drowsily down the stairs. He was barefoot, wearing yesterday's dungarees and working at buttoning the shirt he'd grabbed from the back of a chair. Regan trailed close behind, struggling to properly lace the ties of her robe.

Clay opened the door to Father Ignacio, who was once again wearing his dark brown vestments, tied at the waist with thick rope, and displaying much the same expression as when he'd come to announce the collapse of the orphanage.

Clay ran his fingers through his hair. Was it just the priest, or did everyone come to Regan with their problems? "Howdy, padre. You make a habit of visiting all your parishioners this early in the morning?"

"My apologies, Señor Walker. I know I have made a pest of myself these past few days, but I must speak to Regan. It is *muy importante*. Is she at home?"

"Where else would she be at this hour?" Clay snapped, even as he admitted he was being unaccountable surly. Especially to a man of God. But, dammit, he hadn't slept well last night, and just about the time he'd drifted off, the padre here came banging on the door. He had a right to be cantankerous.

"I'm here, Father," Regan put in gently—and pleasantly, Clay noted with a glower—from behind him. "What's wrong?"

Martha chose that moment to shriek from the other side of her closed door.

Regan started to turn, but Clay put a hand on her arm to stop her. "You see what Father Ignacio wants, I'll get Martha."

Needing no further prompting, the priest stepped

over the threshold and began chattering. "Have you heard? No, of course you haven't," he hurried on, answering his own inquiry. "It's such a tragedy."

"What? What's happened, Father?"

Clay came back into the entryway, pushing Martha ahead of him in her chair.

"It's Nolan Updike," Father Ignacio went on. "His family returned home from town last evening to find him dead. It seems he fell down the steps and broke his neck."

"Fell?" Regan repeated.

Something about the tone of her voice caught Clay's attention.

"*Sí*, it is terrible. Veronica and the children are devastated."

"He *fell?*" Regan asked again.

At her second utterance, the hairs on the back of Clay's neck gave a tiny tingle, the way they often did when something was afoot. He'd been a lawman too long not to heed his body's natural reaction to such things.

"*Sí, sí,*" the father responded distractedly. "That is why I am here. I know that you sat with little Theresa last year when she had the croup. I thought you might like to stay with the family until funeral arrangements can be made." He made the sign of the cross. "God rest his soul. I know some of the ladies in town will drop off baked goods at the house later. It would be a big help if you could go over now, though."

"He fell? Are you sure?"

This time the words were strained. Clay's brow

knit. She seemed either unwilling or unable to come to terms with the details of this Updike fellow's death.

"I can't believe it," Martha breathed. "I've known the Updikes for years."

"Who's Nolan Updike?" Clay asked, wondering why Regan seemed so incredulous at the news of this man's passing.

"He worked at the bank in town," Martha said. "Ran the place, really. Veronica, his wife, organizes Purgatory's harvest festival every year. She must be just beside herself."

Working the wheels of her chair on her own, Martha moved forward a couple of paces, then started to turn in a tight circle. "Clayton, you get the wagon ready while Regan and I get dressed. We won't be long, Father. Then we'll all head over to see what we can do to help."

Regan stood to one side of the room, never so uncomfortable in her life. Veronica Updike sat hunched in the center of the forest green brocade settee, her face buried in her handkerchief, sobbing her heart out. Martha, who had insisted on leaving her invalid chair, sat beside the grieving widow, patting her back and attempting to quell her river of tears.

Veronica and Nolan's three children, Adam, Oliver, and the youngest, Theresa, were hunkered in the corner of the parlor, confused by their mother's behavior and not really understanding that their father was gone forever. Regan felt most aggrieved for them.

Heidi Betts

And worst of all, she was the only one who knew Nolan hadn't truly fallen, but had been pushed. In her wildest imaginings, in the many scenarios that had run through her head when she'd considered herself, Clay, Veronica, or one of the Updike servants finding Nolan's body, it had never occurred to her that people would think his death an accident. Chastising herself for her naiveté, she now realized how unlikely it would have been for them to think anything *but*.

The problem was, she knew the truth. And she had to tell someone . . . or find some way to help them figure it out on their own. She *couldn't* let them go on thinking he'd merely tripped and broken his neck on the way down the stairs. Not when that option meant a murderer would be allowed to roam free, never punished for his crime.

She'd opened her mouth to admit what she knew a dozen times since arriving on Veronica's doorstep. As Veronica had collapsed against her, soaking the front of her dress with tears. As Martha had ordered her into the kitchen to fix a pot of tea for the adults and a plate of shortbread cookies for the children. As Clay had stood off to the side, clutching the brim of his hat and shifting uneasily from foot to foot.

But how could she tell them the truth when that would mean opening herself up to any number of questions about *how* she knew what had happened? About what she was doing in the house—at that hour of the night, when no one was supposed to be home, upstairs in the master bedroom where she had no business being even if she *had* been invited. She couldn't risk raising suspicions, having someone—someone like Clay, with too much time on his hands and so much distrust in his heart—put two and two together and figure out that she was Purgatory's housebreaking bandit.

Stepping closer to the open pocket doors of the parlor, she started to make her way out of the room. She'd been trapped by Mother Doyle and Father Ignacio's demands and Clay's penetrating gaze all day, with no chance to explore the rest of the house. Between sitting with Veronica, playing with the children, and answering the door when other neighbors dropped by to bring food and pay their respects, she'd been trying to think of a way to slip upstairs and see if she could find evidence of the intruder.

She also wanted to return Nolan's pocket watch—resting even now in one of the deep pockets of her gown—to its place in the cherrywood and crewel box where she'd found it. Finding another way to pay for the repairs to the orphanage roof wouldn't be easy, but she couldn't sell Nolan's watch now, not after the way he'd died and knowing how much his family was suffering from the loss. The very thought soured her stomach.

She didn't know what she expected to find. Probably nothing. But she had to be sure. If she could find something, *anything,* she would be able to point Clay and Sheriff Graves in the right direction and let them announce to the town that Nolan's death had not been an accident.

Heidi Betts

She'd just cleared the parlor doors and turned toward the stairwell at the back of the house when a smooth, masculine voice halted her progress.

"Going somewhere, green eyes?"

Chapter Nineteen

Regan stopped in her tracks and took a deep breath, curling her fingers into the folds of her skirts while she struggled to compose herself. She'd been so close, but once again Clay had managed to foil her plans. That was fast becoming one of his most annoying traits.

Turning to face him, she searched for a reason to be heading toward the rear of the house. Everyone had been avoiding the region of Nolan's demise throughout the day. And the stairs to the second floor were situated far opposite the kitchen and dining room, so she couldn't use the excuse of going for more snacks for the children.

"I thought I would . . . check the area," she said, dropping her voice to little more than a whisper and rolling her eyes in the direction of the parlor where

Veronica's weeping echoed into the hallway. "I don't want Veronica and the children to run across something they shouldn't see on their way to bed tonight. It will be hard enough as it is for them to walk through that part of the house."

Clay took a step forward and leaned the right side of his body against the wall, essentially hemming her in as he tapped his dark brown Stetson against his denim-clad thigh. "That's very thoughtful of you," he almost drawled.

She wasn't sure if he meant it as a compliment or was attempting to draw her out, but she had to be extra careful now. It was quite possible that she was closer to being found out at this very moment than the night Clay had chased her from the Finch home.

Hoping she could continue this charade long enough to distract Clay, she feigned morbid curiosity and asked, "Have you seen it yet? Did you see where he actually . . . died?" She glanced down at Clay's dusty boots, not wanting to think about how *she* had last seen Nolan Updike.

"I took a look around," Clay answered, keeping his tone low so as not to be overheard. "Didn't see anything in particular, why?"

Swallowing hard, using the fear she'd experienced last night, she asked a question she thought a meddlesome observer might. "So there wasn't any . . ." she swallowed again, "blood?"

Her innocent inquiry must have relieved any doubts Clay harbored, because he lifted a hand and ran the knuckle of one finger along the line of her cheek. "No blood, sweetheart," he assured her softly. "He fell and broke his neck, but he didn't bleed. And if it makes a difference, I don't think he suffered any."

She nodded. He was right about that. Nolan Updike hadn't suffered, but he hadn't simply fallen, either.

"Do you still want to see where he died?" Clay asked softly.

She did, but not with him. And not for the reasons he thought. He would never understand her desire to go all the way upstairs to look around. And she couldn't replace the watch with him hanging over her shoulder. Maybe she could sneak around the corner later, without Clay tracking her every move.

"No," she told him quietly. "It's all so incomprehensible. I guess I thought that if I saw where it happened, it would make the whole thing more real. I just can't believe he's really gone."

"Were the two of you close?" Clay asked, and she could have sworn a note of aggression tinged his tone.

"To Nolan?" She shook her head. "Not any closer than to anyone else in town, no. Nolan ran the First Bank of Purgatory, so we spoke occasionally when I had business there. I probably had more contact with his wife. Veronica loves organizing social functions, so I often helped with baking or sewing or decorations, along with some of the other women from town."

The muscles of Clay's diaphragm relaxed as he released a pent-up breath. He didn't know why it was such a relief, but hearing Regan shrug off her relationship with the Updikes so easily went a long way toward loosening the tight knot in his gut.

From the beginning, her reaction to the incident had struck him as being a bit off-kilter for the loss of a mere neighbor. He wasn't proud of it, but he'd started to wonder if something had been going on between Regan and Updike before his death. Now, he felt certain his misgivings were unwarranted.

Thank God. He wasn't particularly happy with how relieved he felt—it indicated how attached to Regan he had become. An emotional attachment that scared him.

"How about a walk?" he suggested suddenly, needing to get out of the house. And yes, wanting to be alone with Regan. *There, he'd admitted it,* he thought bitterly. Now maybe his conscience— which kept telling him to pull Regan close and never let her go—would shut the hell up.

She'd just begun to relax, but his question had her spine snapping ramrod straight. "A walk? We can't." And then she seemed to reconsider. "Can we? I mean, we shouldn't. It isn't right to leave Veronica and the children."

Just then, the widow in question gave a wail of despair and Martha could be heard doing her best to comfort her.

Lips curving upwards, Clay pushed himself away from the wall and clamped his hat down on his head. "I doubt we'll be missed, sweetheart. Come on," he encouraged, linking his fingers with hers and dragging her along behind him.

To escape the notice of those in the parlor or others milling around the house, he kept a swift pace, pulling Regan with him. Surprisingly, she didn't struggle as he'd expected. She was probably as eager to get out of the stuffy, grief-ridden house as he was.

They ran through the dry grass skirting the yard, past the wagon and horses they'd left in the shade of a juniper tree, and around the weathered barn a good distance from the house. By the time they'd ducked behind the outbuilding, Regan was laughing and trying to catch her breath at the same time.

Clay watched her press at an apparent stitch in her side, then lean against the barn wall, twining her hands behind her back in a pose of easy friendliness.

She looked breezy and beautiful. Breezy, he thought, rolling the word around in his mind. That suited her, with the hair at her temples pulled back and tied behind her head. The rest was left loose, the long copper ringlets falling about her shoulders and tiny bits of curl coming free around her heart-shaped face. Even in her characteristic black day-dress, she looked young, and for a change, carefree.

He grinned at her wide smile. "Having fun?" he asked.

Caught, her lips immediately thinned and she tried for a more stoic demeanor. It was too late, though, for he'd already gotten a glimpse of the lighthearted young woman hidden beneath the shroud of her widow's weeds.

"I don't think it's at all appropriate that we

211

sneaked away like that," she said, trying to sound prim, but missing proper by a mile when the gaiety in her eyes didn't dim a whit.

"You've spent all day comforting Mrs. Updike, and running around doing both Aunt Martha's and Father Ignacio's bidding. Don't you think you deserve a few minutes to yourself?"

"Time to myself? What a rare and curious concept."

She said it so cheekily that he burst out laughing. The look in her eyes told him she knew perfectly well Martha and the townspeople took advantage of her generous nature.

"So why do you let them run roughshod over you like that? Whenever anybody needs anything, they head straight to you. Even the town preacher comes to you for help and advice."

"They're my neighbors," she replied simply. "If I needed something, they would be there for me."

"And how often do you go to them with your problems?"

Her silence and the slight pinch of her lips was all the answer he needed. She'd never gone to anyone for assistance. Not when her husband died, not when Martha's health deteriorated so much she became nearly house-bound, probably not even for a cup of sugar for a cookie recipe.

But she was always there for others, wasn't she? Martha depended on her to get dressed in the morning, to get ready for bed at night, to prepare her meals and keep the house. Father Ignacio depended on her for financial help with the orphanage and emotional help with the orphans. The Updikes—like most of her other neighbors, Clay would wager—depended on her for support during times of need. And Regan seemed more than happy to comply.

But who took care of her? When would she be pampered and catered to? When did her needs come first?

And if they did, what would those needs be? Clay wondered. Would she long for fancy dresses and fine jewels, or someone to help around the house and with Martha? Maybe she wanted nothing more than to be left alone by friends and family alike. Or perhaps she wanted things exactly as they were; perhaps she liked being needed, wanted people to come to her for help.

Could be, but he didn't think so. Not totally, at any rate. He'd seen the look on her face a time or two when Martha had demanded to be taken to town or wheeled to a particular spot. He'd heard her sigh of resignation today when Martha had sent her off to make tea for Mrs. Updike, or Father Ignacio had listed all of the things she would need to do to help the widow and children get through their bereavement.

"You could say no," he suggested quietly, hitching a thumb in the pocket of his jeans because he itched to run his fingers through the long spirals of her hair.

"Say no?" The tiny spot of skin between her two slightly arched, auburn eyebrows crinkled with perplexity. "To what?"

"Anything. Everything. The next time someone asks you to sit with a sick child or hold the hand of a grieving widow. The next time someone's roof caves in or their cellar floods. The next time someone wants directions to the nearest saloon. You could tell them all to go to hell."

She gasped, her mouth falling open in astonishment. "I could never do that."

He took a step towards her, dipping his head a fraction and fixing her with a determined glare. "Sure, you could. You just say, 'Go to hell.' Try it."

An appalled puff of air escaped her lungs. "I couldn't."

"Come on, Regan. At least give it a shot. Repeat after me: 'Go to hell.'"

She shook her head in denial.

With her back to the barn wall, Clay took the opportunity to move closer, laying his hands flat against the rough planks on either side of her head.

"What are you doing?" she rasped.

"Maybe you just need the proper motivation," he told her, slanting his head to one side and studying her mouth. "I'm thinking about kissing you, Regan Doyle. And if you don't want that, then you're going to have to tell me, plain and simple, to go to hell."

He stepped even nearer, until her skirts wound around his legs and her breasts pressed against his chest. "Ready?"

Her eyes widened and she kept her gaze locked on his lips as they descended toward her own. He stopped a hairsbreadth from her mouth, their warm exhalations of air mingling. Meeting her gaze, he gave her one more opportunity to deter him.

"Last chance, sweetheart. Are you going to say it?" His tongue darted out to wet the spot just below the tiny indentation of her upper lip.

Her fingers curled into his shirt on either side of his waist. Her breathing was shallow and desperate.

"Too late," he murmured as he closed his eyes and let himself be branded by the hot lash of her lips.

She felt like fire, smelled like rain on a hot summer day, and he wondered how he'd gone so long without holding her this way. He'd told himself not to touch her. Not to press for anything she might not be willing to give. They'd made love once, but that didn't mean she ever wanted to repeat the performance. In fact, if her body language the last couple days was any indication, it was entirely possible she regretted letting him near her in the first place.

God, he hoped not. The thought of not being able to kiss her like this, run his hands over her slim limbs and full curves, left him cold.

When had she become such a compulsion for him? She was like whiskey to a drunkard, pennies to a pauper, redemption to a dying man. She was a fever in his blood, creating an inferno that threatened to burn them to cinders at any minute.

And she felt the same. She had to, or she wouldn't be clinging to him like a second skin, winding her arms around his neck and pressing her pelvis into the rigid proof of his arousal.

Their tongues dueled in an intimate battle of

wills. But neither of them cared who won or lost. Instead, they were both intent on searching out the highest level of pleasure possible between a man and a woman. Clay had no doubt they would succeed.

He shifted his hold from the barn wall to the flare of her hips, then up to the swell of her breasts, teasing her nipples through the thin fabric. She moaned in delight and he pressed his thumbs directly over the budding centers.

In response to his increased caresses, her hands drifted from his sides to the front of his shirt. Her fingers moved over the buttons, one after another, all the way down to the waistband of his trousers. Curving the long, ladylike fingers of one hand over his belt, she pulled him even closer, grinding their bodies together.

Her boldness and the elevated friction against that part of his body, already hard and throbbing, made him gasp. He sucked air into his deprived lungs, but didn't stop kissing her. He dragged his lips over her chin, tipping her head back to allow him access to the elegant column of her neck.

She tilted her head even more, inviting him to linger as her other hand burrowed into the opening of his shirt and began to explore. She stroked his chest, circling a nipple and raking her nails through the light matting of hair trailing down to his abdomen.

He thought about lifting her skirts, opening his pants, and taking her right there against the barn wall in broad daylight. The picture they would make caused his hardness to throb even more mercilessly.

Lowering his hand to her thigh, he began to bunch her skirt in one fist, dragging the folds of material up so he could feel the soft, bare skin beneath.

Regan moaned, and it sounded a little too much like a protest for his peace of mind. Not giving her a chance to put voice to whatever thought was crowding around in her brain, he covered her mouth with his own, wrapped an arm around her back, and placed the other on her hip under the bunched-up skirt to direct her balance. Then he bent at the knees and fell backwards, hitting the ground bottom-first and letting her topple onto his chest.

Regan tensed at the sudden lurch. She put her hands out to break her fall and ended up hovering on all fours above Clay. His fingers twisted into the hair at the nape of her neck and held her close as he deepened his kiss.

What was she doing? He looked at her and her knees went weak. He touched her and every sensible thought in her head fluttered off like a flock of crows to a corn field.

She was a grown woman, for pity's sake! And a widow, to boot. Yet here she was, straddling her late husband's cousin in the most unseemly manner. Behind her neighbor's barn. In the middle of the day. While said neighbor was in the house crying a river of tears over her recently deceased husband.

Good Lord, Regan thought, she should be shot.

Drawn and quartered. Dragged through the center of town and hanged for letting Clay muddle her senses again.

And was that his hand sliding beneath the hem of her drawers to cup her exposed posterior?

Aaack! She gave a screech of alarm and tore herself away from him. She sat above him, resting against the tilt of his bent thighs. When she realized the picture they must make—him on his back on the bare ground, shirt ripped open haphazardly to reveal his bronze chest; her sitting astride his hips, her skirts pulled up to her waist, her legs and bottom on display for anyone who might walk around the corner . . . Merciful heavens!

Blood pounding in her brain, she scrambled off of him, yanking her skirts back down as she staggered to her feet.

Clay stayed where he was, letting his head drop with a thump to the ground and staring up at her. His chest rose and fell in rapid succession as he tried to replenish the oxygen supply to his lungs. And then he hitched himself up on his elbows, which only worked to bare even more of his broad, tanned chest.

"Where are you going, sweetheart? Don't you think we should finish what we started?" He shot her a cocky grin. One she itched to slap off his face.

This time, she had no trouble whatsoever getting the words out. "Go to hell, Clay Walker."

Chapter Twenty

When she stormed off—kicking him in the ankle as she passed, no less—Clay rolled quickly to the side and got his feet under him.

"Regan," he called after her retreating back. "Regan, wait!"

Her hips swayed and her skirts swooshed as she marched across the dusty yard, in the direction of the house. Even peeved and prickly, she looked sexy as hell. He'd have liked to watch her backside swish all the way to Abilene, but figured he'd better smooth her ruffled feathers before she got it in her head to never let him touch her again. For he fully intended to explore every inch of her breathtaking body—as long and as often as possible.

He quickened his pace and reached out to grab

her elbow. "Will you hold on a minute?" he puffed out in exasperation.

His hold on her arm effectively halted her progress and she spun around to face him. Frowning with fury, she stacked her balled-up fists on her hips and shot daggers at him from her mossy green eyes.

"Damn, you sure do rile easy," he said.

Her hot-as-coals glare narrowed. "Excuse me?"

"Don't get me wrong, you're beautiful when you're angry. Your cheeks get all pink and your eyes light up." His gaze fluttered down. "And you should see the way your breasts bobble when your breathing speeds up."

Regan inhaled a small gasp of alarm at his audacity and she slapped a hand to her chest like a shield. "You," she bit out, "are insufferable."

"And you," he tapped the tip of her nose with one finger, "are glorious."

Her chest rose as she inhaled deeply, but his comment apparently blew away the better part of her ire.

Taking advantage of her sudden bout of speechlessness, he dropped his grip from her elbow and clasped her hand. "Come on, don't stalk off," he cajoled. "I'm sorry for what happened behind the barn."

One brow and the corner of his mouth both arched at the same time. "Well, not entirely sorry, but I admit that things got out of hand. It's not that I don't want you." He ran the back of his free hand over her cheek and threaded his fingers into her hair. "Nowadays it seems like I want you every minute of the day. But you're right that it shouldn't have gone as far as it did, so for that, I apologize."

He gave her a gentle smile. "Don't let it ruin our outing, though. Let's finish our walk." Tugging on her hand, he tried to get her to follow him in the direction they'd just come.

She hated to admit it, but Clay Walker could charm the scales off a rattlesnake. She tried to hang on to her annoyance, but the look in his gray eyes, the pressure of his fingers around hers, and what sounded like a very sincere apology all worked against her.

So she let him lead her, let him convince her to resume their walk. She only hoped that this time they could both remain upright, all four feet planted firmly on the ground.

She followed him along the length of the barn, but dug in her heels when he made a move to turn behind the structure. "Wait, wait, wait," she rushed. "Where are we going?"

"For a walk. I told you."

Shaking her head with resolve, she said, "Not that way." She had visions of him pressing her tight to the barn wall and having his wicked way with her. Again.

A wolfish glint came into his eyes. "What's the matter, sweetheart? Afraid you won't be able to control yourself once we're out of sight of the house?"

She snorted. "I'm afraid *you* won't be able to control *yourself*. You're an incorrigible brute."

He had the nerve to grin from ear to ear, and

before she knew what he was about, he'd leaned forward to zap a quick, firm kiss to her lips. "I know. That's why you love me." Then he pulled on her arm and propelled her after him as he moved toward a copse of trees far from the house and barn.

Oh, glorious day!

Martha clapped her hands in front of her chest and let out a girlish giggle of excitement. Finally. Finally, finally, *finally* those two youngsters had gotten their heads on straight and were beginning to court one another. It had sure taken long enough!

Once the love-struck couple disappeared into the tree line beyond the barn, she let the heavy velvet drapes fall back into place and made her way to the settee to refresh her cup of tea.

Father Ignacio had gone back to the church a little while ago and the visiting townspeople had followed his lead. They all seemed to understand that the family needed some time on their own.

She had just gotten Veronica and the children to go upstairs for a much-needed nap when she'd realized Regan and Clayton were nowhere to be found. With the house practically to herself she'd been able to peek out every window on the first floor without the encumbrance of her invalid chair.

It had taken her a while to catch sight of them, but eventually they'd come around the side of the barn into full view. She had no way of knowing how long they'd been there, of course, or what they'd been doing.

She certainly had some idea, however. Even from this distance, it didn't escape her notice that Regan's hair was a bit mussed and her skirts had needed a bit of smoothing down. And Clayton . . . why, his shirt had been wide open for all the world to see.

Yes, she had a fairly good idea of what they'd been up to out there behind the barn. It hadn't been *that* long, after all, since she'd shared the company of a dapper young gentleman, herself. Well, Virgil had been seventy if he'd been a day, but once she'd gotten him out of that tight necktie and made it clear exactly how she intended the two of them to spend the afternoon, he'd been as randy as a twenty-year-old.

She should probably be upset by her nephew's and daughter-in-law's activities outside the sanctity of marriage, but the truth was, she was simply too giddy about them sparking to care.

She could already picture the adorable grandbabies—or would they be great-nieces and -nephews?— she would have. Dark-toned boys and freckled little redheaded girls. Or exotic-looking girls and little carrot-topped boys. Now, wouldn't that be darling!

Hmm. The possibility of grandchildren got her thinking, though. It wouldn't do for Clayton and Regan's children to have a grandmother—or great-aunt, as the case may be—confined to an invalid chair. The blasted thing did have its uses, true, but perhaps it was time to give some thought to getting rid of the great contraption.

She lifted her legs and turned both puffy, boot-

covered ankles in slow circles, testing their strength.
Yes, perhaps it was time, indeed.

"Where are we going, and when will we be there?"

"Over here, and soon." Clay's impertinent answer did nothing to soothe her nerves. For the third
time in as many minutes, Regan tripped over the
root of a tree and Clay paused to see that she didn't
fall on her face.

He probably thought she was the most graceless
creature ever put on the earth. At the moment, she
certainly felt like it.

But she didn't think she should be held responsible for her clumsiness at the moment . . . she was
too distracted by the three simple words he'd uttered before dragging her into the woods.

I love you.

He hadn't said them *to* her, of course. He hadn't
declared his undying love and asked for her hand
in marriage; he'd said that his beastly, unmanage-
able behavior was the reason *she* loved *him*. Not
the same thing at all.

Except that it had gotten all the cogs and gears
in her brain spinning in different directions trying
to figure out if he was right.

Did she love him? It was a daunting prospect.

When he'd first arrived, she'd been afraid of him.
Afraid of his status as a Texas Ranger and his ability to take her to jail. She'd been intimidated by his
cocky self-assurance and exceptional good looks.

Later, she'd found his presence quite beneficial.
Although she'd had to go behind his back to accom-

plish a few minor tasks, he'd been a great help with Mother Doyle and a blessing when it came to covering the hole in the barn roof the night of the storm.

Remembering that night sent a tell-tale quiver through her body, her pulse rate accelerated and heat flowed to the most intimate parts of her anatomy.

That, she supposed, was the most telling evidence of all. She'd let him make love to her. *Let?* she thought with more than a hint of irony. Hardly. She'd gone up to the loft with one thing on her mind, just as willing as he to explore the stirrings of longing that seemed to leap between them whenever they were within spitting distance of each other.

She'd never been free with her favors before; not before her marriage to James, and not after his death. She'd done her wifely duty. James had never given her anything to complain about in that regard. But she'd never desired another man or an intimate relationship outside of marriage.

Until Clay.

Clay rode into town and turned life as she knew it upside-down. He filled her thoughts day and night. She longed to touch him and be touched by him. She wanted to spend every hour—awake and asleep—in his presence. He dared her to expose herself, physically and emotionally, in ways she'd never thought possible.

She was very much afraid that she *did* love him.

Which would ruin absolutely everything, damn his handsome hide.

"Here we are," he said, breaking into her thoughts.

How he knew where he was when he'd never been to Purgatory before, and certainly not in the Updikes' backyard, she didn't know. Looking around, she saw nothing but more trees rising far above their heads.

"Where is *here*, exactly?"

"Here," he said with a boyish grin. And then he crossed his legs at the ankles and dropped to the leaf-covered ground.

"What are you doing?" Regan exclaimed.

"Fixing a spot for you to sit without getting your dress all dirty," he told her. And then he yanked her arm hard enough to send her sprawling—right into his lap.

At first she struggled, flipping from her stomach to her back and trying to rise. A burst of laughter escaped Clay as he helped her turn over, but held fast to her waist to keep her from getting away.

"Stop it! Let go!" She slapped at his hands and even elbowed him in the gut, but he only grunted and tightened his grip.

"Settle down, sweetheart, you're just getting leaves on your pretty skirts."

When she realized he had no intention of letting her go, she stopped fighting. "My skirts got plenty dirty when you tried to tumble me out back of the barn a few minutes ago, so I'm sure it doesn't matter if they get a little dirtier now. Let me up."

"True enough," he acquiesced, ignoring her request to be released. "But you have to admit, I did do my level best to keep you as tidy as possible." The splay of his fingers widened to encompass as much of her waist as he could reach. "Wasn't I the one flat on my back, letting you keep your dress hiked up above your knees?"

"Oh!" She gasped at his crude statement and colored all the way to her ears. Pulling back an arm, she rammed her fist into his shoulder with as much force as she could muster.

He laughed and rolled away from her punch— taking her with him, of course—but she didn't miss the wince of pain that crossed his chiseled features.

Good. He deserved it for manhandling her and being so vulgar.

She began to struggle again, but, chuckling, Clay cupped her face and made hushing sounds.

"Regan," he said softly, looking directly into her eyes and holding her attention with nothing more than the mesmerizing warmth of his eyes. "Haven't you figured out yet that I'm only quarreling with you to get a rise out of you? And I'm only doing that because you're so goddamn gorgeous when you've got a bee in your bonnet."

His words stopped her heart faster than a strike of lightning could have. She felt tears prick behind her eyelids and had to blink several times to keep from making a fool of herself by bursting into tears right in front of him.

"Relax, green eyes," he murmured quietly. "I'm not going to touch you—any more than I am right now, at any rate. I just want to sit here and talk. And hold you, if you don't mind too much." He tossed her a lopsided smile.

Blinking again, she fought to contain the lump swelling up from the region of her heart. She'd been wrong earlier; there was no maybe, might, or possibly about it—she was absolutely, positively, head over heels, over the moon in love with this man.

Chapter Twenty-one

Clay noticed the shimmer of tears in Regan's eyes and became immediately concerned. "What's wrong, sweetheart?" he asked softly, brushing the edge of his thumb along one highborn cheekbone.

She swallowed and gave her head a quick shake. Curling her fingers into his shoulders, she said, "You are such an ass, Clay Walker."

His eyes went wide and he leaned back in surprise. "Pardon?"

"You heard me," she retorted, tossing the long strands of her hair over one shoulder. "First you kiss me like there's no tomorrow and get me to nearly copulate with you out back of my neighbor's barn."

"Copulate?" he repeated, biting back a chuckle.

She fixed him with an admonishing glare. "You

229

Heidi Betts

know what I mean. Then you drag me into the woods with you and proceed to both infuriate and insult me."

"I did not insult you," he corrected. "I would never insult you."

"Well, you certainly didn't try to sweet-talk me with that remark about keeping my skirts above my knees."

His skin grew warm as a flush crawled its way up his neck. "You're right. I apologize."

"Thank you. I accept," she said with all the dignity of a crowned princess. "But if you would kindly quit interrupting, I could finish telling you why you're such an ass."

His jaw clamped shut at the reminder of her lowly opinion of him. "By all means," he said through clenched teeth.

"You're an ass," she began, causing his molars to grind together, "because right after insulting me, you say one of the kindest, gentlest, most charming and romantic things I've ever heard."

His brows lifted. "And for that, I'm an ass?"

"A big, stinky jackass," she clarified. Reaching up, she tugged roughly on a lock of his hair. "Don't you know that a woman likes constancy? You can't act like a—"

"Big, stinky jackass?" he supplied, crinkling his nose at her unflattering description of his character.

She nodded. "I've already let you . . ."

"Copulate?" he offered, making sport of her earlier choice of words.

230

"Stop that," she warned and gave his shoulder a light swat.

"Sorry." He pulled a straight face. "Constancy, right?"

"Right. Either be crude and manhandle me, or be sweet and flatter me."

He raised a curious brow. "You're giving me permission to manhandle you?"

"Of course not." Her voice held a tinge of exasperation. "You're supposed to pick sweetness and flattery."

"Ah."

"As I was saying, we've already—"

He opened his mouth.

She held up a cautioning finger. "*Don't* say it. We've already . . . been together intimately, so chances are, we'll do so again."

That proclamation caught him completely off guard. "We will?"

He saw an inkling of doubt come into her eyes. "Probably. Won't we?"

"I don't know. Do you want to?" Just the anticipation of her answer had him going hard beneath the snug material of his trousers. He held his breath, waiting for her response.

Her brows knit and she worried one corner of her bottom lip. "I suppose so," she said finally. "That's probably terribly wrong and sinful of me, isn't it?"

"Not in my book," he answered readily. Far be it for him to try to convince her *not* to make love with him.

231

She cast her gaze downwards, turning shy for a moment, but then she lifted her head and met his eyes directly. "Do *you* want to?"

He threw his head back and gave a rusty laugh. "Does Aunt Martha's voice make your ears bleed? Sweetheart, there's nothing I want more. Why do you think I've been sniffing after you these past couple of days?" He shot her a look. "It ain't 'cause you fry up a mean plate of bacon. The question is: Why haven't you *let* me make love to you, if that's what you wanted, too?"

She looked away, but Clay brought her face back to his with the gentle nudge of two fingers against her chin. The tips of her nails danced along his shoulder blades as she considered her reply.

"At first, I was embarrassed. I've never been with anyone but James," she admitted. "And it really is improper for us to do . . . those things without benefit of marriage."

His grasp on her waist tightened. "Does that mean you want me to propose?" The words scraped past his throat, but he was only half teasing. Until this moment, the thought of matrimony hadn't crossed his mind. He still wasn't sure how he felt about the idea, but now it was there, taking root.

She thought about his question for a minute. "I don't want to marry again. Not for anything other than love."

He frowned. "Didn't you love James?"

Her eyes softened. "I did. I grew to love him, but not the way I should have. He was my husband, and I cared for him very much. He saved me from an uncertain and most likely dire future, and for that I'll always be grateful. More than you can know."

The air caught in Clay's lungs and he was almost afraid to hear more. "What do you mean? What situation?" He'd been under the impression that James had taken a young bride because of a love match. But maybe that affection had been one-sided.

"I was working in a brothel when I met James," she said simply.

If his lungs had seized up on him before, they positively petrified at her confession. It was too much to comprehend all at once. Had Regan been a whore? Had she spread her legs for a dozen men a day? But wait, hadn't she just said that, before him, she'd never been with anyone but her husband? How could that be? He opened his mouth and forced the words past suddenly dry lips. "You were a . . . ?"

"Not yet. But it was only a matter of time. And then one day James Doyle came into Madam Pomfrey's and took a shine to me. I'm not even sure why, exactly, but he said I caught his eye."

Clay knew why. Because Regan was, quite simply, the loveliest woman ever to grace God's green earth. He'd never been comfortable with the notion of young Regan leg-shackled to a man old enough to be her grandfather, but now he was almost pathetically grateful to his cousin for rescuing her from a life of prostitution.

"Pretty soon, he was coming in just to see me,

not even bothering to visit the other girls. And then he started talking about taking me home with him. That scared me," she confided, her voice dropping to a near whisper. "I was afraid he wanted to take me away only to turn me into his mistress. But the next time he came, he brought a ring. He got down on one knee and asked me to marry him, promised me everything my heart desired." She made a small sound at the back of her throat. "To this day, I'm not sure why I believed him, but I did. And I said yes."

"I never knew," Clay grated.

"No one did. James didn't tell anyone where we'd really met. I think Mother Doyle might know; whether James told her, or she merely suspects, I can't be sure."

"You loved him for taking you away from there."

She nodded. "And for treating me like a queen. He was good to me, Clay. When he died, he left me everything. I don't know why." Her bright, expressive eyes grew glossy with tears and a single drop of moisture toppled over the edge. "I don't know why he married me. I don't know why he trusted me to care for Mother Doyle. I don't know why he *loved* me so much."

She gave a little sniff, and Clay wiped the line of the tear away with the curve of his finger, offering her a small smile. "Silly girl," he said softly. "What's not to love?"

Her lower lip trembled and then she buried her head in the crook of his neck. She didn't seem to be crying, merely leaning on him for support. And he was more than happy to hold her as long as she needed.

He wrapped his arms around her slim waist, settling her more securely in the dip of his lap.

It occurred to him suddenly that maybe Regan's real fear, her real bewilderment over James's feelings for her weren't about how a fifty-year-old man could love a young girl he met in an upscale bordello, but about her own feelings of inadequacy. That thought jarred him right out of his boots.

"Regan. Sweetheart." He pushed her shoulders back until she'd straightened a bit, then cupped her face in both of his broad hands. "You're not sitting here thinking you weren't worthy of James's love, are you?"

Before the words were even out of his mouth, her eyes brimmed again and damp trails streaked down her flushed cheeks.

"Oh, darlin'. You poor thing." He wiped the tears away, but a second later new ones formed, so he settled for kissing her nose instead. "All this time, you've felt bad for the fact that James loved you and you didn't love him back in the same way, haven't you? And that you didn't really deserve his time or money or affections."

She nodded and he could see the guilt tearing her apart.

"Well, I want you to stop it. Right now."

She blinked in surprise, but his order had the immediate effect of halting her tears, which had been half his intent, anyway.

"Let me tell you something about men, sweetheart. And you may want to write this down because I *am* one, and that makes me pretty much an authority on the subject. Got it?"

She inclined her head slightly, waiting for the rest of his disclosure.

"Most men have no intention of ever chaining themselves to only one woman. They're just not the marrying kind. Those men who do end up tying the knot usually do it for one of three reasons." He flashed her a secretive grin. "Would you like to know what they are?"

"Please." Her voice was rusty from her crying jag, but he had all of her attention.

"Necessity, sex, or love."

Her chin dipped and she cast her eyes downward at his candid pronouncement.

"Now, that first one can cover a lot of things. A man will marry a woman—maybe a wealthy widow like yourself," he suggested with a playful wink as she peered back up at him, "for her money. Either to pay off his debts, or to live a fancier lifestyle. It doesn't much matter. He could also want children. Or he might just want someone to fix his meals and darn his socks. That's the necessity part.

"The sex part is pretty self-explanatory." He waggled his eyebrows suggestively and gave her waist a squeeze. "But since you can walk into any saloon in just about any town in Texas and get as much of *that* as you want, for only a few silver coins, most men don't go so far as to marry just to have a piece of feminine flesh in their beds."

The blush in Regan's cheeks deepened, but she didn't interrupt him.

"Which brings me to love." Her eyes were wide, waiting for the rest. "When a man is in love with a woman . . . well, there's really no hope for him. He'll be all cow-eyed, with his tongue lolling out, tripping over his own feet to bring her flowers and baubles and doing anything to see her smile. It's a disgrace, if you ask me," he added with a comic expression and earned a watery chuckle from the fairy-like goddess in his lap.

"James loved you, Regan, and you shouldn't doubt his motives for that. It's obvious he didn't marry you for money because he was plenty rich on his own. And I don't think he married you to cook or keep house for him, or to care for his mother when she started to go downhill because he could easily afford to hire someone to do all those things.

"Now, I would be more than willing to believe he'd married you for your body—there are any number of things I'd do to get you out of your frills and lace—except that he met you in a brothel. So we can assume he knew where to go to scratch that sort of itch. That leaves one last possibility," he trailed off, hoping by now that she'd gotten his point loud and clear.

And she had. "Love."

"Love," he agreed. "And something tells me that if James chose to love you, then you were completely worthy of those feelings. James was, after all, his mother's son. Can you imagine Aunt Martha raising a boy into manhood who didn't know his own mind?"

The muscles of Regan's diaphragm constricted at Clay's words and the sudden realization that he spoke the truth. For so many years, she'd felt like an imposter, playing at being a distinguished gentleman's wife. But now she saw that Clay was right. Whatever his reasons, James had chosen her as his bride, and he'd loved her enough to give her a good life, a fine home, and a large enough inheritance to keep her and his mother comfortable for the rest of their lives.

For the first time, she was able to accept without reservation all that had been between her and her late husband.

The only problem now was that she felt a small twinge of guilt over having doubted James's affections all these years. But it was a pinprick compared to the boulder that had rolled around in her belly before.

"I take it back," she said, stroking a hand down Clay's strong-boned, stubbled cheek, relishing the bristly feel of his tanned skin against her palm. "You're not a jackass at all. You're a wonderful, caring man."

"I made the right decision, then?" he wanted to know. "I picked 'sweetness and flattery.' "

With a laugh, she pressed her lips against the inviting velvet swells of his own. "A fine choice, indeed." She followed the trail of her mouth with her thumb, taking the time to study every nuance of his handsome, superbly masculine features.

Opening his mouth, he nipped the pad of her thumb between his straight white teeth. "I'd still like to manhandle you once in a while ... you know, if you were agreeable to the idea."

Using only the very tips of her fingers, she explored his shadowed jaw, the corded muscles of his neck, the adorable curves of his ears. She was like a lover of fine art, studying the lines and angles of a magnificent marble statue. A sculptor contemplating an unmolded block of clay.

"I think that could be arranged," she murmured.

His hands were at her breasts now, his wide palms cupping the heavy mounds, his thumbs drifting over the region of her nipples, making her tingle and shift restlessly on his lap.

"Clay?"

"Hmmm?" He was already kissing the dip of her chin, dragging his lips all around her mouth before narrowing in at the corners.

"How about now?"

His head snapped back so fast, she expected to see it wobble like a top.

"What did you say?"

She smiled at the shock in his stormy gray eyes. "I thought you might like to try that manhandling thing on me now."

His lashes narrowed. "Do you mean what I think you mean?"

"Would you like me to say it more plainly?" she asked sweetly.

"I think that might be a smart idea," he said, nostrils flaring like a stallion on the scent of a mare.

She tangled her fingers into his hair and leveled her gaze on his. "Clay?"

"Hmmm?"

"Will you make love to me?"

Chapter Twenty-two

"Every day of the week and twice on Sunday," he replied staunchly. But inside, he was shouting, *Thank you, God!*

He'd been patient, he thought. Pretty damn patient. But he wanted Regan more than he wanted his next breath. And knowing she wanted him, too . . . It was like a kick to the gut, hobbling him and making him too weak to speak.

So instead, he wrapped one hand around the nape of her neck, placed the other at the small of her back, and leaned forward with her in his arms until she was lying on the leafy ground and he hovered above her.

Her fingers played with the ends of his hair as he settled half on, half off her, trailing light kisses over her cheeks, along her jaw, on her eyelids. He wanted to touch every inch of her all at once.

Moving to the tiny, pearl-like black buttons at the front of her gown, he began to loosen them one by one. As the ebony folds of her dress fell open, the pale white of her skin became visible. Alabaster perfection, with freckles sprinkled like cinnamon across her chest and the upper swells of her breasts.

He continued to free buttons all the way down to her stomach, and lifted his head at the sight of fancy lace running in a line across her chest. She wore a sinfully red corset with hand-stitched embroidery on the satin fabric and black lace bordering. Bones, also accented in black, pulled her waist into an hourglass shape.

She didn't need the figure-changer and Clay was confident she knew it. Chances were, she was wearing the thing for fashion only. Or because she liked the sexy feel of the sheer material against her bare skin. His Regan, he was coming to realize, liked fancy underthings. She might look like a proper young widow on the outside, but beneath all that black taffeta and tulle beat the heart of a wanton woman.

Which was more than fine with him. Just seeing the scarlet satin and lace spread over her porcelain flesh made him want to say a year's worth of Hail Marys.

A row of tiny hook-and-eye clasps fastened up the front of the contraption and her breasts rested in tightly sewn cups of unboned material topped with narrow, frilly strips of black lace.

"This could pose a problem, sweetheart."

Regan lowered her gaze to where he fingered the edges of the upper lacing and ran his thumbs over the prominent corset stays.

"I don't think I can wait long enough to undo all these hooks. But I sure would like to see these lovely baubles of yours."

"Baubles?" She tossed him a shy grin. "I'm sure we'll think of something," she told him with feminine promise. "In the meantime, do you think you could take off your gunbelt? It's digging into my thigh."

He shifted over the layers of her skirts and reached between them to open the buckle of his gunbelt and set the Colts aside as Regan worked the clasps down her front. When Clay raised his head, it was to see the ripe globes of her breasts spilling over the top of her loosened corset.

He groaned low in his throat and started to tug at his vest and shirt and trousers. "Keep it up, green eyes, and this will be over before it's begun."

She batted her lashes beguilingly. "I don't mind."

"Well, I sure as hell do," he returned with a strained chuckle. But he had his doubts, he had to admit. "We already have to make allowances for using the forest floor as a bed. I can't strip you naked and look at you for about an hour and a half the way I'd like."

She averted her gaze and flushed to the tips of her exposed areolas.

"Oh, no, you don't." He turned her head back until she faced him. "This was your idea. Not that

I'm complaining, mind you," he added hastily, "but there's no room for shyness or embarrassment. All right?"

He suspected she still felt a bit timid, but she met his eyes and nodded.

"Since this is bound to be awkward—not being able to take our clothes off and all—I have a suggestion."

She eyed him cautiously. "Yes?"

"Remember what we were doing behind the Updikes' barn?"

One brow arched disdainfully over an emerald orb.

"All right," he modified. "Remember what I tricked you into doing behind the Updikes' barn?"

Her lips curved in an impudent smile. "I seem to have some recollection of the incident."

He snorted. "Then maybe you recall that I had your skirt up around your waist." With his hands under the low hem of her long gown, he started to slowly slide the layered material up the line of her black-stockinged legs. Revealing the high, worn leather of her walking shoes, the tapered column of her muscled calves, her delicate knees. And just above those knees . . .

He let out a guttural moan. "Lord have mercy, woman. You're going to be the death of me."

Just above the curve of her knees were two crimson, lace-covered, completely erotic garters tied about the tops of her silken stockings.

"I can't tell you how grateful I am that you wear these first-class dainties for me."

"What makes you think they're for you?"

One brow cocked upwards while the other narrowed. "Have you been meeting someone else inside or behind barns that I don't know about?"

"Perhaps," she answered, and he could see the teasing glint in her eyes.

"Well, you just let me know the next time you have one of these assignations set up, all right?"

"Why?"

He kissed the tip of her chin, sucking the soft skin into his mouth before saying, " 'Cause I'm pretty handy with a revolver and rifle alike, and I'd like to put a bullet smack in the middle of the bastard's forehead."

"My, aren't we the territorial type."

"Damn straight. I'm not sharing these with anyone." He gave her garter a little snap and she yelped in surprise.

Arching her spine, she pressed her naked breasts into his equally bare chest and nipped at his chin. "What are you going to do now that you have my skirt hiked up to my bottom?"

"How about this?" he asked, and flipped her from her back to her knees, crouching above him. Just like they'd been behind the barn not an hour before.

Only this time, she wasn't going to put a stop to their lovemaking, Clay was sure. If she tried, he'd kiss her mindless and convince her this was exactly where she wanted to be.

But he didn't think he'd have to do any convincing at all, given the way Regan squirmed on his lap while she moved her voluminous skirts aside. Her motions bared his torso to her questing hands and she quickly began to undo the front of his trousers.

Clay sucked in a lungful of pine-tinged air as her nimble fingers dipped beneath his waistband to touch bare flesh, then popped the buttons all the way down the crotch of his pants. He bit his tongue to keep from groaning her name, afraid that if he made a sound, she might be startled into stopping. He liked this new, forward-acting Regan, he just wasn't sure he could survive the onslaught of her strokes and touches.

She tugged at the top of his pants and he lifted off the ground a bit to aid her in getting the bulky material past his hips. Then she tucked back the edges of the fly, exposing his aroused member. It stood at full attention, awaiting her tender ministrations, but instead she ignored his throbbing need and raised her head to meet his eyes.

She licked her lips and her nails dug nervously into the nude flesh of his waist, which was breaking out in goosebumps. "You may have to help me with this next part," she admitted in a wavering voice. "I've never done this sort of thing before."

"You've never been on top?" he asked, finding it hard to believe that her late husband had never taken advantage of her innate sensuality in even this most basic of manners.

She shook her head and looked bashfully away.

"Hey." He brought her face back to his. "There's nothing to be sheepish about. We'll go slow." He fixed her with a knowing grin. "And when we're finished, you'll wonder how you survived all these years without making love this way."

She didn't look completely convinced, but she let him lift her skirts even higher about her waist.

"First, you have to take off your drawers," he told her, holding her skirts out of the way as she wiggled and swayed to remove the slinky crimson garment. "Now, scootch forward. You're going to lower yourself onto me, okay?"

Her eyes widened at his command, and he chuckled. "It's no different from what we did in the barn the other night, sweetheart, except that you're in control this time. Put your hands on my chest, if you want, or lift yourself with your knees and wrap a hand around me to guide me inside."

The cords of her throat convulsed at his frank statement, but he could see her becoming more sure of herself, more at ease with the notion of retaining a dominant position.

"It's all right, sweetheart. Anyone who wears purple drawers and scarlet garters surely has the guts to take an active role in lovemaking. Don't you?"

She swallowed again and then gave a determined nod. Rising up on her knees, she took hold of his manhood—a little too tightly, but he tried not to wince for fear of scaring her off—and aimed it at the very center of her femininity.

He watched that dark, iron-hard part of himself disappear into the moist, copper-curled nest between her legs and let out a strangled sigh.

"Are you all right?" she asked, biting down on her own lower lip.

"Any better and I'd be greeting Saint Peter at the Pearly Gates," he gritted out.

Her own breath snagged as she tried to inhale. "What now?" she asked.

As though he had a thought in his head at this point. His fingers bit into her hips as he fought to keep from ramming himself upwards to completion. "That's up to you, darlin'. Do you want to just sit there, or do you want to move?" *Move! Move!* his body screamed.

She leaned forward a bit, flattening her palms on his bare chest, then curling and uncurling her nails like gentle talons. "I think . . . I want to . . ."

She shifted slightly and his eyes rolled like musket balls in their sockets.

"Move," she finished.

Clay locked his knees, clenched his teeth, and tried not to squeeze her hips too tightly. "Okay. Whenever you're ready," he grated, praying for endurance like he'd never prayed before. "Go at your own pace. You're in charge here."

"I'm in charge, huh?" The breath hissed from her lungs, the only sign she was in nearly the same agitated state as he was.

"God, yes. I'm at your mercy." *Lord, was he ever.*

One side of her mouth quirked up in a grin, but her breath came in short little puffs. "I think I like that."

"Then you might want to, um . . ." He didn't

want to rush her, but if his easy-spoken hint didn't spur her on, he thought he might explode in the next second or two and be worthless to her for the rest of the afternoon.

"Move," she supplied with a sigh and did just that. With her thighs holding tight to his hips, she lifted slightly and then let herself back down.

Stars burst behind Clay's eyes. "This won't last long," he muttered almost to himself.

"What won't?"

If she had to ask, she wasn't nearly as close to the edge as he was . . . which meant he had some work to do. Shifting a hand from her hip to the crux of her thighs, he burrowed a finger between her tight auburn curls and into the cleft hidden beneath. She was already wet and throbbing and he had no trouble finding the tiny bud of her desire.

The minute he touched her there, she gave a gasp of pleasure and rose up on her knees again. When she lowered herself, his finger slipped over the slick nubbin, increasing her ecstasy tenfold.

His other hand moved to the curve of her buttock as he spurred her on. "Faster," he ordered, and she quickly complied.

Her movements increased, up and down, forward and back, until they were both panting with soon-to-be-fulfilled desire.

"Oh, God. Clay!"

He felt the tremors begin deep inside her before her outer body began to shake. "Yes, darlin', that's it." He was so close, he couldn't have held back if his life depended on it. "Now, sweetheart. Now, now, *now*."

She screamed as the orgasm rocked through her, sending her into convulsions above him. She spasmed about him as he shot into her, his own climax causing him to cry out as it squeezed every drop of energy from his worn-out body.

Regan collapsed atop him, her cheek resting along one collarbone, her full head of wild red ringlets falling every which way around them. He hugged her close, stroking the line of her spine through the material of her dress and pulling the skirt down just a little to cover all of the important parts that might be visible to small birds or squirrels high up in the treetops.

"Clay?"

"Hmm?"

"I liked being on top."

He needn't have worried about meddlesome wildlife. His loud guffaw scared them all away.

Chapter Twenty-three

"Clay?" Regan asked a short while later as they were repairing their disheveled clothing.

"What, sweetheart?" He lifted his head to meet her gaze, buttoning the front of his shirt and tucking the tails into his pants.

"Do you think it's possible that Nolan *didn't* fall down the stairs?" She said the words quickly, before she lost her courage. She'd been thinking of how to broach the subject all afternoon, knowing she had to convince someone that the death hadn't been an accident. And now seemed like the perfect time, given Clay's lackadaisical mood.

"What are you talking about?" he returned, distracted by unwinding his gunbelt and fitting the set of revolvers low on his hips.

She finished fastening the clasps at the front of

her corset and adjusted her breasts within the loose top.

Clay closed the distance between them. "Need some help there, darlin'?"

His lips were quirked suggestively and she fought the urge to accept his offer. An offer she was sure would land her right back on the ground, with her skirt up around her ears. "No, thank you," she firmly refused. And then she turned them back to the conversation at hand. "I just mean that . . . don't you think it's a little unusual for a forty-year-old man to fall down the stairs and break his neck?"

"What are you talking about?"

Buttoning her dress and doing her best to fix her hair, she cast him a frustrated glance. "Come on, Clay. The man has probably been going up and down stairs all his life. Why would he suddenly trip and fall? And even if he did, how hard would it have been to throw out an arm to slow his descent and keep him from getting that hurt?"

"Regan." A crease of concern marred his brow as he studied her. "The man fell. It's a sad turn of events, but accidents happen."

"I just think it's unlikely, that's all," she continued, reluctant to quit the subject so easily.

Clay stroked a hand over her hair. "It's a shock for you, I know."

Letting out a sigh of regret, she inclined her head and turned back toward the house. Clay wasn't as open as she'd hoped to the notion of Nolan Updike being murdered, and if they didn't get back soon,

Mother Doyle would bring the roof down shouting for them.

There was something else she'd been thinking about recently, too. "Clay?"

"Hmm?"

It was becoming the typical opening to their discussions.

"You know how you let me try . . ." Her face heated at the very thought of what she was about to say. "Being on top."

"Uh-huh." She could hear the amusement in his grunted reply, which only added to her chagrin.

"There's something else I've heard about, but never tried," she rushed on before she lost her nerve.

"What's that?"

"Well, it's sort of like what you did to me the other night during the storm. When you put your mouth . . . down there." Her face fanned so hot, she was surprised she didn't burst into flames. Her voice dropped to a whisper. "Only I would be doing it to you."

Clay stopped so fast, he tripped over his own feet. "Christ on a cracker, woman," he barked. "You can't just say something like that to a man while you're walking through the woods. It's enough to give him heart failure."

He squinted his gray eyes for a moment as he studied her. "Is that how James died? Did you ask him to let you . . . ?" He waved a hand, unwilling or unable to even finish the thought.

"No!" she gasped, mortified to the marrow of her bones.

"*Hmph*. Well, it's a good thing. A suggestion like that's liable to kill a fellow his age. Now, me, I'm still a young man, so my heart can take it. I'm not so sure about the rest of my body, but that's a whole other matter."

Her fingers clenched and unclenched in the folds of her skirt as she started forward once again. She had felt so at ease with Clay only a few minutes earlier, and now she'd ruined it all by bringing up something she should have kept to herself. "I'm sorry, I didn't mean to embarrass you."

"Embarrass me?" Clay grabbed her wrist and swung her around. "Sweetheart, you should know by now that I don't scare that easy. You just caught me by surprise, is all."

His words softened to a near hush as he bent at the knees and brought his eyes to her level, brushing a thumb over her still-warm cheek. "The fact is, when you said what it is you want to do, it got me so hot, I couldn't see straight. I'm so stiff right now, I don't know how I'm going to walk back into that house without humiliating myself—if I can manage to walk that far at all."

"Oh."

"Yeah, *oh*," he mumbled. "So about this . . . thing you want to do. How about meeting me in the loft tonight, after Aunt Martha goes to bed?" He curled her hand into the crook of his elbow and turned them back toward the house. "We'll have plenty of time to experiment with any number of sexual feats you have in mind."

"I don't know." She did want to try what she'd mentioned, but now that he was putting her on the spot, she felt suddenly squeamish. It wasn't like her to plan a midnight rendezvous. For the sole purpose of physical gratification, too. Lord, but her mother would spin in her grave if she knew what a shameless hussy her daughter had become.

"Are you turning shy on me, green eyes?" Clay teased.

She nodded emphatically. "I think so."

He threw back his head and laughed, then swept her into his arms and kissed her soundly on the lips. "That's why I love you, sweetheart—your utter decisiveness."

Her stomach did a reverse flip and Regan knew it was more because of his declaration than the way he spun her around like a rag doll before catching her against his chest. Did he really love her? she wondered, or was that merely a form of speech?

Before she could give it the proper amount of consideration, though, Clay continued.

"Well, if you change your mind, let me know." He gave her a meaningful wink. "Or maybe I can change it for you."

He pressed a kiss to her temple and she knew that if he put his mind to it, he could reverse her decision in two seconds flat.

"There is something we need to discuss, though."

At his serious tone, she lifted her head to meet his gaze.

"Given our time together, we should probably talk about the possibility of . . ." His words were slow and deliberate, and she saw him draw a deep breath before finishing. "Pregnancy."

Of all the things she'd expected him to say, that had been the farthest from her mind. Unfortunately, the very thought of children, of carrying Clay's baby in the shelter of her womb, all but shattered her already bruised heart.

"If we're going to continue on the way we have been—and I hope to hell we are—then we probably ought to think about some sort of preventive measures. There are steps we can take, a couple of items I may be able to get in town. And if it's already too late . . . Well, I want you to know I'll do the right thing."

He opened his mouth to go on, but Regan pressed her fingers over his lips to halt his good intentions. "Stop, stop, stop. I appreciate the sentiment. That's very noble of you, truly. But you don't have to worry about anything like that."

His brows knit in confusion. "What do you mean?"

Her next words were hardest of all to get out. "I can't have children, Clay," she said quietly, unable to look him in the eye.

For a minute, Clay's lungs locked and he found it hard to draw air. Instead of being relieved that he had not planted a baby in her belly, he was horrified at the abject misery evident on her face.

He tucked a strand of hair behind her ear and gifted her with a sympathetic smile. "Why do you

say that, sweetheart? You're a young woman."
He'd have gone on, but she was already shaking her
head.

"James and I were married for five years. We
never had children." Her explanation, delivered in
a matter-of-fact tone, tore at his heart.

Clay could have argued. He wanted to argue.
James had been more than twenty years her senior.
There was a good chance the fault lay with him and
his age. But Clay felt reluctant to cast aspersions on
her former husband—especially on a subject as delicate as his potency.

Later he would find a tactful way to broach the
subject again. For he knew Regan wanted children
of her own. She was as maternal as they came, and
he could easily picture her with a dozen runny-
nosed brats hanging on her skirts.

That explains the orphans, he realized suddenly,
a lightning bolt of clarity flashing through his brain.
She couldn't have children of her own so she thrust
all of her love, attention, and motherly instincts on
the children at the Home. It made perfect sense.

"I'm sorry," he said softly. "You'd make a wonderful mother." *And beautiful, frizzy-haired babies*,
he thought, puzzled by the pang of disappointment
in his own gut.

Hoping to lighten the solemn mood that had
overcome them both, he brought her flush with his
long frame, flattening her breasts to his chest and
making sure she felt just how much he desired her
when their lower bodies met.

"In a much more selfish vein, I have to say I find

this rather advantageous." He touched their noses together in a gesture even he found extremely intimate and out of character for himself. But if it eased the tension in Regan's slight form, or put a smile on her downcast face, then it would be well worth it. "I can make love to you day and night and never worry about the consequences. You're a dream come true, green eyes." Even so, he would pick something up the next time he was in town, just to be sure they were protected.

His blithe remark didn't quite hit its mark, but she pretended to smile all the same. "I'm glad you find my situation convenient to your over-active carnal appetites," she retorted and gave him a little shove. She pranced off, getting that much closer to the white house sitting in the distance.

"I have it on pretty good authority that you enjoy my carnal appetites," he aimed at her retreating back.

She whipped around, one brow arched so high over her eye, it nearly met her hairline. "And who's authority would that be?" she challenged, hands on hips while she waited for him to catch up.

Never let it be said that Clay Walker didn't possess an ego as big as any other man's. "Mine," he answered, coming abreast to where she stood and looping his arms around her waist. "Meet me in the barn tonight and I'll prove it to you."

She slapped at his tightening hold. "I am not meeting you in the barn."

"Why not?"

"Because you're entirely too arrogant for your own good."

"Oh, but you can help me shed some of that conceit. I've been a naughty boy, Regan. Come to the barn tonight and teach me a lesson."

"No!" Her somber tone was ruined by a girlish giggle.

She twisted in his arms, but he only pulled her against him and bit the back of her neck.

"Stop it! Clay!"

"Hush, someone will hear you." His warning had the desired result. She immediately stilled and he took advantage of her sedate state to nudge her hair out of the way and bite an even more tender part of her nape. "Meet me in the barn tonight."

"No."

"Then come to my room."

He could almost feel her rolling her eyes at his entreaty. "Now, if I won't meet you in the barn, what makes you think I'll come to your room?" she asked.

"My inherent charm?" he offered.

"Highly unlikely," she said with a snort. "Now let me go, you great oaf."

His grip loosened, but he still held her within the circle of his arms. "If you don't agree to meet me, I may be forced to take drastic measures."

She broke away, but didn't run. Instead, she kept one hand on his and pulled him along with her. "Such as?"

"I'll sneak into *your* room and you'll have no one to protect you but that silly black cat."

"Lucy-fur can be quite aggressive when she wants to be. So can I," she tossed out with a superior tilt of her chin.

"What are you going to do, scream?" Clay all but dared her.

"I could. Or I could just kick you somewhere that will affect *your* ability to have children."

Bull's eye. He cringed. "Ouch. You really know how to hurt a man, sweetheart."

She beamed at him, thrilled with the bloodthirsty streak that apparently ran through her veins. "I'll only hurt you if you make me," she promised. "Otherwise, you're perfectly safe from my and Lucy-fur's wrath."

"I'm glad to hear it," he grumbled, watching as she reached out to swipe at a few wrinkles in his shirt and straighten the badge on his vest.

"What are you doing?" he asked. He thought he looked fine already, why was she fooling with his clothes?

"You look like you've been rolling around on the ground."

Cocking his head, he lowered his voice and said, "I *have been* rolling around on the ground. With you."

Two pink spots started in the center of her cheeks and spread outward. "I know that, but we don't have to look like we've spent the afternoon sinning. Tuck the rest of your shirt in before someone sees you," she ordered.

He did as she said, letting her turn back around and head home.

"Um, Regan?"

"Yes?" she shot over her shoulder, carrying herself as regally as a queen.

"Since you're worried about appearances," he offered, an insolent grin turning up the corners of his mouth, "you may want to pull those leaves out of your hair."

Chapter Twenty-four

When they arrived home from the Updikes' house, David was sitting on the porch, waiting for them.

"David!" Regan called out. "What are you doing here?"

Jumping to his feet, he shoved his hands into his front pockets, but didn't say anything. He watched as they climbed down from the wagon and unloaded Mother Doyle, even helping Clay maneuver the heavy chair up the porch steps. But as soon as Clay and Martha disappeared into the house, he blocked Regan's entry and kept her cornered outside.

"Did you hear?" he asked in a low voice, casting a glance over his shoulder to make sure no one was eavesdropping.

"Hear what?"

"About Updike." His eyes went icy and one side of his mouth turned up in a sneer. "He's dead. Serves the bastard right."

"David!"

"My name isn't David, it's Little Badger. That worthless son of a bitch never took responsibility for me, he shouldn't have been allowed to name me."

Regan sucked in a sharp breath of air. She heard Clay's booted stride as he came up behind David, but she didn't move or look in his direction.

"You knew?" she asked, stunned.

David jerked his head.

"But how?" Thanks to Father Ignacio's confidences, she'd known for years now that David was Nolan Updike's illegitimate son, conceived with a Comanche woman from a small tribe outside of town. But never in her wildest imaginings had she thought David knew his true parentage.

"You know about my Indian blood," he told her with a stubborn slant of his jaw. "I knew, too, from an early age that my mother had been Indian, but I wanted to know more about my father. So one day, while everyone else was busy, I broke into Father Ignacio's office. Father Ignacio keeps track of the kids who are abandoned at the orphanage, along with any information he can find when they first show up." David's dark eyes turned hard. "Turns out Nolan Updike is the person who brought me to the Purgatory Home for *Unwanted Children*. He also donated a large sum of money to the padre for my care. I'm not stupid, Regan," he spat. "I know what that means."

"David," she began slowly.

He pulled away, narrowing his gaze on her. "You knew, too, didn't you? But you never said a word. You never did anything to make him pay for how he treated me and my mother."

His accusations were like a saber blade to her heart. "David," she said carefully, "I only came to Purgatory five years ago. I didn't know you or Mr. Updike when all of this happened. And when I did figure out the circumstances of your birth, I didn't think it would be right to say anything. I didn't think it would change anything."

She replaced her hand on his arm. "I love you, David. I couldn't love you more if you were my own son. I wouldn't hurt you for the world, and I thought that telling you could only cause you pain. Can you understand that?"

Several minutes ticked by as David seemed to digest her words and she waited with bated breath for his response.

"I'm glad he's dead," he said finally, almost daring her to reprimand him.

Her eyes met Clay's over David's head and then she nodded. Because no matter how terrible she thought it was to speak ill of the recently deceased, David's peace of mind was of chief concern at the moment.

"You have every right to feel that way," she choked out, opening her arms to him.

Another tense second passed as he decided

whether to trust her. Then he pitched forward into her embrace.

Tears stung her eyes and she blinked to keep them from falling. "Come inside, all right?" she whispered into the hair at his temple.

It was dark by the time David seemed calm enough to return to town. He was still angry—had every right to be—but he didn't burn with fury the way he had when he'd first arrived.

Regan wanted him to stay the night, but he refused. He'd reverted back to his independent demeanor, insisting that he was fine and old enough to make his way back to the Home alone, despite the late hour.

She wouldn't hear of it, of course. Even though it took some doing, she finally convinced Clay to take David home—and David to let him. That part took a stern, motherly glare, but David finally agreed.

As she watched the wagon roll away, she admitted that her reasons for asking Clay to accompany David were two-fold. Yes, David probably shouldn't be wandering around after dark by himself—though lord knew he did it often enough without anyone's permission—but this would also give her a chance to sneak back into the Updike home and return the watch she hadn't been able to replace earlier this afternoon. She only hoped Veronica and the children would be sound asleep after a day of exhausting themselves with tears.

She didn't have much time, and it was quite likely Clay would get back from town long before she did, but she had no other choice. She didn't know when she might get another chance to return the watch, and she didn't want to run the risk of Veronica discovering it missing. She planned to sneak in through the back door, deposit the watch in Nolan's study, and leave without waking the household. She didn't dare to creep into the bedroom where Veronica would be sleeping. Besides, breaking into the first floor room would be much faster. In the confusion surrounding Nolan's death, Regan was sure no one would question why the watch was not in its usual place.

The minute Clay and David trundled out of sight, she hurried to Mother Doyle's room to let her know she'd be out of the house for a while. Used to being left alone from time to time, Martha waved her away, asserting that she was perfectly capable of entertaining herself for an hour or two and needed to catch up on her reading, anyway.

Satisfied that her mother-in-law would be fine until she or Clay returned, she then raced to the backyard to change into her black pants, man's shirt, and well-worn boots. Normally she would have headed for the Updikes' on foot, but with the possibility of Clay's imminent return, she thought it best to ride.

Her two gentle mares were on their way to town with the buckboard, so when she got to the barn, she had no choice but to use Clay's horse, Caesar.

"Easy, boy. It's all right, I won't hurt you." Unfamiliar with any touch but his master's, the piebald gelding was a bit skittish at first, but let her saddle him and lead him out of the barn. She mounted and set off at a brisk trot, giving the horse time to get used to her. Once she felt Caesar had adjusted to his unfamiliar rider, she kicked him into a gallop, praying she would make it to the Updikes' and back before Clay returned.

Clay didn't know why Regan had seemed so anxious earlier when he and David had left, or what all that talk about Nolan Updike being David's father had to do with the spots on a lizard's back, but he was sure as hell determined to find out. He knew Regan was hiding something, and he planned to figure out what. He alternately prayed that she wasn't in some kind of trouble and cursed that she still didn't trust him enough to ask him for help. He drove the horses into a lather in his rush to get home, only to find his own horse missing from his stall.

Caesar's disappearance confirmed his suspicions that something was wrong. And he couldn't wait to question a certain redhead.

He took the time to wipe down the team, simply because it was a routine too important and too ingrained in him not to. But he grumbled and swore the whole time.

The house was dark when he stalked his way up from the barn. A low, yellow glow flickered from Martha's first-story window, but that was it. He found it odd that there was no light from upstairs or the rear portion of the house.

"Regan?" he called, leaving his hat on a table in the entryway.

He heard a shuffling sound on his right, and then Martha returned his greeting. "Clay, is that you, dear?"

Making his way to her bedroom, he eased open the door and found Martha tucked into bed with a book on her lap.

"There you are, dear. Did David give you any trouble on the way back to the Home?"

Giving her room a quick once-over, he shook his head. David hadn't given him any trouble because he hadn't said two words the entire trip. The boy had a chip on his shoulder as wide as the Rio Grande.

He didn't care about that at the moment, though. His main concern was Regan's whereabouts. "Aunt Martha, have you seen Regan?"

"Of course I've seen Regan, Clayton. What a silly question." His aunt craned her neck to look out the bedroom door. "Where is she now?"

Gritting his teeth, he prayed for patience. "That's what I'm asking you. Have you seen her *recently?*"

Folds of skin wrinkled along Martha's forehead. "Not since she came in to tell me she was leaving."

"Leaving?" The word cracked through the room like a whipcord. "For where?"

Brows coming together and mouth turning down in a frown, Martha said, "I can't rightly say, dear. I imagine she had an errand to run."

"Another bloody errand," he grumbled. "How long has she been gone?"

"I'm afraid I can't tell you that, either."

Hands clenching and unclenching at his sides,

Clay fought the urge to snap at his aunt. It would be nice if the old woman paid a lick of attention to her surroundings, especially when it came to Regan's mysterious comings and goings.

Just then, he heard a sound in front of the house. Hoof beats? Caesar, perhaps?

"Are you all right by yourself?" he asked his aunt, but was already on his way out of the room by the time she answered.

When he reached the front of the house, he went to the long, narrow window running vertically alongside the door and used one finger to nudge the lacy curtain open a fraction.

He didn't see anything. No one coming up the steps or wandering around the yard. However the large barn door stood open, even though he was sure he'd pulled it closed after bedding down the cart mares.

And then a figure emerged. The pale moonlight was the only illumination as the stranger slid the heavy barn door shut and darted across the yard. The closer the person got, the more familiar the shape became.

Clay swore, low, long, and viciously enough to send his aunt into apoplexy, if she'd heard.

Regan was dressed all in black, which didn't surprise him in the least. What threw him for a loop was the fact that she was wearing pants. Men's trousers, for God's sake. Where the hell had she been that she'd needed to wear men's trousers?

Her shirt seemed to be of the male variety, too, but if she'd been hoping to hide her gender, she was destined for disappointment. Both pants and shirt were snug enough to emphasize all of her hills and dales, and tell anyone with eyes in his head that she was a woman. And if that wasn't ample proof, her kinky red hair—wholly discernible in the moonlight, pulled away from her face and tied with a strip of ribbon to hang down her back—was a dead giveaway.

For a fraction of a second, the thought that she might be meeting him in the barn the way he'd begged her to flashed through his mind. But she wasn't *entering* the barn, she was sneaking out of it.

And rather than coming up the porch steps and making her way inside through the front door, she crept around the corner of the house toward the back.

What was she up to?

Deciding to cut her off at the pass—and determined once and for all to find out what in blue blazes was going on—Clay hurried down the hall to the kitchen. As silently as possible, he opened the door that led to the backyard and slipped outside, waiting for her to come around the side of the house. When she did, he kept her in his sights, but didn't move a muscle. He wanted to see just what she was prowling around for.

While he watched, she hunkered down near the trunk of a pecan tree and dug around its base, coming up with what looked to be a sack of some kind.

From the burlap pouch, she pulled a balled up wad of clothing and a pair of dainty black evening slippers. Then she began shedding her shirt and trousers until she was crouched in the dark, moonlit night in nothing but her lace-edged corset and red, red drawers from earlier this afternoon when she'd been so beautifully displayed above him as they'd made love beneath a canopy of green leaves and pine boughs.

Before he could blink, she'd wrapped herself in the gauzy black robe, stuffed her feet into the slippers, and was shoving the satchel of discarded men's attire back into the hidey-hole within the roots of the tree. Her chest rose and fell in a staccato rhythm as she straightened from her clandestine chore.

He knew the moment she raised her head and saw him standing against the back of the house, arms across his chest.

"Clay," she breathed, pressing a hand to her stomach. "What are you doing there?"

Her tongue darted out to moisten her dry lips. Lips that had been lying to him since the first day he arrived in Purgatory.

His eyes narrowed. His fists clenched. And an icy shield began to erect itself around his heart. "Shouldn't that be my question?" he asked with disdain, his voice venomous.

She drew the edges of her robe closed and smoothed at imaginary specks of dust. "What are you talking about?" she asked so innocently, it was no wonder he'd been deluded for so long.

"I suppose you're out here looking for your cat." He stepped away from the house, leisurely making his way to the spot where she'd hidden her secret sack of belongings. He knew exactly where the furry little mouse-catcher was at this very moment and was just waiting for Regan to open her mouth and lie to him. The way she'd been lying to him all along.

And yet, deep down, he wanted her to tell him that very thing. Worse, he wanted to believe it. To believe her.

"Well, yes," she answered uncertainly, pivoting as he passed her, watching him stalk straight to the small cavity at the base of the pecan tree. "Have you seen her?"

"She's inside on Aunt Martha's bed," he answered shortly. "The same place I assume she's been all night." Wrapping a hand around the leaf-covered pouch, he lifted it and held it up for her perusal. "And since when do you need a change of clothes to search for your damn cat?"

Her bottom lip quivered as her green eyes turned mossy with unshed tears, and he saw the tendons in her neck flex as she swallowed.

He snapped his back teeth tight to keep from feeling sorry for her. To keep from feeling *anything* for her. The problem was, he did have feelings for her. They'd come up fast and hard, and he didn't know how long it would be before he could exorcise them from his mind and body.

His heart hammered against his ribcage as he began loosening the tie at the opening of the bag. He was afraid—terrified, actually—of what he'd find. There were only a handful of reasons he could think

272

of for her to be running off on these midnight excursions; to lie about looking for her cat; to have a change of clothes hidden under a tree in the backyard; for her to ever wear men's garments at all.

None of them boded well, but that didn't keep him from praying for a blessing from above, for some simple, logical, harmless excuse for everything he'd witnessed thus far. He wasn't quite sure he believed in heavenly favors, but at this point, he'd settle for just about anything that absolved Regan of blame.

"You don't have to go through there," she said softly. "I'll tell you everything."

"Good. I'd like to hear it." He reached inside, but kept his gaze locked on hers. His soul might have been begging for proof of her innocence, but his gut had no problem playing judge and jury. "Maybe this time you can try the truth."

He stretched a hand to the bottom of the sack and pulled out the first thing his fingers came in contact with. It was a mask . . . the same black mask the burglar had been wearing the night Clay had arrived in Purgatory and chased him from the site of his latest robbery.

He raised his head and met Regan's damp eyes. She was the bandit everyone was calling the Ghost of Ol' Morty Pike.

The woman he loved was the thief he'd been sent to Purgatory to arrest and take to jail.

Chapter Twenty-five

"I'm sorry." The words came out in a strangled whisper and the tears she'd tried so hard to hold back slipped down her cheeks unchecked.

If he ever needed more proof of a person's lies, he had only to look at her face. Guilt blossomed on her cheeks, dulled her usually bright eyes, poured from her skin like cheap perfume.

God, he'd been such a fool!

Regan had been prowling around even before he'd come to town—the very first time they'd met, in fact—and he'd let himself be convinced her late-night activities were nothing because he'd *wanted* to believe her, dammit.

Even though his brain had bellowed that she was up to no good . . . even though every law-abiding Ranger instinct he possessed had warned him something was afoot ... he'd ignored them because, quite simply, Regan was the most beautiful woman he'd ever set eyes on. She'd burrowed under his skin and into his heart.

And just this afternoon, he'd been this close—*this close*, goddammit—to asking her to marry him.

Christ, but he must have been three bricks shy of a load to even consider such a thing.

Clasping the material of the makeshift mask in a tight fist, he upturned the burlap bag and let the rest of its contents spill to the ground. He kicked at them with the toe of his boot, scattering the different pieces into individual piles. No other incriminating evidence appeared, and he was almost pathetically grateful.

"Where are the things you stole?" he asked, his tone brittle as he fought to keep the emotions running through his blood separate from the emotions pounding through his heart. He felt like his body was being torn in two. Half of him knew he had to turn her in, while the other half wanted to grab her up, hold her close, and promise to protect her from the culpability of her actions.

"I don't have them anymore."

"What the hell did you do with them? Jesus, Regan, why would you do this? You don't need the money; James left you well enough off—didn't he?"

She opened her mouth to answer, but he held up a hand, reining in his shock and fury, and trying to remember that he was a Texas Ranger. "No, don't tell me. I don't want or need to know."

He bent down to gather the items he'd dumped

275

on the ground, then retied the flap. "You're under arrest," he said simply, thankful when the statement sounded clear and controlled. He certainly didn't feel calm and controlled. He took hold of her arm and spun her toward the house.

"Wait!" Her voice quavered with fear as she hustled along beside him, practically on the tips of her toes to keep up with his long, angry strides. "I can explain. Please, please let me explain."

"And let you worm your way out of this?" he scoffed. "I don't think so." He whipped open the back kitchen door and thrust her inside ahead of him.

"That's not what I'm trying to do, I swear it. Just let me explain. I need you to understand."

He could hear the tears in her voice and steeled himself against them.

"Please, Clay."

The memory of her crying out that very same plea while he was deep inside her blazed across his brain. How could she have been so open, so passionate, and still be a bloody damn criminal? How could she stomp on his guts and still have him wanting to give her the benefit of the doubt?

Remarkably, she did. "Sit down," he ordered, propelling her into the nearest chair.

It rocked back on two legs, but she went willingly enough, smoothing the folds of her wrap, then curling her fingers into the wood on either side of the seat's base.

Leaning against the counter only a few feet away, Clay crossed his arms over his chest and fixed her with his best no-nonsense lawman stare. "All right, talk," he said. "But keep in mind that I already expect every word out of your mouth to be a lie."

She licked her lips and let her gaze drift to the floor before bringing it back up to his. "I've told enough lies. I don't intend to tell any more."

She seemed resigned to her fate, and he tensed to keep from offering even a shred of comfort.

"I'm the burglar you were sent here to catch. But then, you knew that, didn't you?"

He didn't bother to respond. They both knew exactly who she was and what she'd done.

"I don't know how it even started," she went on. "You're right that James left us quite a handsome sum when he died. Mother Doyle and I will be able to live quite comfortably for many years to come."

Then why? Why? he wanted to shout. But he remained stoically silent.

"You know how important the orphans are to me, and while most would consider me a wealthy woman, I still don't have enough of a stipend set aside to finance the Home and children without jeopardizing Mother Doyle's and my futures."

Agitated, she leapt to her feet and began to pace. "So many people in Purgatory *do* have the money, though. Not to fully support the orphanage, but to make a sizeable donation now and again that would keep the Home afloat. The problem is that most of them won't give a dime to a worthy cause."

Her hands bunched at her sides and her shoulders drew taut. "They're so tight-fisted and selfish. So many of them strut around town in expensive clothes, showing off their fancy new jewelry and carriages while Father Ignacio struggles to stretch every penny far enough to feed and clothe and shelter those children. How can that be right?" she demanded, confronting him, and yet not really speaking to him at all.

"I know what it's like to grow up destitute, to watch your sister suffer and die because your parents couldn't afford medical care, to wonder where your next meal will come from. The children at the Home deserve more. They deserve better than that, and if I could give it to them, why does it matter *how?*"

She took a deep, resigned breath, releasing all the animosity from her tirade. "I only stole from those who refused to give of their own free will. Those who made a point of showing me their new baubles and tailored suits and gowns, but then made excuses for not being able to help the orphans. I took only one or two small things from each house. Just what could be easily hawked for cash, and what I thought might make a fair donation to the orphanage. They could afford it, believe me."

"And you think that makes what you did right?" Clay asked, aghast.

"No," she said with a slow shake of her head. "Not right, just necessary."

"Necessary." The word burned like salt in an open wound. "You're a criminal, Regan. A thief. You broke into your neighbors' homes and stole their personal possessions." His voice pitched to a harsh whisper. "I have no choice. I have to take you to jail."

Well, she'd known that was coming, hadn't she?

Regan inclined her head, quietly accepting that she'd broken the law and that Clay had to do his duty and take her to the sheriff. Until she'd turned to find him standing in the darkness, she'd actually thought she might be able to get away with it. But one look in his eyes told her she was wrong.

She thought about Mother Doyle and wondered who would take care of her when she went to prison. About what would happen to the orphans without her there to look after them. About what the townspeople would think of sweet, demure Widow Doyle being the robber who'd plagued Purgatory for the past year.

But most of all, she thought about Clay and how much she'd started to care for him. Love him, even, if she was completely honest with herself.

And now she'd betrayed him. Hurt him terribly, judging by the look on his strong, handsome face.

This afternoon, he'd said he loved her. Or nearly said it. But he couldn't truly love her, could he? Because he didn't really know her.

And even if she loved him back, which she was coming to conclude she did, it didn't matter. She'd deceived him. There was no way he would ever forgive her now.

"If you're going to arrest me . . ." she said finally. His jaw locked. "I am."

She'd known that, of course. It was almost a relief. Not that she'd be going to jail, but that she didn't have to live such a falsehood any longer. She could be honest with him about everything, including Nolan Updike's not-so-accidental death.

"You'll have to take care of Mother Doyle," she told him. "You'll have to stay with her . . . or perhaps you can telegraph your mother and ask her to come be with Martha for awhile."

A muscle ticked in her jaw. "She'll be fine."

"She won't be fine. She'll be devastated. And since I'm the only person who's taken care of her since her health began to decline, it's going to be doubly difficult for her to get used to someone else watching after her. But she's your aunt, so I trust you to see to her. Will you also look after Lucyfur? She's not used to male companionship, but she'll learn to like you if you're kind to her and don't make too many sudden movements or loud noises around her at first."

He rolled his eyes at that. With sarcasm dripping from every syllable, he said, "Anything else? Because if you're finished, we need to go upstairs for the shackles in my saddlebags."

She suspected he'd used the term shackles instead of handcuffs to scare her. But she had more vital things on her mind than how he planned to turn her over to Sheriff Graves.

Her gaze dropped to the toes of her slippers and she twisted her hands together behind her back before lifting her head to once again study his countenance. "There is one thing."

"Uh-huh." He pushed away from the counter

where he'd been leaning stiffly and stretched a hand out to grasp her upper arm. "Come on, let's go. You can fill me in on your cat's favorite meals on the way into town."

Ignoring his flippant tone, she swallowed past the lump in her throat and forced herself to speak. "It's important, Clay. I want you to investigate a murder."

Oh, what the hell was she talking about now?

"A murder," he repeated. "Right. I say I'm taking you to jail and you suddenly have an even bigger crime for me to look into. Did you commit this murder? Because if not, I can't say I give a good goddamn about it." Sure she was trying to throw him off her scent, he tugged her toward the door of the kitchen.

Her body tensed at his accusation and she dug in her heels. "I may be a thief, but I am not a murderer, Clayton Walker."

She yanked her arm from his grasp and took a step back. This time she was the one to cross her arms over her chest. Beneath those luscious breasts, damn her hide.

"Nolan Updike was murdered," she said succinctly, before he could reply to her previous outburst.

"This again?" He forked his fingers through his hair in agitation. "Jesus, the man fell down the steps. How hard is that to accept?"

"He didn't *fall*, Clay. He was pushed." She raised a brow at him and began to tap the sole of her tiny black evening slippers. "Don't look at me like that. I know what I'm talking about."

"And just how did you come to possess this privileged piece of information?" he asked, already moving forward to take ahold of her once more and drag her upstairs with him.

She took another step away from him, evading his grasp. "I *know* he was pushed, *Ranger* Walker, because I was there when it happened."

Chapter Twenty-six

He thought his heart had stopped beating when he found the mask.

He'd been wrong.

It screeched to a halt the minute he pictured Regan in the house with Nolan Updike and his apparent killer.

But maybe she'd been mistaken. She wasn't exactly the most reliable of witnesses at the moment, given her recent occupation as a sneak thief.

"How do you know he was murdered?" he asked carefully, sure her imagination was working overtime.

She relaxed her stance a bit, but remained on guard, watching him for any sudden movements. "I told you, I was there."

His nostrils flared as he prayed for patience. "Where? In the house?"

She nodded. "In the bedroom at the top of the stairs."

"*What?* You mean to tell me you were there when a man was murdered?"

"Isn't that what I've *been* telling you?"

His eyes narrowed. "Where were you *exactly,* in relation to where Updike and his supposed killer were?"

"I was upstairs, in the master bedroom." He saw the muscles of her neck flex before she admitted the next. "I'd just taken a gold pocket watch from the bureau and was on my way back out when I heard voices. I hid behind the door, hoping no one would notice me. And then . . . whoever was with Nolan threatened him. There was what sounded like a scuffle and Nolan fell down the steps. But Clay . . . he was pushed, I know he was."

"How do I know you're not spinning tales again?" he asked, linking his thumbs over the band of his gunbelt, maintaining what he hoped was an unconcerned pose. Because right now, he was very concerned. His heart was squeezing like a vice at the very thought of her being in the house at the same time as a murderer. His mind was screaming that she never would have been in danger in the first place if she weren't a damn Robin Hood-in-training. And his gut . . . well, those Ranger instincts he was so bloody proud of were telling him straight out to believe her.

She might be a lot of things, and there was no

doubt she'd lied before, but she wasn't lying now.

"What would I have to gain by fabricating a story like this?" she returned. "You already know I'm the one who's been breaking into houses. You're prepared to arrest me. How would lying about Nolan's death keep me from going to jail?"

"Maybe you're hoping I'll get so caught up in catching this killer that I'll forget all about your crimes."

"I would never underestimate your integrity as a Ranger. I'm only hoping that you'll believe me enough to search for the murderer. I don't expect any more than that."

She sighed and her rigid posture abated a bit. "To be honest, I'm a little relieved that you finally figured out what I was up to. Don't get me wrong, I'm not looking forward to spending the rest of my life in prison," she added quickly and with feeling. "But I hated misleading everyone. Mother Doyle, the townspeople . . . you."

Their gazes locked and Clay was once again rocked to the soles of his boots by the deep, abiding green of her eyes.

"Especially after all the time we've spent together. The things that we've . . . shared."

"Then why didn't you just tell me?" he demanded, fighting the lure of her softly spoken confession.

"How could I? You came here to capture and arrest Purgatory's resident burglar. How could I tell you the person you were making love to was the same person you'd come to town to apprehend?"

285

Heidi Betts

"You could have said *something*," he growled, and then cursed his own vulnerability. He shouldn't let her get to him this way. He shouldn't want to protect her when she'd broken the law. He shouldn't want to comfort her when she was a damn criminal. And yet that's exactly what he wanted to do. He wanted to carry her upstairs and bury himself in the soft folds of her flesh the way he had this afternoon and pretend nothing had happened, that tonight was nothing more than a nightmare he could put behind him in the bright light of day.

Her criminal behavior went against everything he believed in. He couldn't overlook her actions, and he could never forgive her. Worse yet, he couldn't believe he hadn't figured it out sooner. They'd made love, for Christ's sake, and he had never known the woman in his arms—the woman he'd thought he was falling in love with—was a damn thief. He felt like kicking himself for being seven kinds of a fool.

"I tried to say something," she offered quietly. "Every time I touched you, every time I let you touch me, I tried to tell you how much I'd come to care for you. I fell in love with you, Clay."

The air escaped his lungs in a bitter laugh. "Now's a great time to admit that sort of thing, isn't it? Maybe if you say you love me, I'll capitulate and look the other way while you go on robbing your neighbors blind. Maybe I'll declare my everlasting devotion right back and ask you to marry me. Then I can live happily ever after, pretending my wife isn't the reason a Texas Ranger had to be

286

brought in to stop a string of burglaries." He fixed her with a cold glare. "Don't hold your breath, sweetheart."

Her eyes filled with tears, but he staunchly ignored them. Neither would he let his mind contemplate his own words too closely.

Before tonight, he very well might have asked her to marry him. He'd sure as hell been thinking along those lines. And he had no doubt they'd have been blissfully happy. He'd have kept her in bed half the day and all of the night and she'd have convinced him to adopt a passel of button-nosed tots before their fourth or fifth anniversary rolled around.

Now, he would spend the next four or five years on the trail, chasing down bandits and outlaws, and Regan would rot away in a jail cell.

Christ! He couldn't even picture her in prison garb, her hair tangled and matted with God knew what, her face gaunt from lack of food and proper sunlight, without feeling sick to his stomach. Could he really take her in, knowing that's how she would end up?

The simple answer was yes. It was his job, and she'd broken the law. The path couldn't be blurred when it came to this sort of thing. He had no choice but to arrest her and let the circuit judge punish her as he saw fit.

But he didn't have to do it right this minute, now, did he? The thought came out of nowhere and warmed him from the very center of his soul all the way to his fingertips.

The town of Purgatory had gone this long without knowing who was breaking into houses, what would another few days or weeks hurt? She'd witnessed a murder and could hopefully identify the killer if they figured out who had pushed Nolan Updike to his death. But if she was already under arrest and awaiting trial on charges of burglary, who would ever believe her?

In the scheme of things, murder was definitely a greater sin than a few minor thefts. Wasn't it better to catch a killer than to persecute a woman who had only stooped to stealing to help a bunch of dirty-cheeked orphans?

He was splitting hairs and he knew it. He was trying to justify not only Regan's misdeeds, but his own desire to keep her out of jail. For a while longer, at least.

"You're sure about this," he said, hoping he wasn't making the most phenomenal mistake of his life. "Nolan Updike was murdered."

"I'm positive. I don't know who did it, but someone pushed Nolan down those stairs."

"And you would be willing to testify to that fact, even if it means telling a justice of the peace and the entire town exactly *how* you know what you know."

"Of course. But won't they already figure that out as soon as you take me in?"

He'd eat his boot leather before he'd admit his misguided feelings for her had hindered his oath to uphold the law. After all, he wasn't ignoring her crimes, merely postponing addressing them for awhile.

"If you say a man was murdered, then we should check it out. I'll hold off on arresting you, but only until I have a better feel about this Updike situation. In the meantime, I don't let you out of my sight. You go nowhere, do nothing unless I'm half an inch behind you. Got it?" He grazed her with a stare that warned her not to test him.

Her hands fell from behind her back to fidget at her waistline. "Are you sure about this?"

Despite his best effort, the corner of his mouth lifted in amusement. "Are you trying to change my mind?" he returned.

"No, of course not," she answered quickly. "Whatever you think is best."

"Good." With a jerk of his head, he gestured toward the kitchen table and took a seat across from her. "The first thing we need to do is alert the sheriff."

She raised a questioning brow. "Do you really think Jensen will do anything to help?"

"Maybe not, but this is his town, and I don't want to ruffle any feathers by searching for a killer behind his back. Besides, he may have some ideas about who had it in for Updike. We might also catch the guy faster with more of us out looking for him.

"The second thing we should concentrate on is who might have wanted Nolan Updike dead. Do you have any ideas?"

"Not at all. I can't think of anyone who would want to hurt Nolan. He was a nice man. Everyone liked him."

"Not everyone," Clay interjected, "because somebody killed him."

Dear God. Martha slapped a hand to her breast and collapsed against the papered wall.

Regan? Regan was the bandit she'd asked Clayton to come here to capture? But how? How could Martha not have known? She'd lived under the same roof with the girl for five years now and never once had she *dreamed* her beloved daughter-in-law was the robber everyone called the Ghost of Ol' Morty Pike.

As she began to slowly and silently make her way back to her bedroom, Martha's heart beat off-rhythm in a way it hadn't since the doctor first warned her not to become overwrought several years before. Doctor be damned, though. She'd brought Clayton to Purgatory, and now he was determined to drag sweet Regan off to jail.

Why, if she hadn't been eavesdropping to begin with, she'd have given that boy such a smack on the head! How dare he threaten her darling Regan's freedom. And when he was supposed to be falling in love with her, too.

Martha gave a silent snort. All men, it seemed, were thick as molasses in January. Her own husband and dear son James—God rest their souls—had both been dumb as dirt from time to time, themselves. And it wasn't until she'd given them both a cuff or two that they'd wised up. Now it looked like she'd have to take a switch to her nephew's hide, as well.

In fact, when she first heard Regan's confession and Clay's cold-hearted response she'd been ready to do just that. She'd snapped her spine into alignment and put out a hand to push open the kitchen door, ready to dash to Regan's defense. Then Regan and Clayton had begun speaking again and she'd cocked her head to listen further. What she'd heard next had nearly sent her into palpitations that her physician would be none too pleased about.

Nolan Updike *hadn't* fallen down the stairs, he'd been . . . *murdered*. And Regan had witnessed the entire incident. Martha had been too stunned by this news to move for a few minutes.

Thank goodness Clayton had agreed to hold his tongue about Regan's escapades—of course, only until they'd tracked down Updike's killer. Well, at least that would buy them some time. It seemed her nephew possessed a small lick of sense, after all.

But that didn't mean he would eventually recognize his true feelings for Regan and do the right thing. The right thing being to ignore her past offenses and marry up with her.

Martha wasn't sure what to do about any of the mess she'd helped to create, but she knew she had to do something. If she didn't, her favorite daughter-in-law would end up behind bars, and her bull-headed nephew would never forgive himself for putting her there.

Chapter Twenty-seven

With his elbows resting on the tabletop, Clay pressed the heels of his hands into his eye sockets where Regan imagined a headache must be beginning to pound.

They'd been talking for twenty minutes, going over what she remembered from the night of Nolan Updike's death and anything that might clue them in to who the killer was. Unfortunately, they weren't getting far. She didn't recall any more than she'd already told him, and she hadn't recognized the intruder's voice. Which left them—as Clay had so eloquently put it—ass-deep in castor oil.

"It's getting late. Perhaps we should forget about it for tonight and try again in the morning." She would prefer to get directly on the trail of the killer, of course, but she was practical enough to understand there was very little they could do at this hour of the night.

Clay's hands dropped from his tired face as he studied her. Then he heaved a sigh and pushed back his chair to stand. The spindle legs scraped across the hardwood floor. "I guess you're right. We're not getting anywhere this way, and we could both do with some shut-eye." He held a hand out to her. "Come on."

It seemed more than ordinary to link her palm with his. Even after everything they'd been through tonight and how much she knew she'd hurt him.

He led her through the house and up the stairs, guiding her to her room where he saw her inside, then pulled the door closed silently after her.

He hadn't said goodnight, given her a wink, or even warned her to stay put until he came for her in the morning. He'd simply shut her in her room and walked away.

Well, what did she expect? Regan asked herself silently. She'd betrayed him not only with the robberies she'd committed, but by not confiding in him when they'd begun to grow close. Earlier in the day, he'd implored her to meet him in the barn so they could make love again. Now, he barely wanted to sleep next door to her.

Pain like she'd never felt before, not even when James died, lanced her heart. In a span of mere hours, she'd gone from just beginning to realize she was falling in love for the first time in her life to losing that love because of her own stupid, thoughtless actions.

She yanked at the ties of her robe and pulled the restrictive fabric away from her wrists. Kicking her slippers aside, she proceeded to undo the row of hook and eye clasps running down the front of her red-and-black corset one by one. The tight, form-fitting bones fell away and she took a deep inhalation of relief.

Ahh! She'd been wearing the less-than-comfortable thing all day. Her poor flesh itched at finally being able to move and stretch to its natural capacity.

Suddenly, the door swung open behind her and she gave a shriek as she whirled around, corset pressed to her exposed bosom, to find Clay standing in the entranceway.

"What are you doing?" she charged, her blood still racing from the shock of having him walk in on her.

His dark gray eyes raked her form . . . legs nude, mail-order scarlet drawers covering her lower body, and the rest of her bare but for the corset clutched upside down and backwards to her breasts. "Bedding down," he said.

That's when she noticed the saddlebags thrown over his shoulder and the linens from his bed bundled under his arm. He took another step into the room and kicked the door closed behind him with the heel of one boot.

"You can't come in here," she said, and then recognized the futility of that statement, as he was *already* in.

He paid her no heed, moving forward to deposit

his saddlebags on a chair in the corner and letting the pillow and blankets fall to the floor.

When he didn't react to her assertion, but looked to be making himself at home in the small confines of her chamber, her anxiety increased tenfold. She decided to try another tack.

"You can't stay here," she told him. Her fingers clutched the stays pressed to her chest, attempting to make the rather diminutive garment cover more of her exposed torso. Still, tiny chill bumps broke out on her arms from standing in the middle of the room practically nude for so long.

Clay cocked his head. "Why not?"

"Why not? *Why not?*" she repeated, her voice rising shrilly. "Because it's not proper for you to so much as knock on the door at this hour, let alone be in here with me. Because I'm *naked,* for pity's sake!"

His gaze swept over her once again, causing her to shift nervously and nearly drop the corset. Then he met her eyes, his expression indifferent. "Don't worry, sweetheart, I've seen it all before."

The slight, delivered with so little emotion on his part, bruised her already battered ego. "It doesn't matter. You need to go."

Instead, he started spreading out the thick quilt from his own room on the floor of hers. "I told you I wouldn't let you out of my sight until this matter of Updike's murder is resolved. So you might as well pull your mouth closed and go ahead and change for bed, because I'm not leaving."

"Surely you don't intend to spend the night here,

in my room." She heard Clay's words, saw the determination in his set, square-cut features, and yet she couldn't quite absorb his meaning. "It's after midnight. We're both tired. You can't think I plan to sneak off in the middle of the night."

His hard, dark-as-slate glare bored into her. "Correct me if I'm wrong, green eyes, but don't you do your best skulking around in the middle of the night?"

The accusation vibrated with more than a hint of truth, but still she stuck to her guns. "*If* I tried to go anywhere, I'm sure you would hear me from inside your own room."

"Who's to say you'd pass my room?"

Her brows knit in confusion. "Well, how else would I get out of the house?" she asked. "*If* I planned to run off, which I assure you, I don't."

His retort was immediate. "There's always the window."

She glanced over her shoulder, stunned by the very suggestion. She'd climbed *in* plenty of windows; that was how she breached all of those houses, after all. Not that she had any intention of sharing that little detail with Clay. But it had never occurred to her to climb out one of her own windows in order to perform the thefts without being spotted.

"You might want to cover up there, darlin'."

She swung back around only to note that when she'd turned toward the window on the other side of the room, she'd given him a prime view of her bare back.

"This may be part of my job as a Ranger, but I *am* human."

"Oh!" Well, now she was just plain mad. It was one thing for him to follow his duties as a lawman and step back from their personal relationship because of her deception. But even if he insisted on staying in her room to keep her from running off, he could have averted his gaze from her near-nakedness. He could have turned his back, or waited in the hall for a few short minutes while she threw on a nightdress and got under the covers.

But he was punishing her with his arrogance, demonstrating the power he held over her and letting her know how much she'd hurt him without actually showing his true emotions.

Her Irish temper flared. She felt badly about what she'd done and how her conduct had affected him, but she would *not* stand here fretting about her modesty while he did his best to intimidate her.

Let him stay, then, she thought. But she'd be damned if she was going to make it easy on him.

"I guess there's nothing I can do to change your mind," she said simply. And then she took a deep breath, filling both her lungs and diaphragm with air, and her bones and spirit with courage.

As casually as she could manage, she released her hold on the corset covering her exposed front and let it fall at her feet. She wasn't trying to seduce him, so she didn't cast him any sidelong glances. Instead, she went about the business of readying herself for bed as though he wasn't even there.

Of course, if she just happened to swing her hips

a bit more expansively as she moved across the room, or fling her hair over her shoulder a time or two more often than she ordinarily might . . . well, he deserved it, the wretch.

She sauntered to the bureau along the far wall, forcing herself to pretend that her bosom wasn't hanging out for all the world—or Clay Walker, at least—to see. She ignored the sensations of her nipples budding with involuntary excitement and sifted through the contents of one of the drawers for a particularly slinky shift.

Normally, she would wear one of her ankle-length, rather concealing nightgowns to bed. Something comfortable and demure. For Clay's benefit, however, she chose a garment she usually wore beneath her dresses. A thigh-length, black satin shift with delicate lace making up the slender shoulder straps and filling the V-shaped front.

It was the only expensive piece of frippery she owned in black. While ordering all of the other, more scandalously colored ones, a pang of guilt had persuaded her to order at least one black unmentionable to wear beneath her equally black gowns.

Once she found what she was looking for, she laid it on the dressertop and shimmied out of her red drawers. She felt Clay's gaze on her the entire time and refused to look in the mirror—where she was sure to see his intense image reflected—for fear of losing her nerve.

With the last of her covering pooled on the floor at her feet, she reached for the black shift, lifting it over her head and letting it slide over her arms and down the length of her body.

The hem of the garment came only to mid-thigh and the bodice left much of her chest exposed. That was the idea, though, wasn't it? If Clay insisted on spending the night in her room, then she planned to make it the worst—or at least the most uncomfortable—night of his life.

Christ almighty!

Regan Doyle with her hair pulled into a bun and wrapped head to toe in mourning garb was pretty enough to make his insides sweat. Regan Doyle with her hair falling loose and walking around the room in nothing but what the good Lord gave her made his knees weak and his manhood hard as a hammer in his pants.

What did she think she was doing, strutting around in all her naked glory? Bad enough he'd had to stand here fully aroused at just the sight of her in her fancy drawers, with that sexy red and black fantasy-inspiring contraption pressed to her breasts. But then she'd dropped the shields of those accouterments, and he thought he might explode.

Right here, in the middle of one of the bedrooms of his aunt's home, he expected his blood to boil over, his eyes to cross, and the top of his head to shoot straight off into the ceiling.

Was she insane? Or trying to tempt him? Either way, it had the same effect on his lower anatomy.

He glanced at the pallet he'd put together on the floor, then at the bed Regan was swaying her hips toward and preparing to climb into. It didn't take a high-falutin' university fellow with a diploma on his wall to figure out where he'd prefer to bunk down. Especially with the vision of her beautiful, rose-tipped breasts bobbing as she'd crossed the room, her firm, lush buttocks coming into view as she'd stripped completely, and the whole of that ravishing, mouth-watering image as she'd stood in front of her bureau mirror without a qualm for her nudity.

If she'd raised her head a fraction to meet his gaze in that looking glass, she'd have seen a man nearly driven to his knees by sheer, unadulterated lust.

And the way she'd slipped into that barely there satin nightdress didn't help matters much. Completely naked or decked out in a piece of whisper-thin cloth that wouldn't cover his left Colt, she was inexorably appealing. He wanted to throw her over his shoulder, toss her onto her back on that bed, and remind her of just how virile he could be.

If she thought she could prance in front of him like this and not have him take action . . . well, she was treading on very thin ice, indeed. He was about three short breaths from showing her that his feelings about the robberies she'd committed had nothing to do with his desire for her. Because *that* wasn't going anywhere. Not today, not tomorrow, not a hundred years from now.

While he'd been standing stiff as a post, wondering how loud she'd scream if he took it upon himself to ravage her, Regan had climbed into bed. She sat on the high mattress, the covers folded down and a pillow propped behind her back, one leg crossed over the other, with both knees and most of her pale white thighs visible beneath the hem of her so-called nightdress. The scooped neckline bunched as she moved, giving him several quick, taunting glimpses of her supple breasts and the shadowed valley between them.

He shifted his attention and met her sparkling emerald gaze. She seemed at ease with both her attire and his presence in her bedroom. A definite switch from her attitude when he'd first arrived and announced his intention of spending the night at the foot of her bed.

"Well, you look like you'll be comfortable enough," she said, sparing a glance for his make-shift bedroll on the floor. The hard, unyielding, not-nearly-as-soft-as-her-bed-would-be floor.

He rolled his tongue around his mouth, trying to work up enough spit to speak. But before he got the chance, she continued.

"Goodnight, then," she almost sing-songed as she reached for the lamp on her bedside table and turned down the wick.

In the total darkness that followed, he could see nothing more than the outline of the bed and a slight glow of wan moonlight on the other side of the single small window. Unfortunately, the lack of light didn't block out sound, and he could easily hear the squeak and moan of the mattress as she lay down and settled herself for the long night ahead.

Clay plopped down on the quilt he'd arranged

and began to remove his boots and gunbelt, then undo the buttons of his shirt. It was probably a smart idea to keep his trousers on. If he took off many more layers, the temptation to get up in the middle of the night and crawl into bed beside Regan might be too great to resist. Granted, if the notion really overtook him, a thin barrier of denim wasn't going to be much of an obstacle, but keeping his dungarees on would serve as a reminder to keep his hands—and the rest of his body—to himself.

He heard Regan roll over and release a soft, slumberous sigh, which sent a sharp jab of longing through his bones in a beeline to his groin.

Damn, but this was going to be one hell of a long night.

Chapter Twenty-eight

Clay lay awake for several hours that night listening to the tiny sounds Regan made in her sleep. The sighs and gurgles, even the occasional snort. And he imagined what she looked like, tucked up to her chin in the bedspread with the little yellow flowers. Of course, then his mind would shift to what she looked like underneath those covers—her hands curled at her cheek, her shoulders bare, that slip of a nightdress hitching up her thighs to bunch at her hips or waist.

Thoughts along those lines kept him awake well into the night. And when he finally drifted off, he was still hard as a rock and suspected the chirping he heard in the distance was birds rising to greet the new day.

What seemed like only a moment later, he felt

someone shaking his shoulder and calling his name. His eyes popped open and he saw a fully dressed, well-rested Regan hovering above him.

Sitting up, he ran splayed fingers through his hair and blinked to clear his sleep-blurred vision. "What time is it?" The room was still fairly dark, only a sparse amount of morning light pouring in through the window.

"A little after six. I thought you'd want to get an early start looking for Nolan's killer."

Oh, right. The killer.

He wasn't nearly alert enough to begin the day, but what choice did he have? Climbing to his feet, he reached for his saddlebags to get out a fresh shirt. While he dressed, Regan arranged her hair in front of the mirror lining the back of the low chest of drawers.

And that's when he noticed.

His mouth fell open and his not-yet-fastened gunbelt slipped from his fingers to the floor with a violent *clunk*.

Startled by the loud noise, Regan spun around, her hands still raised to her fiery curls as she fastened a carved wooden comb at the back of her head. "What?" she asked, glancing around for what might have caused his outburst.

"You . . . you're . . . you're not wearing black."

Regan looked down at the bodice of her green gingham gown with thin white lace on either side of the row of pearl-like buttons. "Is it all right?" she asked. "I mean, does it look okay? It still fits, doesn't it?"

She smoothed a hand over the soft fabric. It had been so long since she'd worn anything colorful—on the outside, at any rate—that she wasn't sure her old dresses would still fit properly. And even if they did, people were so used to seeing her only in widow's weeds, they might not take well to her finally putting an end to her period of mourning.

"You look fine," Clay told her, his eyes remaining wide as he goggled at her.

"I don't look *that* different, do I?" His reaction was exactly what she was afraid of. Maybe it was too soon to start wearing regular clothes again. Not that two full years wasn't plenty long enough.

"You look amazingly different," he said. "Or maybe just plain amazing."

That brought her head up.

"What . . ." His Adam's apple bobbed as he swallowed. "Why did you suddenly decide to stop wearing black?"

Fingers bunching at the sides of her skirt, she took a deep breath and considered her answer. "I guess because I woke up this morning and realized it may be the last time I sleep in my own bed and have a choice of what to wear. If I'm going to be forced to wear prisoner gray for the rest of my life . . . well, black is a little too close to gray for my tastes, and I wanted to dress in something bright and cheery for as long as I have left."

She held Clay's gaze a second longer, then turned back to the looking glass to finish pulling the sides of her hair back with the comb.

"Are you about ready to go downstairs? Mother

Doyle will be expecting breakfast, then I suppose we should go into town and have that talk with Sheriff Graves."

Was she that eager to go to jail? Clay wondered. No, she was that eager to catch a killer. While he wanted to just stand there, watching her.

He'd never seen her in anything but black, and the change in her features was breathtaking. Her eyes looked brighter, the green squares on the pattern of her dress enhancing the natural green of her irises. Her hair shone more coppery than ever, the kinky red ringlets framing her face and falling about her shoulders in a cascade that begged for a man's touch. Even her skin seemed more robust, her milk cream coloring now touched with hints of rose.

And he'd thought getting through the night would be tough. Getting through today might just be the death of him.

He bent over to retrieve his six-shooters. "Why don't you . . . um, go on down. I'll be right there."

She turned from her spot at the mirror to face him, one brow raised with skepticism. "Are you sure?" she asked. "That would mean I'd be out of your sight for two, maybe three whole minutes."

His glare narrowed. "Are you mocking me?"

She let out an amused chuckle. "You're the one who's so worried about my whereabouts. Where you expect me to go, I haven't the faintest notion, but I wouldn't want to cause you undue concern. So if you want me to stay half an inch ahead of you at all times," she tossed his words from last night back at him, "then that's what I'll do."

"Good." He was glad to hear it. "But I trust you enough to go down and start breakfast. Just don't go any farther than the kitchen."

She gave him a jaunty little salute. "Yes, sir." As she moved across the room, her petticoats rustled, and when she reached the door, she cocked her head to look at him over the slim curve of her shoulder. "Are eggs all right?"

"Eggs're fine."

She gave an almost imperceptible nod. "I'll see you downstairs."

When the door closed behind her, Clay released the long breath he'd been holding since about two seconds after he spotted her in that brand-spanking new dress. Regan in mourning raiment was difficult enough to disregard. Regan in lovely, brightly colored garments was going to be practically impossible to ignore.

And yet that's exactly what he had to do. He had to keep away from her, and when this was all over, he had to lock her up and let her stand trial for her crimes.

Fastening the large metal buckle at his waist, he shook his head and tried not to contemplate how terrible he was going to feel when that time finally came.

His stay in Purgatory was growing worse by the minute.

The minute Regan closed the door on a still-dressing Clay, she thought she smelled frying ham and flapjacks. Which was impossible, of course, since she was the only one who ever cooked, and she hadn't been downstairs yet to start the morning meal.

But the closer she got to the kitchen, the stronger the scents became.

Her mother-in-law's bedroom door stood open as she passed and she peeked her head inside. "Mother Doyle?" The bed was empty, the covers already pulled up and straightened, and Martha's invalid chair was missing—along with Mother Doyle.

That was very strange, indeed. Mother Doyle rarely woke before Regan, and *never* dressed herself or moved about the house without assistance.

Regan continued through the house, pushing open the swinging door to the kitchen . . . and stopped dead in her tracks.

Three plates were set at the table, filled with stacks of pancakes and steaming slabs of pink (and in some places charred black) ham. Across the room, Mother Doyle was wheeling herself toward the table with a platter of fresh-baked biscuits on her lap.

"Mother Doyle," Regan exclaimed, shocked to the core by what she was seeing. "What are you doing?"

Martha lifted her head at Regan's entrance and beamed a smile in her direction. "Good morning, dear. Why, I'm preparing breakfast, of course. Where's Clayton?"

"Right here."

Regan yelped and jumped a foot at his sudden appearance at her back.

Paying no attention to her startled reaction, he focused on his aunt. "What do you think you're doing, Aunt Martha?"

"You youngsters today," Martha chastised. "Honestly! What does it look like I'm doing? I'm fixing breakfast. Ham, eggs, flapjacks, biscuits . . . I hope you're both hungry."

Clay pushed past Regan and took a seat on the far side of the table. "I sure am." He took a big whiff of the food in front of him and clapped his hands together. "Smells delicious."

Regardless of how good the meal both looked and smelled, Regan was much more concerned about Martha's health and ability to safely cook anything, let alone this large a feast. She rushed forward and reached for the dish Martha was transferring from her lap to the tabletop. "Here, Mother Doyle, let me take that."

To her utter surprise, Martha slapped her hands away. "You'll do no such thing. I'm perfectly capable of putting a plate of biscuits on the table for my nephew and daughter-in-law."

"But you're not," Regan pointed out, agog with both stupefaction and worry. "You're not at all well enough to do this. To do any of this." She threw out an arm to encompass the whole of the kitchen and all Martha had done before Regan and Clay had even risen from bed.

"Well, now, I've been thinking about that," her mother-in-law said slowly. Then she patted Regan's stinging hand and pushed her toward a chair. "Sit down, dear, your eggs are getting cold."

Regan sat, more because her legs were about to give out than because Martha had ordered her to do so. Martha arranged the bulk of her chair beneath the outermost edge of the table and spread a cloth napkin over her knees. Clay, meanwhile, was shoveling food into his mouth like he hadn't eaten for a week.

"You're a dear, dear child, Regan, and you've been an absolute blessing these past few years. Even before my darling James died—God rest his soul—you always took the very best care of me. You were kinder to me than I could have asked. Probably more than I deserved."

"Oh, no, Mother Doyle, never say such a thing." Regan covered her mother-in-law's hand with her own and gave it a squeeze.

"It's the truth, I'm afraid. You've been *too* good to me, and I've taken advantage of your charitable nature. Not that I didn't need someone from time to time," she added quickly. "But I admit that I've let you take over more of the responsibilities around here than I should have. And by doing that, I've allowed myself to become far lazier than anybody has a right to be."

"Mother Doyle," Regan insisted, "that just isn't true."

"It is, dear. And the proof is on the plate in front of you."

Regan's attention swung from Martha's aged, wrinkled face to the heaping meal at her place setting.

"As you can see, while I am not in the bloom of

health, I am certainly capable of caring for myself much of the time. I can dress myself, get around the house passing fine, and even cook a big breakfast for the three of us."

She slanted a glance at Clay, whose mouth was working to chew the large bite of meat he'd just stuffed inside. "There's more ham in the pan, if you'd like it, dear."

Then she turned back to Regan. "My only excuse, I'm chagrined to say, is that I've enjoyed your company too greatly. I look forward to our morning rituals, to having you read to me or share what gossip you might have picked up in town. I've only now come to discern, however, that I needn't act like a helpless child simply to enjoy your company."

Martha's lashes lowered and a sheepish expression stole over her waxen features. "That is, if you can find it in your heart to forgive me for deceiving you all this time."

Regan took a shaky breath and did her best to swallow past the lump in her throat. "Forgive you? Why, I love you, Mother Doyle. I'm thrilled to hear that you're feeling well enough to move around a bit on your own, but I was happy to help you in any way I could, and will continue to do so for as long as you allow it." Clutching Martha's hand in her own, she leaned forward to plead with her. "But please, *please* don't overdo it these first few days you're feeling better. Promise me you'll let me know if you need anything, and that you'll call for either Clay or me if you're overtaxed and need assistance."

Heidi Betts

Eyes glassy with unshed tears, Martha gave her daughter-in-law a solemn nod. "I promise." And then she raised Regan's hand to her lips. "You're such a dear. I thank God for bringing you to me."

Regan's throat closed completely at that declaration and she got up from the table before she made a fool of herself by crying all over her eggs and flapjacks. When she thought she had her emotions under control, she brought the frying pan to the table and offered Clay the last slice of ham.

He gave a vigorous nod and leaned back as she forked it onto his nearly empty plate.

Missing the true depth of the conversation she and Martha had just shared, he shoved an egg nearly the size of his fist into his mouth and asked in true masculine fashion, "So, Aunt Martha . . . you think you can fix a breakfast like this again tomorrow?"

Chapter Twenty-nine

Standing outside the sheriff's office, Regan wrung her hands in front of her. It was bad enough that her new mode of fashion had garnered stares the whole way through town from acquaintances who had never seen—or couldn't *remember* ever seeing her—in anything but black, but Clay expected her to walk into Sheriff Graves's office and report that Nolan Updike's accident had been no accident.

Would the indolent lawman believe her? Would he ask how she knew such a thing? Would she have to admit to being the burglar who had plagued the wealthier populace of Purgatory lo these many months?

Clay had assured her he planned to keep her activities under wraps for the time being, but there was no guarantee that Sheriff Graves wouldn't badger it out of them. Knowing Jensen, he wouldn't want to move a fat finger toward investigating unless he could see no possible way out of it.

But Clay was right that they had to report their suspicions to the sheriff. If they investigated on their own and Graves later found out they'd worked behind his back, he would be even more incensed than if they had made him look into the incident in the first place.

Clay stroked a hand down her arm. "Ready?"

She exhaled a huff of nervous air. "No, I don't think I am. But I don't really have any choice, do I?"

"It'll be fine. Just let me do most of the talking. I don't plan to tell Graves everything, only what he needs to know to do his job."

Inclining her head, she slipped her hand into his and followed him inside. The office was empty, and not very well lit, with only two windows facing the boardwalk and one much smaller, barred window overlooking the cell at the back of the room that held drunks and temporary prisoners. There were more cells in the back for dangerous types.

"Graves?" Clay called out.

They heard dull noises from behind the plank-wood door leading to the other room, and a moment later the sheriff's wide girth appeared. As soon as he saw Clay, his puffy eyes closed to slits.

"Well, well. Ranger Walker, ain't it? What can I do you for?" He leaned against the doorjamb in a lazy pose, fished a toothpick from his front shirt pocket, and began working it between his teeth.

Clay's tall frame tensed at Jensen's entry, and Regan could tell immediately that there was no love lost between these two lawmen, even though as far as she knew they'd met each other only once before. Sheriff Graves, it seemed, had that effect on a lot of people.

"We came to report a crime," Clay said without preamble.

"We?" The sheriff's gaze narrowed even more as he homed in on her, standing slightly behind Clay. "Who's this cute cut of calico you've got with you?"

Used to Graves's attitude, Regan took little offense at his remark. "It hasn't been *that* long since the ice cream social, Jensen. Of course, maybe if you showed up to Sunday services a bit more often, you'd be more likely to remember me."

Before the first three words were out of her mouth, recognition dawned. His brow shot up and his jaw dropped open, causing the damp toothpick to fall to the dusty floor. "Regan? Widow Doyle?"

He took in her uncoiffed hair, gingham gown, and the fact that her hand was still linked with Clay's. "Jesus, Joseph, and Mary. What're you doin' out of your mournin' duds?"

"The typical period of mourning is a year, Jensen. James has been gone more than two now; I think I've grieved long enough, don't you?"

Still a little shaken by her presence in his office with Clay, and her unusual appearance, he stammered. " 'Course, 'course. Didn't mean nothin' by

315

it, I was just surprised to see you gussied up like that, is all."

"Well, thank you, Jensen, I'll take that as a compliment."

"Yes, ma'am, it most certainly was."

"Can we get to the issue at hand," Clay cut in, his patience growing thin at their meaningless banter.

The sheriff glowered, but Regan stepped forward eagerly. "Oh, yes. Jensen, we have a problem, and I'm so hoping you'll be able to help us." The best way to get anything from Sheriff Graves, she'd long ago learned, was to flatter him. And it appeared to be working.

"Sure, sure. What seems to be the trouble?" he asked as he moved to the squeaky rolling chair behind his beaten and battered desk. Lowering his considerable bulk between the weakened armrests, he made himself comfortable and reached into the small pocket of his brown leather vest. He dug around, apparently searching for something, then frowned when he didn't find it. Giving up, he locked his hands atop the mound of his belly.

Now that she'd gotten Jensen's attention, Regan looked to Clay for how to continue this very delicate conversation.

"We believe there's been a murder, Sheriff," he told the older man.

"Murder? What in the Sam Hill are you talking about?"

If she hadn't been there, Regan suspected Jensen's

scowl would be even deeper and aimed much more personally in Clay's direction.

"We don't think Nolan Updike fell down the stairs," she said. "We think he was pushed."

Jensen's jowls blanched and he coughed a few times into his fist before responding. "What do you mean he was pushed? Who told you such a thing?"

"No one told us," Clay answered, "it's just a theory we have. We don't believe his fall was an accident."

The animosity came back into Sheriff Graves's eyes. "A theory, huh? Is that one of your big Texas Ranger words you like to throw around to intimidate small-town lawmen like me?"

Regan felt Clay tense beside her and saw the sheriff's face turning a mottled red. If she didn't step in soon to ease wounded egos, the men might come to blows.

"Now, Jensen, that's not what Mr. Walker was implying at all. In fact, it was his idea to come to you for aid with this matter."

That seemed to appease him. "I still don't see why you'd even think such a thing. Nolan tripped and broke his neck, simple as that."

Catching on to Regan's attempt at treading lightly with Sheriff Graves, Clay moderated his tone when he said, "We thought the same at first. There was no reason not to." He paused and the tension in the room grew. "But it seems there was a witness."

Regan's heart skipped a beat at Clay's announcement. What was he doing? He'd promised not to reveal her involvement unless absolutely necessary. And Clay might disagree, but she didn't think they were anywhere near *absolutely necessary* yet. Biting her tongue to keep from speaking out, she inhaled sharply and told herself not to foil Clay's plan. And he'd *better* have a plan, she thought irritably.

Jensen had grown still, watching Clay with distrust. "What do you mean there was a witness? Who?" he asked curtly.

Clay dipped into his front shirt pocket and pulled out a slip of paper. "I can't rightly answer that one, Sheriff, but this was stuck under my aunt's front door the morning after the accident. Or murder, rather, if this note has any validity."

Regan shifted from foot to foot and craned her neck to get a glimpse of the letter as Clay unfolded it. He hadn't told *her* about any note. Where had it come from, and what did it say? If someone else had seen her at the Updike home that night, she was in a heap more trouble than she'd counted on. But before she could find out what it said, he passed the page to the sheriff.

Graves read it slowly. Or perhaps he read it quickly, but several times over, because a long minute passed before he showed any sort of reaction. He looked up and studied both of them carefully. "You don't know how this got there? Who left it?"

" 'Fraid not. It was as much of a shock to us as it is to you."

Jensen's bushy eyebrows crossed in consternation. "Why in blazes would somebody leave this at the Doyles' door and not come straight to me? I'm the law around these parts." His voice rose and his chest puffed up a bit at that declaration.

Clay handled the situation quite well, Regan thought to herself. He kept his voice level and didn't let Graves's pomposity bother him the least little bit.

"That was my question exactly," he said evenly. "But I don't think whoever it was left the note for me. You can see right there that it addresses Regan specifically. The only thing I can think is that whoever left this at the house saw Regan at the Updikes' the day after the accident and thought she would be close enough to the victim's family to look into this. That even if no one else believed him—whoever saw what really happened—Regan likely would. She's real trusting that way."

The sheriff considered Clay's words, studying the note for any clues. Regan wished she knew what it said, precisely, and how much it might incriminate her.

"Well, when you first came in here, I thought you'd been tipping back a few too many shots of rotgut. But I have to admit this message changes things." His ample gut jiggled as he sighed and pushed up from the desk. "I appreciate y'all comin' to me with this. I'll be sure to look into it." He folded the paper and slipped it into the pocket of his vest. "I'll talk to the folks over at the bank, see if anyone Nolan worked with knows anything. And the funeral is tomorrow, so I'll see if I can't have a word with Mrs. Updike about her husband's personal and business acquaintances."

He didn't seem eager for their assistance, and Clay remained surprisingly silent rather than mention the slight. Regan looked back and forth between the two men, unable to believe they were just going to leave it at that.

"Is there anything we can do to help, Sheriff?" she inquired. "Maybe we can ask around, too, see if Nolan had any enemies, or if anyone heard him having words with someone."

The sheriff's head was already rocking side to side in refusal. "No, thanks, Widow Doyle. I know Walker here is a Texas Ranger, but this is my town. I'll look into who could've left this note, as well as who might have had it in for Updike."

She started to protest. "But—"

Clay's hand clamped around her wrist to shush her, and Graves went on.

"I appreciate your concern, but let me get a jump on this first. If I need your help," he shot a look at Clay, "I know where to find you."

She wasn't sure she liked that idea, but Clay's grip on her arm tightened, so she held her tongue.

"Sounds good to me, Sheriff." Clay offered his hand politely, waiting for Jensen to shake. "I don't particularly want to get involved in this mess, anyway. I'm glad to hear you'll be taking charge of the matter."

Regan's eyes flashed wide. Well, now she was thoroughly confused. She thought they'd come to Sheriff Graves so they could all work together to find Nolan's killer—not to dump the affair in Jensen's lap and forget about it.

Once again, she wanted to say something. She wanted to dig in her heels and demand they get started—all of them. She wanted to ask Clay what he was about, abandoning the issue to a sheriff he didn't even like. But she didn't think a public spectacle would do her any good, so she thanked Jensen, bid him good day, and followed Clay out of the office into the bright noonday sun.

As soon as they were out of earshot of the jail, she grabbed Clay's sleeve and pulled him to a halt in the middle of the boardwalk. "What are we doing, leaving? Why didn't you insist Jensen let you work with him to find the murderer?"

He loosened her hold and placed his hand at the small of her back, urging her forward. "Keep moving," he said. "Talk while you walk so we don't attract attention."

She glanced around, not seeing anyone who would be the least bit interested in her conversation with Clay. But she let him spur her forward and kept her voice to an even keel while they spoke.

"I thought we were going to begin investigating this thing, looking for the killer. Why did you turn everything over to Sheriff Graves and just walk away? And what did that letter say? I didn't know anyone left a note at the house."

Clay tipped the brim of his hat as they passed a young woman carrying packages wrapped in brown paper and string from the mercantile. "They didn't."

Her feet turned to lead, freezing her in her tracks. "What do you mean?"

He nodded to another passerby and spurred her back into motion. "No one slipped that note under the door," he informed her in a low tone. "I wrote it myself this morning before we left for town."

Regan's legs threatened to seize up on her again, but Clay's hand at her spine kept her in step with him.

"It was all I could think of to keep your name from coming up," he continued. "We couldn't tell the sheriff you were the one who witnessed Updike's death, but he wouldn't have believed us if *someone* hadn't claimed to have been there."

"You did that? To protect me?" She was moved beyond measure by his thoughtfulness and nearly stopped walking again in order to thank him.

"For now," he responded. "We don't know exactly what's going on yet, and until we do, the less said about your involvement, the better."

That made sense. And even if it didn't, she was grateful to Clay for not turning the town against her any sooner than he had to. "Thank you," she offered quietly. "That means a lot to me. But what about finding out who killed Nolan? Are you really going to let Sheriff Graves investigate on his own? Don't get me wrong, I'm glad he's willing to help, but I thought we were all going to try to track down the killer. If not, then what are we going to do until Jensen finds the murderer?"

Clay paused then, turning to her with an over-wide smile, and she realized a woman staring at a shop window had heard her use the words "killer" and "murderer." She probably thought Clay and

Regan were up to no good, and hurried off before they could add her to their vile plans.

As the woman bustled away, Clay readjusted his Stetson and fixed Regan with a disgusted look. "One question at a time," he told her. "And keep your voice down. The people of Purgatory aren't exactly used to incidents of murder being discussed out in the open."

She nodded, knowing he was right.

"To keep from stepping on the toes of the local law, we told Graves what we think happened and he's agreed to look into it. He didn't seem to want our help, which is fine with me. I figure he can investigate his way and I'll investigate mine."

"Ooh, you've got a plan." She grinned and bounced on her heels, all but rubbing her hands together in anticipation. "What is it?"

They'd reached the end of the sidewalk where they'd left the buckboard, and Clay offered her a step up.

"I've been mulling this over, and I think I've come up with a pretty good suspect."

Regan paused in the act of straightening her skirts and stared at him, mouth and eyes wide in astonishment. "You have?" She'd been present the night Nolan had died, and even she didn't have a suspect in mind. "Who?"

His answer was short and quick, and turned her blood to ice.

"David."

Chapter Thirty

The wagon bounced beneath her along the rutted dirt road while Regan's mouth worked, but no sound came out.

David? *David?* How could Clay think such a thing? How had he even come to such an outrageous conclusion? Big or small, David would never hurt a living soul. He loved animals and was kind to the other children at the orphanage. He could be surly and distant at times, but that had more to do with his age and the emotions brought up by his Comanche bloodlines than with his true temperament. When David grew pensive, it usually had something to do with the way the townspeople treated him because of the color of his skin. Otherwise, he was an easygoing, fun-loving boy.

How could Clay think he had anything to do with Nolan's death?

They were almost home by the time Regan's vocal chords began to function again. "You're wrong," she said finally, the words harsh as they rasped past her raw throat.

He knew exactly what she was talking about. Had probably known what her reaction would be even before he'd bludgeoned her with the notion that David might be responsible for Nolan Updike's death.

Which he wasn't, no matter what Clay thought.

"I'm not so sure I am. He seems like a logical candidate to me."

"That's ridiculous. It's a wildly outrageous assumption, and it's *wrong*." Wrong, wrong, wrong.

He slanted an indulgent glance in her direction. "You have to admit he didn't sound too keen on Updike when he showed up on your doorstep the day after the man's death. Is it true Updike was David's father?"

A cool layer of perspiration broke out across her skin at his implication. She didn't know all the details concerning David's parentage, but she did know that he was the product of an early relationship Nolan had had with a woman from a nearby Comanche village. When she'd found herself in a family way and gone to Nolan for help, he'd turned her away without a backwards glance. And when she'd fallen ill soon after David's birth, she'd once again begged her son's father for help—to no avail.

It wasn't until after the woman's death that Nolan's conscience had apparently kicked in, and he'd located the child and dropped him off at the Purgatory Home for Unwanted Children.

Regan had always liked Nolan, but she hadn't respected him for the decisions he'd made in his youth, or for running from his responsibilities. In the end, however, he'd seen to it that baby David was taken care of, and that had to count for something.

"Nolan *was* David's real father," she admitted, carefully weighing her answer to Clay's question, "but they never had any contact with each other."

The buckboard rolled into the yard in front of the house and Clay reined the horses to a halt. "David knew who his father was, though, and from what I overheard, it didn't sound like he appreciated being abandoned as an infant."

"I don't suppose anyone would, but that doesn't make David a murderer. He's been well cared for at the orphanage. Probably better than he would have been if Nolan had taken him in and acknowledged him as his son. Possibly even better than if he'd returned to his people."

It was no secret that those who carried Indian blood were most often shunned by society. Even if Nolan had acknowledged David as his son and taken him in, David still would have been scorned for his mixed breeding. He wouldn't have been treated like just another of Nolan's children, but more like a servant. It was also possible that he'd have been treated just as badly had he returned to

326

his mother's village as a white man's by-blow.

"But maybe David doesn't know that," Clay persisted. "Maybe he has visions of living in that big, fancy house of Updike's, with his pretty wife and lily-white, *legitimate* children. Maybe he thinks he deserved better than he ended up with, and when he didn't get the reaction he expected after confronting his real father, he pushed him down the stairs."

She turned on the wagon seat to face Clay more fully, horror seeping through every limb of her body. "How can you think such a thing? He's a child. No matter how much he might have known about the circumstances of his birth . . . no matter how angry he might have been, he would never *kill* someone."

"I hope you're right," he said, but he looked at her as though she was having a hard time accepting the truth. As though he was absolutely certain of David's guilt, and she simply needed to come to terms with an unequivocal fact.

"You're wrong," she insisted for what felt like the hundredth time, pulling her skirts out of the way to climb down from the buckboard. Clay did the same at a less agitated pace, coming around to meet her.

"I heard the killer's voice, and it wasn't David's." But even as she said the words, she knew she couldn't be entirely sure it was the truth.

"Do you know whose voice it *was?*"

"Of course not," she snapped. "If I knew, then

we wouldn't be searching for a murderer, would we?"

"Then how can you be sure of whose voice it *wasn't?*"

"I know you don't like David," she said. "I know you think he's nothing more than a sullen, bad-mannered, half-breed orphan. But he's a *good boy,* and I'm telling you he didn't kill Nolan Updike."

She started to storm off, furious at Clay's accusations, but he stopped her by wrapping a firm hand around her arm.

"I meant what I said; I do hope you're right. I may not like the kid very much, but it won't set well to see a sixteen-year-old boy go to prison, either."

As hard as she tried, he wouldn't let her pull away until he'd had his say.

"This is all I have to go on, Regan. This is how you conduct an investigation. I'll talk to David, see what he has to say. And if something else comes up, I'll investigate that, as well. I don't want to put an innocent person in jail, but I also won't let a guilty one go free. All right?"

Although she still thought his suspicion of David was unwarranted, he sounded sincere and she wanted to believe him. She had to admit, too, that she was a bit overprotective of David. Perhaps she wasn't seeing his anger and resentment toward Nolan as clearly as Clay was. But she still didn't believe he'd *murdered* anyone.

Taking a deep breath, she tried to collect her bearings. She'd trusted Clay enough to let him make love to her, why shouldn't she trust him now? Besides, if he pressed too hard for David's arrest and incarceration, she could always testify in the boy's defense. After all, she'd been there, and she was positive—or almost positive, anyway—it wasn't David's voice she'd heard that night.

"I want you to be nice to him," she said after a moment. "Question him, but don't badger him. Give him the benefit of the doubt. And don't stop looking for the real killer, because I *know* David didn't do it."

Clay's grip on her arm loosened and he gave a quick dip of his head. "Sounds fair to me. As long as you don't interfere with my interrogation or try to protect him if it becomes clear he *did* kill Nolan Updike. Deal?"

Regan swallowed hard, feeling as though she was about to sign a pact with the devil—in blood. But what choice did she have?

She licked her dry lips and met Clay's gaze, silently begging him not to break her heart or destroy David's spirit. "Deal," she repeated, and prayed she wouldn't regret it.

That evening, David sat at the kitchen table, stuffing his face with sugar cookies, apple pie, and anything else Regan put in front of him, washing it all down with a big glass of fresh milk.

Regan was a hell of a cook, Clay had to admit, but he also knew that plying the boy with sweets was her way of softening the blow of Clay's impending questions about his father's death.

He didn't welcome the idea of interrogating a child—and David was still a child, regardless of his size and demeanor—but he was the first person to pop into Clay's mind when he'd considered who might have held a grudge toward Nolan Updike. And as with all of his cases, Clay would start with the obvious and dig until he reached the truth.

Pushing away from the wall where he'd been standing with his arms crossed over his chest, he took a seat at the table and watched David finish the last cookie on the plate. Clay tried to adopt a relaxed pose, not wanting to intimidate the boy.

"David," he began slowly, "I have a few questions to ask you. Do you mind?"

Although Clay still didn't think David liked or trusted him very much, he no longer turned immediately hostile the minute Clay spoke to him, looked at him, or even just walked into the room.

Now, the boy studied him warily, and Regan bustled over with another plate full of cookies straight from the oven. She ran her fingers through his hair, leaving her hand at the base of his neck in a gesture of support for what was to come. As always, her protective and motherly mannerisms grabbed Clay somewhere in the lower region of his midsection and wouldn't let go.

"What kind of questions?" David asked skeptically.

Clay came straight to the point, wanting to save the kid as much pain and upset as possible. "About your father."

He saw David's young body go rigid. "I don't have a father," he hissed.

Regan's fingers massaged David's shoulders as worry lines etched themselves around her mouth and eyes. "He knows Nolan Updike was your father, David."

The boy jumped up, pushing Regan away and nearly overturning his chair. "You told him?" he charged, his dark glare spitting fire as he backed away from them both.

"She didn't tell me," Clay replied calmly. "I heard some of what you said when you came by the other day. You don't have to worry, though, I don't plan on telling anyone."

"No one's supposed to know," David continued almost desperately. "I don't *want* anyone to know."

Clay saw the gloss of unshed tears in the boy's eyes as David struggled valiantly to hold them back. The strings of his heart gave a little tug. He wasn't developing a soft spot for the kid, he told himself. He just felt sorry for a homeless, now fatherless orphan, that was all.

"They don't have to. Not if things work out the way Regan and I are hoping."

David's eyes remained damp, but he didn't look to be fighting so hard against the impulse to cry. "What are you talking about?"

Regan took a step forward, keeping her tone soft as she tried to explain. "David, we don't think your father—Mr. Updike—died accidentally. We think someone might have . . . hurt him."

The boy's face went blank with amazement. "Really? Who?"

And just like that, Clay abandoned the notion that David killed Nolan Updike. The kid might be troubled, might harbor a boatload of anger toward the white man in general and his father in particular. But even a cynical lawman like himself doubted a sixteen-year-old, no matter how world-wise, could be that good an actor. David looked legitimately nonplussed . . . and fascinated by the idea that his father might have been murdered. Considering that the father wasn't a man David liked or respected, Clay figured those feelings were probably both typical and justified.

Breathing easier now that he knew he didn't have to bully a young orphan into confessing to murder, Clay shot a quelling glance at Regan, hoping she wouldn't ruin the rest of his inquiry just yet. He no longer believed David had anything to do with his father's death, but he still had some questions that needed to be answered.

"We don't know, David, that's why we wanted to talk to you. You seemed pretty worked up when you came to see Regan the day after Updike's death. It was obvious you didn't care for the man. Though I can't say I blame you a bit for that one, considering. But do you know of anyone else who might not have liked him? Did you hear anyone talking about him in town, maybe complaining about him or saying they'd like to see him come to some sort of harm?"

From the corner of his eye, he saw Regan studying him with a puzzled expression on her face. He'd obviously shocked her by his sudden shift from planning to accuse David to asking the kid for help with his investigation.

David stuck his hands in the rear pockets of his worn and dirty trousers, squinting as he thought over Clay's question. "I don't remember hearing nothin'," he said finally. "Everyone seemed to like the bastard." He glanced at Regan with chagrin, but a scowl tipped down his mouth nonetheless. "They didn't know what he was really like. They didn't know what he did to my mother and me."

Clay nodded sagely. "He fooled a lot of people," he agreed, thinking David needed the vindication of having someone else regard his father as less of a gentleman than the townspeople all seemed to believe he had been.

"Do you want another piece of pie?" he asked, ushering David back to the table and earning a smile of gratitude from Regan.

Without warning, he found himself reasoning that David wasn't such a bad kid, after all. Just an ordinary child who'd been dealt a lousy hand before he'd even been born. He thought he even understood Regan's fondness for the boy, given what he'd learned in the last few days.

His sudden revelation didn't bring him any closer to finding the real killer, though, and *that* was beginning to annoy the hell out of him.

Chapter Thirty-one

The afternoon after their confrontation with David, Regan, Martha, and Clay attended Nolan Updike's funeral. Afterwards, Jensen Graves was supposed to ask around about Nolan's acquaintances and anyone who might have liked to see him come to harm.

It made Clay antsy not to be in on those conversations, but he wanted to let Purgatory's sheriff take the lead in this investigation, so he kept a tight rein on his tongue and did nothing more than escort Regan and Martha to town and pay his last respects to a man he didn't even know.

Late the following afternoon, however, Clay could no longer keep a lid on his curiosity and decided to head into town.

"Where are you going?" Regan asked, when she saw him heading for the barn.

"I thought I'd see what the sheriff found out after the funeral yesterday."

"Oh, let me come along. I won't be but a minute." Regan began to loosen the apron tied around her waist, turning toward the kitchen where she'd been washing the breakfast dishes.

He caught her arm. "Not this time," he said gently, not wanting to hurt her feelings. "I thought I'd take Caesar, since he needs the exercise, anyway, and I have a feeling Sheriff Graves might open up about what he learned a little quicker if he's not in mixed company."

When she met his gaze, he saw that she wasn't so much hurt as peeved by his line of thinking.

She drew her mouth into a thin, flat line before replying. "Fine. Knowing Jensen Graves, you're probably right. If it weren't for that, though, I'd be coming with you even if it meant riding on Caesar's neck."

He had to chuckle at that. He wouldn't mind, but he imagined Caesar might have something to say about it. The piebald had never been keen on carrying two riders at the same time. Though for Regan, Clay supposed the gelding might just turn charitable in his old age.

"You will let me know what he says, won't you?" she asked anxiously, twisting one corner of her apron around her index finger. She was as eager to catch the murderer as he was.

"Sure." He snugged his hat on his head. "I won't be long."

Regan nodded and stood just inside the front

door while he walked to the barn to saddle Caesar. He pretended not to notice, but he could feel the heat of her gaze boring into his back the whole way. He was almost sorry to enter the barn and know Regan would likely go inside, back to her daily chores.

Caesar snorted a welcome the minute Clay unlatched the door to his stall.

"How ya doin', buddy?" he asked the faithful gelding. Caesar merely snuffled again and pummeled the ground a couple of times with his front hoof.

"Same here," he muttered, a frown pulling down the sides of his face. Taking Caesar's bridle from a nearby peg, he slipped it between the horse's large teeth, then led him out of the stall and into the center of the barn, not bothering to tether him while he went for the saddle.

"I think I'm in trouble, Caes. Real trouble." The horse stamped his hoof to shake off a fly, and Clay took it as an invitation to share his woes.

"It's Regan," he explained. With the saddle hanging from one hand, he arranged the blanket with the other, then lifted the heavy leather seat onto the gelding's back.

Caesar lowered his head and blew out, investigating the straw-strewn floor for bits of fallen hay. Clay had pretty much done nothing but talk about Regan since they'd arrived, so he didn't figure Caesar was surprised by his pronouncement. Tired maybe, but not surprised.

"You know what she did," he went on, giving

Caesar's belly a tap to expel air as he tightened the cinch strap. Once that was done, Clay led him out of the barn and tossed the reins over his head, getting ready to mount.

Try as he might, he couldn't keep his eyes from straying to the house, searching for a quick glimpse of Regan. But she'd gone back inside. The porch was empty, the front door closed.

Stepping into the saddle, he shifted for a comfortable position, then closed his legs around Caesar's sides, asking him to walk.

"She's a criminal, Caes. She robbed all those people and broke the law doing it. But damned if I don't still want her more than any woman I've ever met before."

Almost before Clay signaled him to, Caesar sped up to an easy trot and they were nearly to town before Clay spoke again.

"How am I going to live with myself after I send her to jail?" He was asking himself more than anything, but the horse's short, snorted retort summed up Clay's sentiments pretty darn well—he didn't have the faintest, foggiest notion. He wished to hell he did. Maybe then this sick, heavy churning in his gut would go away.

He brooded about it until they reached the main street of Purgatory, then he at least tried to tamp down the ugliness of his thoughts and focus on the matter at hand: A little thing called murder that *should* bother him more than a simple Irish beauty.

Sure. And maybe later, Caesar would sprout wings and fly him to the moon.

With a sigh, he pulled up in front of the sheriff's office and dismounted, looping Caesar's reins twice around the hitching post to keep him from wandering off. "This shouldn't take long, boy. I'll be back."

Caesar lifted his head, peeled back his floppy black-and-white lips, and gave three quick clicks of his teeth. It was the gelding's way of telling Clay he'd better bring a couple licks of sugar with him when he returned.

He found Graves reclining in his chair, hands linked over the rise of his stomach, boots crossed at his ankles, which were propped up on his desk. The man's eyes were shut and after every breath, a low whistle emitted from his open mouth.

Clay thought about giving a shout, or dropping a book to startle the man out of his midday nap. But he was supposed to be working *with* the sheriff, not against him, and staying on the man's good side probably wasn't such a terrible idea. So he cleared his throat and gave a light knock on the door panel.

Sheriff Graves startled awake, his feet slamming to the floor and his chair nearly tipping over from the sudden shift of weight.

"Afternoon, Sheriff. I hope I'm not bothering you."

Graves was obviously still half-asleep, but he blinked a few times and pushed to his feet. "Not at all, son, not at all. You're just the man I've been meaning to see."

A bolt of excitement kicked through Clay's system. The sheriff must have learned something from his inquiries after the funeral.

"I take it you found something out," he said, trying to appear calmer than he felt.

"Actually," the sheriff drawled, hitching his falling pants up an inch, "I wanted to tell you I think we're sniffing up a dead tree here, Walker. I talked to Widow Updike and some of their servants. Nolan's boss over at the bank, and most of the men he worked with. Even some of the other townspeople I know who were close to him. They all liked Updike just fine and didn't have a bad word to say about him. And none of them seemed to know of anyone who would." He gave a shake of his balding head. "I hate to say it, 'cause you and the Widow Doyle sounded pretty much convinced of Nolan being pushed down those stairs, but I just don't see there's any evidence that claims the same."

Clay's spirits sank. "Did you talk to everyone?" he asked. "Nobody knew of any reason Nolan might have been killed?"

"Well, I didn't come right out and say he had been, of course. I don't need that kind of rumor sweeping through town. But I spoke to all the right people and asked them some pretty leading questions. I think if they knew anything, or suspected anything, they'd have told me."

"Dammit," Clay snarled low in his throat.

"I'm real sorry you got worked up for nothing. Or maybe it was that young widow whose imagination ran away with her. Happens sometimes after a death like this," he said solemnly.

Clay might have had his doubts at first, too, but he believed Regan. Especially since he knew about her nocturnal activities, activities that had led her to be present when Nolan had been pushed down the stairs.

"Maybe we should talk to Updike's wife again. She might have been too upset after the funeral to be thinking straight."

Graves was already shaking his head. "She packed up and took the kids to her mother's over near Killeen. Even sent the help home till they get back. Guess it was too hard for her to stay in that house, what with Nolan dying right there in the hall and all."

Clay grit his teeth and tried not to sound annoyed. "So you're not going to investigate any further." It was a statement, because he already knew the answer.

"Don't see no reason to," Sheriff Graves replied. "Nolan's death was an accident, pure and simple. Thinking anything else will just be banging your head into a brick wall." He returned to his chair and rocked back a bit. "Sorry I can't be of more help."

Extending his arm, Clay shook Graves's hand. "That's all right, Sheriff, I understand. I appreciate you looking into it at all. I hope you won't mind me nosing around a bit more, though. Just to settle my own qualms about the situation."

The man's hand tensed around his, but he tilted his head and smiled. "I can't say as I think you'll find anything, but be my guest. Just don't go getting people riled. You hint at the word 'murder' and suddenly everybody's sitting on their front stoops with shotguns, blasting away at anything that moves."

"I'll be as discreet as possible."

The sheriff settled back in his seat, rapping his stout fingers on the arm of the chair. "Mind if I ask who you plan to talk to?" he asked.

"I'm not sure I'll speak to anyone just yet," Clay said, heading for the door. "I thought maybe I'd go over to the Updike house tomorrow for a quick look-see. As long as the family isn't there. I don't know that I'll find anything, but it can't hurt to have a peek around."

"Well, you let me know, you hear. Bring me some sort of evidence that Nolan didn't just fall and break his fool neck, and I'll be more than happy to help you figure out who done it."

Clay tipped his hat. "Thanks, Sheriff."

Graves waved him off and he made his way to Caesar. The gelding nudged him in the chest, rooting around for a treat, but Clay was too distracted to bother apologizing for his empty pockets. He vaulted into the saddle and turned toward home.

Since Sheriff Graves had already talked to most of Updike's friends, Clay didn't see the point of questioning them again. At least not yet. But he also didn't expect to discover much at the scene of the crime. If the killer had left anything behind, someone would surely have stumbled upon it by now.

His foul mood turned even darker as he realized they may never figure out who pushed a man—a

Heidi Betts

man with a wife and three small children—to his death. He didn't cotton to the idea of a bastard like that getting away.

The only thing he could think of, though, was to talk to Regan again and see if she could remember anything else about that night. If not, they might have no choice but to let a murderer run free.

Regan was on the porch, hands on hips, when he rode into the yard later that evening. Today she was wearing a calico print with tiny blue flowers running rampant over the material and puffs at the shoulders that made her look even taller than her naturally impressive stature. He still couldn't get used to seeing her outfitted in colorful dresses.

As soon as he drew close enough, she ran down the front steps and met him as he dismounted at the barn door. She looped her hand through Caesar's bridle and patted his warm nose.

"What did he say?" she asked breathlessly.

"Not much." He led Caesar around her and into the barn. "He talked to people after the funeral, but says they all spoke highly of Updike. No one seemed to wish him ill or know of anyone who did."

Her face fell. "You mean . . . he didn't find out anything? Nothing?"

"Nothing." He pulled the saddle off and let it rest on the floor as he wiped down Caesar. "He's stopped investigating."

"Stopped?" Her voice echoed his disillusionment.

And then her features hardened, revealing that streak of determination that ran through her a mile wide. "I know what I heard, Clay. Nolan Updike was murdered, and no matter what Sheriff Graves thinks, we have to find out who did it."

He opened the door to Caesar's stall and slapped his rump to move him inside. Then he filled the food trough and left the gelding chomping away merrily.

Turning back to Regan, he hooked his thumbs over the top of his gunbelt and said, "That's kind of what I thought."

Her brows rose. "You did?"

"Yep. Mrs. Updike closed up her house and went to visit her mother for awhile, so I reckoned we'd go over there tomorrow and have a look around."

A glow of anticipation lit her cheeks, but he was quick to stall her enthusiasm. "Don't go getting all excited," he warned. "I don't actually think we're going to find anything, I just can't think of anything else to do."

Though she nodded obediently, she was also grinning from ear to ear. And then she threw her arms around his neck and hugged him. "Thank you for believing me, Clay."

She leaned back a fraction, but was still plastered to his chest, her skirts swimming around his legs like swamp water. "Are you hungry?" she asked in the barest of murmurs. "I started fried chicken while you were gone."

Heat pooled in his groin, sending his temperature soaring. "What if I'm not hungry for chicken?"

Her eyes widened. "I can make something else, I suppose."

"What if I'm not hungry for food?" The words came out in a throbbing growl that matched the pounding of his blood.

A shadow of pain slipped across her mossy green eyes. "I thought you didn't want me anymore, now that you know what I did."

The reminder cooled his ardor a little, but not nearly enough to let her go. "I *always* want you," he said. "What you did is a separate issue."

"You'd be willing to make love to me even though I'm a criminal?"

She sounded perplexed. Hell, so was he. He wished he could explain it to her, but his nerves were a jumbled riot, with his conscience pulling him one way and his desire pulling him another.

At the moment, desire was winning.

"I'd be willing to make love to you if you were the one who pushed Nolan Updike down the stairs," he answered roughly. And then, irritated at himself, he added, "I suppose that bothers you."

Her tongue ran slowly over her bottom lip, drawing a moan from low in his throat.

"It doesn't bother me so much as it confuses me. But what baffles me most is that . . . I still want you, too," she finished on a hushed whisper.

He groaned and pulled her close, his arms wrapping around her waist like a vice. He didn't care why he craved her so strongly, or how much she'd stolen for the orphanage. Right now he wanted her, and if she was willing, there was no way in hell he'd push her away.

"Care to take a little trip to the loft?" he teased, pressing kisses to her soft skin that led ever closer to her delectable lips.

Her head fell back, exposing the creamy underside of her chin and neck. "My chicken will burn."

"Let it." He spread his legs wide enough to encompass her full skirts and began guiding them step by step toward the ladder.

"I make very good fried chicken," she argued. But with her hands climbing his back and her nipples budding beneath the thin fabric of her gown, it was nothing more than a token protest.

"Let Martha handle it." He hoped his aunt noticed the smell of something burning and took the pan off the stove before the house caught fire. Then again, as badly as he wanted Regan, they may be finished and back in the kitchen before Martha even knew they were missing.

Regan turned fluid, going almost limp in his embrace. "I guess you're right," she muttered, her fingers tugging the tails of his shirt out of his waistband. "She did say she wanted to try being more independent."

"Uh-huh."

"Clay?"

Her tone brought his head up and he stared into her passion-clouded eyes, his own hunger mirrored in the emerald green irises.

"Hm?" He barely managed to force the sound through his tight throat.

The corner of her mouth quirked up and he knew he was in trouble.

She turned away, her hand on the rail of the ladder leading to the loft. "Race you." And she was off.

But Clay was never more than one rung behind.

Chapter Thirty-two

She was back in Nolan and Veronica's bedroom, pressed to the wall as two men scuffled on the other side of the very door she was hiding behind.

You owe me.

I don't owe you anything.

I won't let you do this, Updike.

What are you doing? Get your hands off of me! Nooooo!

Regan shot forward like a bullet, inky darkness all around her. Her hands clawed at the bedclothes as she gasped for breath.

"Are you all right?" The mattress shifted as Clay sat up, rubbing small circles on her back to calm her.

She tried to answer, but the air lodged in her lungs.

The bed shifted again as Clay leaned away. Glass clinked and a match flared as he lit the lamp.

"It was just a nightmare," he comforted, brushing the hair away from her damp forehead and curling an arm about her shoulders.

She shook her head, still breathing hard. "It was real," she said. "It was that night. The night Nolan died."

"It's all right, it's over now." He pressed a kiss to her temple and tried to pull her down with him to go back to sleep.

"No. Clay . . . you don't understand." She threw back the covers, heedless of her nudity. The nightdress she'd worn earlier—and which Clay had wasted no time in stripping from her willing body—lay at the foot of the bed, but she dug into the bottom drawer of her wardrobe instead. For the black shirt and trousers Clay had made her take from her hiding spot at the base of the pecan tree. She dressed quickly, dragging the boots on over her otherwise bare feet.

"Where are you going?" Clay was fully awake now and reaching for his pants.

She whipped around, facing him for the first time. "He dropped something. The killer. He dropped something after he pushed Nolan down the stairs."

Clay narrowed his gaze. "Are you sure?"

She swallowed. "No, I'm not sure, but I think . . . maybe. In my dream, I heard something fall. Something light, just a small thud on the carpet in the hallway. I think maybe it wasn't so much a dream as . . . a memory."

"And I suppose we have to do this now," he grumbled, but he was already tucking in his shirt and strapping on his gunbelt.

She tied her hair back in a thick, bushy queue, then covered the redness with a black kerchief, just to be safe and more inconspicuous.

"We'll walk over to keep anyone from seeing the horses," she said as they sneaked down the hall and past Martha's closed door.

They went out through the kitchen and kept up a swift, steady pace through the trees and across several wide-open fields. They stayed off of the main road into town to avoid being spotted by possible passersby, even at this late hour. When they reached the Updikes' house, Regan paused to catch her breath, crouching next to a wide oak and leaning a shoulder against the rough bark.

Clay hunkered beside her, his breathing slow and even. "Now what?" he asked in a low voice.

Since Veronica had taken the children to visit her mother and let the servants have the week off, all the windows were dark. Regan studied her surroundings mostly out of habit and a keen sense of self-preservation.

"Everything looks quiet," she whispered. Then, with the crook of her wrist signaling him to follow, she said, "Let's go."

Silently, they crossed the span of the yard to the house and climbed the few mortar steps leading to the back door. Regan turned the handle and pushed, but the panel didn't budge.

She released a frustrated huff of air. "I was afraid

of this," she said, turning to face Clay. "They locked up before they left. We're going to have to find another way in."

One brow lifted as he studied her. "And just what do you suggest?"

With a grin, she tipped her head to the side and offered, "The window."

This time both brows shot up. "That's right, I almost forgot you've done this before," he said wryly.

A pang of guilt tightened her stomach muscles, but she pushed it away. "Come on."

Sneaking along the side of the house, she stopped beneath the same window she'd gone through the night Nolan had died.

"The last time I used this entrance I needed an overturned bucket from the barn to stand on, but I think you're tall enough to get in without it. Give me a boost?" she asked.

"I sure hope you know what you're doing," he muttered, linking his fingers together to form a makeshift step stool with his palms.

Resting a booted foot in the hollow of his hands, she gave him a small smile. "I've done this before, remember?"

"Hmph." He gave a snort of disapproval, but lifted her high enough to reach the sill.

With Clay balancing her from below, she clutched at the painted wood of the house and forced the glass upwards. Once the window was open all the way, she hefted arms and upper torso into the aperture. The hard wood cut into her diaphragm and shortened her breathing.

"Can you . . . help me a little more?" she called back to Clay.

Before his actions even registered in her shocked mind, he laid the palms of both hands on either side of her posterior and shoved. She gave a squeak of alarm as she flew the rest of the way through the window and tumbled to the floor.

When she turned back around, picking herself up and brushing herself off, Clay was hoisting himself through the opening. He got in as far as his waist, pausing to get a new, better foothold on the smooth boards siding the house.

Repaying his earlier favor, she grasped him under the arms and yanked with all her might, dragging him with a grunted thud into the room.

"Thanks a lot," he grumbled, rotating the shoulder he'd landed on and readjusting his holsters and guns.

She chuckled at his discomfort, then touched a finger to her lips. "Shh. You're not very good at this sneaking around, you know."

His gaze narrowed and locked on hers through the darkness. "I just haven't had as much practice as some people I could mention."

She met his stare evenly, her mouth quirking up in a grin. "True enough. So it would probably be a good idea for you to follow my lead. Now hush and come with me."

They moved to the door of the small bedroom and stepped into the hall.

"Why do we have to be so quiet if the house is empty?" he rasped next to her ear.

"You just do," she whispered back. "It's not right to break into someone's house and then traipse around as though you own the place. It's only respectful to keep your voice down when you're in another's home without being invited." Although they were doubtless both thinking it, neither of them mentioned that it was probably *more* respectful to not break into houses to begin with.

"This is the same way I came in that night," she continued in a low tone. "Through that window and this hallway." She motioned to a door on their left. "Nolan must have been in his office, talking with someone. I didn't hear their voices and I hadn't seen a carriage or mount out front before I came in. I tiptoed down this way," she said as they moved on and came to the base of the stairwell leading to the second floor.

"The struggle took place up there," she told him, pointing into the darkness. Her glance skittered unwillingly to the spot just below the steps where Nolan had died. "And that's where I heard it— whatever it was—fall. Just outside the master bedroom."

With his thumbs hooked over the band of his gunbelt, Clay sighed. "It could be anywhere by now. Let's get a couple of lamps lit and start looking around."

He dug into his front trouser pocket for matches and raised the glass globe of a lantern resting on a table at the foot of the stairs while she went into the other room for a second lamp. Once both were lighted and burning brightly, they began their search.

Regan got on her hands and knees, checking around the bottom of the steps for anything out of place while Clay made a careful perusal of each riser going up the stairs. The job was slow-going, but they kept at it, Regan trailing behind to re-examine the areas Clay had just checked as he moved toward the second story landing.

"That thing you heard drop," Clay's voice boomed through the otherwise silent house. "Could it have been, say, a coin?"

Still searching the steps, Regan straightened and lifted her head to see what he was holding. She knew what he was thinking: that while the coin he'd found *could* be a memento accidentally left behind by the killer, it could just as easily belong to Nolan or Veronica or one of the children and have been dropped and forgotten long before the night of Nolan's death.

He stood just outside the closed doorway to the master bedroom, right where Nolan and his attacker had grappled. Right where she had heard whatever it was bounce on the carpeted floor.

Hurrying to his side, she set her lamp on a hall table with Clay's and took the coin. She held it up to the light, studying the golden disk more closely . . . and gasped as recognition struck. "Oh, my God!"

Just then, they heard a noise. The squeak of a floorboard below, followed by the distinct click of a pistol hammer being cocked. A figure moved up the stairs, but even as Clay reached for his sidearm, the intruder stepped into view.

"Ah, ah, ah," he warned, waving his revolver between the two of them. "Don't even think about it, Ranger. I got no qualms about blowing the little lady straight to kingdom come. It would serve her right, damn busybody."

The gun settled on her, and Clay's hands fell away from his own revolvers.

"Jensen." Regan's eyes went to the gold piece still clasped between her thumb and forefinger. The same coin she'd seen the sheriff toy with a hundred times in the past.

"It was you," she breathed, suddenly putting it all together and coming to a conclusion that turned her blood cold. "The night Nolan died, you're the one he argued with. You're the one who pushed him down the stairs."

The sheriff's glare narrowed on her. "How do you know that?" he barked. And then his brow lifted as he took in her attire, from her boots and men's pants to the black kerchief hiding her hair. He chuckled, his numerous chins trembling with amusement. "I'll be damned. So it was you all the time, eh? Nice work, I must say. No one would ever suspect Purgatory's favorite, kind-hearted widow woman of breaking into houses in her spare time, now would they?" His tone deepened and his dull brown eyes grew sharp. "Same as no one ever suspected Updike of robbing the town blind."

"What are you talking about?" Regan asked,

aware that Clay stood tense beside her, letting her draw Jensen out, learn as much as she could. But despite his quiet demeanor, she knew he was merely biding his time, waiting for the moment when he could get the drop on Sheriff Graves.

"That's right," the sheriff went on, coming up another step. "No one ever suspected their good ol' friendly banker, Nolan Updike, of stealing from his friends, but that's exactly what he was doing. Skimming money off the top of their accounts, and no one was ever the wiser." A sinister grin crossed his sallow face. "I figured it out, though. And that's when me and Nolan became partners of a sort."

Busy focusing on his own furious tirade, Graves never noticed when Clay slowly reached over and took the coin from her tight grip. She didn't dare take her gaze off the sheriff, but she trusted that Clay knew what he was doing.

Jensen's grin turned to a sneer, his words to an angry hiss. " 'Til the bastard decided to back out of our deal. That's why I came here that night. He wanted to stop taking money—stop paying me, the sidewinding son of a bitch. No way was I going to let him get away with that."

"So you came here to confront him. Without anyone knowing, of course, even his wife. And when he wouldn't listen, you killed him."

"It's too bad you figured that one out," he said coldly. "And worse yet that you involved a Ranger. If I'd gotten here a bit quicker and found that coin before you all, you'd never have been the wiser. Nolan was no great loss; people would have gotten over his death soon enough. But now I'm going to have to kill the both of you, and that will be a bit harder to explain. Guess I'll just have to say that when I came around to check on things for the Widow Updike, I found a couple of thieves looting the place. That little get-up of yours sure will help," he added, jerking the gun up and down to indicate her black clothing. "True enough, no one ever would have thought you and Martha Doyle's nephew was the ones behind the robberies all these months, but they'll surely think I'm a hero for catching you at it. Too bad I won't be able to take you in alive."

The barrel of Jensen's gun shifted slightly, now aimed straight at Regan's heart.

Clay raised his hand, the one holding the coin, and shouted, "Catch!"

The sheriff's eyes followed the coin as it sailed through the air and in one lightning-fast move, Clay shoved Regan face-first against the closed bedroom door and whipped out both Colts.

Two shots rang out, nearly shattering her eardrums. Spinning back around, she raced to Clay, running her hands and gaze over his tall frame in search of bullet holes. When she found no marks or blooming spots of blood, she looked instead in Jensen's direction.

He stood unsteadily in the stairwell, blood dripping from his now weaponless hand as it pressed to an equally oozing wound in his shoulder. His gun lay at the bottom of the stairs, spun away by Clay's first, disabling shot.

Clay's bead on Graves never faltered. He returned one gun to its holster, the hammer cocked and his finger on the trigger of the other. His free arm wrapped around Regan's waist, pulling her close to his side.

From somewhere behind the sheriff, they all heard a scuff of footfalls. And then a form appeared out of the darkness. For the second time that night, Regan gasped in shock.

"Mother Doyle!"

"Jensen Graves, you ought to be ashamed of yourself!" her mother-in-law chastised, completely ignoring Regan's outburst.

The sheriff whirled around to identify his latest accuser, but his massive weight and fresh bullet wounds worked against him, causing him to lose his balance. For a moment, he swayed, his arms flailing for a handhold. But his boot heel had already slipped off the edge of the step. With a desperate cry, he fell backwards, giving a great thump as he hit the hard ridges of the steps with his back and clunked his way down the stairs.

He came to rest at Mother Doyle's feet, his head and shoulders crooked awkwardly on the carpeted landing, his legs still canted upwards, hooked on the stairs.

Martha bustled forward, kneeling beside the body to check his pulse and breathing. "Well, that's all He wrote for Jensen Graves, God rest his miserable soul."

Chapter Thirty-three

At Martha's announcement, Regan lifted her head and slipped out of Clay's arms to hurry down the stairs.

"Mother Doyle, what are you doing?" She ignored the prone figure lying lifeless on the polished floor and rushed to her mother-in-law's side. She was down on one knee with her hands on Martha's shoulders. "What are you doing out of your invalid chair?" And then she sat back, her eyes going wide. "How did you even *get* here?"

The steps creaked behind them as Clay made his way downstairs. He checked the sheriff's condition himself, then drew two fingers over the man's face to shut off his sightless stare.

"That's a good question," he said, stepping around the body and cupping a hand under his aunt's elbow to help her to her feet. "What *are* you doing here, Aunt Martha?"

Color seeped to the surface of Martha's thin, wrinkled skin. "Well, now, I was afraid you'd be asking me that," she muttered nervously, twisting the material of her long skirt between her gnarled fingers. "I rode over on Caesar," she admitted. "Followed you, actually. I knew you were up to something and wanted to know what the devil was going on. You've got a fine horse, there, Clayton, but it took the poor thing a while to get used to having me on his back."

She took a deep breath before going on. "You see, my dears, the truth is that I don't need my chair nearly as much as I've led everyone to believe. Don't get me wrong, these old bones aren't as strong as they used to be. I tire easily, and after a while my legs and back can begin to ache. My hearing and eyesight could certainly be better, and sometimes when I'm up too long or try to do too much, I have trouble catching my breath."

She turned to face Regan straight on and grasped her wrist. "When James died, I had that bad spell, remember, dear?"

Regan inclined her head stiffly, stunned by Martha's sudden appearance out of her chair, her confession to not needing the chair at all . . . by *everything* that had happened here this evening. She felt as though the world had turned upside down and she had no dependable grasp on reality any longer.

"That's when Doc Abernathy recommended I order a wheeled chair and use it until I felt a mite better. And you were so good to me back then," she added, her voice warming as she gave Regan's arm a squeeze.

Regan saw her mother-in-law's eyes mist and felt a lump form in her own throat.

"I guess," Martha continued, "I was afraid that if I recovered fully, you would leave me. You know," she said with a rueful smile, "go on with your life, move away, marry again. And I thought—in my feeble old mind—that if I remained incapacitated, you might stay. Even if you did get married again, I figured if I was stuck in my wheeled chair, you and your husband would take care of me."

Martha took a deep breath, drawing herself up and seeming to regain her strength both physically and emotionally. "That was, until I found out what was going on with you and Clayton, here."

Martha shot a glance in her nephew's direction while Regan's head whipped around, her face flaming as she and Clay exchanged looks.

"Not that," Martha admonished, flapping a hand through the air in dismissal. "What the two of you do in the privacy of your rooms . . . or in the barn . . . or in the woods out back of this house . . . is none of my concern."

Regan's face colored with embarrassment and a strangled sound gurgled in her throat as she realized Martha knew of just about every single one of her encounters with Clay. Mortification coursed through her veins, followed shortly by irritation that Martha, apparently not bound to her invalid chair as they'd all believed, had been keeping such a close eye on her.

"Actually, it is," Martha continued. "I've been pining for the two of you to get together, and it does my heart good to know you had the sense to do so."

She gave Clay a light smack on the back of his head, mussing his hair and causing him to duck away from further abuse. "Especially you, young man. For being smart enough to track down criminals for the Texas Rangers, I sometimes wonder if there's anything but un-ginned cotton between your ears."

Clay didn't know whether to glower or gape at his aunt's declaration. He didn't particularly appreciate being slapped upside the head, either, he thought, rubbing the ill-treated nape of his neck.

On the other side of Martha, Regan stifled a giggle and he decided to glower.

"How could you even for a minute consider turning in our dear, sweet Regan?" his aunt railed at him. "If you were a few years younger, I'd take you over my knee. As it is, I'm thinking about finding me a nice switch and tanning your hide."

His eyes went wide. Her threat—empty as it might be—bothered him, but not as much as the apparent fact that Martha had been aware of her daughter-in-law's exploits all along. "You knew?" he charged, dumbfounded. "And you let her get away with it?"

"No, I didn't know," Martha responded

brusquely, tugging at the hem of her bodice. "Not until I overheard your conversation the other night in the kitchen. If I had known, I wouldn't have asked you to come to Purgatory. I would never do anything to jeopardize Regan's freedom or safety."

He looked at Regan, taking in her pale face, framed by dainty copper corkscrew curls that had escaped her hair covering. Even though his heart seized, he uttered the words his position as a Ranger demanded. The ones that had been a part of his upbringing and principles since he was boy.

"She's a *criminal*, Aunt Martha. She broke the law. Robbed your neighbors."

He'd said the same thing to Regan not four nights before, but this time he couldn't meet her gaze. *He* was beginning to feel guilty just for thinking *she* was guilty.

Dammit, why did he have to go and fall for a lady thief? A dull, schoolmarm type never would have given him this much grief.

"He's right, Mother Doyle," she defended him softly. "What I did was wrong, regardless of my intentions. I have to be punished for that."

"Oh, balderdash!" Martha exclaimed. "What you did wasn't the smartest thing in the world, I admit." She turned back to Clay. "And you're right that the law was broken, but she did it with a pure, well-meaning heart. She deserves credit for that, at least."

She reached out and patted Regan's arm. "You won't be doing it anymore, correct?"

Regan nodded, her gaze locking with his rather than his aunt's. "Absolutely. I've learned my lesson, believe me."

"It wouldn't hurt you to ask for help once in awhile, young lady," she chastised. "If the orphanage or anyone else needs help, we'll find some other way to meet their needs, is that understood?"

"Yes, ma'am." Once again, Regan dipped her head earnestly.

Satisfied with Regan's answer, Martha turned on him. She grabbed his ear and gave a twist.

"*Ow!*" he yelped, clenching his teeth against the dull stab of pain.

"And you, young man, need to give this situation a little more thought. You're a lawman. I can respect that. But I also suspect you're well and truly in love with Regan, and threatening incarceration is no way to treat your future wife and the mother of your children."

Though her tone softened, she didn't let go of his ear. "You need to ask yourself what's more important, Clayton: love or duty. If you choose duty, then there's just no hope for you," she muttered with distaste. "But if you really consider your options, I think you'll find that you'll be much happier living in love than bedding down with your righteousness every night. Think about it," she ordered again, finally releasing his ear.

"Jesus, Aunt Martha!" he swore, trying to work sensation back into his throbbing appendage.

She slapped him again, this time on the back.

"And don't use the Lord's name in vain," she scolded.

Giving the dust a moment to settle, they all stood quietly, looking at the body of the sheriff.

"What are we going to do with him?" Regan asked after a minute, breaking the eerie silence. "I mean, he's the sheriff, so we can't exactly *go* to the sheriff to report his crimes or death."

"Does he have a deputy?" Clay asked.

"Not so that you'd know it," Martha answered. "Young Edmund from the livery helped him out once in a while, but Eddie is a few turnips shy of a garden. Jensen never would have given him any more responsibility than rounding up harmless drunks on a Saturday night." She tilted her head to the side and smiled at Clay. "I'd say you're the closest thing to a sheriff we've got in this town at the moment, dear. And you're a Ranger, so people will trust you, believe me."

Clay frowned, playing out the different outcomes of this situation in his head. "I don't know how happy the people of Purgatory will be when they hear I killed their sheriff. They're likely to string me up for murder."

"It wasn't murder."

Regan moved to his side, clutching his sleeve and staring at him with those sad, emerald eyes. This was the second time tonight she'd jumped to his defense. It made him feel about as deserving as a dung pile, given the voice in his head that kept telling him to take her to jail.

"He was going to shoot us," she reminded him.

"You saved both our lives. Besides, your shots only wounded him, they didn't kill him. It was the fall that did that."

Taking a deep breath, she seemed to dip into that bottomless well of strength she possessed. "We'll tell them the truth. That I was here the night Nolan died—and why—and that I knew his fall wasn't an accident. I asked for your help in finding out who pushed him, and that's what brought us back here tonight."

"Nonsense." Martha bustled over to them, hands on hips. "You're not going to go telling everyone you've been robbing houses. There's no need for them to know that." She looked pointedly at Clay. "Not yet, at any rate.

"Clayton," she continued, "you take Caesar home and bring the buckboard over here. Jensen's mount is out front, so when you get back, Regan and I will help you load the body onto his horse. We'll take the wagon home and get Regan changed into something a bit more appropriate while you take the sheriff into town."

With a hand wrapped viselike around his wrist, she dragged him to the door and out onto the front porch.

"And what am I supposed to tell everybody, exactly? They're bound to ask questions when I ride down the street with their sheriff tied to his saddle."

"Don't you worry about that just yet," his aunt told him. "We'll figure that out when the time comes. Now, go," she said, giving him a push toward Caesar. "The sooner we get Regan home and out of these clothes, the better off she'll be. Go, go, go."

Clay followed his aunt's instructions, lifting a booted foot into the stirrup while he wondered when the hell the Rangers had put a seventy-year-old woman in charge.

By the time Clay returned from town, Regan had all but worn a strip off the front parlor floor. She'd been pacing back and forth, back and forth, ever since she and Mother Doyle had gotten home several hours ago.

Mother Doyle insisted she change from her shirt and trousers to a nightdress and wrap so she would look as though she'd been home all evening—if anyone happened to ask or drop by. Soon after, however, Martha had pleaded exhaustion and gone off to bed, leaving Regan wide awake and as jumpy as a rabbit in a rattlesnake pit.

Where was Clay? What was taking so long? Had he told the townspeople the truth—about her secret identity, and how she had witnessed Nolan's murder—or had he made up a slightly different story to protect her?

She honestly didn't know which to hope for. She certainly didn't want to spend the rest of her life in prison, but neither did she want Clay to have to lie. Telling untruths went against everything he believed in, and his honor was one of the things she loved most about him. She didn't want him to betray his integrity just for her.

The sun was rising on the horizon, casting thin

rays of light over the land and turning the sky stunning hues of violet and orange, when the clip-clop of hoofbeats met her straining ears.

Racing to the front of the house, she threw open the door and ran to the edge of the porch. Clay rode into the yard, both man and mount looking sleepy and drained. He didn't glance her way, but disappeared into the barn to settle Caesar.

Regan hurried down the steps and across the yard, following him inside. "Clay," she breathed.

Caesar was already in his stall, Clay loosening the straps of the saddle and lifting the heavy leather from the horse's back. He carried it out of the stall and set it near an empty stall door without looking at or in any way acknowledging her presence.

"Clay," she said again, moving closer. A draft of dread blew through her. Something was wrong. Very wrong, judging by his strange behavior. "Clay, what is it? What happened in town?"

Still refusing to make eye contact, he went about getting fresh hay and water and rubbing down Caesar. "There weren't many people around when I rode in, so I took the body to the doc's office. Told him what happened and left it at that. I'll have to go back in tomorrow," he said without inflection. "Things probably won't be settled for a while."

"But . . . that's good, isn't it?" she asked slowly. "Doctor Abernathy believed you, I'm sure everyone else will, too. It's over then," she said hopefully. "Everything will be fine now."

Latching the bolt on Caesar's stall, he let his gaze sweep over her, then quickly moved past her and

Heidi Betts

out of the barn. He waited for her to catch up, sliding the big door closed behind them, then he started for the house.

"Everything will be fine," he said, but Regan couldn't bring herself to believe it. Something was terribly, terribly wrong, and he wouldn't tell her what. Worse, she had the feeling it had nothing to do with Sheriff Graves's death and everything to do with their relationship.

They reached the house and Clay headed upstairs without a word. She stopped at the bottom of the steps, her nails digging into the carved newel post as she wracked her brain for words that would halt his ascent, that would draw him back and make him take her into his arms the way she'd been imagining for hours.

"Clay," she called after him, softly so as not to sound too desperate or wake Mother Doyle.

He stopped at the entrance to his room, glancing at her for half a second before turning back to the closed door. "I'm tired, Regan. I'm going to bed. Goodnight."

Stepping inside, he closed the door behind him, and Regan's heart shattered. A million sharp, jagged pieces fell to the floor at her feet, along with her tears.

Chapter Thirty-four

For Regan, the next few weeks passed in a blur. Much of that time she spent alone—because she was such bad company that no one wanted to be around her. She slept late into the day and cried herself to sleep each night. She went into town to see how the rebuilding of the orphanage was coming along, but Father Ignacio had sent her home after only an hour because the children kept asking him if she was dying and of what.

Now, she spent most of her time in the house, pretending to read or embroider or clean, but not really doing any of those things. And worst of all, if she and Clay saw each other at all during the day, they acted as though the other didn't exist. He ignored her completely, except when Mother Doyle made a point of trying to draw them together. Regan thought she would prefer his yelling at her, or telling her how disappointed he was, over this display of indifference that drove her absolutely batty.

Thanks to the story Clay and Mother Doyle— mostly Mother Doyle—had concocted, the whole town knew exactly what had happened to the sheriff that night at the Updikes' house, with no mention of Regan's role as the Ghost of Ol' Morty Pike. They knew about Nolan Updike's embezzlement of bank funds, as well as Jensen's part in the swindling, and everyone believed that by catching the sheriff in the act of covering up the murder he'd committed, Clay had accomplished exactly what he'd been sent to Purgatory to do. He was a hero.

A hero who refused to speak to her. Even after he'd gone home to Sweetwater for a few days to take care of some business and returned to wrap up the sheriff's death.

The night Sheriff Graves had been shot Aunt Martha had told Clay to choose between duty and love. He had chosen duty. Maybe he had never loved her. And it was that thought which broke Regan's heart.

Well, enough was enough. She'd spent too much time already agonizing over Clayton Walker. She'd sobbed so long and hard, she'd awakened this morning nauseous, completely emptying her stomach before the sick feeling passed.

But now she felt better . . . determined to stop mooning over a man who obviously didn't want her and regain some control in her life. With that in mind, she twisted her hair into a bun at the nape of her neck and smoothed the lacy front of her pale peach shirtwaist over the darker gabardine of her skirt. She attached dangling pearl earbobs and a matching necklace, then made her way downstairs.

Mother Doyle buzzed around the kitchen, moving platters and trays from counter to table, and taking even more baked goods from the oven. Ever since she'd confessed to not needing her invalid chair, she'd been catching up on all the things she'd missed these past few years. Cooking and baking seemed to be her favorites. Every day, she prepared three full meals for Clay, Regan, and herself, and when she wasn't busy with that, she baked cookies, cakes, and pastries for neighbors and the children at the Home.

The townspeople considered Martha's sudden recovery a miracle the likes of Moses parting the Red Sea and sometimes stopped by the house just to lay hands on one who had been touched by the Lord.

"Regan," her mother-in-law exclaimed when she turned and saw her standing in the doorway. "Good morning, dear. How are you feeling?"

"Very well, thank you," she answered, even though it wasn't entirely true. She still felt a bit queasy and cursed Clay for that, among other things. "Do you need any help?"

"Not a stitch, my dear. I'm just taking the last batch of cookies out of the oven and getting them ready to run over to the church. We're selling them, you know." She shot Regan a sly, sidelong glance. "With the Ghost of Ol' Morty Pike apparently having gone to ground, the orphanage needs extra funds for the repairs to the roof and such. A few of us got together and decided to raise the money with our baking skills. We're going to set up outside the saloon and church and sell cookies to all those men without wives of their own to cook for them."

Martha grinned. "Where there's a will, there's a way, my dear. We're even thinking about holding a potpie dinner. There are plenty of men in Purgatory who would pay for a nice, home-cooked meal. And women who would love not having to cook for one night, I'm sure."

Regan's eyes filled with tears—as they were much too wont to these days. "That's wonderful, Mother Doyle. I'm so proud of you. Of everyone. If people had been this generous in the first place, I never would have had to resort to stealing at all."

Her voice cracked on the last, and Martha bustled forward to envelop Regan in her wide, warm embrace.

"Before the roof collapsed on the orphanage no one realized how needy the Home was. But once they did, they were more than happy to pitch in. I also think they felt a little guilty for not having spotted the problem sooner." She brushed a damp tear track from Regan's cheek. "Are you all right, dear?"

"I'm sorry," Regan apologized, wiping at her running eyes and nose. "I don't know what's wrong with me lately. I cry at every little thing."

"Well, you may want to count backwards and see just when your last woman's time was," Martha said almost off-handedly, and then rushed right on.

"But really, we should all be thanking you. You took the initiative to provide for the orphans in any way necessary, while the rest of us never gave them much thought. Granted, you chose a rather less-than-law-abiding way to support them, but the significance of your actions was there. I haven't said a word to anyone, of course . . . we can never let them know it was you taking their jewels and such . . . but following your inspiration and using a few well-placed kernels of culpability, I've managed to convince the women of this town that we need to be doing more for our community. And the women will make sure their men are equally involved. We're even talking about building a library," she confided with excitement.

At a loss for words, Regan merely nodded, gave Mother Doyle another hug, and sneaked a cookie from one of the plates on the table before heading out back to her garden.

The poor flowers and vegetables were wilting away. She hadn't bothered to water them in weeks, and all of the once-green plants were turning brown, bending toward the ground in a sad assertion of her inattentiveness this past month. But even now, she couldn't bring herself to walk down to the pump and fill a bucket to rescue the desperate vegetation.

What had her mother-in-law meant when she'd suggested Regan count back to her last woman's time?

She wandered around the other side of the house,

along all the beds of Mother Doyle's flowers also shriveling in the hot Texas sun.

Her fluxes had always come like clockwork, so she was confident that wasn't the root of her problems.

Of course . . . Sheriff Graves had died three weeks ago. Clay had come to town a month before that. Which meant she was due . . . Good lord, she'd *been* due. Quite a while ago, in fact.

But it was impossible. She'd been married to James for five years and never been so much as a day late. How probable was it that a few weeks with Clay would result in anything more than a broken heart?

That, she had in spades, thanks to an insensitive Texas Ranger and his rock-solid principles. Which was likely the cause of her body feeling so sluggish and her emotions being so near the surface these days. Wasn't it?

But if she was in a family way . . . oh, lord, a baby. She'd always wanted children; had been so very heartbroken when it had become clear she couldn't have any of her own. And now . . . now, maybe she could. The thought raised her spirits and she began to think that even if Clay never spoke to her again, never returned, she would still have a tiny piece of him to carry with her the rest of her life. Even if he left, he had already given her the most wonderful gift possible—a child to call her own.

She rounded the corner and headed into the shade of a tall oak bordering the barn, thinking she might walk down to the stream less than a mile away, pick some wildflowers to decorate Martha's dinner table tonight.

The minute she raised her head, she saw him. He was making his way from the barn to the house, but stopped dead when he spotted her. For a moment, neither of them moved. They just stood there, gazes locked, her pulse, at least, beating out of control.

And then he changed directions slightly and headed straight for her.

She thought about running. Back to the house, toward the stream, maybe up the tree at her back. Anything to avoid speaking to him. She thought about raising her chin, turning on her heel, and haughtily marching off to let him know just how little she cared to see him.

But in the end, her feet remained rooted to the spot, her muscles tense. If a stiff wind whipped up, she feared her body might snap in two.

As Clay came closer, he swept off his Stetson and ran a splayed hand through his inky black hair. She tried not to notice. Tried not to care. Tried not to remember the feel of his hands on her body.

He stopped in front of her, leaving only a few inches of breathing room between them. Not nearly enough space for Regan's comfort.

"I've been meaning to talk with you," Clay said, tapping the brim of his hat against his denim-clad thigh.

He paused, waiting for some response from Regan. She stood starch-still and ramrod-straight in front of him, her green eyes locked on his, her dusty pink lips pulled in a moue of annoyance.

She had every right to be angry with him, he supposed. They hadn't spoken to each other in close to a month, which was almost entirely his fault. He'd been bouncing back and forth between emotions, trying to figure out what to do about her, her stint as a thief, about Sheriff Graves's death . . . And once he had figured it out—at least he thought he had—it'd taken him another couple of weeks to decide how to say what needed to be said.

Even now, he wasn't quite sure he was ready to just spit it out, but he couldn't think of any more excuses to avoid her. And, he admitted, he was afraid that if he dodged her much longer, she might never forgive him. Which would pretty much ruin the plans it had taken him a full month to map out.

"I don't know if you've heard," he went on, "but they offered me the position of sheriff if I want it."

A dainty auburn brow lifted toward her hairline. He waited for her to say something.

And waited.

And waited.

Her silence grating on his nerves, he began babbling. "I was pretty surprised myself," he told her. "After all that worry about how to explain Graves's death, they not only believed he and Updike had been skimming money from bank patrons, but they offered me his job." He let out a strained chuckle. "The people in this town are far too trusting, if you ask me."

When she still didn't reply, he found himself

stretching for topics of conversation. Anything to keep her in front of him and maybe lead up to what he'd come here to say in the first place. And then he thought . . . why not get right to the point? Tell her what was on his mind and let the cards fall where they may. Even if she slapped his face and told him to go to the devil, she couldn't be any colder toward him than she was at this very moment.

He stopped worrying his hat against his leg and stuffed the Stetson back onto his head, tamping it down tight. "Listen, Regan," he said shortly, "the reason I told you about the offer to take over as sheriff of Purgatory is that . . ." He stuffed his thumbs into his pants pockets. "Well, because I was thinking about sticking around. Turning in my Ranger badge and settling down here."

Oh, God, this couldn't be happening. Regan had bitten down on her tongue, keeping her body rigid and her emotions in check while he'd been talking. But now her nerves were screeching in agony, her mind shrieking in denial.

How could he *stay?* God in heaven, she would never survive. Bad enough she'd had to see him almost every day this past month, both loving him and hating him at the same time; never wanting to be near him again and yet craving his touch; wishing he would disappear, but not sure what she would do if he did.

And now he was telling her that he intended to stay in Purgatory, put down stakes, and live within walking distance of her every day for the rest of her life.

Well, that was easy enough to remedy, she thought with no small amount of bitterness. She would simply have to either die or move away. And while neither of those solutions seemed ideal, there was no way she could continue to live so close to him. Not if what she'd started to suspect turned out to be true.

Clay shifted, cocking one hip and then the other in front of her. "Aren't you going to say anything?"

"I would rather you didn't." The words squeaked out before she'd even thought them through.

He frowned. "Didn't what? Say anything?"

Of course, now that she'd gotten wet, she might as well jump in with both feet. "Stay. I'd rather you didn't stay. You're a Ranger, Clay, not a small-town sheriff. Go back to Sweetwater and be a Ranger." With her skirts bunched in her closed fists, she turned toward the barn and stalked away.

"Regan. Damn it to hell," she heard him mutter. And then he was beside her. "Hold up a minute," he said, taking hold of her arm. "If you don't stop walking away from me, I swear to God I'm going to nail your shoes to the ground."

She turned back to face him, chin high, mouth held firm. She would let him have his say, if she must, and then she would go on with her life as though he'd never been a part of it.

"I don't want to argue with you, Regan. And I sure as hell don't want to go chasing you all over creation just so I can tell you what's on my mind."

Pulling away from his grasp, she crossed her arms beneath her breasts and faced him full-on. "Fine. I'm listening. But be quick about it. I have a lot to do today."

One side of Clay's mouth spasmed into a half-smile. "Did anyone ever tell you you're as stubborn as a two-headed mule? Must be that Irish temper."

Then he muttered, "Maybe this will get your attention," and pulled her flush with his frame, wrapping his arms around her as his mouth swooped down on hers.

Chapter Thirty-five

The kiss was long and deep and as warm as she remembered. So comforting that she leaned into it rather than pulling back the way her brain told her she should. She kept her hands to herself, fighting the urge to flatten them against Clay's broad, solid chest.

He lifted his head and she stared up at him, slightly dazed. Oh, yes, it would be easy to get over this man. And maybe tomorrow when she woke up, the sky would be green and the grass would be blue.

"Now that your sharp tongue is sheathed," he told her, slightly out of breath himself, "maybe I can finish what I started."

Regan wished he would. Maybe then she could go back into the house and work to return feeling to her lips.

"I've been thinking about things these past few weeks. The burglaries you committed and how I felt about them, the time we spent together before I found out. And then this offer to take over as sheriff came up, and I had to consider that, too. Mostly, I kept coming back to what Aunt Martha said about deciding between love and duty."

He sighed on an exhalation of air. "The long and the short of it is, I love you, Regan. I don't care anymore what you stole or why. Especially since you don't plan to do it again, thank God.

"That's why I went to Sweetwater last week," he confessed. "I turned in my badge. Told them I'd gotten a better offer." He shot her an uncertain, lopsided grin. "The question is: Have I got a better offer here in Purgatory? Or should I head back to Sweetwater and beg the Rangers for my old job?"

Regan stared at him, her mouth open in incredulity. Her heart was pounding, the blood rushing in her ears. Had he said what she thought he'd said? No, it couldn't be. She was hearing things. Because she wanted so much for him to love her, she'd created a situation in her head and was now imagining it to actually be happening.

"Regan?" His voice reached her from very far away. "Aren't you going to say anything?"

To test reality, she reached out and pinched him.

"Ouch!" He scowled and rubbed at the spot on his arm. "What was that for?"

All right, so this was real, she thought numbly, ignoring his question altogether. "Could you . . . start over? I don't think I heard you correctly."

He looked at her with raised eyebrows. "Start over?" he asked with a harsh laugh. "Jesus, green eyes, I had enough trouble getting it out the first time."

Her head was spinning, the world lurching viciously, tossing her almost literally upside down. "Just . . . say it again so I can be sure."

"Say what again?" His voice seemed lower this time, like he might know exactly what she was talking about, but chose to tease her.

She glared at him, eyes narrowed. "You know what. If you meant it, say it again."

He dropped all pretense of misunderstanding and grasped her face in both of his hands, tilting her gaze to better lock with his own. "I love you, Regan Doyle. I've been an ass these past few weeks, I know, but that doesn't change how I feel about you. It just took me a while to figure out what was what. Aunt Martha is right: My principles aren't going to keep me warm at night." He closed in until his forehead rested against hers. "Only you can do that, sweetheart. I just have to convince you to forgive me."

Regan blinked rapidly, fighting back tears. But they were tears of happiness. She'd never *been* so happy. "Forgive you for what?" she asked in a watery voice.

"For being such a jackass. You accused me of it once, and you were right. Then I went and pulled the same trick again." His lips brushed over her closed eyelids, then moved to her cheeks and jaw. "I'm guessing I might need regular reminders not to stick my foot in my mouth. Think you might want to accept that responsibility?"

When she looked into his slate-gray eyes, she saw them twinkling with mirth. She smiled back at him, almost giddy with relief and excitement.

"I might," she told him. "After all, I am rather good at it."

Throwing his head back, he let out a loud guffaw, then squeezed her tight, his legs widening to span the volume of her skirts.

"Clay," she began, trying to think straight. "Were you going to ask me to marry you?"

He leaned back, looking her over with a slight frown on his face. "I was thinking about it," he said. "But I was kind of hoping to be the one to bring it up." The lines around his mouth deepened in disappointment.

"Well, you should probably bring it up soon," she told him. With her confidence restored, she had no problem asserting herself once again. In fact, she rather liked the idea of shocking him into a marriage proposal.

One eye narrowed, he studied her closely. "And why might that be?" he asked.

She shrugged a shoulder, the epitome of carelessness as she lowered her lashes. "Only because it seems I might not be as barren as I thought."

Shock brightened his dark eyes and rippled through his body. She felt his reaction in her fingertips and bit back a grin.

He pushed away, holding her at arm's length.

Heidi Betts

"Are you serious? You think you might be . . . are you sure?"

She shook her head and let her happiness show in her smile. "I'm not sure. Mother Doyle's the one who suggested it, otherwise it probably wouldn't even have crossed my mind. But now, I think . . . maybe."

"Holy shit!" A look of wonderment came over his rugged face. "Imagine that. I'm gonna be a daddy. Hot damn!"

Regan laughed. "You're happy then?" she asked. "I was a little afraid you wouldn't be."

"Happy, hell. I'm ecstatic." He hugged her to him, nearly bruising her mouth with the power of his kiss. "You have to marry me now," he said when he finally pulled away. "You know that, right? I don't need to ask?"

"You don't *need* to ask," she said carefully, "but it might be nice if you did. After all, you have been quite the jackass these past few weeks."

He shook his head at her, but his even white teeth belied any annoyance he might be trying to convey. "Don't even have a ring on your finger and already you're harping at me. Something tells me you're going to make an ideal wife."

"I will try," she replied primly.

"I'll just bet," he said on a laugh. And then his tone softened, his eyes burning into hers. "So, Widow Doyle . . . Regan. Will you marry me?"

She nodded, tears once again brimming on the tips of her lashes. "I'd better. Folks might not mind me breaking into their houses, but I'll definitely get

384

a reputation if they find out I'm in a family way without the benefit of a husband."

"Mmm. That could be a problem. Good thing you won't be without one much longer than it takes to ride into town and fetch the padre." With his hands locked tightly about her waist, he lifted her off the ground and started backing her toward the barn door. " 'Course, I was thinking we might get an early start on our honeymoon. The cart having already gone before the horse and all, it can't matter too much, can it?"

She wrapped her arms around his neck and her legs around his waist. "It's certainly not proper, but . . . I don't suppose it would hurt all that terribly."

"Good. 'Cause I've been meaning to take another trip up to the loft, see if things up there are as good as I remember."

"I'll bet they are," she whispered, nibbling at the lobe of his ear.

When he answered, his voice was raspy and choked with sensation. "I'll bet they are, too."

He started up the ladder to the loft, letting her scuttle ahead of him in a flurry of skirts and petticoats. As he set his boot on the next rung, he caught a glimpse of bright red amidst the otherwise snow white ruffles.

With a shake of his head, he climbed the rest of the way up the ladder, patting himself on the back for falling in love with the greatest woman in the world. Burglary skills, red drawers, and all.

* * *

Kneeling on the settee, Martha pressed her nose to the front parlor window, watching her nephew and daughter-in-law out by the barn.

Things hadn't looked good at first, and she'd nearly worried herself right back into her invalid chair. But then Clayton seemed to come to his senses and whatever he said put a smile on Regan's pretty porcelain face.

Only moments later, there was no mistaking the youngsters' intent as Clayton picked Regan up and headed straight for the barn.

Martha almost rubbed her hands together in glee. It had worked. Not exactly as she'd planned, given Regan's unknown hobby as a thief and Clayton's obstinacy when it came to breaking the law, but it had worked nonetheless.

If she wasn't mistaken—and she seldom was—things were going to be a mite different around here from now on.

During all of her matchmaking machinations, she'd never given much thought to what would happen to her if she did manage to get Regan and Clayton together. She didn't know if she would continue living here with them or move to Sweetwater with her sister. Perhaps she would even end up living by herself, be it in the house James had built or elsewhere. The important thing, though, was her daughter-in-law's and nephew's happiness. Everything else would fall into place.

And, she thought impishly, she might even enjoy being on her own again. Perhaps she could renew her less-than-proper friendship with her dear friend,

Virgil. He had to be pushing eighty by now, but she suspected that if she put her mind to it, she could still get him as randy as a sixty-year-old.

Abandoning her post at the parlor window, she hurried down the hall to her bedroom. She could still see the barn from this part of the house, so she would know when Regan and Clayton started back toward the house.

Taking a seat at her writing desk, she pulled out an envelope and stationery and began scribbling as fast as her aging hands could move across the paper.

She needed to tell her sister to pack her best dress and hop a train to Purgatory as soon as possible. They had a wedding to plan.

Epilogue

Two weeks later, to the day, the entire town of Purgatory, Texas, stood in the courtyard outside the orphanage awaiting the bride's arrival.

A lot of changes had been taking place, lately. Changes Martha Doyle was proud to have played a part in—and in most cases, instigated.

The Purgatory Home for Unwanted Children was now called The Purgatory Home for Adoptive Children. And she, Father Ignacio, and the other women of the newly formed Ladies' Auxiliary were working hard to place as many orphans as possible in kind and loving homes. Martha made sure to drag one or two of the younger orphans along with her to the Auxiliary meetings, quilting circles, and afternoon teas, so people were beginning to realize just how adorable and lovable most of the children were. In her many years on this earth, Martha had learned that a little plucking of the heartstrings never hurt.

David, who had gotten along so horribly with Clayton early on, now stuck to him like a burr in a blanket. At first, the young man had been wary and quite unhappy at the news of Regan's impending marriage. But once Clayton and Regan had both made it clear they intended to marry with or without David's approval, and once Clayton had welcomed him with open arms, man and boy had become almost inseparable.

And, miracle of miracles, Regan and Clayton had plans to legally adopt David just as soon as they were legally attached themselves. The boy had already moved into the house and was getting along quite well in the role of son—and soon-to-be older brother, though Martha didn't think he was aware of that small fact yet.

Regan had met Clayton's mother when she arrived to help with the wedding arrangements, and the two had hit it off immediately. And neither Martha nor her sister said anything about the fact that Clayton slipped into Regan's room each night after he thought everyone else was asleep, and slipped out of her room again in the morning before he thought anyone was awake. The two older women had many a time whispered about these little late-night trysts and decided that, with the horse already out of the barn, so to speak, it really didn't make much sense to run behind and close the barn door. They were just happy the youngsters were tying the knot and seemed to be truly in love with each other.

And though it had been decided—more by Clayton and Regan than by Martha herself—that Martha would continue living with them, she'd already made plans to return to Sweetwater with her sister for the next few weeks to give the newly wed couple some time alone.

The piano, which had been moved from the saloon to the churchyard for the ceremony, began its halting notes and everyone's attention turned toward the door where the bride would be making her entrance.

Clayton stood on the other side of the parted crowd with Father Ignacio, awaiting his bride. Martha and his mother had insisted on a special outfit for the big day, but had only been able to talk him into black denim trousers, a black leather vest over white dress shirt, and a brand-spanking new black Stetson. He looked handsome and dapper and likely made several unattached young ladies in attendance feel near swooning.

And he appeared only a tad nervous—nowhere near ready to bolt, Martha thought with relief. It had taken so much to get these two together, she hated to consider that anything might drive them apart. God willing, nothing ever would.

The side door of the church opened and David stepped out ahead of Regan. He was dressed much the same as Clayton, with a black jacket instead of a vest and wearing no hat on his head of straight black hair, which they'd finally talked him into having cut. He held out a hand, waiting to do his duty.

In the next moment, Regan came into view, looking lovelier than a spring meadow . . . or all of the angel babies in Martha's Cherub Room rolled into one.

She wore a beautiful new ivory gown covered with pearls and lace, and cut in a manner that both accentuated her generous curves and hid the one tiny bulge she preferred not to reveal just yet. Her wild copper curls were caught up at the sides and fixed with a delicate garland of daisies and blue-bonnets.

But it was Regan's smile that caught the crowd's attention as David led her down the makeshift aisle toward her groom. She looked completely, deliriously happy. Happier, Martha thought, than any other bride throughout history had ever looked.

Martha's heart skipped a romantic beat and she dabbed at her running eyes with a handkerchief from her sleeve.

David delivered Regan to Clayton's side and paused to buss her cheek in a mature, gentlemanly fashion before stepping back to observe the rest of the ceremony with everyone else.

Father Ignacio began the service, his Spanish accent ringing through the air. He asked the bride and groom to love, honor, and cherish, and with an exchange of rings, they both pledged to do just that. From the looks on their faces and the adoration in their voices when they each said, "I do," Martha had no doubt they would keep the promise for many years to come.

As the ceremony came to a close, Clayton was allowed to kiss his bride—which he did with utter abandon, giving no mind to the large group of witnesses surrounding them. Regan's cheeks glowed a rosy red when Clayton finally let her go, and they turned to face their wildly applauding neighbors for the first time as man and wife.

From there, the exuberant crowd moved down the street to the saloon where tables of food and drink had been set up for the guests. Always the perfect hostess, Martha bustled around making sure everyone's glasses were filled and that they tried the pecan pie. After all, it was her own special recipe and she'd made twelve of them; she intended to see them properly appreciated.

Not thirty minutes into the reception, Martha noticed a distinct absence. The bride and groom, it seemed, had disappeared. She considered getting her sister to help her search for them, then thought better of it. Clayton and Regan were young, full of life, and newly married. Let them run off and do what young, newly married couples did; there would be plenty of time later on to visit with friends and well-wishers.

Clay didn't take his hands or eyes off Regan as they made their way down the boardwalk toward the jail. He'd wanted to get away from the reception, get Regan alone, and walking down the street to visit his new office was the only thing he could think of—other than tossing her over his shoulder and hieing off to parts unknown.

He opened the door to the empty building and ushered his new wife in ahead of him.

His wife. Lord in heaven, but he wasn't sure he'd ever get used to that. Before coming to Purgatory, he'd never wanted a wife. Never thought there'd be room for one in his life as a Texas Ranger. Now here he was: town sheriff, husband, soon to be a father. And he'd never been happier.

Just the thought of Regan, just a glance in her direction, had his pulse picking up and his palms sweating like an untried boy.

He cleared his throat, shaking off his sudden nervousness. "What do you think?" he asked, closing the rough plank door behind them.

It wasn't her first time inside the office, but she acted as though it was. She took in the front jail cell, the scratched and stained desk, and the wall of Wanted posters lined up behind.

"I think you're going to look much better here than Jensen Graves ever did." With her hand still linked with his, she turned to face him and stepped close, smiling. "You're going to make a wonderful sheriff. Purgatory is a very lucky town." She lifted up on her tiptoes and pressed a kiss to the line of his jaw. "And I'm a very lucky woman."

Clay let his hands drift over her waist, coming to rest on the very slight swell of her belly where his child safely slept. "I'm the lucky one, sweetheart. I was a lonely, empty husk of a man before I met you."

She gave a low chuckle at his over-exaggeration. "You were a very attractive husk."

He shared her smile, then grew serious once again. "I don't know what I'd do without you, green eyes."

Her mouth moved to his, her arms winding up around his neck. "I'll do my best not to let you find out."

"Good," he said with feeling, squeezing her tight. "I love you, Regan."

"I love you, too, Clay," she whispered in return.

He kissed her hard and deep, bending her back over his arm as they shuffled step by awkward step across the worn floorboards.

They were both breathing heavily when they broke apart and it took him a minute to regain his equilibrium. "So, Mrs. Walker," he managed finally. "Is there any chance I might interest you in a tour of the back room? I understand there's a cot back there."

"A cot," she teased. "How romantic."

She was right . . . a ratty old cot in the corner of a jail cell wasn't exactly the ideal spot to spend a wedding night—or afternoon, as the case may be. But damned if he wanted to take the time to find a better place to make love to his new bride.

"We could head home," he offered. "Mother and Aunt Martha probably won't return for a few hours yet. Or we could run over to the hotel and see if anyone's there to give us a room."

"Clay." She took his face between her hands, smoothing her thumbs over his rough cheeks.

"We've made love in a barn loft, in the woods, and in our bedroom with your mother across the hallway . . . do you really think where we make love now matters to me?"

God knew it didn't matter to him; he'd take her anytime, anywhere. But she deserved better. "I just want you to have the best of everything. Always."

"I *have* the best of everything," she said, kissing first one corner of his mouth and then the other. "I've got you."

Reaching behind her, she opened the door that led to the back of the office and took Clay's hand in her own. "Care to carry me over the threshold?"

Needing no further invitation, he swept her off her feet and into his arms. "Darlin', it would be my pleasure," he drawled as they moved through the doorway and toward the rest of their lives together. Clayton Walker, ex-Texas Ranger, and his former-burglar bride.

Damn, sometimes life was sweet.

Heidi Betts

ALMOST A

Lady

Pistol-packing Pinkerton agent Willow Hastings always gets her man. Until handsome, arrogant railroad security chief Brandt Donovan "gallantly" interferes in an arrest, costing Willow a collar and jeopardizing her job. And now she is supposed to collaborate with the dashing, distracting bachelor to catch a killer? Never! Brandt is shocked yet intrigued by this curvy, contrary, weapon-wielding brunette. Willow's sultry voice, silken skin, and subtle scent of roses make him ache to savor her between the sheets. But go undercover with the perplexing Pinkerton? Chastely pose as man and wife to entrap a killer? Such unthinkable celibacy could drive a bachelor to madness. Or to–shudder!–matrimony. . . .

___4817-5 $4.99 US/$5.99 CAN

Dorchester Publishing Co., Inc.
P.O. Box 6640
Wayne, PA 19087-8640

Please add $2.50 for shipping and handling for the first book and $.75 for each book thereafter. NY, NYC, and PA residents, please add appropriate sales tax. No cash, stamps, or C.O.D.s. All orders shipped within 6 weeks via postal service book rate. Canadian orders require $2.00 extra postage and must be paid in U.S. dollars through a U.S. banking facility.

Name_____
Address_____
City_____ State_____ Zip_____
I have enclosed $_____in payment for the checked book(s).
Payment <u>must</u> accompany all orders.☐Please send a free catalog.
    CHECK OUT OUR WEBSITE! www.dorchesterpub.com

A Promise of Roses
Heidi Betts

Spunky Megan Adams will do almost anything to save her struggling stagecoach line—even confront the bandits constantly ambushing the stage for the payrolls it delivers. But what Megan *wouldn't* do is fall headlong for the heart-breakingly handsome outlaw who robs the coach, kidnaps her from his ornery amigos, and drags her half across Kansas—to turn *her* in as an accomplice to the holdup!

Bounty hunter Lucas McCain stops at nothing to get his man. Hired to investigate the pilfered payrolls, he is sure Megan herself is masterminding the heists. And he'll be damned if he'll let this gun-toting spitfire keep him from completing his mission—even if he has to hogtie her to his horse, promise her roses . . . and hijack her heart!

___4738-1 $4.99 US/$5.99 CAN

Cinnamon and Roses
Heidi Betts

A hardworking seamstress, Rebecca has no business being attracted to a man like wealthy, arrogant Caleb Adams. Born fatherless in a brothel, Rebecca knows what males are made of. And Caleb is clearly as faithless as they come, scandalizing their Kansas cowtown with the fancy city women he casually uses and casts aside. Though he tempts innocent Rebecca beyond reason, she can't afford to love a man like Caleb, for the price might be another fatherless babe. What the devil is wrong with him, Caleb muses, that he's drawn to a calico-clad dressmaker when sirens in silk are his for the asking? Still, Rebecca unaccountably stirs him. Caleb vows no woman can be trusted with his heart. But he must sample sweet Rebecca.

Lair of the Wolf

Also includes the second installment of *Lair of the Wolf*, a serialized romance set in medieval Wales. Be sure to look for future chapters of this exciting story featured in Leisure books and written by the industry's top authors.

___4668-7 $4.99 US/$5.99 CAN

Dorchester Publishing Co., Inc.
P.O. Box 6640
Wayne, PA 19087-8640

Please add $1.75 for shipping and handling for the first book and $.50 for each book thereafter. NY, NYC, and PA residents, please add appropriate sales tax. No cash, stamps, or C.O.D.s. All orders shipped within 6 weeks via postal service book rate. Canadian orders require $2.00 extra postage and must be paid in U.S. dollars through a U.S. banking facility.

Name_____
Address_____
City_____State_____Zip_____
I have enclosed $_____ in payment for the checked book(s).
Payment <u>must</u> accompany all orders. ❏ Please send a free catalog.
       CHECK OUT OUR WEBSITE! www.dorchesterpub.com

⌐ ENTER TO WIN A $50.00 ⌐
GIFT CERTIFICATE TO VICTORIA'S SECRET!

You fell in love with the passionate tale of Regan and Clayton. Now you can share romantic moments with your own special someone courtesy of Heidi Betts herself! *Walker's Widow* is part one of three in Heidi's exciting new series set in the Western town of Purgatory, Texas. Keep your eyes open for *Callie's Convict* in July 2002 and *Hannah's Half-Breed* in January 2003!

This contest is co-sponsored by Dorchester Publishing Co., Inc., and Heidi Betts. For additional news, upcoming releases, and exciting contest information, please visit their websites at www.dorchesterpub.com and www.heidibetts.com.

OFFICIAL ENTRY FORM

No purchase necessary. Simply fill in the information below. (Type or print legibly.)

NAME: _____

ADDRESS: _____

_____

PHONE: _____

E-MAIL ADDRESS: _____

MAIL ENTRIES TO:

DORCHESTER PUBLISHING
DEPARTMENT HB
276 FIFTH AVENUE, SUITE 1008
NEW YORK, NY 10001

OFFICIAL CONTEST RULES: No purchase necessary. Must be at least 18 years old to enter. Only one entry per envelope. Use of a photocopy of an original entry form is acceptable. Entries must be postmarked by July 15, 2002. The contest is open to all residents of the U.S. and Canada, excluding employees and families of Dorchester Publishing and the Comag Marketing Group. A random drawing for all entries will be held at the offices of Dorchester Publishing on or before July 30, 2002. Odds of winning are dependent on the number of entries received. Any illegible, mutilated, altered, or incorrectly filled-out entry forms will be disqualified. Not responsible for lost, late, misdirected, damaged, incomplete, altered, illegible, or postage-due mail. Entries become the property of the sponsor and will not be returned. The gift certificate will be mailed to the winner on or before August 15, 2002. If the prize is returned to Dorchester Publishing as undeliverable, the prize will then be awarded to an alternate winner in a random drawing. Void where prohibited by law.